Dov Silverman, win
Merit Award for M
Brooklyn, New Yor
He served as a US
has worked as a railroad conductor, auctioneer,
college lecturer and high school principal. For the present,
he writes, teaches and serves as a Safed city councilman.

By the same author

Legends of Safed
The Fall of the Shōgun
The Black Dragon
The Shishi
The Good Shepherds (in Japanese)
Tairo

DOV SILVERMAN

To the Gates of Hell

This edition published 1994 by
Diamond Books
77–85 Fulham Palace Road
Hammersmith, London W6 8JB

A Grafton Original 1992

A catalogue record for this book
is available from the British Library

ISBN 0 261 66505 7

Set in Times

Printed in Great Britain

Dedicated to the memory of
Jules Rubinstein

Acknowledgements

To my wife Janet,
Editor of all my works.

For Support and Encouragement Along the Way

Act I Creativity Center, Lake Ozark, Missouri
Dr Morris and Dora Molinoff
Char Plotsky, Supreme Adviser
Malka Rabinowitz
Eleanor and Morty Radden
Sylvia and Mel Springer
Paula and Leslie Tint

Preface

The Japanese have a different image of themselves from
that which is seen by others.

Dov Silverman

The Year of the Rat
1936

1

The radio of the lead T-95 fighter plane crackled and Captain Hino Arai's voice came through. 'We're only doing 180 miles an hour! We'd need a typhoon up our arses to reach the 250 that marks a first-class fighter plane!'

Captain Kenji Ishikawa looked to the plane off his left wing and spoke into his microphone. 'Genda, what do you think?'

'More power,' came the reply.

Kenji laughed. His cousins would ride their engines to Hell and still ask for more power. 'A bigger engine would shake this plane apart,' he said.

'Junk it!' Hino exclaimed.

'We're paying for these kites, not the government,' Kenji said.

'I call a meeting of the board of the Ishikawa zaibatsu – conglomerate – right here in the sky,' Hino announced.

'I'll go back to the drawing board,' Kenji said. 'We need a stronger fuselage without added weight so we can install a more powerful engine in this single-wing plane.'

Hino and Genda Arai both grunted.

Kenji gazed down at the whitecapped ocean, wondering if it could be farmed to feed the people of Japan. He scribbled his question on a memo pad strapped to his leg. Seven years of rising birthrates and severe economic depression had weakened the morale and morals of the Japanese people. Female infanticide was being practised again. Young women were sold to brothels. Robbery on the roads and theft in the cities had increased tenfold. For

9

many Japanese, starvation was one meal away. The army is demanding the invasion of China to solve our economic problems, Kenji thought. Others favour communism. Most of our people accept their fate and do nothing.

'Land coming up,' Kenji said. 'Reduce speed to 120 miles!'

The three pilots throttled back and flew low over the coastal mountain range of central Honshu. Kenji noted the long narrow funnels of rice paddies that petered out on terraced heights in the valleys. Rows of tea bushes clung to steep slopes. Orchards and vegetable gardens ran right up to the houses of the villages below. Every inch of land is being used, he thought, but it's still not enough to feed seventy million people. If I had studied oceanography instead of aeronautics at Cal. Tech., would I have been in a better position to help my country? He looked around the cockpit of the plane. No. I can't solve every problem. If I try to do it all, I'll accomplish nothing. My studies have given me the knowledge to build planes. Our zaibatsu has made the commitment to perfect a world-class combat aircraft. Japan will need that for her survival.

The zaibatsu's money had been used to purchase land in California, Australia and New Zealand, but those countries now barred Japanese from owning property. The imperial navy wanted to force its way south into Malaysia and the Dutch East Indies; the army favoured pressing north into China from its bases in Korea and Manchuria. The air force, in which Kenji and his cousins held the rank of captain, had nothing to say. They were subordinate to the older military establishments.

Static in Kenji's earphones was followed by the familiar voice of the flight controller. 'Experimental flight T-95, this is Gifu tower at Ishikawa field. I have you in sight and you are clear for landing. The wind is from the west at twelve miles an hour. Visibility fair and beginning to cloud.'

10

'Flight leader reading you loud and clear,' Kenji answered. 'Prepare the beer!'

A blue smoke rocket soared above the red windsock on the open wooden tower. Kenji waggled his wings to get his cousins' attention, then hand signalled them with a diving motion towards the tower. Hino and Genda signalled Kenji with thumbs-up. The three pushed their throttles forward. The Mitsubishi engines roared. The planes' wood frames shuddered and the canvas wings rippled as they dived towards the landing field.

'No, no,' the flight controller cried. 'Don't do that! It's against regulations!'

Kenji chuckled into the microphone. The man in the tower jumped from side to side. He waved his arms to turn away the three planes, then dived to the wooden floor. Kenji's plane roared in. He pulled his control stick back, clearing the tower by only twenty feet. Genda and Hino roared by on either side.

The controller's shaky voice came over the radio. 'There'll be no beer if that happens again. It's a good thing you three own the company or I'd report you. Come down. There's an urgent message.'

Kenji signalled Hino and Genda to land. He stayed aloft to watch the storm clouds moving in from the sea. Then he flew over the field, flipped the plane into a barrel roll, up into a reverse loop, and touched down in a perfect three-point landing.

At the hangar, the ground crew took over Kenji's plane. The flight controller served Dutch cheese and steins of German beer on the polished roof of a brand-new four-door Lincoln Continental.

Kenji read the note placed in his hand. 'Call this number immediately. Ask for Mangiro.' He showed it to his cousins and the three eyed each other, but said nothing. The telephone number was one of many at imperial army headquarters in Tokyo; the name was of someone long dead.

11

'I don't see how you can drink cold beer in the winter,' the flight controller said to Kenji. 'At least your cousins know enough to take it warm.'

'They acquired their tastes in London, but mine comes from the States. That's the difference between Americans and Englishmen, cold beer.' Kenji shoved the stein into the controller's hand. 'Try it.' He strode to the company telephone.

The number Kenji dialled was answered immediately. 'Mangiro, please,' Kenji said.

'Kenji Ishikawa?' an unfamiliar voice asked.

'Speaking.'

'Mother of autumn.'

'Father of spring,' Kenji responded without hesitation, although he had never before used the secret passwords.

'I warn you of a coup attempt in the capital this evening,' the voice said. 'Your uncle, Hiroki Koin, lord keeper of the privy seal, is to be assassinated. I am unable to reach him.' The voice gave additional information, and signed off.

Kenji cranked the telephone again. 'Operator, Captain Ishikawa of the imperial air force speaking. This is an emergency! Call the following numbers . . .'

Kenji charged out of the hangar, shouting to Genda and Hino as he ran. 'Leave everything and get in the car!'

The two pilots handed their steins to the flight controller and jumped into the Lincoln. Kenji slipped behind the steering wheel and kicked the starter switch. The big twelve-cylinder engine purred with power.

'Are we off to the Gifu pleasure quarter for wining and wenching?' Hino asked.

'Tokyo in three hours,' Kenji said.

'That's 180 miles. What did army headquarters tell you?'

The whitewall tyres spun and the car shot forward. Kenji ignored the exit road and drove out on the half-mile airstrip. The Lincoln's speedometer read 110 miles when the car left the tarmac and hit the dirt service road paralleling the Gifu–Tokyo turnpike. The big black automobile careened down the narrow road; a cloud of dust billowed up behind. Kenji swerved right; the car hit the rise at the entrance to the turnpike and catapulted on to the paved road.

'My stomach's in my socks,' Hino said. 'Why can't we fly to Tokyo? What's going on?'

'Tokyo airport is closed,' Kenji said. 'Army headquarters and Central Police Station have no outside communication. A coup attempt is about to take place!' He jammed his foot to the floor and reached down for a German luger automatic in the leg pocket of his flying suit.

'Who informed you?' Genda asked.

'The voice was unfamiliar but he said Uncle Hiroki is in danger and can't be reached. I had the operator check the lines. They're dead!'

'The political assassinations of five years ago were a bloody slaughter,' Hino said.

'Hang on,' Kenji shouted. He braked the car to avoid a group of villagers returning from the fields. The car skidded, narrowly missing the farmers.

'If there's an attempt to take over the government, then Tojo's involved,' Genda said.

'Tojo is pulling the strings of the puppet governments in Korea and Manchuko,' Hino said.

'He's also involved with Koda-ha, the Imperial Way Society,' Genda said. 'They've vowed to abolish the constitution and return absolute control of the country to the Emperor.'

'Hirohito doesn't want to govern,' Kenji said.

'I've listened to younger officers in the Imperial Hall of Martial Arts,' Genda said. 'Tojo has them convinced he knows what the Emperor really wants. They believe that Uncle Hiroki and others in the Diet are preventing his majesty from expressing himself.'

13

'What does military intelligence have to say?' Kenji asked.

Genda grunted. 'There've been rumours of a coup.' He reached under the front seat and pulled out a Thompson submachine gun. He fitted the round drum of .45 calibre lead-nosed bullets on to the barrel and drew back the bolt.

Fat drops of sleet splattered the windscreen. Grey clouds darkened the sky as they sped north.

2

Raiko Minobe's large, dark eyes dominated her smooth young face. She was slim and elegant in a beige kimono with a purple obi around her small waist. Lord Hiroki Koin, wearing a cutaway tuxedo, seemed fascinated by the tiny young woman before him.

'Is it true you were patron to the artist Auguste Rodin?' Raiko asked.

Hiroki, aware of Raiko's background, took no offence at the un-Japanese bluntness of the question. 'Twenty years ago the depression in France was as bad as it is here now. The French government withdrew its support of many fine artists. It was possible to purchase superior works of art for the price of a week's lodging and a few bottles of wine.'

'From the stories Father tells of you and Madame Koin, I'm certain Rodin received a fair price for that.' Raiko pointed at a huge sketch that covered an entire wall. It portrayed a maze of twisted, tortured figures in the throes of intense agony.

Noriko Koin entered the room and placed a bowl of fruit on the table. She too wore the traditional kimono. Her graceful movements and eloquent speech projected a quiet dignity. 'That was Rodin's gift to my husband. Hiroki supported the artist until his death. The sketch eventually became a huge metal door.'

Raiko looked again at the mass of human suffering, and shuddered. 'I could not keep such a thing. It is too painful.'

'Your father used to meet Noriko and me in Europe,'

15

Hiroki said. 'We often travelled together while you were growing up in New York. He influenced me to accept Rodin's gift and keep it prominently displayed.'

'Father prefers softer paintings at home. Nothing so harsh. He has several Monets.'

'There is a photograph of your father, Noriko and me with Claude Monet,' Hiroki said. 'The waterlilies in the picture, and those in Monet's paintings, were grown from lotus roots out of our pond in the rear of this house. This sketch, which so disturbs you, is called "The Gates of Hell". It reminded your father of the Russo–Japanese war in which we served together.' Hiroki remained silent for a few moments, then recalled, 'I met your father for the first time in the trenches outside Port Arthur. That was in 1904. We served in aerial reconnaissance during the Manchurian campaign. He received a bloody nose when our observation balloon was shot down.' Hiroki tapped his left leg with his cane. 'I broke this in three places. Your father went on to become a professor at Tokyo University and Japan's leading authority on constitutional law. I am now the first adviser to the Emperor.' Hiroki shook his head. 'It is remarkable how lives progress. Upon my appointment as lord keeper of the privy seal, your father convinced me to accept this sketch as a reminder of the horrors of war. Japan lost 100,000 men in the Russo–Japanese war. Before I attend any session on military matters, I look closely at the picture. Then I counsel against war. Of late though, the army heeds neither the Emperor, your father, nor me.'

'Do you refer to our Kwangtung army in Manchuko?' Raiko asked.

'Hiroki and I prefer the true name of Manchuria,' Noriko said. 'General Tojo renamed it Manchuko when he placed the Chinese Emperor Henry Pu-yi on a false throne. Tojo has Emperor Henry addicted to opium. The general tells him what to say, and when.'

'Korea is also under Tojo's thumb,' Hiroki said. 'The Kwangtung army milks Korea and Manchuria in the same way that the Europeans drain their foreign colonies.'

'Our occupation of those areas has some positive aspects,' Raiko said.

Noriko smiled. 'I am pleased you said our. Because of your American education, I feared you might have dual loyalties. And you should know that this is the first time I have ever heard my husband discuss economics and foreign policy with a woman.'

'Raiko is an extremely intelligent young woman,' Hiroki said. 'The girl has a BA in mathematics from Vassar, and two MAs summa cum laude from Harvard in statistics and history.'

'See how my husband boasts about you,' Noriko said. 'Your father has kept us informed of your progress. Hiroki always wished to have a daughter.'

Raiko saw a look of sadness pass between the couple and knew the conversation reminded them of their two sons who had died in the 1923 earthquake. Hiroki led the two women out on to a glass-enclosed porch at the rear of the house.

'Father told me you planted a tree when I was born,' Raiko said.

'The very day.' Hiroki pointed. 'See that snow-covered cryptomeria between the lily pond and the storeroom?'

'It doesn't look very tall for twenty-three years,' Raiko said.

Hiroki chuckled. 'Neither are you. But the cryptomeria is a long-lived, healthy and lucky tree. That is what Noriko and I wish for you.'

'At your age a Japanese girl should have a husband,' Noriko said. 'I know a wonderful marriage broker.'

Raiko bowed, and smiled. 'I prefer to choose my own husband.'

'Ah,' Noriko said. 'Your American education shows

17

itself. It is contrary to the way things are done in Japan. May I ask where you are working now? I called the English section of Japan Broadcasting Company and learned you were transferred. I had to ask Hiroki to locate you.'

Raiko cast a quick glance at Hiroki. 'I am temporarily assigned to the Classified Translation Department. Their telephone number is unlisted.'

Noriko frowned at her husband. 'Do you have this poor young thing involved in the Cherry Blossom Society?'

The look of dismay on Raiko's face prompted Hiroki to touch her arm. 'You answered correctly. My wife knows all my secrets.' He laughed out loud. 'In 1904 Noriko and I walked through North Korea to the Manchurian border and gathered intelligence on the Russian army. She is a senior member of the Cherry Blossom Society.'

'Have you exposed your friend's daughter to danger?' Noriko demanded of Hiroki. She turned to Raiko. 'My husband will do anything to learn other people's secrets.'

'The most formidable opponent I've met is the new Remington electric typewriter,' Raiko said.

Hiroki leaned on his cane and bowed low to Raiko. The bald spot on the back of his head reflected the electric lights.

'Stand up,' Noriko chided her husband. 'You are embarrassing the girl.' She smiled at Raiko. 'He always does that to beautiful women.'

Hiroki laughed. 'This young lady has nothing to be embarrassed about. She finished a test puzzle sooner than 100 others at the radio station. Wantabe promoted her to the Classified Translation Department.'

'The Black Chamber.' Noriko shook her head. 'There are no windows in that room. Is Raiko the only woman?'

'Not to worry,' Hiroki said. 'Mini's daughter showed them all.'

Raiko had never before heard her father's nickname,

18

but recognized it as suitable to a man less than five feet tall, exactly her height.

'At first Wantabe tried to humble Raiko with a merchant marine code we thought unbreakable,' Hiroki said. 'She returned the plain-text message within a week. Wantabe immediately promoted her to number-one desk. He is teaching her to use our new cipher machine.'

'I've always sensed patterns in jumbles of letters and words,' Raiko said. 'They challenge me.'

'Your knowledge of German and statistics was instrumental in breaking the Nazi's diplomatic code,' Hiroki said.

'I thought we were on good terms with the Germans,' Noriko said. 'Our foreign minister is now in Berlin, isn't he?'

'It is the Nazis who cannot be trusted,' Hiroki said. 'And Mini's little girl tricked them. With Wantabe's help she prepared misleading information about our military. I passed it to Richard Sorge, the senior German news correspondent in Tokyo, whom we know is Gestapo. Raiko monitored the German Embassy's coded radio transmissions to Berlin until she recognized her own message by length and word formation. Because she knew the message content, it was easier to break their code. Raiko also helped in cracking a French business code and a senior Dutch diplomatic code. The Cherry Blossom Society worked on that Dutch code for two years.'

The sound of gunfire came from the front of the house. They heard the gatekeeper's cry. 'Assassins!' More shots were fired. A bullet whipped through the paper walls of the house and shattered the large porch window.

'Come quickly,' Hiroki said, leading the way out of the back door through falling snowflakes. 'I have a hunting rifle in the storeroom.' He hurried ahead around the pond, and slipped to the ground. His cane snapped and the jagged end speared his left forearm.

19

Sitting up in the snow, Hiroki pulled the bloody piece of wood from his arm. Raiko removed her obi and bound the open wound. The two women helped Hiroki to his feet.

'Stand where you are!' The stern voice came from a lieutenant flanked by six soldiers with rifles. 'We do not wish to kill the ladies,' the officer said. 'Please step away from the lord keeper of the privy seal!'

Kenji wheeled the dented limousine through the snow-covered streets of Tokyo. The car had skidded into ditches, trees and stone walls, but the engine still roared with power. Kenji turned into their uncle's street. He gauged the distance to the driveway of the Koin house, then slammed on the brakes. The car skidded up on to the grass. Before it stopped, the three pilots were out and running.

Genda snapped off the safety catch of the submachine gun and ran around the side of the building. Hino and Kenji bolted past the gatekeeper's body. They moved up the front steps and through the open door, shouting for their aunt and uncle.

'Beware the assassins,' Hiroki cried.

The lieutenant whirled and fired in the direction of the approaching voices. Hino shot through the back-porch window, hitting him in the stomach. Kenji's bullet slammed into the officer's chest, knocking him over backwards.

The six soldiers turned from their prisoners and levelled their rifles at the two air-force captains. Their officer lay dead and they hesitated. Genda came around the side of the house and fired his submachine-gun, killing all six.

Kenji saw a girl and his aunt supporting his uncle.

'There were shots from the prime minister's house across the street,' Hiroki said. 'Go quickly!'

'Little one, stay with my aunt and uncle!' Kenji said to Raiko. 'Hino, Genda, come with me!'

The three ran back through the house and out the front door. Kenji led the way across the road, through shrubs surrounding the prime minister's house.

With a burst from the submachine-gun, Genda cut down two infantrymen guarding the front door. Three more soldiers came running around the left side of the house, and died in a hail of bullets from the Lugers and the Thompson. Seven more men charged around the corner, firing as they came. The Thompson roared; the Lugers cracked.

Only two infantrymen remained standing. 'We surrender,' they cried. 'We surrender.'

'Where's your officer?' Kenji demanded.

They pointed to one of the bodies surrounding them. Kenji turned the officer face-up. His body was riddled with bullet holes, blood seeped from between his thin lips, but he was alive.

'Where is the prime minister?' Kenji asked.

'Dead,' the officer whispered. 'The coward ran out of the house screaming. We caught him.'

'Why did you do this?'

'For the Emperor.'

Kenji ran to the side of the house. The tuxedo-clad body had been shot, stabbed and hacked. He turned it over and stared at the distorted features. His heart jumped. 'They didn't kill the prime minister,' he shouted as he ran back to the front of the house. 'Genda! Hino! They murdered the wrong man!'

Genda fired the Thompson and the remaining two soldiers went down.

'Why did you kill them?' Hino asked.

'They knew the prime minister still lives,' Genda said.

'We could have isolated them,' Kenji said.

'We may be the ones who are isolated,' Genda said. 'Who knows how widespread this rebellion is. Let's find the prime minister.'

21

Kenji called into the house, identifying himself as the adopted son of the Koins. An elderly couple appeared at the front door. The prime minister helped his wife step over the two dead soldiers. The woman's eyes were glazed.

'We have a car,' Kenji said, taking the woman's arm.

'My brother understood what was happening,' she mumbled. 'He ran outside screaming to make them believe he was the prime minister. And they killed him.'

'His sacrifice must not be in vain,' Kenji said. 'Please walk faster, Mrs Okada.'

Hiroki, Noriko and the girl were already in the limousine. Kenji drove slowly, careful to avoid all military patrols. Genda was correct. They had no idea who supported whom.

There were no guards outside the walls of the imperial palace. The car passed through the main gate and was surrounded by the Emperor's personal bodyguard.

The commander of the guard saluted. 'Prime Minister Okada. Lord Hiroki Koin. The Emperor wishes to see you.'

3

The peaked roof of the Fifth Moon Inn housed powerful
radio transmitters. False chimneys camouflaged the aerials
of Kwangtung army headquarters located outside the
Manchurian capital of Mukden.

Inside the long, three-storey building, General Hideki
Tojo sat at a government-issue desk in a sparsely furnished
office. Dubbed The Razor for his keen mind, he had
been first in his class at the Military Academy and
first at the Army Staff College. He had singlehandedly
modernized the Japanese army. His greatest achievement
was least known, even in military circles: the integration
of civilian spies into army intelligence. Through 50,000
agents, Tojo had his finger on the pulse of mainland
China, Formosa, India, Malaysia and the Dutch East
Indies. Nationalistic Japanese groups, such as the Black
Dragons, White Wolves and Pink Lotus Society, all led
by retired army officers and funded by patriotic businessmen, reported to military intelligence, to Kempetai –
the National Secret Police – and Koda-ha, all controlled
by Tojo.

He watched the intelligence officer decode the latest
communiqué from Tokyo. The beaming officer looked up
from his desk. 'Sir, the message is signed by the League
of Blood. That is the code name to indicate all is as you
planned. The National Diet, the War Ministry and Central
Police Station are in our control.'

Tojo planted his elbow on the desk top, cocked his little
finger and motioned the intelligence chief forward. The

officer jumped from his seat and quickstepped to Tojo's desk. He snapped to attention.

'Who was assassinated?' Tojo asked.

'The inspector general, the finance minister, the grand chamberlain and minister of education.'

'The prime minister?'

'He escaped with Lord Koin.'

Tojo frowned. 'Hiroki Koin and the prime minister are powerful enemies. They represent the strongest factions in the Diet against our expansion into China.'

'Sir, the remainder of this message is more positive. Inspector General Tsubota reports from outside the occupied buildings that no one of importance in the government has condemned our actions. The army ministry has not rejected Captain Ando's demands to replace the Emperor's advisers. Dr Tsubota reports newspapers and radio stations are silent, most politicians wish to avoid a military confrontation in the capital, and several industrialists have urged the government to support our cause.'

'What of the general staff?' Tojo asked.

'No word.'

'And the Emperor?'

'Nothing.'

A flick of Tojo's little finger sent the intelligence officer back to his desk. The Razor stared into space for several minutes. He knew the coup was far from successful. Prime Minister Okada and Hiroki Koin controlled the Diet and the Emperor would not act without a majority. A word from Hirohito would cause the Koda-ha members to lay down their weapons and commit seppuku – ritual suicide. 'I will gain public support for the invasion of China!' he said aloud, and summoned the intelligence officer. 'Code the following message to Dr Tsubota at the Yasukune shrine! "Should you judge the coup attempt a failure, implement Plan B!" Code the following to Captain Ando

24

and the men of Koda-ha! "Warriors of Japan! You have struck a glorious blow to free the Emperor from those misguided advisers who isolate his imperial majesty from his people! Pamphleteer the public and fellow soldiers throughout the capital to join you! Maintain discipline, obey your officers and you shall be written well in the history of our nation! The Emperor must be freed from those who deceive him! Keep a strong heart, a clean rifle and we shall triumph!" End of messages! Sign them The Razor!'

Half a mile from downtown Tokyo

The National Diet, the War Ministry and Central Police Station in the government compound had been occupied by Koda-ha in a fierce but short battle. The three large buildings stood side by side in a semicircle, connected by communication wires even before the regular telephone lines were cut. Koda-ha propaganda units immediately began using the government printing presses to condemn Prime Minister Okada and all those against war with China. They called for the invasion of China for the Emperor's sake.

'Reduce the alert to fifty per cent and feed the troops in two shifts,' Captain Ando ordered his adjutant. 'All three buildings have well-stocked cafeterias.'

'Sir, the men are nervous about firing on their fellow Japanese soldiers who surround us.'

'They're to shoot only those who enter the compound!'

'We could use the mortars.'

'The mortars are for show,' Captain Ando said. 'Integrate the mortar crews into the rifle companies! The mortar shells can be thrown like grenades if necessary.'

'Sir, I too hesitate to kill Japanese soldiers,' the adjutant said.

'You are Koda-ha, sworn to restore the Emperor to

25

power! Those who attack us threaten his imperial majesty! They are traitors!'

A runner entered the room. 'Sir, an officer of the imperial guard approaches under a flag of truce.'

'You cannot meet with him,' the adjutant said. 'Your identity must be kept secret. Dr Tsubota's last radio message confirmed Plan B in effect. I'll go out in your place.'

'You know what that could mean for you,' Ando said.

'It would be my honour, sir.' The adjutant exchanged his insignia with the captain, and left.

A short time later the adjutant returned. He bowed, and reported. 'Sir, we have been given an ultimatum from the general staff. Surrender or die.'

'Traitors,' Ando cried. 'Damned traitors to Japan!' He slammed his fist into the palm of his hand. 'I'll fill the courtyard with their dead!'

'They won't attack,' the adjutant said. 'They intend bombarding the three buildings with artillery.'

'All Tokyo will hear the guns! The people will rise up and join us!'

'The government has closed all newspapers and radio stations. Tokyo is under martial law. The pamphlets we tried to distribute were confiscated. This area is sealed off.'

'How much time do I have to answer the general staff?'

'Two hours.'

'Good. Have our propaganda units in all three buildings use their loudspeakers to influence the soldiers surrounding us! Print up more fliers and distribute them to those troops outside! Prepare for action!'

Prime Minister Okada had bathed, shaved and changed clothes. 'Your nephew may have saved our lives, but I still think Kenji is a gadabout,' the prime minister said to Hiroki. 'I know him because I watched him grow up.'

'I admit he is sometimes reckless.' Hiroki adjusted the sling on his arm. 'But that is what it may take to reach the US Embassy. Kenji speaks English like a native and is acquainted with John Whittefield III, who is the American cultural attaché and senior US intelligence officer. Kenji is prepared to take risks.'

'Risks.' The prime minister laughed. 'That is the understatement of the year. He was arrested for parachuting into the centre of Hibiya park during the Plum Blossom festival. For climbing public buildings while intoxicated.' Okada laughed again. 'Remember his advertisement in the newspaper petitioning the government to build a proper mountain suited for international climbers?'

'Genda and Hino will keep Kenji in line. You can trust the three of them to deliver your message.'

'Kenji keeps a white mistress. Aren't Japanese women good enough for him?'

'Sex is not the issue,' Hiroki said. 'The bombardment of the government buildings has been going on for several hours, without results. The foreign embassies are complaining about our censorship of their newspapers and radio stations. The new American ambassador demands to know why Western Union telegraph and international telephone communications have been suspended. The Reuter's bureau chief presents an hourly demand for freedom of the press. We can respond to all of them through the American ambassador.'

'Bring Kenji,' Okada said. 'I will brief him.'

US Embassy, Tokyo

Ambassador Joseph Grew pointed to the window and the sound of artillery fire. 'Please explain that noise to me, Mr Whittefield. My wife is nervous. I'm concerned for the safety of my family, the embassy and its staff.'

'There's a coup attempt in progress,' John Whittefield

27

said. 'It's the reason I couldn't meet your ship yesterday. The Koda-ha rebels are surrounded. I perceive no danger to anyone in the embassy.'

'Then why the continued shooting?'

'Unfortunately the Koda-ha show no sign of surrender despite being trapped. The Japanese soldiers outside the government buildings have orders to bombard the compound to rubble. The Emperor is furious over the assassinations. His order to the general staff to relieve all pro-Koda-ha commanders in the military and police has been carried out. The Japanese navy is moving two heavy cruisers into Tokyo bay. If you'll look out the window, you can see the Imperial Hotel at the end of the street.' John pointed. 'There are naval gunnery officers near the top, on the observation platform for tourists. They'll range the cruiser's heavy guns on the rebels.'

'It would appear the Koda-ha cannot defeat the imperial forces,' Grew said.

'The rebels aren't in revolt against the Emperor. The Koda-ha honestly believe they know what the Emperor wants. Or better yet, what he really should want.'

'Hirohito is not an intellectual recluse,' the ambassador said. 'He holds a university degree in marine biology. He's a scientist in touch with the world and its realities.'

'The rebels are convinced the Emperor is surrounded by corrupt advisers who keep the truth from him. They believe military expansion on mainland China is necessary to solve Japan's economic problems. That anyone opposing such a policy must be killed.'

'The American government is against a Japanese invasion of China,' Grew said.

John spread his hands. 'There you have it.'

'Have what?' the ambassador demanded.

'Even many Japanese who aren't extremists believe America is strangling Japan. Your tour of duty here may not be too pleasant. Americans are no longer in favour.'

28

'But the United States has never taken an inch of Japanese soil, or one yen in tax. We haven't tried to govern Japan's seaports as the Europeans did. America has contributed to Japan's progress in education, agriculture and industry. How did our image become so tarnished?'

'Many Japanese still remember 1905 and President Theodore Roosevelt's settlement of the Russo–Japanese war. They claim the Russians surrendered and Japan won the war. But Theodore Roosevelt stepped in and forced the Japanese to return all their hard-fought gains. And he won the Nobel Peace Prize for saving a white nation from paying a cash indemnity to Asiatics.'

'That is an unfair simplification of Theodore Roosevelt's policies.'

'Mr Ambassador, you know history as it's taught in America. I know it as taught in Japan. The Japanese were our allies in the Great War. The Treaty of Versailles was orchestrated by President Wilson to cheat the Japanese out of an indemnity. Germany was forced to pay large cash settlements to all the allied countries except Japan. The final insult was Wilson's influence on England and Australia. The statement of the three allies to the League of Nations indicated that Japanese are racially inferior to Caucasians.'

Grew cleared his throat. 'I had hoped that incident was forgotten.'

'Neither forgotten, nor forgiven,' John said. 'Every action of a Japanese from birth to death is related to status. Westerners translate status as honour. But the Japanese see it differently. They can perform deeds, which in Western eyes would be dishonourable, and not be troubled by what we call a Christian conscience. But if someone causes a Japanese to lose status, no matter whether at home, work or in an open forum before other nations, that shame will never be excused. Some day, in some way, the Japanese will repay the three insults to them by the American government.'

29

'I cannot believe Japan would, or could wage war against America. The distance separating our countries is too great. The ties binding us are too strong. In addition, our military superiority is overwhelmingly obvious.'

John shrugged. 'Science and technology have reduced distance. Another Roosevelt in the White House opposes Japanese expansion into China. The Japanese don't measure strength by the number of men or machines, but by spirit. Last month Billy Mitchell agreed with me.'

'I was in Washington at the general's court-martial,' Grew said. 'I don't know how a brilliant officer could make such wild claims. But let's return to the problem at hand. Why the coup attempt now?'

'I think you should hear the answer from my Japanese cousin. Prime Minister Okada commissioned him to explain the situation, and Kenji is due here soon.'

'What position does this cousin of yours hold?'

'He's the largest single shareholder in the most powerful zaibatsu in Japan. The Ishikawa conglomerate owns twenty-five per cent of the world's merchant fleet. It has banks, trading companies and industries throughout the world. Kenji Ishikawa manages his own aircraft company. He designs, develops and flies his own fighter planes.'

'How did this whiz-kid come to be your cousin?'

'He'll tell you.' John pointed out of the window. 'That's him with the swagger stick. The other two are his cousins – Genda with the submachine-gun and Hino with the Luger.'

'Keep the two armed men outside. You and I shall speak with Kenji Ishikawa alone.'

4

'Captain Ishikawa, may I ask how you are related to John Whittefield?' Joseph Grew questioned.

Kenji bowed. 'Mr Ambassador, John is my cousin by adoption three times removed. His great-great-grandfather rescued and adopted my great-grandfather Moryiama Ishikawa.'

'I read about him on my trip over,' Grew said. 'In America he is referred to as John Mung, the man who brought Western knowledge into Japan after centuries of isolation.'

'The Ishikawa name is also adopted,' Kenji said. 'He was named Mangiro at birth. When he and Saiyo Ishikawa fell in love, her family was among the most ancient and respected in the empire. But they were without male heirs. As part of the marriage arrangements, Mangiro agreed to take the Ishikawa name.'

'He certainly enhanced the reputation and fortune of the Ishikawa family,' the ambassador said. 'But lately you have brought notoriety of another sort to the Ishikawa name.'

'I assume you refer to my arrest for climbing a city building.'

The ambassador winked. 'I refer to leading the Japanese team that conquered the Matterhorn.'

'Yes, sir,' Kenji said, and looked questioningly at John.

John shrugged, raising his eyebrows to indicate he had not informed the ambassador.

'The most admirable of Captain Ishikawa's many adventures . . .' Grew paused, holding the two young men in a moment of suspense. '. . . was to paint the bull's-eye on

31

the backside of the archery instructor in the Imperial Hall of Martial Arts.'

For a long moment Kenji remained frozen. Then he began to rock back and forth. Gales of laughter welled up from his broad, powerful chest. His legs weakened and he staggered to keep his balance. 'My cousin Genda held the paint can,' Kenji gasped.

'I would like to know the ambassador's source of information,' John said. 'That incident was the talk of Tokyo, but no one knew who did it.'

'May we please change the subject before there are more of my secrets revealed,' Kenji said, his face beet-red. 'I will present my official report.' He cleared his throat and stood at attention. 'Prime Minister Okada regrets any inconvenience caused to the American ambassador because of the shooting. At the first opportunity, an official ceremony will be arranged for your excellency, the ambassador, to present your credentials.'

Grew motioned Kenji to a seat. 'You've suffered enough from my sense of humour. I suggest we forgo formalities. Please brief me on the military situation in Tokyo.'

Kenji handed over a list. 'These are the names of the four senior advisers to the Emperor who were assassinated yesterday by Koda-ha rebels.'

'Have there been uprisings in other parts of Japan?' Grew asked.

'Few people outside Tokyo know what has happened,' Kenji said.

'That brings us to another question,' the ambassador said. 'Freedom of the press. All transoceanic telephone and telegraph services have been disrupted. Radio stations are shut down.'

'These closures will continue until this Koda-ha episode is ended.'

'When will that be?' John asked.

'Soon,' Kenji said.

'Why have they taken up arms in the first place?' Grew asked.

'It's a reaction to the recent elections which swept the liberal party to power. The Koda-ha wish to replace those advisers close to the Emperor. They want his imperial majesty to dissolve the Diet, take personal charge of the government and sanction an invasion of China.'

'Would the Japanese people forgo their democratic form of government?' the ambassador asked.

'Hungry people care little for political philosophy, and less for the morality of military expansion,' Kenji said. 'The depression has taken its toll on the national attitude towards democracy. Recent articles in newspapers, talks on radio and speakers in the street advocate an imperial dictatorship. Japan is the most literate country in the world. Our people have read about the progress in Italy under Benito Mussolini and in a Germany under Adolf Hitler. Even your American press blames Wall Street for the depression. Japanese equate Wall Street with the United States. The Koda-ha rebels have put out pamphlets against America's policy of Ring Fence – keeping Japan from expanding into China. We do not wish the Koda-ha's propaganda to spread. Therefore, all communications will remain suspended.'

'How do you predict the outcome?' the ambassador asked.

'Mass suicide by the surviving rebels would make them martyrs. It could eventually topple the government.'

'Are those 1,500 men prepared to die for their cause?'

'To a Japanese soldier, an honourable death is preferable to an honourable life,' Kenji said.

'Allow me to explain, Mr Ambassador,' John said. 'There is a saying in Japanese – "The fear of disgrace makes one brave." If the last act of a man's life is honourable, then he has served his Emperor and his purpose for being born. If his entire life was a legend

33

of honourable deeds and his last act disgraceful, he has failed the Emperor.'

'Why not have the Emperor inform the rebels of his displeasure?' the ambassador asked.

'Unthinkable,' Kenji said. 'A message from his imperial majesty, even if it was filtered through his advisers to the lowest clerk in the empire, could not be handed to the rebels. It would be unseemly. Incorrect form. There is no precedent for such a thing.'

'Bombing the rebels would create martyrs for their cause,' John said.

'That's it,' Kenji cried. 'You've given me the way to end it!' He shook the ambassador's hand, then John's. 'I must return to the palace.'

'You cannot consider aerial bombing in the centre of the city,' John said. 'It's extremely inaccurate. Bombing would endanger the civilian population. Fire in a city built of wood could devastate the entire capital!'

'My bombs won't explode,' Kenji said.

Wantabe, the heavyset intelligence chief, and Raiko, the newest decoder in the Black Chamber, followed the scent of the Koda-ha radio code. Like jungle cats who smelled blood, they stalked silently between cluttered desks, crouching over clacking typewriters and telegraph machines. Raiko was first to identify the period at the end of a sentence. Wantabe soon recognized the code as a variation of an outdated army cipher. He divided his men into units working on ideogram, letter substitutions, frequency of letters and transposition of homophones.

A shout from the radio operator at the far end of the room brought Raiko and Wantabe running. They were handed copies of the latest message to the rebels.

Raiko pointed at the last two words. 'This signature has different and more letters than the previous messages.'

'Nulls,' Wantabe said. 'They're using characters without

34

meaning to confuse us.' He placed the first three intercepted messages side by side and stepped back.

Raiko pencilled out certain letters in each signature. She examined the messages. She erased . . . pencilled . . . contemplated. 'There is a pattern here but I can't define it.' She sighed.

Wantabe took the pencil and spoke as he worked. 'Raiko, you are a natural. With experience and training you might well become Japan's best code expert. Take my advice. Always work with a partner. This business can drive one crazy. What is peculiar about this code is the use of Japanese ideograms for Latin letters. You are thinking of a mono-alphabetic language and they are using a poly-alphabetic code with nulls. Come, I'll show you on the cipher machine.'

Wantabe set up a second alphabet under the first. He rotated cylinders in an attempt to transpose the plain-text of the letters. For two hours Raiko watched the chief spin dials, with no results.

'Try numbers,' she said, and reached out to manipulate the dials. Her big, dark eyes burned into the cipher machine.

Wantabe inched away, hushing everyone in the room for fear the slightest noise would break the mystical spell binding the girl to the machine. He remembered the times he had become one with such a machine.

Fifteen minutes later Wantabe whispered to Raiko. 'That's a null. Delete it.' His hand shook as he touched the number dial. 'Repeat the last sequence.'

'181261018,' Raiko said.

'Everyone stop what you are doing,' Wantabe shouted. 'Translators, on me!'

Men rushed from their desks and surrounded the chief.

'Gentlemen, this series of numbers may represent a signature or the formal conclusion of a message sent to the Koda-ha rebels,' Wantabe said. 'Write out the alphabets in your speciality languages! Assign a number to each letter! Bring me something that makes sense!'

Raiko worked in English, assigning number one for A, number two for B, and on through the alphabet. In a single letter to number transposition there was no meaning. Double numbers proved another dead-end. Combinations of double and single numbers sent her heart racing. The number 18 became R, 1 equalled A, 26 equalled Z, 10 equalled O. Raiko pronounced each letter, 'R..A..Z..O..R. Razor,' she whispered. 'RAZOR!' She translated the word into Japanese for Wantabe. 'The first three numbers must be "the".'

'Shush,' Wantabe said. 'Not another word. You have decoded seven letters in plain-text. With this much I can break any cipher.' He turned from Raiko and shouted, 'Everyone stop! I have broken the Koda-ha code! You may all return to your normal work. Raiko, bring these papers to my office.' He picked up the cipher machine and whispered, 'If anyone asks, tell them I solved the problem!'

Raiko stared at the back of the man she most respected in the Black Chamber. He had given her status, treated her with respect. If the chief wants credit for my work, I'll gladly give it to him, she thought. But there was disappointment in her heart.

With the Koda-ha messages decoded, Wantabe put the plain-text into a briefcase and called Raiko back to his office. He handcuffed her left wrist to the case. 'The prime minister waits at the palace for this. A car with armed guards will take you. You are to relay the signature orally. The Razor is the nickname of Hideki Tojo, general of the Kwangtung army. He was given that label in staff college because of his sharp mind. Tojo can be a vengeful man. Credit Mr X, my code name, with solving the problem.'

Raiko understood, and bowed. 'Why are you protecting me?'

'Our country will need your abilities for the war that is coming. I can see it from the flow of messages across my desk. It is a repeat of the onset of the Great War when the Germans sided against France and England. Where Japan will fit into this war I do not know, but we have become too powerful not to be involved.' Wantabe spread his hands in a futile gesture. 'I was once able to force the answers from a cipher machine, as you did today. But my mind is almost burnt out. Yours is fresh. You will be very important to the future of our country. I will teach you everything I know.'

Michi no Myia Hirohito, the 124th descendant in an unbroken line on the throne of Japan, sat behind a polished ebony desk. Lord Keeper of the Privy Seal Hiroki Koin bowed and approached the Emperor. He bowed again, then stood at attention.

'Is the prime minister dead?' the Emperor asked.

'Mr Okada is shaken but in good health, your majesty. I suggested we act as if he was assassinated. According to constitutional law, upon his death you may initiate military action without the Diet's approval.'

The normally mild-mannered ruler of seventy million people leaned forward. 'There will be no negotiations with the rebels! Seppuku, surrender, or dishonourable death in the ruins of those three buildings!'

'There is a problem,' Hiroki said. 'It is unprecedented to deliver a message from the descendant of the Sun Goddess Amaterasu-no-Kami to anyone in rebellion against the throne.'

'It is your problem. Solve it. Now tell me about the men who were assassinated. How did they die?'

Hiroki held his wounded arm close to his body, unconsciously massaging it as he spoke. 'Sire, the attacks took place in their homes. Viscountess Saito placed herself in front of her husband, the grand chamberlain. She begged to be killed in his stead, pleading that Japan needed her husband. She held on to the muzzle of the assassin's machine-gun and he killed them both.

'The minister of the navy bade his family farewell and discussed the reasons for his death with the Koda-ha men. He called them an inarticulate bunch of rowdies and requested they shoot him before he was bored to death. They did.

'The wife of the education minister clung to her husband and they shot through her, killing both.

'The minister of finance was stabbed and hacked to death.'

Hirohito's lips puckered. He squinted through his wire-frame glasses and repeated, 'Seppuku, surrender or death to the rebels.'

Hiroki bowed and stepped back. 'So it is ordered, so it is done.' He backed out of the Emperor's presence into the anteroom.

Genda, Hino and Kenji were waiting. 'It must end tomorrow,' Hiroki told them.

'I suggest printing the Emperor's orders,' Kenji said. 'If we stuff large paper sacks and drop them from the planes at a low altitude, the sacks will burst on impact and scatter the message.'

'That suggestion may have saved my life,' Hiroki said. 'I thought to deliver the message myself, then commit seppuku for breaching protocol.'

'What if they don't surrender?' Hino asked.

'We'll shell the buildings into a pile of rubble and take no prisoners,' Hiroki said.

A guard caught Hiroki's eye from the doorway, and bowed. 'A young lady brings an important message from Mr X.'

'Admit her,' Hiroki ordered.

Raiko entered the reception room clutching the brief-case to her breast. Kenji stared at her for a moment, then blurted out, 'You're the child who helped my aunt and uncle.'

'The lord keeper of the privy seal is quite capable of caring for himself,' Raiko said.

'And this young lady is not a child,' Hiroki snapped.

Unaccustomed to being corrected by a woman or reprimanded by his uncle, Kenji stammered, 'I saw you as a beautiful child that night. Your eyes . . . I mean they are so . . .'

'So close to the floor?' Raiko said, and curtseyed. Although people often mistook her for a youngster, she had the tall, handsome captain on the defensive and saw no reason to let him off. 'Sir, I may be short in height, but you are short in manners. The distance of my head from the floor gives no indication of what is inside.'

'No insult intended,' Kenji said, and bowed, wondering why he was apologizing to a female. He saw Genda's stomach shaking and was annoyed at his cousin for enjoying the situation.

'This is Raiko Minobe,' Hiroki said. 'Her father teaches at Tokyo University.'

'Old Mini's daughter?' Kenji asked.

Raiko restrained a smile. She had the captain again. 'My father is not old. And if you refer to him as Mini in the English sense of miniature, you are revealing your perverted judgement of people's physical attributes once again.'

'But . . . Your father was my teacher. I have great respect for him.'

Hiroki saw the glint in the young woman's eyes and thought it time to rescue his nephew from her quick tongue. 'Raiko, I would like to present Captains Kenji Ishikawa, Genda and Hino Arai.' He pointed to the briefcase. 'Is that for me?'

Raiko slipped the handcuff off her tiny wrist without opening it. 'Sir, I respectfully request that the captains

39

leave the room. I have an important verbal message from Mr X.'

'We are all members of the Cherry Blossom Society,' Hiroki said. 'Kenji finances the Black Chamber.'

Raiko nodded, and bowed to the three pilots. 'Wantabe has identified the code name Razor as General Hideki Tojo. The Razor has ordered Koda-ha rebels to die fighting unless commanded by the Emperor to capitulate. In that case only the captain of the rebels is to commit seppuku. The others are to surrender and demand a civil trial in open court.'

'I thought they would all die before giving up,' Genda said.

'Tojo is clever,' Hino said. 'He wants a show trial to bring the Koda-ha cause to public attention. Then he'll order them to commit seppuku.'

'They will receive my attention,' Hiroki said. 'You three can see Raiko home. By the time you return, the leaflets will be packed into paper sacks.'

Kenji was fascinated by Raiko's large, dark eyes, and disappointed to hear her say, 'I have an escort home, thank you.'

Kenji bowed low. 'I request the opportunity to apologize properly. Could we meet?' But when he looked up, Raiko was closing the door behind her and his cousins were laughing. He wondered why he had apologized twice to this woman when he had never before apologized to anyone. 'And such a little person too.' He grunted.

5

Sixty hours of intermittent shelling had taken its toll on the Koda-ha rebels. At dawn, during a one-hour truce arranged by the Red Cross, the dead and seriously wounded were evacuated from the compound.

Among the medics and physicians who picked their way through the rubble at Central Police Station was the army's inspector general, head of Koda-ha, Dr Nikkya Tsubota. A graduate of Tokyo and Heidelberg Universities, he had received his doctorate at the Sorbonne and his military instructions from General Hideki Tojo.

Dr Tsubota looked up from the lung wound of a young sergeant and saw Captain Ando watching him. 'I see you've changed your insignia,' the doctor said.

'Yes, sir,' Ando said.

The doctor drew blood from the wounded man's arm, left the needle in the vein and detached the syringe. He filled another syringe with a milky substance, fitted it to the needle and injected it. 'You were ordered to keep your identity secret because of your expertise with explosives,' he said to Ando. 'Change clothes with this sergeant!'

Ando's brow wrinkled. He looked into the doctor's dark eyes, magnified behind the thick lenses of horn-rimmed glasses. 'This man is seriously wounded,' Ando said.

'He is dead,' Tsubota replied, pointing to the empty syringe. 'I killed him. Change! We'll get you out of here.'

'He was a good soldier,' Ando said.

'In death he serves the Emperor. Now! Change immediately!'

Tsubota plastered the sergeant's bloody bandages on to

Ando's body, then squirted him with blood from the first syringe. 'Stretcher bearers,' the doctor shouted.

Supposedly dead, Shira Ando was carried to an ambulance, and driven out of the compound.

The hour-long truce ended, but the shelling did not resume. At 7:30 a.m., the sound of three Mitsubishi seaplanes caused a stir among the Koda-ha men. The planes swooped in low over the government buildings. On the third pass, bundles were dropped into the compound, and burst apart. The morning breeze blew leaflets in every direction.

As each soldier finished reading the Emperor's order to surrender, he unloaded his weapon, placed it on the ground and marched out with his hands up.

The adjutant wearing Ando's insignia cut an X in the soft lead nose of a .45 bullet and ordered his first sergeant to shoot him through the back of the head. The dumdum bullet tore away the lieutenant's face. His body was later identified as that of Captain Shira Ando.

The Great Hall of the Imperial Palace

Hiroki addressed the members of the general staff, the survivors of the Privy Council and senior military officers. 'There will be no public trials for the rebels! Cremate their dead! Koda-ha officers will receive a military court-martial in closed session! Their names are not to be publicized! The Emperor has heard the pleas of weeping families of Koda-ha enlisted men. They will remain in barracks until the tenth of March. On that date they will embark for Manchuria. The Emperor commands it!'

'So it is ordered, so it is done,' the assembly chanted in unison.

At the rear of the great hall, Kenji and his cousins stood with John Whittefield. 'I assumed all the rebels would be executed,' John said.

'They should have been,' Genda growled. 'I agree with their cause, but not their methods. Hiroki erred in influencing the Emperor not to shoot the whole lot.'

'A practical solution has been reached,' Kenji said. 'Most of the soldiers are from the Tokyo area. We've had food riots here. A mass execution might have sparked more protests. Twenty officers will be shot and the rest sent to prison.'

'You mean the military court has already made its decision?' John said.

'The Privy Council decided several days ago that the rebel officers would be shot,' Hino said. 'The enlisted men of the First Division will never see Japan again. They'll be integrated into the Kwangtung army in Manchuria and forgotten. That is the Emperor's decision.'

John opened his briefcase and handed Kenji a flat, round can labelled *Pathé News Films. The Court-Martial of General Billy Mitchell*. 'Ambassador Grew wishes to show your uncle and the Emperor what happens to American military-men who stir up trouble between Japan and the United States. The ambassador also requests to know why the Japanese foreign minister has been so long in Berlin.'

4 March 1936, Berlin

The lean and sallow-faced forty-year-old Joseph Goebbels pointed to the robust Japanese foreign minister across the dance floor. 'The man must have been vaccinated with a victrola needle. He never shuts up.'

Ruth Kuhn laughed. She pressed her thigh against Goebbels's hand and he stroked her. Those guests who noticed, looked away. The Nazi minister of propaganda was feared by friend and foe.

'How much longer will the little fellow be your guest?' Ruth asked.

'He leaves tomorrow. This is his farewell and good-riddance party. Herr Hitler has given him permission to make an announcement of international importance tonight.' Goebbels sighed. He turned and looked directly at his mistress, his thin lips turned up in a sarcastic smile. 'This is your farewell party too.' His eyebrows raised as Ruth Kuhn's heart sank. 'Would you mind accompanying the Japanese foreign minister to Tokyo?' Goebbels asked. 'He has requested Caucasians to work for him.'

'I would die before sleeping with that fat little yellow bastard!'

'Well put. Herr Hitler also considers the Japanese an inferior race. Germany's relationship with them is one of convenience, to upset the Russians. However, the Japanese wish to train you and your father to spy on the American Pacific fleet. With their slanted eyes and yellow skin, they are too conspicuous among Caucasians. It would mean gracious living for you on a tropical island.'

'And our relationship?'

'When your father brought you to me it was understood to be a temporary arrangement,' Goebbels said.

Ruth saw the deadly expression in his eyes and tensed. She knew of those who had misread that look and disappeared for ever. 'My father and I will go with the Japanese,' she murmured.

Goebbels's eyes came alive. He clicked his heels and bowed. 'Excuse me. It is time for our guest to speak.'

Ruth Kuhn felt herself swaying. She caught her balance, took a glass of cognac from the table and downed it. A strident chord from the orchestra silenced everyone in the hall.

Goebbels led the Japanese foreign minister to the podium. 'Ladies and gentlemen, fill your glasses. Mr Matsuoka has a special toast.'

The foreign minister raised his glass and spoke in accented German. 'To the Emperor. To Herr Hitler. To the Anti-Comintern Pact signed in the Reichstag yesterday by our two great nations. From this time forward, Germany and Japan will exchange information regarding the activities of international communism. We shall work to stem socialism. In the event either country is attacked by the Soviet Union, the other will strengthen the military pressure on Russia's border. Banzai,' Matsuoka shouted. 'Banzai! Banzai!'

The Germans threw up their right hands and roared, 'Heil Hitler! Heil Hitler! Heil Hitler!'

Goebbels took Matsuoka by the arm and leaned down to whisper in his ear. 'You do understand this agreement is not a military alliance.'

The Japanese foreign minister smiled. 'Neither does Japan wish to be linked to Germany's future armed adventures. However, my statement should give Stalin a headache. That serves both our purposes, does it not?'

Goebbels nodded. 'In response to your request for Caucasian spies, Otto and Ruth Kuhn shall accompany you to Japan. Of course they will need training.'

2 May 1936, Haneda Air Force Base, Tokyo

Entrance to the lecture hall was by invitation, and that only with permission of Kempetai – the Japanese secret police. Staff officers and ranking pilots filled the seats. Army, navy and civilian intelligence agents stood in the crowded aisles.

Genda followed Kenji on to the speaker's platform. They both bowed to the assembly.

'Gentlemen,' Kenji said. 'I am proud to announce that Captain Hino Arai has broken the world's long-distance airspeed record in an original Mitsubishi T-97 fighter plane from Tokyo to London. He covered the 9,537-mile route in ninety-four hours and seventeen minutes, including refuelling.'

The hall erupted with cheers. 'Banzai! Banzai! Banzai!'

Those who had taken part in the preparations for the record-breaking transoceanic flight climbed on to the stage to congratulate Genda and Kenji and take their own bows.

When order was restored, Kenji addressed the assembly again. 'Gentlemen, two months ago I was handed a Pathé News film by the American ambassador. It is entitled *The Court-Martial of General Billy Mitchell*. Although the subject of the film is the insubordination of a senior US army officer, of greater significance to us is his new bombing technique.' Kenji stepped back. 'Lights! Switch the sound off! I'll translate.'

The room darkened and the screen lit up. An American army officer was surrounded by reporters. 'The location is Washington DC,' Kenji said. 'General William L. Mitchell, a soldier's soldier who came up through the ranks to command the US army air force, was first introduced to the flying machine by Orville Wright in 1908. Mitchell commanded the US army air force in France during the Great War. His belief that air supremacy will win the next war has led to many confrontations with his superiors. The following test resulted in his court-martial.'

Kenji signalled and the film stopped. 'What you are about to see is the first of two bombing runs. General Mitchell went outside regular channels to arrange this demonstration. His friends in the American Congress forced the military to test the new air-attack theory. You should understand that there is rivalry between the army and navy for congressional funds. The American air force is part of the US army signal corps. In other words, the last rice bowl to be filled after the army, navy and marine corps. Mitchell claims small aeroplanes can destroy large naval targets – in this case a retired navy frigate. His superiors ordered him not to use the new tactic. Instead to bomb from an altitude of 3,000 feet.'

Kenji motioned and the film began again. The stiff faces of American military-men filled the screen. 'The civilians are Congressmen and newspaper people,' Kenji said. 'The ship in the background is the target. Those three specks high on the right of the screen are old biplanes. They are now over the target. Bombs away, from 3,000 feet as ordered. Geysers appear fore and aft of the target. No bomb is close enough to damage the ship. Notice the relaxed faces of the military-men aboard the observation craft. The first test was a failure, as Mitchell expected. He returned to base and begged for modern planes to use his new tactic in the second run, but permission was denied. Mitchell commandeered the newest American single-wing planes and loaded them with a 500-pound bomb each. Now watch the second run.'

Kenji remained silent. He saw every man in the audience lean forward, eyes glued to the three dots at the right of the screen moving swiftly towards their target. Almost over the frigate the planes nosed down, growing larger and larger. Like three hawks, they swooped towards their prey. Four hundred feet above the target, the bombs were released and the planes arched back up. Two bombs hit amidship, the third a close miss to starboard. The frigate broke in half and sank.

'Lights,' Kenji ordered.

The brightened hall remained silent. Men continued to stare at the blank screen with the vision of destruction still impressed on their minds.

'Divebombing,' Kenji said. 'The target sank in two minutes, forty-five seconds.'

'Mitchell was put on trial for insubordination,' Genda said. 'Japan should give the man a medal. Tomorrow we begin divebomb training. Those who wish to volunteer may sign up with me at the end of this meeting.'

'Because Mitchell was a general, his superiors could only reprimand him at a public trial for disobeying orders,'

Kenji said. 'They gave him the opportunity to resign but he refused, and used the courtroom as a platform to attack Japan. Mitchell was stationed in Kyoto and Nagasaki for two years. He knows our country. But his testimony resulted in dismissal from the army. That is the reason this film was given to me. An apology from the American government for Mitchell's accusations.'

Kenji motioned and the lights went out again. A military courtroom appeared on the screen. 'Mitchell is taking the stand,' Kenji said. 'I'll translate the general's closing remarks. He says, "The manoeuvre used to sink the frigate is called divebombing. This tactic should be incorporated into US air-force training programmes. The effectiveness is clear. I disobeyed orders because I believe a war between Japan and the United States is imminent, and inevitable!"

'Note the confusion among the spectators,' Kenji said. 'The army lawyers are trying to silence Mitchell. The judge disagrees. Mitchell continues speaking: "Unless enlightened statesmen in Tokyo and Washington resolve our differences, Japan and America will be at war within three years. The devastation of Europe in the Great War, and the present worldwide economic depression, have resulted in a withdrawal of European forces from the Pacific. This has created a vacuum between Japan and the United States. When the seal on that vacuum is broken, America and Japan will be sucked into confrontation. The recent assassination of liberal Japanese politicians, the disappearance of pilots Amelia Earhart and US Marine Major George Evans near Japanese-occupied islands in the north Pacific, and the refusal of Japanese authorities to allow visitors to those islands, indicates they are being fortified. The recent Anti-Comintern Pact signed with fascist Germany, and Japan's violation of the agreement with the Allies not to build more battleships and aircraft carriers, are indications that the Japanese are preparing for war."'

Kenji was surprised at the lack of reaction in the hall to Mitchell's accusations. He continued translating. 'Notice the officer standing on the left. He's laughing. And now he shouts, "I suppose you can tell us where the little yellow buggers will strike first." The courtroom quiets and Mitchell answers, "It depends on the location of the US Pacific fleet. Japan must neutralize the fleet. To do it they will attack without warning, as they did against the Chinese fleet in 1895 and the Russian navy at Port Arthur in 1904. I expect the attack will take place on a holiday. The fleet is in harbour on holidays, without the ability to manoeuvre, and most of the men go on shore leave. The attack will come from the air as swiftly as I sank that frigate."

'Lights,' Kenji said. 'That last, and most ambiguous statement, resulted in General Mitchell's dismissal from the American army without rights to pride or pension.'

Again his audience surprised Kenji. Every man in the room, including the senior officers, stood and bowed to the blank screen. Kenji turned and bowed also, to General Billy Mitchell, a fellow soldier who had sacrificed his honour for his country.

'Those who wish to begin training on the new dive-bombing technique may now sign up with me,' Genda announced.

Kenji whispered to his cousin, 'I expected reaction to the accusation that we're fortifying the Pacific islands, or that we're responsible for the disappearance of the marine major and Amelia Earhart.'

Genda shrugged. 'Mitchell's accusations are probably true.'

A note was handed to Kenji:

Well done, Captain Ishikawa. Send the film to my head-quarters. Remain available in Tokyo.

Vice Minister of the Navy,
Admiral Isokoro Yamamoto

6

Raiko Minobe imagined the grinding sound was part of her dream about Kenji. Half asleep, she experienced warmth in her loins, and wondered what it would be like to touch her body to his. The sound persisted and Raiko opened her eyes to see Ruth Kuhn sharpening pencils. The beautiful blonde woman was a diligent student, quick to grasp new ideas. In the five weeks of living and studying with Raiko, Ruth's English had improved dramatically. She was already proficient at coding radio messages.

'You're up earlier than usual,' Raiko said in German.

'I wish to be prepared for this morning's test,' Ruth answered in English.

'Excellent. That was part one of today's examination. Always react in English. You can't disguise your accent, but we can make it sound sexy.'

'My duties will be to observe and report on the Pacific fleet,' Ruth said. 'I'm not going to sleep with the American navy.'

'In Hawaii, beautiful, unmarried white women are rare. Officers will be panting to impress you with knowledge of their ships, their destinations and training schedules. If you wish to invite them to your villa overlooking Pearl Harbor, or to the new cottage near Hickam Field, that's up to you. Will you and your father be living together?'

Ruth chewed the inside of her lip. Her father had taken her to Goebbels as a virgin, in return for prestige and wealth. He had agreed to spy for the Japanese rather than be cut off from his source of power. 'Otto is unable to learn the codes,' Ruth said.

'Wantabe has decided that only you will receive and

50

transmit on the radio. Your father will be trained in aircraft identification, plus the mapping of ammunition, food and fuel storage facilities.'

'Otto will be relieved to hear that.'

'Wantabe wishes to reduce the pressure on you,' Raiko said. 'Pass today's examination and I'm instructed to take you night clubbing in the Roppongi. The chief will escort us, and we'll speak English.'

'Then the evening's entertainment is part of my training.'

'That too. But more of a reward for supplying Rudolph Hess's doctoral thesis on Japan's intelligence service. Our people didn't know he studied here.'

'Those papers are on public record in Heidelberg University,' Ruth said. 'In Berlin I often heard members of the German general staff deride the Japanese intelligence service. But from what I've learned here, Hess's information is outdated.'

'Loyalty to Germany may require that you report this observation to your foreign office,' Raiko said. 'Please, for your own sake, don't mention it within hearing of other Japanese. The Kempetai are everywhere.'

'Like Hitler's Gestapo,' Ruth said in German. 'That bastard Goebbels and his Nazi friends won't hear a word from me. I feel like getting drunk tonight. Where are we going?'

'The Jazz Club.'

Although outranked by everyone in the waiting room, Genda, Hino and Kenji were admitted first. Admiral Isokoro Yamamoto glared at them as they stood at attention before him. 'I earned an engineering degree from Meiji and Harvard Universities,' the admiral said. 'According to the horsepower ratio and r.p.m. rating of the Mitsubishi aircraft engine, it was impossible to break the long-distance speed record. Did you three fake the claim?'

'No, sir,' Hino answered. 'We worked as a team. I am a navigator with a knack for catching air currents. I charted the course and took the southern route because of following winds. My brother is the tactician.'

Genda bowed. 'Sir, I trained the ground crews along the route to refuel and service the plane in a minimum amount of time.'

Yamamoto grunted. 'According to your own reports, the T-97 fighter will not do 250 miles an hour. My calculations indicate that speed was necessary for the plane to arrive in the time stated.'

'Sir, I found the solution in an old German scientific journal,' Kenji said. 'In the Great War, during the siege of Paris, German artillery-men attained greater distances by firing high into the atmosphere. The author explained that above 30,000 feet the thinner air has less friction on shells or aeroplanes. Hino flew at 35,000 feet.'

'But it is known one cannot breathe, and could freeze at that altitude,' Yamamoto said.

Hino smiled. 'I dressed like an Eskimo.'

'He also used an oxygen mask and breath regulator designed by the staff of Tokyo University's medical college,' Kenji said. 'Hino discarded the oxygen tanks before each landing. Our ground crews put new ones aboard during refuelling without anyone's knowledge.'

'Why the secrecy?' Yamamoto asked.

'Eventually we'll perfect high-altitude flying for all our pilots,' Kenji said. 'It increases range and attains tactical advantage in aerial combat. It would give us the ability to fly higher and dive out of the sun to surprise enemy planes.'

'Do you suppose we would use such a tactic to fight the Americans as General Billy Mitchell predicted?' Yamamoto asked.

'I hope so,' Hino answered. 'I want to be tested against the best. The Americans have surpassed the world in military aeronautics, and they've never lost a war.'

'Japan has never been defeated, and we are 2,000 years older,' Genda said. 'There will be war. The American policy of Ring Fence makes it inevitable.'

'We cannot fight the Americans,' Kenji said.

'Impossible to avoid,' Genda replied. 'The land deals our zaibatsu made in Australia, New Zealand and California for peaceful resettlement of our citizens were nullified by new laws against property sales to Japanese.'

'We cannot defeat the United States,' Kenji said. 'If we are to expand, it must be on the Asian mainland.'

'Do you advocate Tojo's policy of invading China?' Yamamoto asked. 'If so, my advisers believe Franklin Roosevelt will stop the Kwangtung army.'

Kenji began to sweat. He held strong feelings for America. He had studied there and had many friends. He was about to voice a suggestion that could result in war if he was wrong. 'Admiral, our alternatives are limited. I believe a restricted incursion by the Kwangtung army into the five northern provinces of China would not prompt an American or European military reaction. The United States has followed an isolationist policy since the Great War. The Europeans are trying to appease Germany and Italy. Mussolini annexed Ethiopia, Hitler took the Rhineland and nullified the Versailles Treaty without opposition from the Western powers. If we invade northern China, American politicians will have a dilemma. They know the Chinese Nationalist army is trained by German officers. That Chiang Kai-shek also uses Italian pilots. Mao Tse-tung's Chinese Communist army receives its weapons from Moscow. Roosevelt and Anthony Eden are against Stalin as well as Mussolini and Hitler. They consider all three to be fascist states.'

'The English-language newspapers call us fascists too,' Yamamoto said. 'We may be forced to let Tojo loose in

China, but I fear Roosevelt's reaction. I was chief naval attaché in Washington DC for two years, and know the military power of America. We cannot defeat the United States.'

'It is not in our interest to try,' Kenji said. 'Without the American market, Japan's economy would be ruined.'

'The Chinese market is larger,' Genda said. 'If we control it, Japan will become rich.'

'No one can control China,' Yamamoto said. 'Not even the Chinese. Chiang's Nationalists are fighting Mao's Communists, and the rest of their country is ruled by thieving warlords. Whether we fight the Chinese, Russians or Americans, Billy Mitchell is correct. Air power will determine the outcome. Keep me informed of your high-altitude flying and divebomb training. Put the stress on carrier-based planes. We are an island nation which must depend on our navy to protect us.'

The Roppongi was aglow from one end of the broad avenue to the other. Flashing lights advertised nightclubs, bars and restaurants. The street was crowded with uniforms and young people dressed in European styles. But at the corners of cross streets, elderly people begged. In back of the club kitchens, orderly lines of children formed at garbage cans.

The air-force officers who piled out of the large Lincoln did not notice the poor or the hungry. Kenji, his Russian girlfriend Natasha and his two cousins were escorted into the Jazz Club by two uniformed doormen.

Hino began to sing along with the Negro band from Chicago. He danced behind the headwaiter towards the group of airmen seated under their squadron flag. Empty beer bottles littered the table.

'Over here,' the airmen called. The senior sergeant stood up and saluted the three captains.

'There's no rank at this table,' Kenji said. 'We worked together for the record. Together we celebrate.'

'To the world record,' Hino said. He pointed at the empty bottles on the table. 'We're far behind. The custom is for Japanese officers to lead their men into battle.' He handed Kenji and Genda full bottles.

Kenji pointed at the flag. 'To the finest squadron in the world. Here's to the record we broke and the records we will break. Here's to us.'

'Drink! Drink! Drink! Drink! Drink!' The airmen chanted until the three captains emptied their bottles.

Kenji massaged the rump of his redheaded mistress and kissed her mouth. 'Now it's time for serious drinking. More beer,' he shouted.

The band finished their number and a woman called in English from across the large room. 'If that's what you call serious drinking, I'll drink any of you or the entire Japanese air force under the table!'

There was stunned silence. Hino's eyes brightened at the sight of a big-busted blonde standing across the room. 'I accept the challenge,' he called in English. 'Will you and your party please join us?'

Ruth Kuhn removed Raiko's hand from her arm. 'I spoke in English.' She nodded to Wantabe. 'Tell the chief not to worry. We Germans invented beer.' Ruth strutted across the dance floor, challenging the airmen with every movement of her voluptuous body.

'Wow!' Hino said to Kenji. 'This blonde is as beautiful as your Natasha.'

'And her tits are almost as big,' Genda said.

Kenji's eyes were on the Japanese girl following the blonde. Raiko wore a Western-style dress that showed her every curve. Her legs were shapely in high heels and her eyes sparkled like the black sequins on her dress.

'My name is Ruth,' the blonde said. 'This is Raiko, and our escort, Mr Wantabe.'

Raiko tried to keep from looking at the beautiful redheaded woman clinging to Kenji's arm.

'Please join our party,' Hino said. 'You, Miss Ruth, are excused from the drinking challenge.'

Ruth moved very close to him. She inhaled slowly, which pushed her large breasts further out of the low-cut dress. Hino's eyes were lost in the cleavage between the two quivering mounds of white flesh.

'Does the imperial air force concede defeat to a woman?' Ruth asked.

Hino gurgled, and grunted.

'Bring on the beer,' Genda shouted.

Ruth turned to Raiko, having to grasp her arm to get her attention.

Raiko finally translated what Ruth wanted to say in Japanese. 'The challenge stands.'

'Drinking from a bottle bloats the belly with air,' Ruth said. 'Fill some pitchers.'

'Do you remember me?' Kenji asked Raiko in Japanese.

She nodded at his mistress. 'I see you found someone your own size.'

'Why do you make it so difficult to be friendly?' Kenji asked.

'Is this a proper place to discuss friendship?' Raiko asked.

'But we're here. Where would you like to discuss it?'

The question and the concern on Kenji's face angered Raiko. She sat down with her back to him.

Beer-bottle caps popped and water pitchers were filled with frothy golden brew.

'Captains three, do you accept my challenge?' Ruth Kuhn laughed deep in her throat.

'What is the wager?' Hino asked.

Ruth had seen Sorge, the senior German correspondent, and his embassy cronies sitting at the rear of the nightclub. She knew her actions would be reported and Goebbels would hear. She raised her arms over her head and pirouetted. 'The prize is me, if you win.'

'And if we lose?' Hino asked.

Ruth embraced the young flier and gave him a long kiss on the mouth. 'My prize is you and your officer friends.'

'All three of us?' Hino gasped.

'Those who can walk out that door with me.'

Wantabe's eyes rolled in his head as Raiko translated. 'What will Kenji do with his mistress?' he asked.

Raiko punched the table, ignored the question and turned in her seat to watch the contest.

Ruth raised her pitcherful of beer to the three captains. 'Drink,' she cried.

'Drink! Drink! Drink!' the airmen chanted, and the band took up the beat. Except for Raiko and the Germans, everyone in the club joined the chant.

Hino grasped his pitcher with two hands. Beer flowed down his chin as he reached the halfway mark. Genda drank more slowly, but steadily. When Ruth put her empty pitcher down and reached for another, Kenji bowed and conceded defeat. Hino and Genda gulped their pitchers empty and took up full ones.

The crowd chanted and the drums rolled as the contestants swallowed more and more beer. The second pitcher slipped from Hino's lips, spilling beer down his uniform. He plopped into a chair.

Genda's slow steady drinking caught up with Ruth's. His eyes rolled to the right as he drank, noting they were even. With one great gulp he finished the pitcher, and slammed it on the table. 'I win you,' he roared at the buxom blonde.

Hino staggered forward. 'What about me?'

'The fräulein is going home with us!' Two of the four Germans stood behind Ruth. Both were young, athletic-looking men. Their Prussian-style haircuts marked them as military. The first one reached out and took

57

Ruth's arm. 'It is time for you to leave!' he said in German.

Kenji did not notice the third muscular German move behind him. 'The lady is with us!' Kenji said in German. 'Please leave before there is trouble!'

'The yellow monkey speaks the mother tongue.'

Kenji started forward but was grabbed from behind. Genda rushed the first two Germans and was punched hard in the stomach. He let out a giant belch, spewing beer all over them, and fell to the floor holding his belly.

Hino slipped a heavy glass ashtray into a cloth napkin. Using it as a blackjack he clubbed the man holding Kenji. Kenji leapt forward with the swiftness of a jungle cat, wedge-punching the first German under the nose. He kicked the other in the groin and judo-chopped him behind the neck. The airmen hustled the three Germans out of the club.

Hino focused his bleary eyes on Ruth Kuhn. 'Who takes the lady home?'

Ruth looked to the rear of the club where Sorge sat alone. 'You!' she said loudly, and pointed at Genda sitting on the floor, his eyes still glazed. 'He can't get up and Kenji has enough to handle with his redhead.'

'First we must advertise our squadron's success,' Hino said. He pointed at the flag overhead, then at Kenji. 'Captain Kenji Ishikawa, you are famous for climbing high mountains and tall buildings. I request that you hang our banner from the flagpole of the Imperial Hotel where the Emperor will see it in the morning.'

Raiko's mocking eyes angered Kenji. 'Of course!' He smiled down at her. 'Will you join us?'

Raiko stood up. 'You're drunk. Climbing the Imperial Hotel in your condition is a deadly risk.'

'Those are the only ones worth taking,' Kenji said.

'Not while I watch,' Raiko said, and stalked out of the club.

7

'Why is a junior officer, who wishes to advise a senior, like a bull without balls?' Dr Tsubota giggled and answered his own question. 'Because no matter how hard he tries, he cannot.'

'What advice would you give Tojo?' Captain Ando asked.

'Do not kill Chang Tso-lin.'

'We've been tracking the marshal for six months. The explosives are in place.'

'Patience is the supreme virtue,' Tsubota said. 'I would use Tso-lin's troops to hold back the Russians on the Mongolian border. We can always get him out of Tojo's way. If he dies now, part of his army will become bandits, some will join Chiang Kai-shek's Nationalist army in the south, and others Mao Tse-tung's Communists in the north. Sooner or later we'll have to fight all of them.'

'But Tso-lin was bribed by our own prime minister to move into central Manchuria.'

'The prime minister fears Tojo and the Kwangtung army. When Chiang Kai-shek moved the Chinese capital from Peking to Nanking, it was an invitation for our army to march. That is when Hiroki Koin decided to station Tso-lin's Chinese troops behind the Kwangtung army, to prevent Tojo from invading China. Hiroki fears the Americans would step in to save Chiang Kai-shek and there will be war between the United States and Japan.' Tsubota cleaned his glasses, squinting at Ando. 'Whatever my opinion, you and I do as we are told.

Tso-lin must die before he reaches Mukden. Tojo has ordered it.'

'And so it will be done,' Ando said. He donned the uniform jacket and cap of a colonel in the Kwangtung army, then accompanied Tsubota to a waiting Chinese staff car.

'The train should approach the tunnel about two this afternoon,' Tsubota said. 'Watch for the colour red on the right side of the tracks. If you survive, we will meet in Mukden and I'll introduce you to the pleasures of the Fifth Moon Inn.' The two men bowed.

Ando was driven to the storage-yard of the Tientsin–Mukden railroad. The Chinese guards searched him and confiscated his pistol. They led him across a maze of tracks. Two thousand Chinese soldiers waited to board a forty-car freight train.

'You'll have luxurious accommodations,' a guard said. He pointed at a train of twenty-one parlour cars headed by three steam engines. It was protected by hundreds of armed guards. 'The middle car is the marshal's. It once belonged to the Dowager Empress. You can enter only from the far sides of the dining cars on each end. We cannot be too careful.'

Dressed as a colonel, Ando was assumed to be the senior of four other Japanese officers travelling in the front compartment of the de-luxe car. Marshal Tso-lin had also brought along senior Communist and Nationalist officials, to ensure his safe arrival in Mukden. The remainder of the parlour cars contained Tso-lin's personal possessions, 500 handpicked bodyguards and, unknown to Tso-lin, 300 pounds of TNT.

Five days earlier, with the help of railroad workers bribed by Tsubota, Ando had installed the large explosive charge in the undercarriage of the dining car just ahead of Tso-lin's de-luxe parlour car. The yellow nitrogen compound had been melted, moulded and painted to blend into the car's frame.

Now, Ando was taken directly to meet the marshal, and was surprised by the soft voice and scholarly appearance of the most feared warlord in China.

'Colonel, please be seated,' Tso-lin said through an interpreter. 'Your four colleagues are in the next compartment. You will remain here. May I offer you some tea?'

'Yes, thank you,' Ando said, relieved he did not have to sit with fellow Japanese officers he would soon kill.

The stilted conversation, conducted through the interpreter, waned. When two Chinese generals joined the marshal, Ando bowed and moved to the opposite side of the large, ornately decorated compartment. The train began to move and Ando's watch showed it was leaving on schedule. The marshal's train had priority over all opposing trains on the Tientsin–Mukden railroad.

Two hours later, the train reached the outskirts of Peking. Ando saw soldiers posted every hundred yards on both sides of the track all along the way through the old capital city. The countryside became more rugged. Wheat fields instead of rice paddies. Hills and mountains replaced the flat-lands. The scenery reminded Ando of home and he grew lonely. He missed his wife and two sons. Perhaps he would never see them again. He longed for things Japanese – the language, the smells, the jokes. 'Red is the colour,' he mumbled, and looked around to see if anyone had overheard. I must concentrate, he thought. Tsubota hired a hundred-man work gang to stand three miles from the longest tunnel on the route to Mukden, all wearing red shirts. When I see them, I'll go forward to the dining car and light the fuse to the TNT. Detonated inside the tunnel, the explosive power of the 300 pounds of TNT will be quadrupled. If, by chance I'm not allowed to move forward and set off the charge while travelling, I'll do it at the Mukden station and die in the act.

He looked at his watch. It was noon and lunch was scheduled to be served at 2 p.m. He might be dead before then. He took pen, paper and ink from his briefcase and tried to compose his death poem. He dropped page after page on the seat beside him.

'Marshal Chang asks if you are having trouble,' the interpreter said, pointing to the pile of crumpled papers.

'Thank the marshal for his concern.' Ando bowed. 'I am an amateur poet. Would it be permissible for me to go forward and get a bite to eat? I had no breakfast. Food might accelerate the creative process.'

Chang Tso-lin nodded his agreement to the interpreter. 'You might wish to send lunch to your fellow officers in the forward compartment,' the interpreter said to Ando.

Again Ando bowed. He shoved the last poem into his pocket and looked at his watch. It was almost 2 p.m. He was shocked the time had passed so quickly. He forced himself to appear calm as he walked forward. The voices of the Japanese officers were audible through the compartment's closed door and he prayed it would not open.

He reached the end of the coach and went out on to the open platform between the cars. Two guards eyed him. The rush of fresh air brought him relief. Holding the handrail, Ando cautiously descended the steps and stuck his head out of the speeding train. He squinted into the wind. Far ahead was the long line of red shirts standing on a hillock. His heartbeat quickened. He backed up the steps and entered the dining car.

The first toilet on the right was locked. Ando cursed himself for becoming caught up in his death poem. He had to get inside the toilet and set the fuse. He knocked on the door and the occupant knocked back. Ando pounded the door with his fist and the occupant pounded back. Ando braced himself to kick the door in, and it flew open. An irate Chinese officer trundled out, cursing and hitching up his trousers.

Ando pushed past the man and slammed the door shut behind him. His heart pounded. He leaned over the Western-style toilet and pried out a square floor plate. Wind rushed up into his face. He groped for the two-minute fuse, found it and struck a match. The force of air from under the speeding train doused the flame. The air extinguished match after match. He reached into his pocket and pulled out his death poem. The paper caught fire on the next match and he thrust the flame against the fuse. It sizzled, then burned brightly, faster than normal because of the wind. Ando dropped the floor plate over the hole and rushed out of the toilet. He pushed by people in the dining car and rushed forward as quickly as possible, cursing himself for not having taken the wind factor into account.

Ando pushed by the officer he had disturbed in the toilet. The man's angry shout was lost in the roar of wind and darkness of the tunnel. The increased wind pressure in the tunnel would cause the fuse to burn even faster. Ando bolted forward blindly, pushing passengers out of his way, knocking others over. He reached the far end of the dining car and dashed across the open platform into the rear of the next car. He started to run and the floor lifted under his feet. A blinding light lit up the car. A tremendous roar threatened to crush Ando's head. His knees buckled and he was catapulted forward through the darkness. His shoulder caught the back of a seat. He flipped in the air, landing on struggling bodies. People fell on him. The high-pitched screeching of iron wheels on steel rails, the sound of tearing metal and screaming wail of the engine whistle seemed to go on for ever. The train skidded half a mile with its brakes locked, and finally came to a stop outside the tunnel.

Soldiers helped Ando to his feet. The bright sunlight hurt his eyes. He crawled through a shattered window and down from the train. Dark greasy smoke billowed from the mouth of the tunnel. The three big engines had dragged the front half of the train out into the sunlight. The rear of the dining car had blown off. Bodies were plastered against walls, ceiling and floor.

Men rushed back into the smoke-filled darkness. They began leading and carrying a line of wounded out of the tunnel. Marshal Chang Tso-lin's body was placed with a hundred others.

Shira Ando slipped away from the carnage. He rendez-voused with a squad of Kwangtung army cavalry and began the cross-country journey on horseback to the Fifth Moon Inn.

7 October 1936

John Whittefield placed a pile of papers on the ambassador's desk. Both men waited for the secretary to leave and lock the door.

'You may report,' Joseph Grew said.

'After February's attempted coup, elder statesmen close to the Emperor, led by Hiroki Koin, disciplined the coup leaders. Some young officers were shot. Many were jailed. Others were exiled to the Kwangtung army in Manchuria.' John placed his hands on the documents before the ambassador. 'Here is proof of Tojo's responsibility for the assassination of Marshal Chang Tso-lin. He used two Japanese officers to carry out the murder. I believe we should make this public. It may anger the Chinese people enough to unite them, and prevent the invasion of northern China by Tojo.' John tapped the papers. 'That invasion is outlined here.'

Grew leaned over his desk and fixed John with cold, hard eyes. 'How did you come by this information?'

'As chief of intelligence, I have agents throughout China, Manchuria and Japan.'

Grew held John's eyes with his stern gaze. 'Come now, Mr Whittefield. This is the American ambassador you're speaking to.'

John coughed. 'Sir, I broke into the Kyoto headquarters of Koda-ha and copied these documents.'

'You what!' Grew leaned further over his desk. The veins in his forehead pulsated, the tendons in his neck jumped. 'You are First Secretary of this embassy! Wars have been started with less provocation! If you had been caught the least it would have meant was expulsion for you, possibly me too, and certain embarrassment for the United States government!'

'It was quite safe,' John said. 'A Yakuza night watchman led me in and out.'

'You're working with Japanese tattooed gangsters! My God, man, are you crazy!'

'Sir, look at the information and you'll agree the risk was worthwhile.'

'I'm too disturbed to read! Brief me!'

John held up the batch of papers. 'It took three nights to copy all this.'

'Three nights,' the ambassador moaned. 'Next time I ask how you accomplished something, don't tell me.'

John's eyes brightened. 'These papers prove Koda-ha was involved in the assassination of Chang Tso-lin. Tojo actually wanted him killed in China, not Manchuria.'

'What is the difference?'

'The Japanese would have blamed Chiang Kai-shek and used it as an excuse to invade China.'

'A staged incident to start a war?'

'That's how Japan got control over Manchuria and Korea,' John said. 'They acted out a phony battle along the Manchurian railroad for an excuse to invade that country. According to these papers, Tojo's primary interest is northern China and the Yangtze valley. Those areas can supply raw materials for Japan's industries, markets for her products, and enough land to resettle ten million Japanese who will raise food for the homeland.'

'Does Japan have the military strength to fight China and resist pressure from America and Europe?'

'Koda-ha's evaluation is that since Hitler's and Mussolini's rise to power, the Europeans can no longer exert military pressure in the Far East. That leaves only the United States.'

'How do we compare in armaments with Japan?' Grew asked.

'The answer is in these documents,' John said. He rifled through the papers and found what he was looking for. 'The Japanese navy has ten battleships, thirty-eight cruisers, 119 destroyers, 108 corvettes, sixty submarines and four aircraft carriers. We're outgunned at sea.'

'Last month's naval evaluation report indicated that we have more military naval tonnage than Japan.'

John walked to the wall map and pointed. 'America has two oceans and only one navy. That navy has to patrol both oceans and maintain a presence on both coasts for defence. We have four times more area to cover than Japan.'

'Are you saying the Japanese have more naval power than America?'

'In the Pacific ocean, twice as much. Furthermore, Admiral Yamamoto has had every Japanese merchantship fitted with gun mounts, weapons, ammunition, and staffed with gunnery officers and radio-men. Yamamoto is also a strong advocate of naval air power. He's building two of the largest, most modern aircraft carriers in the world. They'll be faster than anything we have or plan to have in the next ten years. Would you like a comparison of land and naval air power?'

Grew nodded, and listened to the long list of fighter, bomber and reconnaissance squadrons of both countries.

'To sum up,' John said. 'America has 4,104 military

machines, of which 1,752 are considered first-line aircraft. Japan has 1,639 combat-ready planes.'

'And America being a two-ocean country means that in the Pacific, Japan outflies us two to one.' Grew stood up and shook John's hand. 'You are to be congratulated. How you could remember the names, places and numbers of the American naval and army aircraft squadrons to compare them with the Japanese equipment, amazes me.'

'I didn't memorize anything. It's all listed in the Koda-ha files.'

The ambassador turned chalk-white and fell back into his chair. 'You mean to tell me the Japanese have spies in the United States?'

'Extremely efficient spies. They may even have American military personnel working for them.'

'John, send this information to Washington by the quickest method possible!'

'Yes, sir. I'll use the grey code.'

8

Natasha was as tall as Kenji in her high-heeled shoes. Her long red hair cascaded over soft shoulders, on to full breasts with large pink nipples. Kenji never tired of her nude body. He thought of her as his living *objet d'art*.

Natasha turned and looked at him over her shoulder. 'Which side do you prefer?'

Kenji undid his robe and Natasha's eyes roamed his athlete's body. His muscles rippled down like a washboard that narrowed between powerful thighs. She pointed at his golden rod. 'You'll be late for your meeting.'

Kenji pressed his palms against Natasha's. He rubbed his body against hers, brushing breast to breast, belly to belly. He spread her arms wide, holding her hands in his. She leaned closer and kissed his lips, his neck, his chest. Kenji shuddered. The emergency meeting of the Cherry Blossom Society would wait.

Raiko sat in the Koin living room. The tortured figures in Rodin's sketch reminded her of the attack on Hiroki six months before, and she shuddered. 'Who or what is Kenji Ishikawa?' she asked.

Noriko Koin sensed more than a casual interest in the question. 'He is probably the richest, most sought-after bachelor in the empire.'

'I didn't mean his marital status,' Raiko said. 'I've read that he's an aeronautical engineer who finances, builds and tests his own fighter planes. That in itself is a great responsibility. Then he performs a dangerously foolish act like climbing the Imperial Hotel to get his picture in the newspapers. And he flaunts his White Russian mistress to the photographers.'

'I doubt publicity was the reason for his performance,' Noriko said. 'Kenji owns at least one newspaper in Tokyo, and several more around the country. He doesn't worry what others think of him.'

'That must sometimes be embarrassing to you and Hiroki. Kenji is like your son.'

'He is very conscious of our feelings, but he is also impulsive. As for his Russian mistress, my husband Hiroki is responsible for that.'

For a moment Raiko lost her poise. 'Did Hiroki force Kenji to take a white concubine?' The intensity in the girl's eyes confirmed Noriko's suspicions.

'You seem to have a Christian concept of sexual morality,' Noriko said. 'Having a mistress, a concubine or a favourite girl is natural to those Japanese men who can afford it.'

'With the Ishikawa fortune, Kenji could buy every White Russian woman who fled the Soviets,' Raiko said.

'I think your question really refers to why a white woman, not why a White Russian.' Noriko smiled. 'Hiroki's brothers took Kenji to his first pleasure-house. They told him a story about Hiroki, who was born and raised in Korea. Upon his return to Japan, Hiroki's brothers had taken him to a pleasure-house. Hiroki could only perform with a Chinese girl. He explained that having been out of Japan for so long, sex with a Japanese girl was like relations with a sister. He could not. It is the same with Kenji. He has spent years in America and he emulates Hiroki in many ways.'

'I am a Christian,' Raiko said, watching Noriko's face to gauge her reaction.

'Did your father convert?'

'Father follows the teachings of Confucius. He's polite to the possibility of gods and Heaven, but never prays to any god. I investigated the Christian religion at Vassar college. Their beliefs are illogical, but I found it comforting to sit in church with my friends.'

'Kenji's great-grandfather was baptized a Christian in Honolulu,' Noriko said. 'Mung reverted to the Japanese religion when he returned to Japan. He was buried by a Buddhist priest.'

Sounds from the front of the house distracted .he two women. 'That should be Kenji,' Noriko said. 'He makes a great noise kicking off his shoes. You must have brought important information for such a gathering on such short notice.'

'Wantabe sees war coming,' Raiko said. She motioned to Rodin's picture on the wall. 'I believe Japan may be approaching the Gates of Hell.'

Wantabe appeared in the doorway and beckoned to Raiko. She bowed to Noriko and followed the heavyset man.

'Do not be frightened,' he whispered.

Several men were seated on either side of a long table in the study. Raiko recognized a government minister, two generals, Admiral Yamamoto, Kenji and Hiroki at the far end of the table. Wantabe motioned her to a seat opposite his.

Wantabe cleared his throat and addressed Raiko. 'As senior members of the Cherry Blossom Society, we are devoted to the Emperor, the empire and the people of Japan. We also espouse Pan-Asianism and over the years have supported revolutionaries throughout Asia. More recently, because of the economic depression, the Cherry Blossom Society has concerned itself with domestic issues. Now the society has again become involved in international events. There is no official government approval for our activities. We do maintain close ties with members of the National Diet and the military. Raiko Minobe,' Wantabe pointed at her, 'I have sponsored your

70

admission to the Cherry Blossom Society. You are the most talented code-breaker I have ever met and I see you as my replacement. If you decide to join us, it will no longer be as an employee. You will become one of us. I must caution you that it could be dangerous. Your life would be subject to our orders. You would have to ask permission to travel, even in Japan. You could not marry nor have children without the society's approval.'

Kenji's heart went out to Raiko. Her small breasts were barely visible above the table top. He found himself hoping she would reject the long list of obligations Wantabe read to her. Then his heart swelled with pride as she took the oath.

'I swear to obey, without question, the orders of the Cherry Blossom Society and its officers, no matter the consequences to my family, friends or myself,' Raiko repeated after Wantabe. 'I will carry out the society's dictates to the best of my ability in the service of the Emperor.'

'Gentlemen,' Hiroki said, 'rise and receive the newest member of the Cherry Blossom Society.'

Some of the most powerful men in the empire stood, and bowed. Wantabe placed another chair beside Raiko's. Noriko, who had been standing behind her, sat down.

'Now we are two females in the group,' Noriko whispered.

'Members,' Wantabe said. 'The following report is a result of Miss Raiko Minobe's ingenuity, talent and diligence. During and after the February coup attempt, Raiko directed my staff in monitoring all foreign-embassy radio messages around the clock. Knowing the embassies were sending details of the fighting, and later of the trials, made breaking the codes easier. Last week the German and American embassies used the same codes Miss Minobe had deciphered in February. She will explain.'

The fear Kenji had of Raiko being intimidated by the

men seated around the table was dispelled by her confident stance and the determination in her voice.

'A radio message from Berlin, to a Mr Sorge in Tokyo, instructed all German correspondents stationed in the Far East to use every effort to embroil Japan and the Soviet Union in a military confrontation. The Germans are ordered to go beyond written despatches. Unlimited funds and diplomatic connections are available for them to implement military intrigues.'

'Sorge is chief German correspondent in the Far East,' Wantabe said. 'He is also an officer in the Gestapo. This message to Sorge reveals Hitler's intention to keep Russia busy with Japan while the German army gives its full attention to Europe.'

'I suggest we inform our military, the government and, in this case, the Kempetai,' Hiroki said.

Wantabe nodded at Raiko. 'This young lady broke the American grey code last February. It is a cipher used by the US diplomatic corps. Miss Minobe will explain.'

Raiko read out a list of Japanese warships, aircraft carriers, their armaments and ships' complements. She then detailed the make-up, location and armaments of the Japanese air force, as John Whittefield had done for Ambassador Grew. She went on to speak of high-altitude flying, the use of oxygen and divebombing techniques. When she looked up, she was met with stunned silence.

Kenji's face was drained, his eyes glazed. He upset the teacup in front of him. 'Someone has betrayed Japan! This information is most recent and top-secret! The traitor must be found!' He began questioning Raiko, as did the others.

Wantabe continued the report. 'The third part of Miss Minobe's account involves our Kwangtung army. General Tojo has ordered Koda-ha to arrange the kidnapping of Chiang Kai-shek by the Communists. The analysis of our Black Chamber political section is that without Chiang's

72

personal leadership, the Nationalist army will crumble. Tojo will invade China unopposed, especially since Chang Tso-lin's army dispersed after his death.'

'What about Mao's Communists in the north?' a military officer asked.

'They are a much smaller, ill-equipped, ragtag group,' Wantabe answered. 'The Nationalists have pursued them for years. Alone, the Communists present no problem to our Kwangtung army.'

'I am uncertain of what action to recommend,' Hiroki said. 'I oppose war. However, food riots in Japan have become more frequent. We could make good use of the natural produce, raw materials and trade that would come to us from China.'

'Let Chiang be kidnapped and killed,' the government minister said.

Another man of military bearing in civilian clothes spoke. 'Chiang Kai-shek's abandonment of the northern capital is our signal to take Peking. Japan's objective should be limited to the five northern provinces. We cannot afford to involve ourselves in a prolonged land war. The Chinese people are too many, their country so vast it would swallow us up.'

'I do not see how Tojo could possibly finance a major military move into northern China,' a banker said. 'The prime minister has directed the national treasury to tighten the purse strings of the Kwangtung army.'

'Tojo is trading Manchurian wheat and soybeans for German military equipment,' Raiko said.

All eyes again fixed on the tiny woman at the end of the table. 'General Tojo is now holding large-scale military manoeuvres near the Chinese border,' she said. 'Koda-ha has ordered a military alert in Manchuria . . .'

After two more hours of intensive discussion, Hiroki summed up the majority decision. 'For the good of the economy, events in Manchuria should be allowed to take

73

their course. The government will not be informed of Koda-ha's plan to kidnap Chiang Kai-shek, nor of the Kwangtung army manoeuvres on the Chinese border. The government will be informed of a breach in military security, and asked to find the traitor or spy.' Hiroki bowed. 'This meeting is adjourned.'

Noriko served green tea and rice cakes, then took her husband aside. 'Kenji should escort Raiko home.'

'I see a naughty gleam in your eyes,' Hiroki said. 'What are you up to?'

'Raiko is interested in Kenji.'

'She is very small for such a big, husky fellow.'

'That little woman is the first female I have met who has the courage and mental ability to handle our Kenji.'

Kenji parked his car and strolled up the neat gravel path to his villa. He admired the sparkling, dew-soaked pines. He listened to the water rushing over meticulously-placed rocks in the garden. They splashed a melody he had never heard. He kicked off his shoes at the door.

'Where have you been?' Hino asked. 'We're due at the airfield.'

Kenji grinned at his cousins in their aviator coveralls and leather flight jackets. 'Have you seen Natasha?'

'Sleeping,' Genda said. 'Where were you all night?'

'Talking. I was talking with Raiko Minobe.'

'You mean that little one with the sharp tongue?'

'We parked at Chiba Point overlooking Tokyo bay,' Kenji said. 'Raiko believes the Japanese national problem is the conflicting interests of our army's actions abroad, and the necessity for those actions. Meaning Tojo's occupation of Korea and Manchuria and our need for the food that is sent to Japan from those places.'

'Are you telling us that little girl had you talking about politics, economics and morals?' Hino asked.

'I'm going to buy her several new International Business Machines tabulators.'

'I can understand IBM equipment for our businesses, or for the banks,' Hino said. 'But what does the little one want with them?'

'For the Black Chamber,' Kenji said. 'Raiko will use the new machines to process information more rapidly. I'm buying them for the country's security. There are Japanese spies working for the West.'

'Spies, my eyes,' Genda chided. The brothers winked at each other.

'You could have taken the girl to a good hotel rather than hump her in the car,' Hino said.

Kenji's shoulders hunched and his eyes narrowed. 'It wasn't like that,' he growled. 'We talked about radios, about signal interception equipment and direction finders. Raiko says knowledge of the sender's location and message frequency is often the key to decoding alien radio transmissions.'

'I think she's located your direction finder,' Hino said, pointing between Kenji's legs. 'I believe the frequency rate of message interceptions between the two of you will increase.'

'You can tell us more about the girl when we get back from flying,' Genda said. 'You're already up in the clouds.'

'Do I know this Kenji Ishikawa?' Ruth Kuhn asked.

'You went home with his cousin Hino from the night-club,' Raiko said.

'You mean the big, good-looking one who climbed the building? With the Russian girlfriend?'

'You don't understand anything about Japanese men.'

Ruth grinned. 'Hino taught me a thing or two that night. Japanese men aren't too different from Germans. Won't spending all night with this Kenji ruin your reputation as a chaste Japanese maiden?'

'We talked. Nothing physical happened. And if you don't tell, no one will know. It was like we each knew what the other was going to say, but still wanted to hear it.'

'What did you talk about?'

'Aeroplanes. Kenji designs them. They have problems with wing armament. The weight of the machine-guns causes vibrations at high speed. Manoeuvrability is affected. Kenji had a glass wind tunnel built in his house. He puts birds into the tunnel to watch them fly. He keeps fish in large glass tanks so he can watch them swim.'

'I thought he was a pilot.'

'He is, and an aeronautical engineer too. By watching the fish he hopes to learn more about air currents and wind friction.' Raiko jabbed her finger in the air. 'That is the most important problem to solve at this time – friction.'

Ruth Kuhn laughed. 'That was the problem the last time you and Kenji met.'

Raiko smiled. 'I have an appointment with him next week. He wants to show me a site for building a radio-interception and direction-finding station.'

'Your antennae seem to be in tune with his. Am I hearing heart-to-heart messages?'

They both laughed, and began the day's lessons. Ruth recited the key to a particular cipher, but Raiko's mind remained on Kenji and their next meeting.

9

Shira Ando lay back among the silk pillows and sighed. His vacation was ending. Two of the pleasure-girls dressed while the third massaged his body. They would all be gone before Tsubota arrived. Ando turned on his stomach and the girl stood on his back, kneading his muscles with her toes and the soles of her little feet. He gazed at the carved Chinese dragons, the exquisite jade figurines and the intricately sculpted elephant tusks artistically placed around the room. His reward for killing Chang Tso-lin was the best the Fifth Moon Inn had to offer.

Ando pointed to his uniform. The girl stepped off his back and picked up the jacket. She plucked a thread from the epaulette that carried his new rank of major. 'Success pays well,' he said, and rose to his feet. He threw his shoulders back and savoured having her dress him.

Two large jugs hung from the ends of a peasant's pole slung across Dr Tsubota's shoulders. Ando bowed, and motioned to the table set with fruit, sweets and rice cakes. 'Please be seated and I'll serve tea.'

Tsubota set down his load. 'Aren't you going to ask what I'm carrying?'

'It would be impolite.'

'True,' Tsubota said. He removed the wicker covers from the jugs and waved Ando closer. 'Come. This is for your next assignment. What do you see inside the jugs?'

'Fish.'

'Not just fish. Goldfish. There are 621 varieties and

77

these are among the rarest. I had them sent from Bangkok. Huang-sen, Secretary of the Kuomintang – the Nationalist Chinese Army – is an avid collector. Goldfish are his most compelling passion.'

Ando peered into the jugs. 'What will the secretary have to do for them?'

'Assist in the capture of Chiang Kai-shek. If Huang-sen takes this bribe, he'll lure Generalissimo Chiang Kai-shek to visit him in Sian, northern China. There, the generalissimo will become Mao Tse-tung's prisoner.'

'Huang-sen is a Chinese traitor.'

'Yes,' Tsubota said. 'Your assignment is to see that Mao Tse-tung executes Chiang Kai-shek. If not, you will kill the generalissimo yourself.'

'Chiang has been fighting the Communists for years,' Ando said. 'His scorched-earth policy has caused hundreds of thousands to starve. Mao must kill him.'

'Not so. This Mao is an unpredictable idealist. Chiang would cut out Mao's heart and have it for dinner without a thought. But Mao has publicly stated he is prepared to suspend the communization of China and combine forces with Chiang Kai-shek to stop Japan's invasion. Mao and Chiang are old comrades in arms. They trained together in Moscow. Until the Germans stepped in to help Chiang, both their armies were supplied by Russia. In the 1920s Chiang founded the Whampoa Military Academy, China's West Point. Mao was his second in command. They may be enemies on the battlefield now, but Tojo wants to be certain old friendships do not cloud Mao's thinking. Generalissimo Chiang Kai-shek must die while in Communist hands. It will leave the majority of the Chinese forces leaderless. A weakened China suits Tojo's purpose.'

'Do the newspaper reports that Japan was responsible for Tso-lin's death have anything to do with this kidnapping?' Ando asked.

'Exactly. The Americans gave that information to the press after their agents broke into Koda-ha headquarters in Kyoto and learned of Tojo's plan to invade China. The United States want to stop us from expanding. By releasing the information, they have stirred up Chinese nationalism against us. If Chiang and Mao ever did come to an agreement, it could unite all China against Japan. But if Chiang Kai-shek dies while in Communist hands, there will be a Chinese civil war. Our Kwangtung army can then cross the border unopposed.'

Baoding, Northern China

Fifty armed guards protected Secretary Huang-sen's sprawling villa. Barbed wire topped the mud-brick wall around the compound. Machine-guns covered the gates.

On the porch, Captain Ando speculated how many bangalore torpedos would be necessary to breach the wall at a point where the machine-guns could not traverse. Two in the corner, he thought. That would be enough to allow a company of men racing through the gap to take the house in one quick rush. But such an attack would not be necessary. The sad-faced Huang-sen had taken eager possession of the exotic goldfish. He had arranged for Ando to accompany him and his staff to the meeting in Sian where Chang Kai-shek was to be taken prisoner. He had given Ando a personal tour and detailed explanation of the 200 glass fish tanks located throughout the elegantly furnished house. Each tank had an overhead electric light. Every twenty tanks had an attendant who cleaned them and fed the fish specially prepared food. These men were trained to work silently, and each carried a pistol. They were Huang-sen's personal bodyguards.

Ando joined Secretary Huang-sen and his entourage aboard a Ford tri-motor plane. The two-hour trip to Sian passed in silence. Just before the landing, Ando was informed that Huang-sen's troops had already taken Chiang Kai-shek captive. Mao Tse-tung was in charge. Ando opened his briefcase and touched the thermos bottle in which he had melted and moulded two pounds of TNT. A turn of the top and bottom caps in opposite directions would ignite a fifteen minute fuse. It would kill the generalissimo if Mao did not.

Hiroki Koin greeted the three pilots when they were ushered into Admiral Yamamoto's office. 'Gentlemen,' Hiroki said, 'the Emperor has accepted our recommendation to improve our economy. The Kwangtung army will invade China's northern provinces. Tojo's first step was to engineer the kidnapping of Generalissimo Chiang Kai-shek by the Communists. Chiang is alive, but I doubt he will remain so for long.'

'We must know what reaction there will be to Chiang's death among the Westerners in Peking,' Yamamoto said. 'Specifically the British and Americans. How will they react when our army invades China?'

'Doesn't the Cherry Blossom Society have agents in Peking?' Hino asked.

'Yes,' Hiroki said. 'But not among the Westerners. You three pilots have been chosen because no-one else could reach Peking in time. Kenji's relationship to John Whittefield, the senior American intelligence officer in the Far East, is a major factor. Whittefield broke into Koda-ha headquarters in Kyoto and stole military information. He is now in Peking. This alone indicates that important events are about to take place there. Kenji's relationship with Whittefield may give us a direct line to the American ambassador in Peking. We must know how Britain and the US will react when the Communists kill Chiang and our army invades China.'

'Where is Generalissimo Chiang being held?' Kenji asked.

'In Sian, northern China,' Hiroki said. 'You three will fly to Peking and report to our ambassador. As yet, none of the foreign embassies have left Peking for the new Chinese capital of Nanking.'

'When do we leave?' Genda asked.

'Immediately,' Yamamoto said. He unrolled a map and the men moved around it. 'You will also be testing a new plan of mine called carrier-hopping. The distance from Tokyo to Peking is 1,300 miles. With a range of 600 miles for our T-96 fighter planes, you should make Peking in three hops.' The admiral pointed to an X on the map in the Korean strait near Pusan, and another in the Yellow Sea off Port Arthur. 'I have ordered my aircraft carriers to wait at these locations. Planes will be warmed up and prepared to go as soon as you land. How long should it take?'

'What are the weather conditions along the route of flight?' Hino asked.

'Snow from here to the coast,' Yamamoto said. 'Good from there to Korea. No reports yet from the Yellow Sea squadron.'

'We'll be bucking head-winds to Korea, and following winds from there on,' Hino said. 'I estimate eight to ten hours in the air.'

'What if you were to fly with oxygen at high altitudes?' Yamamoto asked.

'We'll have to stay low to navigate from ground markers,' Hino said. 'The Tokyo-to-London flight was planned, practised and co-ordinated with radio operators along the route. They kept me on course.'

'Then low-level navigation it is,' Yamamoto said. 'You'll land in China at a makeshift airstrip fifteen miles outside Peking. You'll be taken directly to our embassy. Official contact will be through our cultural attaché. Informal contacts outside the foreign compound will be through Jade Joe, a Chinese antique dealer. You'll use the password, "Father of Spring".'

'And he'll reply, "Mother of Autumn",' Kenji said, looking from his uncle to the admiral. 'I know that's the correct countersign, but don't know why. When I received warning of the coup assassinations last February, the voice used those passwords. Where do they come from?'

'Those were the passwords of the Black Dragon Society,' Hiroki said. 'Your great-grandfather Mung was the last chief of the imperial secret service. After Mung's death the Black Dragons were incorporated into Koda-ha.'

'Whoever warned you of the February assassinations must be an old family friend,' Yamamoto said. He handed each of the three pilots a briefcase. 'Your flying instructions, maps, call letters and radio frequencies are all there. From Peking you'll radio your information to Mr X in Tokyo. That is Wantabe's code name. Good luck.'

Haneda Air Force Base

Snow floated down in fat flakes that stuck to the runway. Inside the hangar, Hino concluded his orientation briefing to Genda and Kenji. 'We can fly over these snow clouds and the weather will clear before we reach the Sea of Japan. We should have good visibility after that, and pick up the first aircraft carrier off Pusan in four hours. Our army in Korea will guide us with radio signals over the southern peninsula. Once we leave the Korean west coast, there'll be no navigational guides but the stars. We'll be over the Yellow Sea until we spot the second carrier near Port Arthur.' Hino frowned. 'Radio contact hasn't been established with our second aircraft carrier. That usually means bad weather.'

'You'll find the carrier for us,' Genda said.

'How can we miss with the best navigator in the imperial air force,' Kenji said, and slapped his cousin on the shoulder.

'That brings me to the last item,' Hino said, folding the

82

map. 'If one of us develops engine trouble over water, he must inform the others which point of land he is heading for, and keep in radio contact as long as possible.'

Kenji and Genda nodded. The three pilots buttoned their flying suits and went to their planes.

Kenji handed a note to the flight chief. 'Call this number and read the message over the phone! Do not mention anything about this flight!'

'Kick them over,' Genda shouted from his cockpit. The engines in the three T-96 fighters roared to life.

Ruth Kuhn watched Raiko tilt the picture on the wall. 'I saw you do that once before just as we were leaving the house,' Ruth said. 'Why?'

Raiko smiled. 'Sometimes I put a statue near the edge of a shelf or pull a book out of line. The landlady works for Kempetai. She's a natural fussbudget. If the out-of-place item is adjusted when I return, I know she's been here and made a report to the secret police.'

'Is it because I live with you?' Ruth asked.

'Her visits are more frequent since your arrival. We Japanese are very spy-conscious.'

'The Gestapo too. I never got used to being spied upon. Possibly that's why I took this assignment. To spy on others.'

'Does it bother you that you'll be working for Japan and not Germany?' Raiko asked.

'Goebbels told me that in return Japan will send Germany information from the Near and Far East where Occidentals are too conspicuous. Since the Anti-Comintern Pact, most Germans see Japan has an ally. Our countries have similar problems. Germany has the European enemy on one side and Russia on the other. Japan has China on one side and America on the other.'

'But we're not a fascist state,' Raiko said. 'Hitler is a dictator.'

'Japan could use fascism to bring prosperity to its people. Democracies are too slow. It takes months, sometimes years, to make decisions. In Germany and Italy, unemployment has been reduced. New roads are being built and even the trains run on time. German intellectuals feel a dictatorship is needed for five or ten years to recover from the economic depression.'

'If we're to be on time for my father's lecture, we should leave now,' Raiko said. She was well aware how much her American background influenced her political concepts. A Japanese dictatorship was an upsetting idea. 'Dress warm,' she said. 'It's snowing hard.'

The telephone rang and Raiko answered. 'I have a message from Captain Kenji Ishikawa,' the voice said. 'I'm reading the captain's note: "Excuse me for not being able to keep our appointment tomorrow. Business has called me away. I apologize. The IBM tabulators will be forwarded by my shipping agent in Hong Kong, via Shanghai. They should arrive before my return. I'll call you soon."'

'Do you know where the captain has gone?' Raiko asked.

'I am not permitted to say,' the flight chief said.

From his stiff, cadenced speech, Raiko felt he was a military man. 'What air base are you speaking from?' she snapped.

'Haneda,' came the reply.

'When did Captain Ishikawa take off?'

Raiko heard a swift intake of breath on the other end of the line. 'Miss Minobe, I have said too much. Without meaning to offend, I beg your pardon and now hang up the telephone.'

Raiko looked out of the window. The trees and shrubs were bending under the weight of falling snow and she was certain Kenji was flying.

'Is something wrong?' Ruth asked.

'I'd like to stop at a shrine on the way to the university,' Raiko said. 'I have a prayer to say for someone's safe return.'

Through the window, Ruth saw headlights slice through the falling snow and turn into the driveway. 'The taxi is here. You can tell the driver which shrine you want.'

Raiko opened the front door and found Wantabe standing there. 'You must come immediately,' he said, puffing white vapour clouds into the cold air. 'I have decoded a message from The Razor to Koda-ha. Chiang Kai-shek has been captured by the Communists.'

'But if you've decoded it, why do you need me? Ruth and I were on our way to my father's lecture.'

Even though he spoke in Japanese, Wantabe looked over Raiko's shoulder to be certain the German girl could not hear. 'After we decoded that message, our radio operators caught the same strange Russian code you monitored last February,' he whispered. 'It's coming from somewhere in Tokyo and resembles The Razor's message in length and form. We might be able to break it.'

10

A thousand feet above the snow-laden clouds, the three T-96 fighter planes flew in loose V-formation towards the Sea of Japan. Hino gazed through his cockpit canopy at familiar stars. Navigating is easy with the frequent radio contact from the ground, he thought. The final leg, over the Yellow Sea, will be different. He looked to Kenji and Genda's planes on his right and left. Kenji's latest modification had increased their airspeed to 200 miles per hour.

Kenji saw Hino's cockpit light go on and watched his cousin examine a map. 'We should now be over the Japan Sea,' Hino said on the radio. 'The cloud cover is breaking up and there'll be good visibility. This head-wind is stronger than I expected. Nothing to do now but straight flying until we pick up the carrier's radio signal.'

'The head-wind could mean a better tail-wind from Korea to Port Arthur,' Genda said.

'Possibly,' Hino said. 'I hope we'll reach Peking about six in the morning.'

'I'll buy breakfast when we land,' Kenji said.

Their small talk died away and the three aviators flew on through the dark night. As they moved further out over the sea, they saw fewer running lights of fishing boats below.

The steady drone of the engine relaxed Kenji. Our planes are sturdy, although not fast enough in the turns, he thought. This aircraft will have to be improved to match reports of the latest German and American planes. Our armament is insufficient compared to the Western models. He had given the problem of more powerful guns to the Mitsubishi zaibatsu.

Kenji's thoughts of aircraft designs drifted to Raiko. She was short, but a long elegant neck flowed from under her well-defined chin into gentle shoulders. Her collarbones seemed more prominent than those of other women. Her breasts, though small, were pleasantly noticeable. Her long eyelashes curled. Her large eyes could be sparkling pools of black light that shot angry fire, or soft and deep lagoons that called to him. They dominated her face. Raiko was beautiful and childlike, womanly and exquisite at the same time.

'Kenji! Kenji!' Hino's voice came over the radio. 'You're straying. You'll drift off to Vladivostok.'

'Don't fall asleep now,' Genda said. 'My little brother has led us directly to Yamamoto's X on the map.'

The carrier below was lit up and easily visible some twenty miles away. Kenji heard the ship's flight chief giving them landing instructions. Three flares burst at their altitude several miles ahead.

'This is flight leader,' Kenji said. 'Mark those flares! That'll be the scout plane to guide us in. I'll land first, Genda second! If there's a problem I'll inform you. Hino, as navigator you're most important to this mission. Be certain rather than quick when you land!'

Kenji followed the scout plane in a pass over the carrier. Instructions from the flight officer were as calm as the sea, yet night landings were always tricky. On the second approach, Kenji lined himself up for the landing with the nose of his plane between the two lines of deck lights, and descended. The rows of lights on the carrier's flight deck narrowed as he closed in.

The deck officer, his arms spread, a light bar in each hand, showed Kenji the tilt of his wings as he came in. Kenji concentrated on the deck, on his altitude and airspeed, automatically adjusting the trim of his wings according to the light bars. He swooped over the deck, slapped the flap handles down, shut the magneto switch and stopped the engine. There was a moment of silence before the plane smacked down. It bounced over the first catch wire. The tail hook caught the second wire and Kenji was thrown forward. His safety straps cut into his shoulders. He was rocked backwards as the plane jerked to a stop. Men rushed at the plane from all sides, pushing, pulling it off the flight deck, making way for Genda, and then Hino.

The three pilots gulped hot miso soup and stretched their legs on the flight deck.

At the last moment before they climbed into the cockpits of the three readied planes, Hino ordered the engines shut down. 'I want the fuel tanks topped off to the last possible drop,' he ordered. 'There's rain on the west coast of Korea and still no communication from our next carrier off Port Arthur.'

The crew worked swiftly and the three planes were soon on their way to an uneventful flight over Korea. At the last radio check from a Japanese army base on the west coast, they were informed of high winds, dense cloud formations over the Yellow Sea, and still no word from the second carrier.

Soon after they lost sight of land, their windshields were splattered with raindrops. Hino began regular five-minute compass and altitude checks. Kenji could hear the tenseness in his cousin's voice. The rain increased and visibility was limited outside the cockpits. Hino directed a change of altitude in a search for stronger tail-winds.

At 2 a.m. the rain turned to sleet and the cockpits grew colder. The three pilots buttoned up and put on their gloves.

'We should be ten minutes ahead of schedule,' Hino said at 3 a.m. 'I'm getting a distorted radio signal. I think from the carrier.' He switched on his transmitter and called, 'Carrier! Carrier! Flight T-96 requesting permission to land.'

88

The ship's transmission was masked by uninterrupted static. Hino kept calling, with no better results.

'I've got snow on my windscreen,' Genda said.

'Get out and clean it off,' Kenji answered.

'Keep quiet,' Hino snapped. 'I can't make sense of the carrier's transmission. I'm not even sure if it is the carrier. Descend to 1,000 feet! The signal may be clearer there.'

The three planes dropped down from 10,000 feet into thick clouds.

'Getting snow build-up on windscreen and wings,' Kenji said.

'Mine too,' Genda said.

'I can no longer see either of you,' Hino said. 'It's all snow.'

'This is flight leader,' Kenji said. 'Level off! On my command we climb out of this mess at a thirty-degree angle! Prepare to execute! Execute!'

The three planes turned upwards. Each pilot strained to see the running lights of the others, but driving snow blocked all vision.

Hino, in the lead, called out the altimeter reading, '15,000 feet and still in the snow cloud.'

'Maintain speed and direction,' Kenji ordered.

'20,000 feet . . . 25,000 feet.'

'We should have taken Yamamoto's advice and brought the oxygen,' Genda said.

'I'm through at 27,000 feet,' Hino shouted.

'Damn,' Kenji growled. He throttled back, so close to Genda's tail he thought his propeller would chop it off.

'This is Navigator,' Hino said. 'Form up! Reduce speed to 160 and follow me! We have to stretch 600 miles of gas to 700, or else bathe in the Yellow Sea.'

'No chance of finding the carrier?' Genda asked.

'Couldn't land if we did,' Kenji said. 'Hino's right. We can't waste any more time.'

'Keep a tight V-formation,' Hino said. 'I'll be flying up and down to look for tail-winds.'

Several times in the tension-filled hours that followed, the planes broke the 30,000-foot level to stay above the clouds. Hino led them up into the thinner air until he grew dizzy, then down again. In the clouds, with obscured vision, their formation loosened. Steady chatter between the three planes told them they had drifted too far when their voices began to fade. It was blind flying of the worst kind.

'My gas gauge reads empty,' Genda said.

Hino glanced down at his lap pad covered with scribbled computations of fuel capacity, wind factors and airspeed. 'If I've done my job correctly, we should be over land. We can try to put down on a road while we still have the power, or go on until our tanks are dry and glide into the snow.'

'We go down with power,' Kenji declared. 'I'll take the lead! We fly in step formation to the right! I'm low man!'

Kenji eased his plane forward. Genda took a position off Kenji's right wing and 100 feet above. Hino took a similar post above Genda.

'We're going down,' Kenji said. 'Descend at a fifteen-degree angle! Throttle back to 120 miles an hour!'

The planes slipped into dark clouds and were lost to each other.

Kenji called out the altimeter readings, '10,000 . . . 9,000 . . . 8 . . . 7 . . . 6,000 feet. Are there mountains in this area?'

'Makes no difference to me,' Genda said. 'My engine has quit.'

'Maintain your glide pattern!' Kenji said. 'Read out your airspeed! Hino and I will adjust to it. Hino, you scout to the right for a place to land! I'll head left.'

Kenji throttled back according to Genda's speed. The altimeter read 500 feet. Kenji wondered if the cloud cover was at zero feet and they were about to crash

90

into a mountain. The cabin temperature was zero degrees Fahrenheit, yet sweat steamed his goggles. He expected the earth to loom up in front of him at any moment.

'A road,' Hino shouted. 'Swing right and I'll lead.'

'I see you,' Genda shouted. 'I'm following.'

Kenji broke through the cloud cover and saw Genda's tail section on the right through a blizzard of snowflakes. He followed. They were almost at stall speed, 200 feet above the ground when Hino and Genda made the left turn.

'Oh shit,' Hino shouted, 'it's a goddamned river!'

'Look for a road on either side,' Kenji ordered. 'Roads always parallel rivers.'

'I'm going in the river,' Genda said. 'No choice.'

Kenji gunned his engine and pulled alongside Genda. He saw Genda's flaps lower, saw the wheels touch the water, and slide.

'It's frozen,' Hino shouted. 'He's skidding on ice!'

Genda's plane did a slow-motion turn and slid backwards into a snowbank.

'Hino, look for a place for us to put down,' Kenji ordered.

'I see a large open field ahead,' Hino shouted.

'That's it,' Kenji cried. 'My engine is dead!' He dropped his flaps and held his breath. The wheels touched the ground, and he felt the plane skidding. Kenji tensed for a crash, snow built up under his wheels and wings, and he came to the softest stop in his flying career.

The world was silent. With trembling hands Kenji pushed the cockpit canopy back. A rush of cold air and snowflakes on his face helped to bring his trembling body under control. He saw Hino's plane ahead, its wing broken and angled up. Hino climbed out of his cockpit and came running across the snow. Kenji pulled himself out. He grabbed a handful of snow and bit into it to relieve the dryness in his mouth.

'Where are we?' Kenji called.

'On a frozen lake. Genda must have landed on a feeder river.'

'Genda!' Kenji forgot his own fear. 'We've got to find him!'

It was 5 a.m. and growing light. The two aviators trudged back through the snow. Suddenly a red rocket curved up towards the grey clouds.

'Genda's well enough to signal,' Kenji said, and began to run.

They found Genda's plane tail-down in a snowbank on the frozen river. One wing was torn away, the landing gear had collapsed. Genda sat on the engine cowling with a flare pistol in his hand, smiling. 'Kenji, where's my breakfast? You promised to buy it when we landed.'

'I'll buy a whole goddamned restaurant for you,' Kenji shouted. 'Get down from there and let's decide what to do.'

'Come up here,' Genda said. 'The engine's still warm. We had lucky landings, but could freeze to death in this damned weather.'

Raiko was asleep on a cot in Wantabe's office. She had made little progress with the Russian code, and planned to attack it in the morning when her mind was rested and clear. Wantabe entered the office and touched her shoulder. She jumped up, seeing concern in the chief's eyes.

'What is it?' Raiko asked.

'Kenji Ishikawa, Hino and Genda Arai are missing over the Yellow Sea.'

Raiko's stomach contracted. 'When? How long?'

'They're eight hours overdue and storm conditions prevail along their route. No word since they left the west coast of Korea. Reports indicate gale-force winds. The storm has closed all roads from the Chinese coast to Peking.'

92

Tears streamed down Raiko's pale cheeks. Her mouth opened but she could not speak.

Wantabe took her hands in his. 'I was going to ask you to inform Hiroki and Noriko Koin, but I'll do it.'

'No,' Raiko said. 'Please, not yet. Don't call them yet. Let's wait. There's still a chance of their having reached land. Wait eight more hours. Then, if necessary, I'll tell the Koin family.'

Wantabe dried the tears on Raiko's cheeks with a rice-paper tissue.

'I know he's not dead,' she said. 'Don't call.' Her large, tear-filled eyes begged.

'I must inform Admiral Yamamoto,' Wantabe said. 'He will decide. Why don't you try that Russian code again? Best to keep yourself occupied.'

Raiko nodded, and went to her desk. She was tense and short-tempered with the Russian translators. She strained her neck repeatedly to glance at the desk for incoming messages. She tried to eat, and could not. The Russian code was impenetrable. The clock would not stop. No matter how hard she prayed to Jesus, Buddha and the Shinto gods, no incoming message reported Kenji's safety.

The eight hours Raiko had requested passed. Seeing Wantabe get up from his desk and walk towards her, she jumped up and rushed into the toilet.

The chief waited. He checked his watch once more, then entered the toilet room. Raiko stood in a corner weeping. He grasped her shoulder and whispered, 'I'll tell the family.'

'No,' she gasped. 'It will be easier on them if the news comes from me.'

'I'll call a cab for you.'

It's almost the new year, Raiko thought as she entered the taxi. What a terrible present I bring for the Koin family. The car crossed the Sumida river near the imperial palace.

'Driver, I've changed my mind. Take me to the Yasukune shrine.'

Raiko walked up a short hill, past winter grass covered with snow. The well-tended gardens and buildings had been dedicated by the Meiji Emperor in 1869 to honour those who died reinstating imperial rule. Officially this place was called Shrine for Establishing Peace in the Empire. But its popular name had become Shrine of Fallen Soldiers.

Raiko walked by old stone lanterns and dwarfed pine trees. She took the bamboo dipper and cleansed her lips with spring water from a small stone basin. She stood at the entrance to the shrine and fumbled in her purse. Tears blinded her as she threw coins into a wooden box. She clapped once to command the attention of the gods, folded her hands in prayer, and bowed. 'Gods, if you do not already have the souls of Kenji Ishikawa, Genda and Hino Arai, I wish their speedy and healthy return to us. I insist on their return! Oh gods who dwell beyond the clouds, please help them! Don't take Kenji away from me!'

The Year of the Bull
1937

11

Stars glittered in the cold night air above the Koin residence, but Raiko Minobe did not see them. She stared at the decorations for the new year – a sacred rope with prayer notes hanging from the lintel of the front door to keep evil spirits away; pine branches and bamboo stalks arranged at the gateway to ensure prosperity, good health and a happy life.

None of it will help, Raiko thought. I'm the wicked spirit and bearer of evil tidings. Kenji is dead. She stumbled at the gate, grasped the fence and wept. She looked up at the stars and cried out, 'When I need you most, you fail me! Kenji is the only man I ever cared for. The only person I want to be with. You who dwell beyond the clouds betrayed me! I hate you! Christ! Buddha! All the Shinto deities!'

Raiko cleared her throat and marched up to the front door. Turning her back to the house, she bent to loosen her shoes. The door opened behind her and she was swept inside the house by Noriko and Hiroki. They embraced her, both speaking at once. She could not understand them.

'Kenji is dead,' Raiko whispered. She repeated the words louder, feeling the strength leave her legs. The older couple helped her to a chair. 'I'm sorry,' Raiko sobbed. 'I'm so sorry to have to tell you about Kenji's death.'

Noriko's smiling face appeared to Raiko through a mist of tears. Noriko's lips were saying, 'He is not dead.'

'We just spoke to Kenji and the boys on the telephone,' Hiroki said. 'Wantabe called us. He is searching for you.'

'But I don't understand,' Raiko said. She saw her hands flutter, and collapse in her lap.

Noriko pressed a cup of saké to Raiko's lips. 'Drink this and believe it when we say that all three are alive and well. Hino's brilliant navigation led them safely through the storm.'

'They crash-landed on a frozen lake,' Hiroki said. 'Then scared some Chinese farmers half to death when they appeared in flying suits, leather helmets and goggles. Genda said the farmer kept repeating, "On my life I never saw human beings like these."' Hiroki giggled.

Raiko downed a second cup of saké. 'Thank the gods,' she murmured.

'Yes,' Hiroki said. 'Wantabe told us that just after you left the Black Chamber he heard from an Ishikawa purchasing agent in Peking. Kenji had ordered a money voucher to buy the Seven Sisters Brothel outside Peking.'

'You mean the first thing Kenji did after surviving a crash-landing and a blizzard was to buy a house of prostitution?'

Hiroki saw colour rise in Raiko's cheeks and hastened to add, 'Not for himself. It was for a bet he made with Genda.'

Raiko leaned forward, eyes narrowed, jaw set. 'I'm certain Kenji Ishikawa will join his cousins with the seven sisters.'

Noriko pressed a third cup of saké into Raiko's hand. 'I do not believe the boys had time for prostitutes. They are already at our consulate in Peking. They telephoned from there.'

Hiroki and Noriko were both grateful for the knock at the door that distracted Raiko. They were pleased to see Wantabe.

'Isn't it a miracle they're safe,' Wantabe said.

Raiko began to laugh. 'I would like to give thanks to the gods,' she cried. 'And apologize to them. If we go to a Buddhist temple, we'll hear the new-year bells!'

'All 108 chimes,' Wantabe said.

'We can dine on year-crossing noodles and drink saké as we listen,' Hiroki said. 'This is a night to celebrate!'

Noriko took Raiko's hand. 'We will all go together and bring in the Year of the Bull.'

Manchuria

In the long reception hall of the Fifth Moon Inn, General Hideki Tojo sat at a low table facing row on row of Kwangtung army officers. The general raised his cup. 'To the Year of the Bull! We drink this toast with manushizake – snake wine – and raw eggs, the diet of the Japanese fighting bulls. Like the bulls, we will become endowed with increased energy and courageous spirit in preparation for Operation Marco Polo!'

'Banzai! Banzai! Banzai!' the officers roared. They drank the snake wine and sucked raw eggs from intricately decorated lacquer bowls. Faces flushed, hearts swelling with pride, the men sat back to hear their leader.

'The Kwangtung army will not be stopped by Chinese Nationalists in Nanking, nor buried in the backwater of Manchuria by liberal Japanese politicians in Tokyo,' Tojo said. 'I have planned a two-pronged offensive – political in Japan and military in China. For several days now Chiang Kai-shek has been a prisoner of the Communists. Mao Tse-tung will kill the generalissimo and our propaganda units in China will stir up civil war between the Nationalists and Communists. My intelligence chief, Dr Tsubota, has agents behind enemy lines operating against both sides. Warriors of Japan! Fill your cups once more and toast our success in the Year of the Bull!' Tojo flicked his little finger and the first of 108 chimes was sounded on a Buddhist

temple bell. Waiters entered carrying platters piled high
with the long, year-crossing noodles.

2 January 1937

Raiko entered the Black Chamber and was delighted to
find that an IBM tabulator had arrived from the United
States. 'How did it get here so quickly?' she asked
Wantabe.

'A diligent Ishikawa shipping agent dispatched it in the
care of a trained Japanese key-punch operator. They came
on the silk-train express from Hoboken, New Jersey to San
Francisco. Then by Ishikawa steamer direct to Yokohama
in just twelve days.' Wantabe handed Raiko a file folder.
'Another message in the strange Russian code was received
in Tokyo and relayed to China. The IBM machine is
already in operation on that code. This is what we have
so far. Come and see.'

Raiko watched the key-punch operator eliminate hours
of pencil-pushing drudgery in minutes on the tabulator.
She then looked over the shoulder of a code clerk using
that information to fill in one of the work-sheets she had
designed.

'The machine appears to produce more material than
one person can handle,' Raiko said.

'That is not the problem here,' the clerk replied. 'I am
stymied.'

From across the room, Wantabe saw the familiar mystical expression cross Raiko's face. She became totally
absorbed in the clerk's work-sheet. The burning light in
her eyes indicated to Wantabe that Raiko's mind was
transposing the jumbled figures on the paper into mean-
ingful words. He waved his hands, signalling everyone
nearby to be silent.

'You aren't making progress because you're working on
a two-tier cryptogram,' Raiko said to the clerk. 'This is a

three-tier system.' She pulled up a chair, snatched a clean work-sheet and began to write.

Sixty hours later, Raiko crept to the couch in Wantabe's office and dropped off to sleep. Twelve hours after that, she ate a breakfast of smoked fish and pickled vegetables, and returned to work on the code. In a short while she handed in the clear-text of the Russian message sent from Tokyo to China.

'This cannot be,' Wantabe said.

'It is,' Raiko answered. 'The first outgoing message from Tokyo to Moscow parallels information from Tojo to Koda-ha about Chiang Kai-shek's capture by Mao Tse-tung. That means whoever is sending this Russian code has broken the Kwangtung army code also. The outgoing Russian message to China is addressed to B, whoever that is.'

'Borodin,' Wantabe said. 'Mikhail Borodin is the Russian agent who drafted the Kuomintang's constitution for Chiang Kai-shek. He deserted the generalissimo for Mao Tse-tung when the two Chinese leaders parted ways.'

'So my translation is logical,' Raiko said. 'Does Borodin have the authority to order Mao Tse-tung to release Chiang Kai-shek?'

'No.' Wantabe pointed at three initials on the work-sheet. 'But JVD has the power. You say this message was relayed from Moscow to Tokyo and on to China.' He scratched his balding head and wondered out loud. 'Who the hell in Tokyo is so important that Joseph Vissaronovich Dzhugashvili sends him direct messages?'

'Who is Dzhugashvili?' Raiko asked.

'Joseph Stalin.'

Hiroki bowed before the Emperor. 'Sire, I have requested this private audience because Joseph Stalin has become personally involved in the abduction of Generalissimo Chiang Kai-shek. He has ordered that the Nationalist

101

leader be released. If Chiang were to die while in Communist hands it would divide China, and Stalin wants to prevent civil war there. He wants Chiang Kai-shek's army to oppose our Kwangtung army. Should I inform General Tojo?'

'Immediately,' the Emperor said. 'If Chiang's death will mean an easier conquest of the five northern Chinese provinces, so be it. According to my military advisers, our control of northern China will improve Japan's economy.'

Sian, Northern China

Secretary Huang-sen tugged at his drooping moustache and raised his sad eyes to Major Shira Ando, motioning him to a seat in front of the desk.

'When will Chiang die?' Ando asked.

'That is a problem,' the secretary of the Kuomintang said. 'Mao received a secret message three days ago. Since then he and Chiang have been closeted in conference. The relationship between them has changed. The generalissimo will be freed.'

'The Communists cannot be allowed to make peace with the Nationalists!' Ando said. 'I have orders. You accepted the goldfish! Chiang must die here in Sian!'

Huang-sen shrugged. 'I carried out my part of the agreement by delivering Chiang into Mao Tse-tung's hands. If they want to make peace, it is good for China. I am Chinese.'

'You will be a dead Chinaman if Chiang leaves here alive!'

Huang-sen nodded. Two guards stepped behind Ando and pressed their pistols to the back of his head.

'Never threaten,' the secretary said. 'You are leaving Sian for Manchuria on my personal plane. I will host the generalissimo for a short stay at my villa in Baoding.

Accept fate, my friend. Your plan for Chiang's death cannot be implemented.'

'You lying bastard,' Ando growled.

The first guard pistol-whipped Ando across the face, knocking him off the chair. Both guards took turns kicking him across the floor towards the door.

'Pick his head up,' Huang-sen said, and pointed at the bloodied, battered face. 'Because those goldfish are priceless to me, I will let you live. Tell General Tojo all is not lost. Chiang Kai-shek is a viper. Mao has erred in freeing him. Chiang's one goal is to destroy the Communists. He thinks the Americans and British will stop Japan from invading our northern provinces. I personally doubt either Western country would take military action for moral reasons in the Far East. They consider us an inferior race.'

The frustration of betrayal, the kicks to his groin and stomach caused bile to rise in Ando's throat. He retched. The guards flung him out the door and he vomited in the dirt. His briefcase was slapped against his chest and he was dragged by the feet to a waiting car.

At the airfield, Ando was thrown aboard the Ford tri-motor warming up on the runway. He slumped in a seat, hugging his briefcase, spitting blood into a bucket the guard shoved between his legs. They ignored him throughout the flight.

Ando heard the Chinese pilot repeat landing instructions for the Kwangtung army airbase outside Mukden, then request permission for an immediate take-off. Ando removed the thermos bottle from his briefcase and tucked it under his seat.

The Ford tri-motor circled the airfield, then descended. Ando was hustled out of the plane and left standing on the tarmac. The aircraft taxied down the runway and turned right.

A Japanese army staff car pulled up and the driver

started to get out but Ando jumped in. 'To the tower as fast as possible,' he ordered.

The car roared across the airfield. Ando leaned over and held the horn button down. The car skidded to a stop and a head appeared at the control-tower window.

'What the hell is going on?' the air controller shouted.

'I'm Major Ando of military intelligence! Give that Ford tri-motor priority to take off immediately! I set a bomb aboard the son of a bitch! It's about to explode!'

The head disappeared back into the tower. Seconds later the plane raced down the runway and lifted off. It climbed 1,000 feet into the blue sky, banked left in a graceful turn and flew away.

The driver looked questioningly at Ando. The head appeared in the window again and the air controller shouted, 'When?'

Ando smiled through his battered lips and swollen eyes, and pointed to a small dirty cloud on the horizon where none had been before. They heard the echo of a dull thud in the distance.

'Take me to the Fifth Moon Inn,' Ando ordered. 'I have a plan to kill more goddamned Chinamen!'

12

'This is the Japanese ambassador in Peking speaking. I request a direct telephone connection with General Hideki Tojo.'

There was a pause. Then a voice said, 'General Tojo here.'

'Sir, I have been ordered by Lord Keeper of the Privy Seal Hiroki Koin to put you in touch with Captain Kenji Ishikawa. I now relinquish the telephone to the president of the Ishikawa zaibatsu.'

'General Tojo,' Kenji said. 'The Cherry Blossom Society has decoded a message from Joseph Stalin ordering Mao Tse-tung to release Chiang Kai-shek. We have every reason to believe Mao will comply.'

There was a long period of silence before Tojo responded. 'Your society has never shared information with Koda-ha. Why now?'

'For the good of Japan we must co-operate.'

'Your information confirms and clarifies what a battered agent of mine has just reported,' Tojo said. 'The question is, how to react.'

'The Cherry Blossom Society believes your plan to eliminate Chiang Kai-shek is correct,' Kenji said. 'It would save thousands of Japanese soldiers.'

'What do you know of my plans?'

'Our people have also decoded the Kwangtung army cipher.'

Tojo grunted. After a pause, he said, 'We believe the generalissimo has gone to Baoding to recuperate, but that is not confirmed due to a snowstorm in Manchuria. Chiang Kai-shek's Flying Palace is the only twin-engine plane

105

in the Far East painted pure silver. Chiang sometimes pilots it himself, and rarely uses automobiles to travel great distances. If we can verify the plane's presence from the air at the airfield near Huang-sen's villa in Baoding, I will order a commando raid to eliminate the generalissimo.'

Kenji looked out the window. 'The weather here in Peking is good enough for flying.'

'Do you have a plane at your service?'

'I'll buy one.'

'Buy a large one,' the Razor said. 'We'll need it to transport our marine commandos. I will have the airfield here cleared of snow for you. Our weather is expected to change for the better in six to eight hours.'

'Genda and Hino Arai and I request permission to take part in the raid, sir.'

'You may be president of Japan's largest zaibatsu, but you are a captain in the imperial army. You would have to follow orders.'

'Yes, sir!'

'Put your famous navigator cousin on the line. Major Ando will explain where Huang-sen's villa is.'

The largest plane Kenji's purchasing agents in Peking could locate was a three-year-old seventeen-passenger Hugo Junker. Its owner was reluctant to sell, until he heard how much money was offered.

While Hino made up the flight plan and Genda checked the plane's mechanical system, Kenji worked with the former German owner to label the instrument and radio panels in Japanese. In three hours, the gas tanks were filled and the plane positioned for runway number one. Its Lufthansa sign stood out in large white letters against the corrugated aluminium skin.

'Pilot to navigator,' Kenji said. 'Begin take-off procedure.'

Hino read from the operating list. 'Test flaps . . . Rudder . . . Brakes . . .'

Kenji manipulated the various switches, handles and pedals. 'Contact on the starboard engine. Contact on the port engine. Contact on the main engine.' He squeezed the magneto switches and the three 750-horsepower BMW nine-cylinder radial motors roared to life.

Genda turned from the radio set. 'Permission to take off is granted.'

Kenji moved the throttle forward and the Hugo Junker rumbled down the runway, faster than he expected. It lifted off with half the airstrip unused.

'By Buddha's rosy red arse, what power,' Genda cried. 'If we could put a couple of these engines in a fighter, we could outfly anything in the world!'

Hino called out compass readings and directions.

'How does this tin box fly?' Genda asked.

'Like a dream with a motor up its tail,' Kenji said. 'The Germans build solid equipment.'

'If BMW would sell the Ishikawa zaibatsu some of their motors, we could copy them,' Genda said.

'They already have.' Kenji laughed, pointing out the window at the plane's three engines. 'We'll present these to the engineers at Mitsubishi after we've completed our mission. I've asked the engineers to design a 1,000-horsepower radial engine to be fitted into a wood-frame, canvas-covered monoplane. An all-metal plane like this is good for transports or bombers, but a fighter's got to be light, fast and quick in the turns.'

'A thousand horsepower,' Genda marvelled. 'I could ride the wind out of the sky with an engine like that. Let me at that control stick.' He and Hino both took turns flying the large plane.

Kenji returned to the pilot's seat and Hino directed him. 'Continue along the rail-line until you see a broad road crossing it at a right-angle. There'll be an army base on the left side of the tracks. The villa is on the right. According to Major Ando, the wide road past the villa leads directly to the airfield. It was built especially for Secretary Huang-sen.'

Twenty minutes later, Kenji motioned to look out of the front window. 'Those rows of black spots in the snow must be the army base. Take note of everything you can about the villa. Keep your eyes peeled for the Flying Palace.' He banked the plane to the right. 'That road going by the house is as wide as the Berlin autostrada. Keep a sharp watch. I want to make only one pass over the airfield.'

Kenji checked his altimeter. At 5,000 feet, he could make out people on the ground, and counted seven cars around the villa. He tipped the Junker's nose down in a gradual descent in order to see over the centre engine. The ground had a light dusting of snow. Small bodies of water were frozen in the ditches on either side of the wide road. Concerned that the silver Flying Palace might not be visible against the white background of snow, he lowered his altitude once more.

They flew over the airfield, over army trucks and cars lined up near large low buildings. Three single-wing Russian Yak fighter planes were parked in front of their hangars, marked by the multi-pointed sun of the Chinese Nationalist army painted on wings and tails.

'If the Flying Palace is inside one of the hangars, we'll never know whether Chiang Kai-shek is here,' Hino said.

'By the gods, there it is,' Genda cried. 'She is giant! What a wingspread!'

'She's a beauty,' Hino said. 'I've never seen anything so streamlined. She must look wonderful in the air.'

'There's no hangar in the Far East large enough to hold her,' Kenji said. 'Genda, get on the radio to Major Ando. Tell him what we've seen. Hino, navigate us to the Kwangtung army base outside Mukden.' Kenji turned the plane north. 'That silver giant is the first Model One,

Douglas Curtiss passenger plane,' he said. 'Our agents in Washington heard rumours that President Roosevelt made a gift of it to the generalissimo. It's not painted silver. The body is a special processed smooth aluminium.'

'What powers the monster?' Genda asked.

'The DC-1 has two 1,200-horsepower Cyclone engines with three-blade variable-pitch propellers,' Kenji said. 'She carries thirty-two passengers, plus freight.'

'Why don't we buy those engines and stick them in our fighters?' Genda said.

'The Americans won't sell to us. But that doesn't matter. The motor is too long for what I have in mind. When I find the correct balance between engine length, weight and power, Japan will have the greatest fighter plane in the world.'

The cloud ceiling over Mukden was 11,000 feet and the weather clear as the Hugo Junker approached the Kwangtung army airfield. Snow was piled on either side of the main runway, which was lined with burning oil pots. Kenji landed the Junker, then taxied behind a bicycle rider who led the plane to the storage and maintenance area.

Major Ando, with swollen eyes and stitches in his split lip, bowed to the three pilots. 'Captain Ishikawa, we need this aeroplane for our operation against Huangsen's villa.'

'On condition we take part in the action,' Genda said.

'That is General Tojo's decision,' Ando said. 'How many soldiers will this plane carry?'

'It was built for seventeen passengers, but I've studied the blueprints,' Kenji said. 'By removing the seats, luggage racks and toilets, we can carry at least twenty-seven.'

'Please instruct our maintenance people to that effect,' Ando said. 'Then we'll meet with General Tojo.'

At the Fifth Moon Inn, the four officers entered Tojo's office and snapped to attention. A tall sallow-faced civilian with thick glasses stood next to the desk of the general of the Kwangtung army.

The bald-headed general raised his hand, motioning Kenji and his cousins forward with his little finger. 'You are certain the Flying Palace is at Huang-sen's villa?' Tojo asked.

'The aeroplane described as the generalissimo's is parked on the runway of the airport near the villa,' Kenji said.

'Allow me to introduce myself,' the civilian said. 'Dr Tsubota is my name. In your opinion, Captain Ishikawa, could three transport planes land at the airport and with 100 men hold that position and attack the villa?'

'Not successfully,' Kenji answered.

'If the planes and commando unit are expendable, could they succeed in killing Chiang?' Tsubota asked.

'No,' Kenji said. 'According to the number of cars and trucks parked at the airfield, more than 100 men must be on duty there. It's three miles from the airfield to the villa. I assume Huang-sen will have more guards than usual with Chiang Kai-shek as his guest. I saw at least seven big cars parked at the villa.'

'With twenty imperial marines, I can take that villa,' Ando said. 'I've been inside.'

'You would be facing more than Huang-sen's guards,' Genda said. 'By the time our men ran the three miles from the airport, troops from the army camp would have crossed the railroad tracks to the villa.'

'We could land on the road,' Hino said. 'That road from the villa to the airport is wide enough and long enough. Our marines could get to the villa's front door in minutes.'

'An excellent suggestion,' Tsubota said. 'But the noise would alert the guards. For Ando's plan to work, surprise is necessary.'

'Paratroopers,' Genda said. 'The marines are trained in night-drops. We've worked with them.'

110

Tsubota came around the desk and peered through his thick spectacles at Hino. 'Your long-distance flight achieved international fame for Japan. If your brother's plan of paratroopers is feasible, could you land a transport plane on that road and pick them up?'

'My speciality is navigation. Kenji could pilot the plane.'

'Hmmmm,' Tsubota mused. 'First parachute the marines in, they attack the villa, then you land. It's an idea.'

'If you have qualified pilots for the other two transport planes, I'll fly the Junker with Hino as the mission's navigator,' Kenji said. 'And Genda is one of Japan's best fighter pilots.'

'We have no need of fighter planes now,' Ando said.

'How do you expect us to escape after the mission?' Genda asked. 'The Chinese army base will be alerted by the firing. They'll come charging across the railroad tracks. I saw four biplane fighters on the airstrip when we landed here. With those, I could delay the Chinese at the railroad crossing.'

'The four planes you saw are old models,' Tojo said. 'We use them for reconnaissance.'

'Sir, they're French Vouens,' Genda said. 'Each carries two water-cooled 9mm machine guns. There are five hand-racked twenty-pound bombs on either side of the cockpit.'

'One modern Chinese fighter plane could knock down all four biplanes, catch the three transports and blow us out of the sky,' Kenji said. 'We saw three single-wing Yak fighters parked outside the hangars near the Flying Palace.'

Genda grinned. 'We can bomb the hangars and strafe the fighters on the ground. Then we'll guard the railroad crossing.'

'The attempt to kill Chiang Kai-shek will be made,' Tojo declared. 'Major Ando, are you capable of co-ordinating this attack at dawn tomorrow?'

'Yes, sir!'

'Be certain that Kenji Ishikawa and his cousins are not assigned to the same plane. The nation cannot afford to lose three of its heroes in one day.' Tojo motioned Ando closer with his little finger. 'You will jump with the paratroopers and lead them in!'

'But I've never jumped from a plane.'

Dr Tsubota smiled. 'After your fiasco in Sian, Major Ando, you are fortunate the general allows you the use of a parachute to make that jump.'

'Dismissed,' Tojo barked. He watched the four officers do an about-turn and march out. When the door closed, he turned to Tsubota. 'Mr X decoded our army cipher, and is probably responsible for warning the prime minister and others about the assassinations in February. Have Koda-ha in Tokyo kill him!'

Dr Tsubota bowed. 'Wantabe will die.'

13

Piloting an overloaded plane, at night, in a complicated commando operation over unfamiliar territory, Kenji's teeth clenched so tight they ached. He had used the entire runway before the overloaded Junker became airborne. The thirty marine passengers did not know they had come within fifty yards of crashing, but Kenji's co-pilot did. Fear was still plastered on his face.

'Sir,' the radio operator said to Kenji. 'Captain Hino reports fifteen minutes to jump-time.'

Kenji wondered if his cousins felt as tense as he did. Genda had taken off earlier and was somewhere forward with the slower-moving old fighter planes. Hino was leading the mission through the dark in the transport plane. I should compliment him once again on his navigational ability, Kenji thought. Each checkpoint on the flight plan was reached within minutes of the designated time.

'Sir,' the co-pilot said. 'A flashing light to starboard.'

'That must be Genda's group,' Kenji said. 'Those old crates have no radio. Flick the cabin lights on and off three times.'

'How will Captain Genda know when to attack the air base?' the co-pilot asked.

'Major Ando and the marines will fire a green star rocket. That's also our signal to land.'

'Sir, if we have to use the machine-guns, I think the vibrations will damage the metal wing covering.'

Kenji looked out of the side windows at the tripods he had ordered bolted on to the wings between the engines and cockpit. 'They'll hold. Don't worry. The Germans build sturdy stuff.'

'I've never fired a Lewis gun.'

'Have you?' Kenji asked the radio operator.

'Yes, sir. I'm receiving a message from Captain Hino. He says three minutes to jump-time. Sunrise in twenty minutes. He can see the Baoding airport tower lights. The paratroopers jump after we pass the airfield.'

Kenji leaned back and shouted, 'Marines, prepare to jump!'

In the lead plane, Hino turned to Ando. 'Major, open the cargo door and prepare to jump!'

Ando patted Hino's shoulder, and made his way back between the double row of paratroopers. He staggered under the weight of his parachute, submachine-gun and ammunition belt.

'Prepare to jump,' Ando shouted.

A grizzled master sergeant pulled the cargo door in and a great rush of air filled the plane. The fuselage rattled. Ando edged his way to the open door and looked out, glad for the plane's vibrations so the men would not know his legs were shaking. 'Sergeant, remember our agreement,' he whispered. 'If I freeze, push me out.'

'Yes, sir. But if you don't hook your rip-cord to the overhead cable, your 'chute won't open.'

Ando forced a weak smile, and snapped the rip-cord to the cable.

'Go,' Hino shouted from the cockpit.

Ando felt himself catapulted into space. He saw the plane's tail-section pass by. He was floating down but looking upwards, watching men from the Junker bail out above him. He forgot the instructions to cross his hands over his chest and keep his chin down, and his body was jerked to an abrupt halt. His head snapped back. He fought for consciousness, then opened his eyes in complete floating silence, with marines all around him. A feeling of peace filled his body. He saw the airfield tower

114

lights ahead and knew the villa must be at his back. The enemy below seemed unaware of the attacking force.

'Keep your legs together and tumble,' someone shouted.

Ando looked down between his booted feet and saw the ground racing towards him. He hit with a jolt, rolled and stood up. But, tangled in the 'chute cords, he fell again.

The sergeant looked down at Ando. 'Are you all right, sir?'

'Most exhilarating,' Ando said. 'I never before experienced such a thrill.'

'Yes, sir. Let me help with that harness. We've been fortunate. The enemy hasn't detected our drop. The demolition team is waiting.'

Ando stood up and shrugged out of the straps. Scouts led him and the demolition team across the field, using a drainage ditch for cover. They reached the outer wall around the villa undetected. Behind them, the marines moved silently into position. Several ran for the railroad crossing.

Ando directed the demolition team to dig two holes under the dirt wall. He was now in his own element. He placed the bangalore torpedos and set the detonator, waving the other men back and counting to himself as he moved away. He pointed at the sergeant, who fired a flare pistol at the moment of explosion. Chinese machine-gunners on the villa porch were surprised by the noise and shocked by the concussion. The marines rushed through the smoking gap in the dirt wall, halfway across the compound before the first shot was fired at them.

Ando slipped through the breach in the wall, confident his plan was working. When the Chinese machine-guns did fire, they could not traverse far enough to bear on the marines. Several of the men around him fell to enemy rifle fire, but the outside guards were quickly overwhelmed. Marines surrounded the villa, throwing grenades inside through windows and doors.

Ando's heart lurched. There were only three limousines parked by the gate, not the seven Kenji had reported. He dashed inside the house. Water from smashed fish tanks soaked the thick Persian carpets. He ordered the secretary of the Kuomintang dragged forward in his night clothes. Huang-sen looked around at his dead guards, the flopping fish, and wept.

'Where is the generalissimo?' Ando demanded.

Huang-sen reached down and scooped up a long-tailed goldfish in his hands. 'Look what you've done to my fish,' he moaned.

The Flying Palace was gone, but without a radio there was no way for Genda to relay the information that Chiang Kai-shek had escaped. At sight of the green star rocket, he led his planes in a strafing attack on the three Yak fighters still parked outside the hangars. Long bursts from the Lewis guns set the Yaks ablaze. The attacking biplanes, their rising-sun insignia covered over with fresh paint, released twenty-pound bombs by hand.

Genda flew to the far end of the field and machine-gunned the large fuel storage tank. He dropped two bombs to ignite the gasoline. Turning towards the army base, he fired a red star rocket from the open cockpit of his plane. The other fighter pilots broke off their attack and followed him to cover the railroad crossing.

Hino had anticipated the green star rocket and was in position to descend. His pilot led the two empty transports down over the army base, past the railroad crossing and on to the road just beyond the villa.

Kenji's plane was last in line on the road. He and his radio operator climbed out of the cargo door and up on to the wings. Through the cockpit's windows, the co-pilot handed each man a Lewis gun and five ninety-seven-round pan magazines.

116

Kenji set his machine-gun up on the tripod bolted to the wing. He inserted a magazine and snapped a round into the firing chamber. He lay down facing the tail and sighted on the railroad crossing, then shouted to the radio operator on the other side of the fuselage. 'Be careful not to shoot off our own rudder or tail wings!'

The concussion of the exploding gas storage tanks three miles away reached the plane. Kenji looked behind and saw a large dirty fireball mushrooming up into the morning sky. Machine-gun fire from the railroad crossing brought his attention around in the opposite direction. He saw a Chinese army motorcycle with sidecar careen off the road into a ditch. The twenty-man Japanese marine roadblock fired at an army car racing for the crossing, until it burst into flames. A Chinese staff car and two trucks were destroyed at the railroad crossing by Genda's fighter planes.

Kenji saw marines streaming back from the villa and boarding the planes ahead of his. The wing rocked under his belly as marines piled into the Hugo Junker. He counted only ten men. Ando and the marine sergeant had killed the more seriously injured, left their bodies in the villa and burned it. The two planes ahead revved their motors for take-off.

A Chinese armoured car came rumbling towards the railroad crossing. The fighter planes sprayed it with machine-gun fire, but the bullets bounced off. The pilots' hand-held bombs missed the target. The iron monster kept coming, spitting fire from its machine-guns, shells from a light cannon in the turret. It tore up the marine roadblock.

Ando, at the cargo door of the Junker, shouted to the co-pilot, 'Take us out of here! Now!'

'What about the men at the roadblock?' Kenji shouted.

Ando sliced his hand across his belly in the sign for seppuku.

117

The armoured vehicle rumbled closer to the Hugo Junker and Kenji fired a burst from the Lewis gun. His bullets ricocheted off the vehicle in a spray of sparks. He saw the turret cannon swivel in his direction. 'Get us out of here,' Kenji shouted to the co-pilot from the wing.

A shell whizzed by and exploded in front of the plane. Kenji saw a marine jump out of the ditch on the side of the road and run towards the armoured car, carrying a satchel-charge. He was cut down by the bow machine-gun. The turret cannon fired at the plane again, this time on the mark, but the Junker had begun to move. The shell burst behind the tail. Another marine dashed out into the road and grabbed the satchel-charge from his dead comrade. He ran only a few steps before he was killed, but his sacrifice gave the Junker time to pick up speed. Kenji saw a third marine grab the satchel-charge and fling it under the armoured car. The big iron vehicle lifted into the air, and landed upside-down on ice in the roadside ditch, spinning like a top.

The Junker raced down the road. Kenji shouted to the radio operator to climb back into the plane. Kenji released his Lewis gun from its tripod and let the extra magazines slide off the wing. He stood up to grab for the cockpit window and was almost blown away by the backwash of the propeller. He pulled himself halfway through the window, face to face with the terrified co-pilot at the wheel. Ando pulled the radio operator in through the opposite window and turned to Kenji.

'Don't touch me,' Kenji said. 'This pilot is scared stiff.' He eased himself back out. Standing on the wing with just his head and shoulders inside the cockpit, he spoke softly to the panic-stricken co-pilot. 'You have another two miles of road and plenty of time. Are your flaps lowered?'

The wild eyes swivelled towards Kenji. The young pilot shook his head no.

'Reach down on your right side and pull back gently on

the first black knob. That will lower the flaps and give the plane more lift.' The fierce wind tore at Kenji's body. He lost his trousers and underpants, but he continued to talk the co-pilot through take-off procedures. The plane became airborne. 'Keep her nose up. That's it. Now give her full power.'

'We're up,' the co-pilot shouted. 'I've never flown anything other than a trainer!'

'And I've never given instructions while standing bare-arse on the wing of a flying plane. Up flaps and pull me in before I freeze my backside off!'

The plane roared over the burning airfield. Ando and the radio operator pulled Kenji in over the lap of the co-pilot.

'Let me at those controls,' Kenji said. 'I've got to see if Genda and his fighter planes got away.'

'No!' Ando said. 'That's an order! There's nothing you can do except get this plane shot down! From the looks of that airfield, they destroyed everything on the ground. But Chiang Kai-shek flew out an hour before we arrived. He's on his way to Nanking for a press conference to show his people and the Western world he's still alive.'

'What about Huang-sen?'

'Dead on the floor with his beloved fish in the burning villa.'

'Will Tojo cancel the invasion of northern China because we missed Chiang?' Kenji asked.

'He may delay the plan,' Ando said. 'Whether he'll let me live to see it implemented is another question.'

'Meanwhile, get me something to wear,' Kenji said. 'I'm not flying this thing back to Mukden in my birthday suit.'

14

Knowing it would change American foreign policy, John Whittefield very carefully worded his message to Ambassador Grew in Tokyo.

'All the following information was purposely given to me by Mikhail Borodin, senior Soviet agent in the Far East: Japanese commandos assassinated Secretary Huang-sen of the Kuomintang and burnt his villa in Baoding. Although Chiang Kai-shek was their original target, he escaped. The Japanese are preparing to invade China. Their army is on manoeuvres twelve miles from Peking. A firebrand, who had been jailed for involvement in the 26 February coup attempt in Tokyo, has suddenly appeared here as commander of the manoeuvres. General Kingoro Hashimoto's release from prison and Prime Minister Okada's retirement were arranged by Hirohito. The Emperor was supposedly influenced by President Roosevelt's one-billion-dollar naval budget.

'Borodin claims the military, secretly guided by the Emperor, will soon be running Japan with General Tojo as Hirohito's chief of staff. That Tojo's attempt to assassinate Chiang Kai-shek was sanctioned by Hirohito personally, in recognition of Chinese nationalism as the greatest threat to Japan's economy. Borodin believes that moderate Japanese leaders are being pressured indirectly by the Emperor and by Japan's economic depression to accept war as a solution. Since Japan's withdrawal from the League of Nations, their government leaders feel that their policies of expansion are misunderstood by the West. (I disagree with Borodin's claims about the Emperor. Hirohito is a reserved man who shuns politics.)

'Russia is concerned that Japan may join Germany and Italy in signing their new Axis Alliance. It is meant to co-ordinate and pivot the power of fascist states against communism; to encompass the world in a new order to solve the international economic crisis. My sources confirm Borodin's revelation that Stalin's latest purge of Soviet army officers has weakened the combat capability of Russian troops on the Mongolian–Manchurian border. Borodin requests that we supply Chiang Kai-shek and Mao Tse-tung with weapons to enable them to resist the Japanese invasion and keep Tojo's attention away from the Russian border. Although both Chiang and Mao were trained in Moscow, I recommend that we back the Nationalists. Mao takes his orders from Stalin. Chiang is more ruthless, but also more independent and apt to take American guidance.

'Borodin referred to my break-in at Koda-ha headquarters in Kyoto. He asked if we would be interested in the plans for the new British Spitfire fighter plane, which has flown at more than 350 miles an hour. The plans will remain in the British Embassy's safe in Peking for a week. They're en route to Chungking where the repair and supply depot for Chiang Kai-shek's new mercenary air wing is to be located. The Flying Tigers will be commanded by retired US General Claire Chenault, who is my agent. I employ him through the US External Survey Department. We'll eventually get the Spitfire plans through him. If you wish me to secure the documents immediately through other methods, respond quickly. Respectfully yours.'

John walked to the embassy code-room, marked his message urgent and put the symbol of the grey code at the top of the first page.

*   *   *

'Loyalty of the people for the Emperor and their desire to serve him is Japan's strength,' General Tojo said to Dr Tsubota. 'When our man is appointed prime minister, national conscription will become a reality. The size of the imperial army will triple.'

'Many members of the National Diet oppose conscription,' Tsubota said. 'America's protective tariffs have crippled our export industries. The politicians will cry about the cost.'

'But the industrialists will applaud. An expanded army means large military contracts and reduced unemployment. You and Ando will have your propaganda people encourage public emotion to override legislative logic! Arrange an incident that will anger our people! The Marco Polo bridge would be a good location to start a war. Co-ordinate your activities with General Kingoro Hashimoto!'

'Our first objective should be Peking,' Tsubota said. 'The Nationalist army has all but left that city for Shanghai. The only viable force Chiang Kai-shek has is on the border between the Marco Polo bridge and Peking.'

'Give Hashimoto a valid pretext to attack!'

'Kingoro needs no pretext,' Tsubota said. 'He hates the Chinese more than the round-eyes. He claims the Chinese are traitors to our race for not accepting Japan's leadership in a greater Asia.'

'Good,' Tojo said. 'Now, I want to know if we have a traitor in our midst. Or is it that Wantabe knows all our secrets? First our army code was broken. Secret files were stolen from Koda-ha headquarters in Kyoto, the prime minister was warned about our assassination teams and Chiang Kai-shek escaped an hour before our commando attack.'

'Wantabe will die as I promised,' Tsubota said. 'Chiang's escape was pure luck.'

'Bad luck for Ando. He is to be forbidden food between

sunrise and sunset, and all sex or entertainment in any form until China is invaded!'

'Understood.' Tsubota bowed. 'I'll send Major Ando to Kingoro Hashimoto. And then on to Peking where he'll direct my agents in contriving the incident.'

'He'll be held personally responsible!' Tojo said. 'This is his last chance to redeem himself! Now, tell me why Lord Koin and Admiral Yamamoto are taking you from me at this time. Are they trying to reduce my power?'

'Neither seeks your friendship nor your animosity,' Tsubota said. 'Both respect your power. They wish to utilize my agents and my knowledge of French Indochina and the Dutch East Indies. Roosevelt's one-billion-dollar naval bill and America's protective tariffs convinced them that Japan must contest the United States for control of South-East Asia. The Dutch and French have begun to transfer their naval forces back to Europe because of Mussolini and Hitler. Admiral Yamamoto convinced Lord Koin and other liberals that Japan must be prepared to protect her sources of oil, tin and rubber in South-East Asia.'

'I thought the admiral and the lord keeper of the privy seal were against war with the United States.'

'Definitely,' Tsubota said. 'But with Charles Lindbergh and other personalities leading an "America First Movement", Yamamoto and Koin are certain America's isolationist policy will prevent it from taking military action, unless of course the US is attacked.'

'What orders has Yamamoto given you?' Tojo asked.

'To develop a large espionage network, with Saigon as my base, to plan infiltration and subversion of the French and Dutch colonial authorities. I am to gather all possible information regarding invasion sites, airfields and harbour facilities. Yamamoto has given me three years.'

'The admiral may be for peace, but when it comes to war he is a genius,' Tojo said. 'Do a good job for him. And be sure to pass copies of all information to my army intelligence and Koda-ha in Kyoto.' Tojo stood up and walked to a cabinet. He unlocked it and withdrew an old, thick folder marked SECRET. He handed the folder to Tsubota. 'Read over this account of the activities of General Honjo. He was the most unscrupulous and successful agent Japan has ever had. Prior to the Russo–Japanese War, he used sex, drugs, blackmail and assassinations to infiltrate, sabotage and subvert tens of thousands in Manchuria. He addicted Emperor Henry Pu-yi to opium and set up the puppet government of Manchuko. His methods may be the key to your success.'

'If you must send someone to Kenji at Kwangtung headquarters, why not Raiko?' Noriko said. 'She has travelled around the world by herself. The two of them will never see each other if she doesn't go now.'

'Raiko alone in China?' Hiroki shrugged. 'Her father will not permit it.'

'I think otherwise,' Noriko said. 'Mini has a twenty-three-year-old unmarried daughter whose advanced age, Western education and manners severely restrict her marriage prospects. Mini's interpretation of constitutional law has frightened away most prospective suitors. On a professor's salary, he cannot provide a very attractive dowry. The girl will be an old maid unless he allows her to go to China now.'

Hiroki raised his teacup towards Noriko. 'To the Japanese cupid. You know that love matches in Japan are rare. Marriage for most men is only a necessary step towards advancing their station in life. The ideal Japanese wife bears sons, keeps a good house on a modest budget, and does not complain about her husband's inattention.'

'Ours was a love match.'

'How can you say that?' Hiroki teased. 'The first time we

124

met in the Imperial Hall of Martial Arts, you pummelled me with your kendo sword.'

'Then you rose up and kicked and punched me unconscious with karate blows,' Noriko said, knowing her husband would blush.

Hiroki still asked Noriko's forgiveness for striking her whenever he thought of the day they had been tricked into fighting each other. But he also knew that whenever she mentioned it, she was trying to persuade him. He saw her eyes fill with tears. She only cried when she thought of their two dead sons.

'If our boys were alive, I would want one of them to marry Raiko,' Noriko said. 'She is a special person.'

Hiroki went to his wife and kissed away her tears. 'Kenji is almost our son. If you think Raiko is best for him, I will speak to Mini after his lecture tonight. Actually I could make use of Raiko's presence at Kwangtung army headquarters to send false information via the Kwangtung code. We know the Americans have broken it. Raiko deciphered a message from John Whittefield to Ambassador Grew. Sending her to China will justify her absence from the Black Chamber. She has completed Ruth Kuhn's training. Ruth and her father will soon leave for Honolulu. The more I think of it, the better an idea it is. Raiko can leave tomorrow morning on the China Clipper.' Hiroki did not mention he was thinking of having her fly with two of Japan's best safecrackers. He and Yamamoto had decided it was necessary to obtain the plans of the Spitfire fighter from the British Embassy safe in Peking.

15

Tokyo University

'Make no mistake,' Professor Tatsukichi Minobe said. 'Those Black Dragon bully-boys will attempt to disrupt tonight's lecture.' The little man gathered his notes and put them into a neat pile. 'I did not see any city police.'

'We cannot trust them or Kempetai,' Hiroki said. 'Kodaha controls both. But Wantabe has stationed members of the Cherry Blossom Society in the audience. They are trained in combat judo.'

'If violence should break out in the auditorium, please see Raiko safely home.'

'It is because of Raiko I am here,' Hiroki said. 'She has been overworked in the Black Chamber and needs a rest. I must send someone to Manchuria for a short period, and am considering her.'

'There is talk of war in China,' Minobe said.

'Raiko would be sent to the Kwangtung army headquarters, and escorted from Tokyo to Peking by two armed escorts. My nephew Kenji will meet and chaperone her upon arrival. You know Kenji.'

'Yes. He is a remarkable and versatile young man, although a bit undisciplined. My daughter has mentioned him once or twice.'

'Favourably, I hope.'

'No,' Minobe said, cocking a thick eyebrow at his friend. 'In fact, Raiko took exception to his penchant for notoriety and public drunkenness.'

'I will come directly to the point,' Hiroki said. 'Noriko

126

believes your daughter and Kenji have feelings for each other. She thinks the two should be together.'

'Oh my.' Minobe smiled and rolled his eyes. 'When your Noriko sets her mind to an idea, I know we two will capitulate.'

'She says their independent personalities and Western backgrounds make them suitable for each other, just as those attributes make them incompatible with others.'

'You and I have been through two wars and long difficult periods of peace. There is no other family I would rather see my daughter marry into than yours. I have reservations about Kenji, but Raiko will make her own decision.'

'Then Raiko has your permission to leave on the morning flight to Peking?'

'If she wishes.'

Hiroki let out his breath. 'After your lecture, I shall host everyone to dinner.'

Minobe motioned to the door. 'The noise may be an indication of a short speech.'

'You are the nation's champion of democratic constitutionalism. Your teachings and theories have influenced our government's leaders for a decade and a half. You have many supporters out there.'

'But are they prepared to fight for their democratic beliefs?'

Hiroki, Noriko, Ruth and Raiko sat in the last row of the crowded lecture hall. Wantabe positioned himself behind them. Several of his agents were stationed inconspicuously nearby, while another twenty sat in the front row. More Cherry Blossom men were on the way.

The atmosphere was charged and the mood ugly when Professor Minobe was introduced. He strode on to the stage with his papers in one hand and a wooden box in the other. Placing the box on the floor, he stepped up on it behind the podium.

127

Raiko estimated that half the people applauded. The others remained silent and stone-faced.

'You have your father's attractive large eyes,' Ruth Kuhn whispered. 'He appears to command the audience to silence with his eyes.'

Raiko thought the quiet in the hall more ominous than the noise. Young toughs, wearing silk jackets with Black Dragons embroidered on the backs, stood in the aisles and against the walls. With arms folded across their chests, they glared at her father. Rows of uniformed cadets sat at attention with that same hateful stare directed towards the podium.

Professor Minobe's voice boomed from the loudspeakers. 'Many in Japan believe the Emperor to be the embodiment of moral order. They believe that imperial authority to rule is established by lineal descendancy from the gods. Most Japanese have never spoken the Emperor's name, nor ever heard it said aloud. It is Michi no Miya Hirohito.'

A hissing sound of people sucking wind through their teeth swept the lecture hall.

The professor leaned forward and smiled. 'You see. I was not struck dead. Hirohito! There, I've done it again and the gods have not punished me.'

'We shall punish you,' an angry voice shouted from the aisle.

Many voices joined in the denunciation. 'Traitor!'

'Step down!'

'You filthy liberal!'

The little man placed his fists on his hips and waited. His dark eyes roamed over the audience. With his powerful voice, he silenced everyone. 'For some of you, the Emperor is the ultimate source of all values! He represents what is good, true and beautiful!' Minobe lowered his voice, drawing the audience to him. 'For many, the Emperor is the head of our national family. Upon him depends the survival of Japan. What foolish reasoning!

128

Historians and genealogists have proven that the lineal descent of the imperial house was often broken. The Emperor's bloodline is not pure, and the mental illness suffered by his father certainly indicates disfavour in the eyes of the gods. In the twentieth century it is absurd to believe that all Japanese have common folk ancestors identified with the Emperor, who is himself supposedly one of the gods. Archaeologists and anthropologists trace our ancestry, language and culture to China. The only pure Japanese are the Ainu people, those hairy folk whom our ancestors drove to the mountains of the north centuries ago.'

The uproar in the hall was deafening. Raiko believed her father had alienated everyone there.

'Those uniformed cadets remind me of Hitler's youth groups,' Ruth whispered. 'They're the most dangerous ones in this hall. They wait quietly while everyone else shouts. They have a plan.'

'There's never been a riot in Tokyo University,' Raiko said. 'We Japanese are a civilized people.' She looked at the contorted faces around her and shuddered. She heard vicious threats shouted at her father and was afraid for him. 'At least we're supposed to be civilized.'

'This is a new era,' Ruth said. 'Look at those Black Dragon toughs with their hate-filled eyes.'

At the rear of the auditorium, three men edged their way through the angry crowd to a position behind Wantabe. Unaware of their presence, he leaned over and whispered to Hiroki, 'I suggest we leave.'

'Not yet. That could precipitate a mass exodus of Minobe's students and supporters. He would be left alone. Let me know when our reinforcements arrive.'

The Black Dragons in the centre aisle began shoving and threatening people. A place was cleared for a young university professor.

'The love of a child for his parents comes from nature,'

the professor shouted. 'Japan is one great family! The imperial house represents our national parents! It is natural for us to worship the Emperor as the head of our national home. The spirit of loyalty and piety are bound up as one in the Emperor and Japan's character. The power of the Emperor to guide Japan is necessary for the survival of our people. His majesty's right to rule is god-given. We don't need a constitution! We don't need a National Diet! And certainly we don't need traitors like Professor Minobe in this university!'

'Is my father safe?' Raiko asked Wantabe.

'Reinforcements have just arrived. Those young men forming up on either side of the stage are from the Cherry Blossom Society.'

'Watch the uniformed hooligans,' Ruth said.

'If something does happen, follow me,' Wantabe said. 'My men will clear a path for us to the rear door.'

Tatsukichi Minobe's voice boomed from the loud-speakers, shocking people into silence once again. 'I am second to none in my conviction that our unique national policy regarding the Emperor is our greatest glory! Therein lies a part of our nation's strength! But the state should also be considered a legal entity! That entity must have sovereignty, and the authority to rule above all individuals! The Emperor is the highest organ of the state. He carries out the executive functions as our national leader, but he must be subordinate to the law of the land. The legal authority of our constitution is far more vital to the country than Hirohito's lineal descent!'

'Anyone who compares his imperial majesty with a scrap of paper should be shot,' the young professor shouted.

With a snarling roar like that of an enraged animal, the toughs in the centre aisle rushed the stage, and were met head-on by Wantabe's agents. The Black Dragons were kicked, karate-chopped and punched. They were forced backwards. In their frustration and rage they turned on

130

the audience. Fighting erupted in between the seats, in the aisles, up in the balcony.

'Listen,' Ruth said. 'What are the cadets chanting?'

Raiko strained to hear above the uproar but could not make out the words.

The cadets stood, chanting at the tops of their voices, and the fighting stopped. The hall was quieted by the strength and unvaried pitch of the unfaltering cadenced call, 'One voice! One blood! One command! One voice! One blood! One command! The Emperor! The Emperor! The Emperor!'

The cadets surged forward, trampling chairs and people in a co-ordinated rush towards the stage.

It was the signal for the three men behind Wantabe to act. Two cleared a way for the third, who slipped a long, thin-bladed stiletto from his sleeve into the palm of his hand. He cocked his arm to drive the pointed shaft into Wantabe's back, and was struck a karate chop at the base of his skull by a Cherry Blossom agent. The assassin fell dead. His two companions were beaten senseless.

Surrounded by agents, Wantabe, Hiroki, Raiko and Ruth were rushed towards the rear door. Raiko jumped up on a chair to look for her father. She saw that many had come prepared for a riot. Bottles, stones and bricks flew through the air. Young men ripped chairs from their footing in the cement floor and battered each other.

Wantabe pulled Raiko from her perch. 'Your father is protected,' he said. 'He'll meet us at the rear entrance to the stage.'

Raiko had to jump up to see what was happening as Wantabe's men led the way towards the exit. The wave of uniformed cadets had reached the stage, but they broke against the line of Cherry Blossom defenders. The Black Dragons piled into the fight and the mêlée worsened. Many fell with crushed skulls and smashed bones. Bodies fell from the balcony.

The crowd around Raiko was crushing her and she began to panic. Suddenly she felt herself propelled forward like a cork popped from a bottle, and was carried outside with Wantabe and the others. Surrounded by university policemen, they were escorted to Kenji's 1937 Lincoln Continental.

'Professor Minobe will be waiting for us at the rear of the building,' Hiroki told the driver. 'Then on to the nightclub of Miss Kuhn's choice. This is her farewell party.'

Wantabe saw the shocked look on Ruth's face. 'Foreign Minister Matsuoka gave orders that you and your father are to proceed by passenger ship to Honolulu,' he said. 'Our agents have arranged Dutch passports. They'll be waiting in Hawaii to give you the keys to a house overlooking Pearl Harbor.'

'This is so sudden,' Ruth said to Raiko. 'I'll miss you.'

'We'll have time for a last talk tomorrow,' Raiko said.

'I'm afraid not,' Wantabe said. 'You are also leaving early in the morning on a well-earned vacation. You two must say your farewells tonight.'

Raiko's father entered the car and her relief at seeing him replaced thoughts of her surprise vacation and Ruth's departure. 'Father, are you hurt?'

'Not at all, although I can't say the same for constitutional government. At least no-one slept during that lecture.'

Hiroki was certain several people were permanently at rest on the auditorium floor.

16

The Imperial Reception Room

There were no tatami mats to cushion the sound of Hiroki Koin's patent-leather shoes on the hardwood floor. The chairs were European, as was the desk behind which sat the Emperor of Japan. His thin, sallow face and dark eyes, framed by wire-rimmed spectacles, were reflected in the polished desk top. A gold inkstand, pen, blotter and single sheet of paper were set before him. Hiroki bowed.

'Describe last night's disturbances at the university,' Hirohito said.

'Sire, five people were killed and thirty-one hospitalized. The attack on Professor Minobe was planned by Koda-ha and co-ordinated with the Black Dragons to express public rejection of constitutional authority over imperial rule.'

'I assumed the people would prefer Japan to be governed by law rather than decree,' the Emperor said. 'My grandfather made the constitution a gift to them.'

'Sire, Emperor Meiji instituted democratic reforms by virtue of his power as monarch. The people had no choice. Your grandfather ordered the National Diet to abolish inherited rank. He gave the people the right to vote, and declared compulsory education. Personal achievement rather than birth became the criterion for upward social and economic mobility.'

'The new prime minister prefers that lineal descent take precedence over ability,' Hirohito said. 'Mr Konoe espouses aristocratic authority, but wishes the army to rule.'

'You, sire, are supreme commander of Japan's armed forces.'

'This new constitutional amendment approved by the Diet requires one army officer and one naval officer as permanent members of the cabinet. If either military representative resigns, the government falls. Koda-ha may champion my power publicly but, with this new law, they have actually limited it and the Diet's ability to make change. The military controls the government of Japan.'

'If the military-men were to bring down the government by resigning, the reins of power would be entirely in your hands,' Hiroki said.

The Emperor of Japan sat motionless. Minutes passed before he looked up. 'Were you in danger last night?'

'I was protected, although my chief of intelligence was almost murdered. One assassin died. The other two were captured and interrogated. They are Koda-ha men. Wantabe's decoding of the Kwangtung army code appears to be the reason for the assassination attempt. I suspect the order for his death came from General Tojo.'

'Then why is Professor Minobe's daughter on her way to Tojo's headquarters?'

Hiroki's surprise at the Emperor's knowledge showed on his face. Hirohito smiled and explained, 'The departures on the China Clipper for Peking were printed in the morning newspaper. Is the girl in danger?'

'Raiko Minobe will be safe,' Hiroki said, making a mental note to order all passenger lists of ships and planes cleared in the Black Chamber prior to publication. 'She is carrying several messages to General Tojo. We are co-operating with the planned invasion of the five provinces of north China.'

'Why a young female messenger?' the Emperor asked.

Hiroki grunted, and excused himself. 'Sire, I have used my office for personal reasons. My wife wishes Miss

Minobe and our nephew Kenji Ishikawa to spend time together.'

'My wife . . .' The Emperor paused, then said, 'The Empress was quite impressed with Captain Ishikawa's feat of climbing the Imperial Hotel and raising his squadron's flag. We could see it from our balcony. I personally was more taken by Captain Hino Arai's world speed record. Where are your nephews?'

'Training with a fighter squadron in Manchuria,' Hiroki said.

'How or where will war with China begin?'

'Reports indicate Tojo's agents in Peking, Shanghai and other major cities have been ordered to antagonize the Chinese. If no incident results to give Tojo an excuse for war, I believe he will create one. His senior *agent provocateur* has dropped out of sight. When Major Ando surfaces, the action will begin.'

The Emperor glanced at the pocket watch presented to him by King George VI of England. 'I have invited the prime minister to join us. He should be waiting outside.'

Fumiaro Konoe was tall for a Japanese. His long face and thin figure added to the appearance of height. His short Hitler-style mustache identified him as Koda-ha.

'Mr Konoe,' Hirohito said, 'I wish you every success in all your endeavours as prime minister. If foreign press reports are correct, your first crisis may be a military confrontation in China. Are you prepared?'

'Yes, sire.' Konoe bowed. 'My predecessor was most diligent in the transfer of office. Our military in Manchuko are on alert for Chinese acts of aggression.'

'Have you made provisions for peace as well?'

'The Chinese are quite hostile. They do not wish peace. Societies have been formed to boycott Japanese products. Nationalist and Communist political units have emerged with anti-Japanese themes. They threaten those Chinese who do business with us. Until recently the Chinese people were wedded to their ancestral past and thought little of themselves as a nation. But now a political solidification is taking place that is dangerous for Japan.'

'The rise of Chinese nationalism is in direct proportion to the Kwangtung army's aggressiveness,' Hiroki said. 'I refer to the occupation of Formosa, Korea and Manchuria. Now we prepare to invade China itself. I agree Japan must expand. But delicately. Otherwise, 500 million Chinese will rise against us.'

'Peaceful penetration of China proper is no longer possible,' Konoe said. 'Time is of the essence. The relationship between Japan's population, our landmass and food production is a matter of life and death. We have fifty times more people per square mile than America. Eighty per cent of our land is untillable, and we are virtually without natural resources. For Japan, the alternative to war is starvation.'

'I agree to a limited incursion into China,' Hiroki said. 'But many of your Koda-ha people are espousing a Nazi-type New Order, a Greater Asia, a Japanese-controlled Pacific Ocean. The Kwangtung army's objectives must be limited. Their immediate goals should be to make the Chinese countryside safe from warlords and protect the cities from tong chiefs. Japan must develop vibrant trade with the Chinese people.'

'Japan has proved its ability to govern Korea, Manchuko and Formosa,' Konoe said. 'In each country the birthrate has risen, the death-rate fallen and the level of education improved. General Tojo's incursion into China will be geographically restricted to the north. He promises victory in three months. The Chinese people will benefit from our agricultural experience and industrial expertise.'

The Emperor adjusted his spectacles and perused the sheet of paper on the desk before him. He looked up at the prime minister and said, 'Japan cannot afford an extended foreign war. We must reap immediate financial

136

benefits. The Cherry Blossom Society has decoded messages indicating Mao Tse-tung and Chiang Kai-shek will combine forces to oppose Tojo's invasion. Joseph Stalin has ordered it.'

'Sire, the scorched-earth policy used by Chiang's German generals against the Communists makes full co-operation between the two groups unlikely,' Konoe said. 'In addition, we have agents on both sides who are assigned to sow dissension.'

Hiroki saw the Emperor's eyes wander and knew the audience would soon end. It was common knowledge that Hirohito preferred his laboratory and marine specimens to political discussion.

The Emperor looked at the two men standing before him as if for the first time. 'Those whose careers depend on war, want war,' he mused. 'It would be a mistake for Japanese forces to be drawn into central or southern China.'

'General Tojo recognizes the consequences of attempting to occupy the vast Chinese landmass,' Konoe said. 'Our troops will be restricted to the north.'

The Emperor nodded to Hiroki, who said, 'America's Ambassador Grew informed the Emperor that in the event of a Japanese invasion of China, the United States might well decide to intervene. Such a decision would bring our two nations into conflict.'

'Military intelligence discounts such a threat,' Konoe said. 'The United States has maintained an isolationist policy since the Great War. Presently there is a sizeable delegation of German-Americans from the Midwest here in Tokyo. Their purpose is to convince Japan to sign a military pact with Hitler. They are convinced that if we do, the Americans will follow our lead.'

'That is absurd,' Hiroki said. 'The American president and US Congress are against Hitler. American anti-Nazi sentiment was highlighted at the Berlin Olympic Games in the incident of discrimination by the Nazis against the American Negro Jesse Owens.'

'I agree,' Konoe answered. 'But the appearance of this German-American delegation supports my argument that America will never commit troops in the Far East to protect a non-white nation such as China. The great Charles Lindbergh is only one of the popular leaders in the powerful "America First Movement". They support better ties with Germany and an isolationist policy in the Far East.' Konoe bowed to the Emperor. 'Your imperial majesty. I must point out that democracy is a confused and cumbersome way to govern. America will not help China because of their belief in white racial superiority.'

'Admiral Yamamoto does not agree,' the Emperor said. 'Naval intelligence indicates a US military movement to support China. If, as you have pointed out, the Nationalists and Communists will soon be at each other's throats, then I will allow more time. It would save Japanese lives.' The Emperor indicated the paper on the table before him. 'This order delays the invasion of China.'

Konoe fell back as if struck. His face turned red and beads of sweat formed on his brow. 'It may be too late.'

'You may approach me next year with facts and figures listing the economic benefits Japan would derive from the occupation of northern China,' the Emperor said. 'Bring me conclusive proof the Americans will not go to war against Japan.' He took the pen from its golden holder and signed the paper.

Hiroki stepped forward and used the blotter to dry the signature. He handed the order to the prime minister. The two men bowed, and with lowered heads backed towards the door. The Emperor's voice stopped them.

'Mr Konoe, the harmony of my soul and my peace of mind are disturbed by incidents such as the riot that took place at Tokyo University last night. In the future I will hold you responsible for such unsettling events.'

The China Clipper flew from Tokyo to Nagasaki, over the Yellow Sea and on to Peking in an uneventful journey. The senior safecracker sat in front of Raiko, the other behind her, silent, solemn men who gave no indication they were protecting the beautiful young woman. Tattooed Yakuza gangsters from Section Ten of Kempetai were often used by the secret police for espionage and sabotage.

Raiko dozed, and thought about the attack on Wantabe. She recalled that he had taken credit for breaking the Kwangtung army code, and was ashamed for having doubted his intentions. At her insistence, Wantabe had promised he would always travel with two bodyguards. Hiroki had vowed to her that guards would remain with Wantabe wherever he went, day or night.

Raiko snapped on the overhead light and opened her book, the new worldwide bestseller *Gone with the Wind*. Rhett Butler embraced Scarlett and it was Kenji holding Raiko. She felt his strong hands on her shoulders, his body against hers, and she shivered. Scarlett's lips met Rhett's and Raiko sighed.

She finished reading the last page of the book and looked out of the window, surprised to see the sun's first rays, the crimson horizon over mainland China. There were tears in her eyes. She reread the last few pages as the plane descended to Peking International Airport, and wondered if Kenji Ishikawa would leave her as Rhett Butler left Scarlett. Her body, her soul yearned for Kenji.

17

An atmosphere of organized frenzy pervaded the US Embassy. Rumours of war were rampant. Invasion seemed imminent. American residents of the former capital sought assurances from the embassy that their neutrality would be honoured if Japan's Kwangtung army crossed the border. Businessmen demanded guarantees for their financial institutions if the Japanese occupied Peking. The entire US marine detachment was needed to keep order on the quarter-mile queue for visa and passport validations.

In this charged atmosphere, in an overcrowded office, John Whittefield, head of the American Far East Intelligence Service, shared a desk and telephone with the embassy security chief. John had worked day and night to learn when and where the invasion of China would take place. In an attempt to forestall the Kwangtung army's crossing of the border, John's agents had spread false rumours of American intervention.

John held the telephone receiver to one ear and a hand to the other ear to block out the noise around him. 'What information do you have?'

'Kenji Ishikawa just left the Japanese Embassy,' Jade Joe said. 'He signed out a car for Peking International Airport. Mr X is arriving on the China Clipper. Ishikawa will escort this Mr X to the Kwangtung army base to meet General Tojo. Do you know who Mr X is?'

'No,' John lied. Jade Joe sold information and co-operation on the open market and John was not about to give him anything free. The curio merchant was also on the Japanese payroll.

'Mr X has two companions who'll stay with me until their mission, whatever it is, is completed,' Jade Joe said.

'There's a substantial bonus if you learn what it is.' John hung up the telephone, and shouted out. 'Anyone in the room have a clean shirt I can borrow?'

The security chief reached into a drawer and handed John a paper-wrapped shirt. 'My sources in Nanking claim Chiang Kai-shek will let the Japs take Peking. The generalissimo believes that will draw us and the Europeans into the war on his side.'

'What makes him think that?'

'Don't forget we pulled the Chinese chestnuts from the fire during the Boxer Rebellion. For the present, Chiang thinks the American economy needs the Chinese market, and he knows the Europeans have 200 years of vested interest in this country. If the Europeans let China go to the Japs, they could lose Malaysia, Indochina and the Dutch East Indies too.'

'The West is busy lining up against fascism in Europe,' John said. 'Chiang is mistaken. They won't come to his rescue. Neither will Roosevelt. The Democrats would lose the next congressional elections if Roosevelt initiated armed intervention. Chiang might well forfeit northern China if he's not careful.'

'That also fits into the generalissimo's plans. He'll withdraw and let the Communists fight the Japanese. His idea is to wait until after Mao Tse-tung is defeated and the Japanese are weakened. Then he plans to attack.'

'We live in interesting times,' John said. He buttoned the shirt, donned his jacket and topcoat. 'I'm off to meet Mr X.'

John Whittefield stood in the doorway of Armfield Shipping, a front for the US Intelligence Service, on the second-floor balcony. The airport's reception, departure and customs areas were located on the first floor of the long, two-storey brick building. The benches in the railroad-style waiting room faced north and south and people had to swivel to watch the east and west doors. Porters and taxi drivers mingled with the crowd. Chinese policemen were everywhere.

'See anything?' the office manager asked.

'Not yet. There are so many Japanese uniforms down there, it's hard to pick him out.'

'The Japs strut around as if they already own the place. They're sent here on liberty from Manchuria with orders to cause trouble. But the Chinese police ignore any fracas involving a Jap soldier. I spotted Ishikawa before. He's bigger than the other slant-eyes.'

John flashed an angry look at the manager. 'They're Japanese. Not Japs, not slope-heads or slant-eyes!'

'Yes, sir,' the manager said. 'I was stationed in Japan and had great respect for them as a people. They're clean, industrious and polite. But they seem to change when they're overseas. After they've lorded it over you once or twice, you'll understand.'

'There's Kenji Ishikawa.' John pointed. 'Standing to the right of the main entrance.'

'Listen. They're posting the arrival of the China Clipper.'

They heard the announcement made in Chinese, French, English and Japanese. They saw the police form a line at the passenger entrance and sweep the crowd back beyond the customs area. Several Japanese soldiers purposely held their ground, but the Chinese police passed them by, pretending not to notice.

'It looks like the Kwangtung army has the run of the airport,' John said.

'You haven't seen anything. They drive against traffic, refuse to pay bills in restaurants and beat up those who complain.'

'How long has this been going on?'

'Since Chiang Kai-shek retreated to Nanking.'

On the first floor, Kenji Ishikawa was also searching the crowd of incoming passengers, expecting a short fat man who waddled. He spotted Raiko, almost lost amid the taller people around her, and started forward, but caught himself. His heart and mind raced at equal speed in opposite directions. He wanted to rush to Raiko, take her hand, speak to her. But Wantabe wasn't with her, which signalled to Kenji there might be danger.

He watched until the last passenger entered the customs line and he was certain Wantabe had not arrived. Raiko was struggling to lift a suitcase on to the customs table. His heart leapt with each step as he strode towards her. The Chinese police fell back to let the tall Japanese air-force captain through.

'Allow me,' Kenji said. He reached with one hand to lift the large bag, and grunted. Raiko's big dark eyes twinkled and they both laughed. 'Have you got Mount Fuji in here?' he asked.

Raiko pointed behind her to the second suitcase set between two solemn middle-aged Japanese men, and grinned. 'Fujiyama is in that one.'

'Are you Mr X?' Kenji whispered.

'Yes, isn't it wonderful. I didn't realize how much I needed a vacation.'

'I wasn't told it would be you. I expected Wantabe.'

'Disappointed?' She watched his face.

'Not at all. What will you be doing at Kwangtung army headquarters?'

Raiko's plan was to not lose Kenji as Scarlett had lost Rhett Butler. Her first step was to remain with him as long as possible in Peking. 'There is much to explain. First stop will be Jade Joe's where these two gentlemen are to be housed. Do you know the place?' She moved closer to him.

'Yes,' Kenji said, breathing in her perfume, wanting to hold her. He glanced at the two men.

'Could you pass that second suitcase through customs without it being examined?' Raiko whispered.

Kenji cleared his throat. 'That's enough,' he informed the customs agent. 'These people are with me. I vouch for them!'

The Chinese official snapped the lid of the first suitcase closed. 'Yes, Captain. You and your party may proceed.'

Kenji motioned a porter to the luggage and signalled the two men to follow him. He took Raiko's arm and moved into the crowd.

'Did you notice the custom man's face?' Raiko asked. 'He was smiling when you told him to let us pass, but his eyes were filled with hate.'

'What's in the second bag?' Kenji whispered.

'Burglar tools under a false bottom.'

'What on earth for?'

'To steal the plans of the British Spitfire fighter plane. I thought you knew. The two men with me are the best Yakuza safecrackers in Japan.'

Kenji glanced behind at the men. 'Wonderful company you keep.' When he turned around, the blond head of John Whittefield was moving towards him above the crowd, smiling broadly.

Just as Kenji lifted his hand to wave, two Japanese soldiers blocked the American's path. John tried to walk around them but a third and fourth soldier stepped in his way, forming a four-man wall.

John bowed to the soldiers. 'May I please pass?' he said in flawless Japanese.

'Where did you learn the mother tongue?' the first soldier demanded.

Another soldier grabbed John's arm and pulled him around. 'We're talking to you, Round-eye!'

'And I am talking to you, Soldier!' Kenji said from behind. 'Remove your hand! You are fortunate my friend is in good humour. This round-eye learned Japanese from my mother and karate from my father. He holds a fourth-degree black belt in karate.'

The soldiers tried to salute Kenji, apologize to John and disappear into the crowd at the same time. Kenji ignored them and turned to John. 'Are you all right?'

'Fine. But I never met your parents and the only black belt I have is holding up my trousers.'

'I hold a karate black belt,' Kenji said. 'There was nothing to fear. I apologize for the rudeness of my countrymen. Please meet Miss Raiko Minobe.'

John bowed, immediately placing the beautiful young woman as Professor Minobe's daughter. Ah, she is Mr X, he thought. I need to find out why she came. 'Please allow me to repay your kindness by inviting both of you to dinner tonight,' John said. 'I insist.'

Kenji jumped at the excuse to spend more time in Raiko's company. 'We would be delighted. John Whittefield is the cultural attaché at the US Embassy in Tokyo,' he told her.

'Mr Whittefield must be meeting someone,' Raiko said.

'Just seeing someone off,' John said. 'Where are you two staying?'

'The Japanese Embassy,' Kenji said.

'Just around the corner from our embassy,' John said. 'I'll come by at seven. See you later.'

The luggage was stored in the Lincoln's boot and the

two Yakuza were seated in the rear. Raiko turned to Kenji at the wheel. 'Before you start the engine, I must tell you your friend was lying. I read the departure board. There are no planes leaving Peking for the next six hours.'

'Lying is part of John's profession,' Kenji said. 'He's senior US intelligence officer in the Far East.'

'Should we be having dinner with him considering what they're going to do?' Raiko indicated the two silent men in the rear seat.

'Exactly what is their assignment?'

Raiko explained as Kenji drove to the foreign quarter. He pulled up in front of Jade Joe's curio shop.

'I'll take the men inside and return shortly,' Kenji said.

Alone in the car, Raiko leaned her head back against the seat and imagined Kenji's arms around her. She read his grim face when he came out of the shop. 'What's wrong?'

'Jade Joe's contact in the British Embassy was fired for taking bribes. He's inside now, weeping at the loss of his job and sketching the location of the safe where the Spitfire drawings are. They're so numerous and large, they're being kept in a big vault on the third floor. The Yakuza believe they'll be able to open the vault. That is if they can get to it. Without the guard to help us, that may prove difficult. Jade Joe suggests climbing.' Kenji put the car in gear. 'I'll drive by the British Embassy and take a look at the building.'

'Are the drawings that important?' Raiko asked.

'All artists, architects and engineers steal ideas from each other. That's how improvements are made. It's called progress. There've been rumours of British innovations that solve wing vibrations at high speed. If so, then my Zerosen fighter may become a reality.'

'Why do you call it Zerosen?' Raiko asked.

'We're up to model T-97 in experimental fighters,' Kenji

said. 'I've dreamed of building the perfect fighter plane. And even if it comes out as T-98 or 99, I would still call it double zero. T-100 doesn't sound right to me.'

They turned a corner and Raiko motioned to the British Embassy. 'There's a long line of people waiting at the gate.'

'For visas and passports. Half of Peking has moved south to the new Nationalist capital of Nanking. The other half are either too poor or too wealthy to leave. They're expecting our Kwangtung army to invade.'

'Not for a year at least,' Raiko said. 'That's the Emperor's order.'

'Tojo will be unhappy to hear that,' Kenji said, and pointed. 'The corner of that stone building on the third floor, second window from the right, is where the drawings are. We have no time to waste. Jade Joe's contact says they'll be moved tomorrow. The British fear that if our army invades, Tojo won't honour their embassy's neutrality. They've begun moving all top-secret documents to Singapore.'

Kenji stopped the car and got out. He lifted the engine cowling. Raiko saw him pull the coil wire from the distributor cap and feign fixing the engine, all the while examining the building, the embassy grounds and the guards.

He re-entered the car and Raiko said, 'It seems impossible to break in without being caught.'

'Climbing is the only way.'

'But those building blocks are so tightly fitted there's nothing to grip.'

'Yes, there is. On the corners every other row of stone has a protruding block. I can go up that way.'

'The Yakuza are supposed to break in, not the owner of the Ishikawa zaibatsu.'

'Those old boys can't make that climb without help.'

'Neither can you,' Raiko said. 'If you use the blocks on

147

both sides of the building's corner, the guards at the main gate will see you.'

'I'll only use the blocks on the far side.'

Raiko looked at the building and shook her head. 'That's physically impossible. You would have to pull yourself straight up three floors. I judge there's only about an inch or two grip on those blocks.'

'I've gone up the face of cliffs with smaller hand-holds.' Kenji did not mention that he would be carrying heavy rope to help the Yakuza up, or that the protruding ledges on each floor had been extended to obstruct climbers.

'Won't there be guards inside the building?' Raiko asked.

'They remain outside the offices,' Kenji said, looking directly at her. 'You know, you're very bright. You caught Whittefield lying at the airport, and here your comments are right to the point.' He leaned towards her and she seemed to sway towards him, but he pulled back. 'Climbing is the only way,' he said. 'Tonight, after our dinner date with John.'

'I'm coming with you.'

'Not up that wall you aren't,' Kenji said.

'I'm afraid of heights, but I can drive the getaway car.'

Kenji laughed. 'You've seen too many American gangster movies.' He started the engine and drove on. 'I'll call Jade Joe's and tell the Yakuza to get ready.'

'I'm coming with you,' Raiko repeated.

'There are certain things that women are not meant to do. Espionage is one.'

'Your Aunt Noriko spied in Manchuria with your Uncle Hiroki. You need a lookout.'

Kenji laughed again. 'If those guards catch me hanging on the side of that building, I'll either need a good doctor, a lawyer or an undertaker.'

18

Upon his return to the embassy, John Whittefield was given a message. He telephoned Jade Joe.

'My car will come by in ten minutes,' the curio merchant said.

'I have an important dinner engagement this evening,' John said.

'You'll return in time to meet Captain Ishikawa and Miss Minobe. Bring $5,000 American.'

John made no comment to his having been spied upon. 'I've never paid that much before,' he said, knowing the Chinese merchant was dealing from a position of strength.

The phone went dead and John shrugged. He went to the security chief and signed requisition slips for the money and a snub-nosed .32 revolver. He slipped the weapon under his elastic stocking brace. He pulled the .45 automatic from his shoulder holster, snapped a round into the chamber, reholstered it and left the embassy.

A chauffeured limousine with shades drawn waited in front of the embassy. The rear door swung open as John approached and Jade Joe motioned to the seat opposite him. John sat with his back to the driver and the bodyguard.

Jade Joe wore the traditional long black silk gown of a merchant with a pearl-grey, wide-brimmed fedora, and held a thin, black cheroot underhand with a pair of golden tweezers. 'Slide the window closed behind you,' he said. 'Our business is private.' He stomped his foot and the car started up. 'Do you have the money?'

'Information first,' John said. 'For $5,000 I could buy Peking.'

'With the Japanese prepared to invade, you would be overpaying. But $5,000 is not much to pay for the plans of the Spitfire fighter plane.' The smile on the cherubic Chinese face exuded confidence.

John had tried, without success, to convince Ambassador Grew in Tokyo and naval intelligence in Hawaii that it was worth the risk to steal the British plans. Now here was his chance to buy them. His excitement was difficult to contain. 'Have you found a way to get the plans?'

'Not me. Your dinner guests have. They brought two Yakuza safecrackers with them.'

'If they steal the plans there'll be hell to pay,' John said. 'The British and Chinese secret services will stop at nothing to prevent them from leaving Peking. The plans must be photographed as we arranged. Is my equipment still in place?'

Jade Joe puffed his cigar, and spoke through a cloud of smoke. 'The camera, lights and window shades are in a crate next to the vault the plans are in.'

'How and when are the Japanese going to try to get at that vault?'

Jade Joe pursed his lips and blew smoke into John's face. He rubbed his thumb and forefingers together. 'Money talks and bullshit walks.'

'How did you come by this information?'

'The Cherry Blossom Society requested me to set up the theft just after you cancelled your plan.'

'How much are they paying you?'

'More than you.'

'You sold my idea to them,' John growled. 'People have died for less.' His hand moved to the automatic in his shoulder holster.

The merchant's placid face showed no emotion. 'The

150

Japs knew the Spitfire plans would be here for a week. They called me.'

An arm wrapped around John's throat and a knuckle was driven into his spine, stiffening his body. Jade Joe reached over and gingerly plucked the .45 from the shoulder holster, dropping it on the seat.

'Asking my guest to close the window behind him gives him a sense of protection from my bodyguard and driver,' the Chinese merchant said. 'They slipped the window out as soon as you turned around.' He waved his cigar and John was released.

The American dropped forward with his head between his legs, gasping. He palmed the snub-nosed .32 from his sock, caught his breath and sat up. 'How could the Japanese know about the Spitfire plans without you telling them?'

Jade Joe shrugged his round shoulders. He caressed the brim of his fedora. 'The Japs knew. I didn't tell them, or anyone else.'

'Why should Kenji Ishikawa reveal so much?' John demanded.

'Because I told him our man who was to let them into the British Embassy was fired. Ishikawa and his Yakuza had to come to me for an alternative plan.'

'What is your scheme?'

'To go up the wall. Ishikawa says he can climb three storeys, drop a rope and help the Yakuza up, all without being seen.'

'Climb,' John mumbled, remembering Kenji's escapades in Tokyo. 'When?'

'The money first,' Jade Joe said.

John began to withdraw a wad of $50 bills from his jacket pocket. He heard the guard move behind him, and froze.

'Just pass me the cash and all will be fine,' the merchant said.

John leaned forward and handed over the money. He fell back in his seat and, in the same motion, lashed around with his elbow, catching the bodyguard across the nose. The crack of bone was audible inside the car. Jade Joe reached for the automatic on the seat but John pushed out his right hand and pressed the snub-nosed .32 against the merchant's temple. He slipped over next to the fat man, holstered the automatic and pocketed the $5,000. Putting the muzzle of the pistol in Jade Joe's ear, he repeated, 'When?'

The merchant's eyes swivelled left to stare into the ice-blue orbs of the American agent.

'If you don't tell me and I don't kill you, my career is ruined,' John said. He pushed the gun harder. 'When?'

'No need to get angry,' Jade Joe said. 'It's tonight, after your dinner date. I told them the plans will be moved tomorrow morning.'

'That's not true,' John said.

'I lied. It often pays well.'

'It will again if I get those plans for my country. There's an extra $1,000 payable for success. Tell your driver to let me off at the US Embassy! Take your bodyguard to a doctor. His nose is all over his face. Don't forget, $6,000 for you to make certain everything goes smoothly tonight!'

John led Raiko and Kenji into the Quan Ju-de restaurant in the centre of Peking. 'Our embassy recommends this as the best place for Peking duck.'

'You order for us,' Kenji said.

'I enjoyed Chinese cuisine in New York,' Raiko said.

'You'll find northern Chinese food different from Cantonese cooking,' John said. 'In the north they use more wheat than rice, and spices rather than sauces. Peking duck is coated with honey and smoked over the wood of date trees in those open ovens.'

'I hope we won't have long to wait,' Kenji said. 'I'm hungry and Raiko and I have an early-morning appointment.'

'I ordered ahead,' John said. He pointed to the chef at the largest oven with several ducks hanging over it. 'He tests to see if the birds are done by weighing them in his hand. When they've lost one-third of their original weight, they're ready.'

'What are you doing in Peking, Mr Whittefield?' Raiko asked.

'Please call me John. I came to prevent, or delay, the Japanese invasion of China.'

Raiko saw a wary look cloud Kenji's eyes. He leaned forward and asked, 'How do you intend to accomplish that?'

'By sending messages through friends like you to inform Tojo that if his troops cross the Marco Polo bridge, they may be facing American soldiers.'

'The general could take that as a threat,' Kenji said.

'He should,' John replied. 'A serious threat. My mission in Peking is to defuse a potentially explosive situation.'

'Our meeting at the airport wasn't by chance,' Raiko said.

John laughed. 'I expected to see fat old Wantabe, and Mr X turned out to be the beautiful Miss Raiko Minobe.'

Kenji signalled Raiko to remain silent with a slight nod of his head. They watched the chef approach carrying two golden roasted ducks. He skilfully peeled the crispy skin on to one plate, the succulent meat on to another. The waiter brought platters of Lotus-leaf pancakes, Hoi-sin sauce, shredded onions and cucumbers.

John picked up his chopsticks. 'The correct way to eat Peking duck is quickly, while the meat is steaming hot.' He demonstrated as he spoke. 'Spread the sauce on a pancake, add some duck, a little onion and cucumber, then fold the pancake closed, and enjoy.' He stuffed the filled pancake into his mouth, chewing and smiling at his Japanese guests. They watched him in silence. 'Please eat,' John said. 'We'll talk about Wantabe, the Cherry Blossom Society and Mr X later.'

The chief of US intelligence has revealed himself for a specific purpose, Kenji thought. He nodded to Raiko. They both prepared pancakes and began to eat.

'I'm looking forward to an interesting conversation,' Kenji said. 'Meanwhile this duck is delicious.'

When John left the table to settle the bill, Kenji leaned towards Raiko. 'We'll let him speak first.'

'Americans often give the impression of being open and naïve,' Raiko said. 'Whittefield is quite clever.'

'He's also in a great hurry. Otherwise his approach would be more subtle. He expects our army to invade and is trying to bluff us out of it.'

'He doesn't have to. I told you the Emperor ordered the invasion delayed for a year.'

'Tojo may not obey that order,' Kenji said. 'General Hashimoto is in command of our troops at the border. He's a wild-eyed nationalist who thinks like a kill-crazy samurai.'

'Would Hashimoto or Tojo defy an imperial decree?'

'They'd stage an incident that could not be ignored in Tokyo.'

John returned to the table and led the couple to his car. He drove in silence until, several miles outside of Peking, he parked the car off the road. He led Kenji and Raiko to a grassy knoll overlooking a river. Moonlight reflected in the slow-moving water.

John pointed up-river where the bright moon outlined the graceful arches of a bridge. 'Seven hundred years ago, Marco Polo crossed that same bridge and became a favourite of the great Kublai Khan here in Peking. The Venetian merchant brought with him knowledge of the West. He returned to Venice with insight into Far Eastern culture. Kenji, your great-grandfather did much the same when he returned from my grandfather's home in Massachusetts to Tokyo. John Mung helped bring Japan out of 250 years of isolation.'

'And now Mung's adopted country may soon be at war with the country of his birth,' Kenji said.

'Not if the Kwangtung army remains where it is, on the other side of that bridge.'

'Japan is being strangled by Roosevelt's policy of Ring Fence. We have a right to colonies as well as you and the Europeans.'

'America is not a colonial power,' John said.

'Puerto Rico, Cuba, Hawaii, Samoa and Panama are all under United States control,' Kenji said. 'How much land did you steal from Mexico? The American Fruit Company runs most of South America with the help of US marines.'

'You have Formosa, Korea and Manchuria,' John said. 'Your engineers suck the natural resources out of the earth and send them to factories in Japan.'

'Where we make products that are barred from the American market by Roosevelt,' Kenji replied.

Raiko watched the two men – both patriots with a love for the other's country. Both angered and frustrated by the actions of their leaders and the economic situation which brought them into conflict.

'One-third of the American workforce is unemployed,' John said. 'Our gross national product has been halved and our people are starving.'

'So are my people,' Kenji said.

'War won't solve either country's problems,' Raiko said.

'Tojo recently quoted Hitler that war creates employment,' John said. 'The Germans either farm to feed their army, work in factories to supply their army, or they're in the army.'

155

'That is the fascist response to an economic problem,' Kenji said. 'A confrontation between Japan and the US over China serves no-one's interest. Chiang Kai-shek has abandoned the northern provinces and Mao Tse-tung is too weak to control them. The Kwangtung army can bring order and prosperity to that region.'

'Keep Tojo out of China!' John said, flexing his hands.

'Open the American markets to Japanese goods,' Kenji declared, the muscles in his neck twitching.

The Oriental and the Occidental faced each other within sight of the Marco Polo bridge, their eyes locked. Raiko sensed fearful historical significance. 'Why did you reveal your knowledge of Wantabe, Mr X and the Cherry Blossom Society?' she asked John.

He tore his eyes away from Kenji's and said, 'To impress upon you my knowledge of your plan to break into the British Embassy tonight!'

Raiko sighed. Wind whistled through Kenji's teeth. He set his feet, balled his fists and moved his body into the karate attack position.

John's hand moved towards his .45 automatic as he said, 'I proposed stealing the Spitfire plans, but my superiors decided against it.'

'You and the British are allies,' Raiko said. 'Why would America have to steal from them?'

'There is still a great deal of anti-British feeling in the United States. Tens of thousands of our men died to save Europe in the Great War. Americans don't want to be drawn into another European conflict. Six of our midwestern states are actively pro-German. There's a delegation of American farmers in Tokyo right now trying to convince your government to join Mussolini and Hitler in the Axis Alliance. German-Americans have a powerful pro-Nazi lobby in Washington. The British fear that if the Spitfire plans were given to the United States, there's a possibility the Germans would soon have them. The

156

British would rather sell us the plane, than have us produce it. England would benefit with income, jobs and the military advantage in Europe.'

'Is the plane that good?' Kenji asked.

'Our agents clocked it at 341 miles an hour over a ten-mile flat course.'

'Japan must have those drawings,' Kenji cried.

'America too. I suggest we co-operate.'

'What do you have to contribute?' Kenji asked.

'Can you really climb that building and get the safe-crackers inside?'

'Yes. I'll lower a rope for them.'

'Lower it for me too,' John said. 'Those drawings are too many and too large for you to sneak out of that building.'

'I'm an aeronautical engineer,' Kenji said. 'I'll know what to take.'

'And if they're found missing in the morning, the British and Chinese secret services will be all over Peking. It could take months to get them out.'

'Not if our army invades,' Kenji said.

'I have photographic equipment inside the building, and I know how to use it. You select the plans, I take the pictures and the British will never know.'

'Everyone seems to know,' Kenji said. 'Jade Joe must be working for you.'

'He works for money.' John held out his hand. 'Can we do this together?'

Raiko sighed in relief as Kenji and John shook hands.

'We'll make the break-in after midnight,' Kenji said.

19

Kenji followed Raiko up two flights of steps in the Japanese Embassy. He watched the play of light on her jet-black hair, the swing and sway of her hips under the silk dress, the soft play of muscles in the calves of her shapely legs. He wanted to run the palms of his hands around her hips and belly, to put his mouth on hers. He was breathless when they reached the second floor.

'Your face is flushed,' Raiko said. 'Are you rested enough to climb that wall?'

Kenji's heart pounded. 'Here's our room . . . I mean your room. I thought to share it with Wantabe. I'll take my things and find another place.'

'Leave them for now,' Raiko said. 'There isn't much time and I'm going with you.'

'My uncle, your father and the Cherry Blossom Society would hang me if you were caught.'

'The British will do the hanging if you're caught. But they won't bother me. I'll be outside in the car. And I have a diplomatic passport.' Raiko ran her fingers over the wood-panelled door. 'I'll be ready in fifteen minutes. Then you can shower and dress.'

'See you in quarter of an hour.' Kenji went down the stairs, resolved not to take her on the mission.

'I need a man who can drive,' Kenji said to the embassy security chief.

'I need 100 who can walk,' the chief snapped.

'What did you say?' Kenji growled.

The security chief looked up into the scowling face of the young captain. He shook his head and sighed. 'Excuse me, Captain. I'm acting telephone operator and embassy

158

information clerk in addition to my own job. If they put a broom up my arse, I'd be able to clean the floors too. Everybody is out in the field. We're expecting the Chinese to attack our Kwangtung army. There's no-one to spare. I'm sorry.'

Kenji grunted. You've been misled, my friend, he thought. The attack will be made by our Kwangtung army on the Chinese. Kenji shrugged, accepting that Raiko would have to drive, and feeling pleased. He wanted her to see him climb that building.

'Have three pairs of tennis shoes, a screwdriver, a bottle of whisky and fifty feet of rope sent to my room in a duffel-bag,' Kenji ordered the security chief.

Raiko sat on the double bed and watched the closed door of the shower-room. She listened to the change of sounds of the water as Kenji showered, and pictured his wet and glistening body, the large veins in his muscular arms. The shower stopped and she envisioned Kenji towelling himself. She felt warm all over.

Raiko answered a knock at the door and the security chief handed her a duffel-bag. 'These are the things Captain Ishikawa ordered. And here's a message for him.'

Kenji emerged from the shower-room, face glowing, hair perfectly parted. He wore evening clothes with a starched white shirt and black bow tie – the handsomest man Raiko had ever seen. She pointed to his feet. 'Barefoot?'

'No socks.' Kenji emptied the duffel-bag on the bed.

'Why do you need three pairs of tennis shoes?'

'To find the smallest size I can wear. I have to feel the wall with my toes. That's why no socks.'

'What is the whisky for?'

Kenji winked, and began trying on the shoes. He put the best pair back into the bag, then slipped his patent-leather shoes on his feet. He read the message and looked up at

Raiko. 'Jade Joe wants us to wait until 1 a.m., when the British Embassy will stop receiving people for passports. That should cause enough of a commotion at the main gate to divert the guards' attention. We'll meet John at the curio shop. He's briefing the Yakuza.' Kenji stepped closer and looked down at Raiko. 'I want you to promise me that if there's any trouble, you'll drive away.' He studied her face and became lost in her beautiful eyes. 'Promise!'

'You're frowning,' Raiko said.

'This is not just spying you're involved in. Active espionage is punishable by death.'

'I promise,' Raiko said. 'Let's forget about espionage while we wait. Tell me about your crash-landing in the snow. I went to inform your aunt and uncle that you and your cousins were dead.'

'We missed our rendezvous with the second aircraft carrier due to a snowstorm, and our fuel ran out. Hino led us to a safe landing on a frozen lake. We burned our planes to keep warm while we searched for a road. That road led to a group of farmhouses. By the time we reached there we were stiff as zombies with toes and fingers frozen. We were wearing our flying suits and goggles, with scarfs wrapped around our faces because of the severe cold.' Kenji laughed out loud. 'Those farmers had never seen an automobile, much less a pilot. They took one look at us and fled. We followed them from house to house, until finally the children approached and recognized us as humans. We were taken by cart to the nearest town.'

'It's a miracle the three of you survived the landing and the severe cold. Where are your cousins now?'

'At the Seven Sisters.'

Raiko bounced off the edge of the bed. Her large eyes narrowed and her nose scrunched up. 'I forgot you bought a brothel!'

Kenji cursed himself for mentioning the Seven Sisters. 'It's just an inn on the road to Peking.'

160

'I'm certain the seven sisters know how to accommodate their guests.' Raiko pouted.

'They're old women,' Kenji lied. 'People go there to eat, not for sexual pleasures.'

'I saw your cousins panting after Ruth Kuhn. The seven sisters must provide quite a menu for them. Did you dine at their table?'

Kenji leapt to answer the knock on the door.

'Captain, I have someone to drive for you tonight,' the security chief said. 'The perfect man has just arrived. Major Ando is military intelligence.'

'So you lied again,' Raiko fumed at Kenji. 'You were planning not to take me!' She threw on her coat, flounced past Kenji and snapped the car keys from the security chief's hand. 'I'm going, Major Ando or not!'

Kenji followed Raiko down the stairs to the lobby, where she approached the man waiting there. 'Major Ando?'

Shira Ando smiled at the beautiful woman. 'Yes?'

'I am the personal representative of Lord Keeper of the Privy Seal Hiroki Koin,' Raiko said. 'My credentials are upstairs. Will it be necessary to show them to you?'

Shira Ando looked at Kenji, who shrugged. Ando bowed. 'I recognize you, Miss Minobe. Part of your mission was to inform General Tojo that the invasion of China must wait a year longer. The second messenger arrived earlier at the Fifth Moon Inn. He flew there by fighter plane. I'm sure you are aware that at least two couriers are always sent with important messages. Since the message aborted my mission, I am at your service.'

'Very well,' Raiko said. 'We're going to break into the British Embassy to steal their Spitfire plans. If you'd like to join us, you may.' She walked out the front door, watched by the three men with open mouths.

161

'Are you going right now?' Ando asked Kenji. 'Neither you nor the lady seem dressed for such a mission.'

'She is driving. As for me, a tuxedo is what I always wear when climbing a wall.'

'I've been curious to see the inside of the British Embassy,' Ando said. 'By the way, what is a Spitfire?'

'I'll tell you on the way,' Kenji said. They hurried out to the car.

Raiko motioned Ando to sit in the front seat next to her, and Kenji in the rear. It pleased her to see Kenji's annoyance. I'll show him, she thought.

At Jade Joe's, Kenji got into the front seat, which pushed Ando closer to Raiko. The two Yakuza sat in the back with John. Kenji was becoming jealous of the handsome major.

They neared the British Embassy. 'Do you need two men to open that safe?' Ando asked.

'One,' the chief safecracker answered. 'My name is Issei.'

'And me to photograph,' John said.

'Good,' Ando said. 'Issei goes up the wall after Kenji. His assistant comes with me. The diversions at the main gate will be serious enough to allow three men enough time to go up the wall without being seen. The diversion for coming down will be our job. Miss Minobe, you'll signal me when the mission is complete. Stop the car!'

Raiko pulled to the side of the road to let Ando and the Yakuza out. She drove around the block to approach the embassy grounds from the opposite direction, and parked the car behind others along the road. John, Issei and Kenji crouched on the floor.

'What do you see?' Kenji whispered.

'The royal marine guards are trying to keep the crowd of people in order at the main gate. Ando's being pushed away. There, he's seen us.'

'It's two minutes after one,' John said.

'They're closing the gate,' Raiko said. 'Oh my! People are starting to throw things at the guards!'

'Don't get excited,' Kenji warned.

Raiko turned and saw Kenji open the bottle of whisky. Before she could reprimand him, he swished some in his mouth and spat it on his sleeve. He loosened his bow tie, poured a little whisky over his shirt and tuxedo jacket, then smiled up at her from his position on the car floor. 'If they catch me, let's hope they'll think I'm still the crazy playboy.'

Raiko looked out of the window again. 'Get ready. People are climbing the gate. More guards are rushing from the consulate.'

'Time to go,' John said, and opened the door.

'Remember your promise,' Kenji whispered as he slipped out the door. 'If there's trouble, get away fast!'

'Please be careful,' Raiko said.

But Kenji did not hear her warning. He was away and running across the lawn. Raiko saw him vault a hedge. The three men scaled a six-foot picket fence. She lost sight of them until they appeared at the corner of the building. Kenji slung the rope over his head and shoulder and put the screwdriver in his lapel. He tightened the laces of his tennis shoes and peeked around the corner of the building.

'There's a full-blown riot at the main gate,' Kenji whispered to John. 'The guards are trying to drive the crowd back with fixed bayonets. I'm going up this first floor using both sides. Nobody will notice me. They're too busy.' Gripping the protruding stones with fingers and toes, Kenji scrambled up the wall like a spider.

Raiko saw him stop at the first-floor ledge that stuck out three feet from the wall. She gasped when he reached up with his right hand, crossed his left, gripped the ledge and swung out. He gripped the ledge with his left hand and swung with his back to the wall, holding on with two hands.

He swung back and forth, then jack-knifed his body up and on to the ledge.

'Oh gods, protect him,' Raiko prayed. She saw him rise, turn and peek around the corner of the building.

The sound of gunshots came from the main gate. The British guards were chasing rioters. Kenji went up both sides of the wall to the second ledge. He performed his acrobatic feat again, but this time took a longer rest on the ledge before he peeked around the corner of the building. The crowd had dispersed. Stretcher bearers were helping wounded and carrying off dead bodies. The guards were back at their posts, on alert.

Raiko saw Kenji take the screwdriver from his lapel. He chipped hand-and foot-holds on the next protruding stone of one side of the building. Digging his fingertips in, he pulled himself up one block. Holding on with one hand, he chipped with the other, then pulled himself up another block. It took fifteen minutes of muscle-straining work to reach the third ledge.

Raiko watched Kenji cross hands, grip the ledge and swing out with his back to the wall. He swung back and forth, then jack-knifed up, and his legs slipped off, leaving him dangling by his fingertips in mid-air.

'Do it, do it,' Raiko cried. 'You're losing strength!'

With his back to the wall, Kenji knew there was no way he could turn and grasp it. He had to make the ledge, or fall forty feet.

Raiko watched him swing back and forth, then jack-knife up again. One leg slipped off, the other held. She saw him wriggling upside-down, forty feet in the air. He won't have enough strength for another try, she thought. His second foot caught hold and he pulled himself up on to the ledge, face-down. He lay there, not moving.

Raiko gripped the steering wheel. Her body trembled. Sweat and tears poured down her face. It was another ten minutes before she saw Kenji stand up and jimmy the

164

window open with the screwdriver. She held her breath until he poked his head out of the window and dropped the rope down.

John and Issei climbed up the rope and through the window.

'Kenji, that was a magnificent climb,' John said. He closed the window and coiled the rope on the floor.

'Where's the photographic equipment?' Kenji demanded.

John switched on his flashlight. 'Look for a wooden crate labelled PLATTE BROTHERS GEOLOGICAL SURVEY EQUIPMENT.'

'This room is filled with boxes!' Kenji said.

'It should be to the right of the vault as you look at it. This is a storage room for large, expensive items. Here it is. PLATTE BROTHERS. Help me pry the lid off.'

The three men worked swiftly. They pulled out long pieces of black cloth and fixed them over the windows. John rolled up his jacket and placed it to block the space under the door. Then he switched on the lights. 'My God, Kenji, what happened? You're full of blood!'

'There was broken glass embedded in the ledges.' Kenji turned to Issei. 'Open that safe!'

The Yakuza bowed to Kenji. He pointed to the big iron door with the golden letters, MORLEY VAULT AND CASH BOX LIMITED. 'To open this is not a problem. To stop the bleeding of your body is. You are a brave man, but even those with courage need blood to live.'

'I'll bind the cuts on my legs,' Kenji said. 'My shirt will keep the others from bleeding. Get to work!'

Issei pointed to the floor. 'If you do not wish people to know we were here, you should wipe up the blood.' He took a stethoscope, pad and pencil from his pocket and spun the dial on the safe door. He listened to the tumblers fall and listed numbers.

Kenji tore the sleeves off his jacket. He ripped them into strips and tied them around his bloody legs.

165

John set up the Leica camera, the lights and screen. 'Why is it taking so long to open that safe?' he asked.

'You've seen too many movies,' Issei said.

Kenji laughed. 'That's what I told Raiko when she demanded to drive the getaway car.'

'Got it,' the Yakuza said, and pulled open the vault door.

'There must be 100 three-foot drawings in there,' John said.

Kenji reached for one of the large scrolls and John pulled him back. 'Clean your hands. We don't want any blood on the plans.'

Kenji spat into his palms. 'Wipe them on my trousers,' John said.

Kenji rubbed his hands on John. He held his palms out and the other two spat into them – wiping, spitting, until his hands were clean.

'I'll do the selection!' Kenji said. 'You two unroll and photograph! Keep them in order!'

Down in the car Raiko tried not to doze, and was angry with herself each time she awoke. The street was quiet. Only four British guards stood at the embassy gate.

At a quarter to five Raiko saw a light in the third-floor window. She opened and closed the car door just a crack to flash the interior lamp. The light in the window went out and Kenji climbed on to the ledge. Raiko saw white sleeves on his jacket, and wondered why. He dropped the rope down the side of the building and the three men descended.

Raiko opened the car door twice, signalling Ando with the interior light. He and the second Yakuza ran up the street with loud shouts at the British guards. They each fired two shots. The guards unslung their rifles and ran out to shoot back. Both men ducked behind parked cars, shouting obscenities as they fled.

Raiko held her car's back door open. John, Kenji

166

and Issei piled into the back seat. 'Did you do it?' she asked.

'We've got the film,' John said.

'Where's Ando?' Kenji asked.

'The guards chased him and the Yakuza.'

'Find Ando,' Kenji ordered. 'I can't go with John to develop the film. Ando must be there to get our copy.'

'Kenji needs a doctor,' John said.

Raiko roared away from the curb, making a U-turn on two wheels. She screeched the tyres around the next corner. 'Why does Kenji need a doctor?' she demanded.

'If I survive this ride, I'll be fine,' Kenji said.

'There's Ando,' John said, pointing. 'Pick him up and drive us to the American Embassy. We'll take a car from there.'

Raiko screeched the car to a halt and Ando jumped into the front seat. She sped to the US Embassy, dropped John and Ando off, then raced to the Japanese Embassy. She and Issei helped Kenji out of the car. Raiko blanched at sight of his bloody clothes.

'Send the embassy doctor to Captain Ishikawa's room immediately,' she ordered the guard at the entrance.

In Kenji's room, Raiko helped the doctor strip off the bloody clothes. Kenji's body was covered with cuts and scrapes.

'What happened?' Raiko asked.

Through half-closed eyes, Kenji looked up at her and smiled. 'Glass. Broken glass embedded in the cement on the ledges. The British aren't so dumb.'

Raiko recalled seeing Kenji rest for ten minutes on the last ledge. He had been lying on the jagged points of broken glass.

'He doesn't seem to have lost enough blood to make him pass out,' the doctor said. 'Most of the cuts on his body are superficial.'

'How much more blood can he have left? His clothes are soaked!'

The doctor frowned. 'He's young and strong. He shouldn't be unconscious.'

Kenji snored and Raiko began laughing and crying at the same time. 'He's sleeping. He hasn't slept for two nights.'

The doctor smiled. 'With a few stitches in his legs and iodine on the rest of his wounds, he'll be fine.'

Raiko looked down at Kenji's battered body. 'I'll remain here with him.'

She awoke in an armchair next to the bed. The wall clock showed 9 p.m. She had slept for sixteen hours. Kenji was sleeping peacefully. She knelt on the edge of his bed and watched his diaphragm rise and fall, rise and fall. Her body filled with desire and she lay down next to him, feeling his warmth. She put her arm around him and Kenji snuggled closer. She pressed against him and heard his breathing change to quick shallow gasps. She felt him grow hard and large, pressing into her. He caressed her buttocks. She stared into his face but he was still asleep. She grew frightened of the hardness pressing at her, and excited with the thought of having it enter her body. She looked down and gasped. His penis was swollen; large and angry. Veins stood out along its length, pulsating as if with a life of its own. It looked too large to enter her small body, yet she desired to press herself forward. Then Kenji rolled closer to her. He cried out and grasped his injured knee. Raiko jumped from the bed, trembling with fright and desire. Kenji turned and tossed, and fell back to sleep.

20

'I'm ordered to accompany you and Raiko to Kwangtung army headquarters in Mukden,' Ando said.

Kenji concealed his disappointment. For the past week of his recuperation he had been sleeping late, walking and talking with Raiko and enjoying her company. She made certain he ate well and took afternoon naps. Each evening she read aloud to him. With the return of his strength, his feelings for her grew stronger. He dreamed every night that she lay with him in his bed. But they were never alone. All personnel on the embassy grounds were restricted because anti-Japanese feelings ran high in the streets of Peking. Angry Chinese crowds often fought with police at the embassy gates. They attacked Japanese soldiers on leave in the city.

'The ambassador has offered his personal limousine for the drive to the Fifth Moon Inn,' Ando said.

'Thank the ambassador,' Kenji said. 'But my purchasing agents located a 1935 Dusenberg in excellent condition. I prefer my own car.'

'It's a ten-hour trip,' Ando said. 'Driving could disturb the wounds on your legs. I'll be glad to chauffeur you. We can leave as soon as you're ready.'

From the crossing point at the Marco Polo bridge to the outskirts of Mukden, they drove past endless lines of Japanese troops, artillery and supply convoys.

'Two years ago it would have taken sixteen hours to reach Mukden,' Ando said. 'Our army laid this road especially for the invasion. We have agents inside China who have restored bridges and repaired roads in order that our trucks, tanks and artillery can move faster once they cross the border.'

'Isn't the Chinese government aware of all this activity?' Raiko asked.

'I'm certain their spies report our work to Nanking,' Ando said. 'But there is no Chinese government in the northern provinces. Generalissimo Chiang abandoned the area. The villagers benefit from our road-building and bridge-mending, so they help us. Only in the cities do the Chinese sabotage our efforts. Nationalism is strong there.'

It was evening when Ando wheeled the big Dusenberg into the driveway of the Fifth Moon Inn.

Raiko was puzzled by the long, red-brick two-storey building with yellow tiled roof. 'This doesn't look like headquarters of the Kwangtung army.'

'It was bought by army intelligence prior to the Russo–Japanese war,' Ando explained. 'The bottom floor was a restaurant, bar and gambling house, the top floor a brothel. The girls were trained in the art of lovemaking and extracting information from their Chinese and Russian clients.'

'Kenji recently purchased a place like that called the Seven Sisters,' Raiko said. 'Have you heard of it?'

'No, and I'm unlikely to for some time. General Tojo has restricted me to eating and drinking only between sunset and sunrise. I'm forbidden sex or entertainment until my mission is completed.'

'What is your mission?' Raiko asked.

Ando leaned closer to her and whispered, 'Are you good at keeping secrets?' Raiko nodded, and he said, 'So am I.'

She laughed. 'Can you tell us why you've been punished?'

'I killed the wrong man,' Ando said as he stepped from the car. He was saluted by an orderly.

'Major, you are to come with me,' the orderly said. 'The captain and lady will please wait.'

170

Ando entered Tojo's office. He quickstepped to the front of the desk and saluted. A general stood to Tojo's right. The man's powerful shoulders and bull-neck appeared about to burst the seams of his uniform jacket. His large round skull was shaven clean.

'General Kingoro Hashimoto meet Major Shira Ando,' Tojo said. 'This young man is in charge of our espionage and sabotage units in northern China. He will create the incident you need to begin the invasion.'

'In August,' Hashimoto grunted. 'The ground will be dry and reinforcements integrated into the line companies by then.'

'I thought the Emperor ordered the invasion postponed for a year,' Ando said.

'The reason for the delay is not because of the Emperor,' Tojo said. 'Our prime minister and the Koda-ha faction in the Diet struck a bargain with Hiroki Koin and his liberals to pass a national military conscription bill. The army will treble in size within three months.'

'Another three months to integrate the new recruits and then we'll kick Chinese arses to Nanking and beyond,' Hashimoto rumbled.

Ando stiffened at attention. 'Sir, I respectfully remind General Hashimoto that whoever rules the five northern provinces of China, effectively controls the rest of the country. Our strategists never envisioned occupation of central or southern China.'

'They have poor eyesight,' Hashimoto said.

'Sir, we could be swallowed by the vastness of the country and multitude of its people.'

Hashimoto's shoulders hunched, his eyebrows lowered. 'You, Major, will help me reduce that multitude and fertilize the vastness of Asia with dead Chinese.'

'Yes, sir,' Ando said, remembering Tsubota's analogy of advice to a senior officer and a bull without balls. In fifteen years of army duty he had learned when to remain silent.

171

'Are Captain Ishikawa and Miss Minobe with you?' Tojo asked.

'Yes, sir. The captain succeeded in stealing plans of a fighter plane from the British. He claims the information may give Japan air superiority for several years. Miss Minobe carries a special message from the lord keeper of the privy seal to General Tojo. It has been a long drive from Peking, but the lady insists on seeing you as soon as possible.'

'Is this Professor Minobe's daughter?' Hashimoto asked.

'Yes, sir.'

'Perhaps we could get back at that intellectual pacifist bastard through her.'

Tojo looked at Hashimoto. 'What are you suggesting?'

'Addict her to drugs, compromise her sexually and control her through shame. She could be used to influence her father.'

'Kenji Ishikawa has a deep affection for this girl,' Ando said. 'He could be a powerful enemy.'

'They die too,' Hashimoto said.

'I will see both of them now,' Tojo ordered.

Kenji snapped to attention before Ando and the two generals. Raiko folded her hands and bowed. Tojo motioned them both forward with his little finger.

'Captain Ishikawa, I admire success. But in the future, do not place yourself in unnecessary danger! Your value as an aeronautical engineer surpasses your worth as a pilot or a spy.'

'Sir, risks make life worth living,' Kenji said.

'Spoken like a true samurai,' Hashimoto said. 'What have you learned from the British plans?'

'I have not had the opportunity to examine them closely. But two innovations I saw while photographing have already justified the risk. The British use a variable pitch propeller, and folding landing gear. Both will save fuel, reduce vibration and increase airspeed. These changes will

172

enhance our fighter plane's capability, extend its range and reduce maintenance.'

'From what Major Ando has told me, the Americans also have the British plans,' Hashimoto said.

'The mission could not have been accomplished without John Whittefield's help,' Kenji said. 'His photographic equipment was essential. I have only to change the negatives into positives and project them on a screen for thorough examination and evaluation.'

Hashimoto turned to Ando. 'Why haven't you killed Whittefield?'

'There was no opportunity,' Ando said. 'He had a man covering me from the moment we entered the film laboratory. I expected to be killed. After bringing the film to our embassy, I returned to the curio shop with the two Yakuza and finished Jade Joe. I recovered this.' Ando placed two stacks of bills on the desk before Tojo, one in dollars, the other in yen.

'Jade Joe could have been useful to us in the future,' Kenji said.

'Major Ando's judgement was correct,' Tojo said. 'Because of that Chinese merchant, the Americans may have a fighter plane equal to yours when we invade China.'

'If so, they'll not use it to defend the Chinese,' Kenji said. 'John Whittefield made several slips in our conversation which confirm my belief that America is bluffing. He said if we cross the Marco Polo bridge, we *could* be facing US soldiers. Could is a conditional term, not positive affirmation of intended action. Whittefield also used words such as prevent or delay the Kwangtung army from crossing the border. The Cherry Blossom Society believes Roosevelt will maintain his isolationist policy. He won't allow America to become involved militarily. And the killing of a man like John Whittefield could only bring trouble on our heads.'

173

'Doesn't Roosevelt's massive spending for naval armament indicate otherwise?' Ando asked.

'The build-up of the Pacific fleet is more of a defensive measure than offensive,' Kenji said. 'It will be five years before the first new American warship funded by this congressional bill is launched. The fascists of Europe have the American public looking west, not east.'

Tojo turned to Raiko. 'It is a pleasant change to have someone so beautiful in my office. Why were you sent?'

Kenji held his breath. He had warned Raiko that on no account was she to reveal her membership in the Cherry Blossom Society, nor her position as second to Wantabe. She was to pose as a decoder from the Black Chamber acting as a courier.

'Sir, the first part of my mission was to bring word of the Spitfire plans,' Raiko said. 'Second was to convey the message I understand you have already received, the Emperor's order to delay the invasion of northern China. Thirdly, I am to impart the key to the American grey code to your intelligence people. I am to offer my services in sending false information through your Kwangtung army code, which US naval intelligence has deciphered.'

'The Americans have ceased using the grey code since the night you stole the Spitfire plans,' Ando said. 'Whittefield must have guessed it was your deciphering of their code which revealed the plan's existence and whereabouts.'

'Mr Wantabe deciphered the grey code,' Raiko said.

'Your knowledge of the grey code is of no benefit,' Hashimoto said.

'Not exactly,' Raiko answered. 'Mr Wantabe broke your army code because it was based on an outdated cipher he was familiar with. This might be the case with the new American replacement code. Or we could try a technique Mr Wantabe used to break other foreign codes. You send information in the Kwangtung army code. The

Americans pick it up and transmit it in their new code. With knowledge of the message's contents, decoding is simpler.'

Tojo looked to Ando. 'In the absence of Dr Tsubota, you are senior intelligence officer. What is your recommendation?'

'Give Miss Minobe access to our Black Chamber. She'll need the facilities to encode and send ahead the more important information on the Spitfire to Ishikawa industries. She and the captain will work together.'

Tojo gave a non-committal nod. 'Is that all, young lady?'

'I am to tell you there is an information leak in Tokyo. Joseph Stalin's order to free Chiang Kai-shek was relayed to Borodin in China from someone in Tokyo. Borodin was also informed of General Hashimoto's early release from prison, the discontinued resettlement of Japanese farmers in Manchuria, and the information that Japan will soon be guided by a military government under your leadership, General Tojo.'

'Let us hope Borodin is as correct about me as he is about the rest,' Tojo said. 'But who in Japan is important enough to receive direct communications from Joseph Stalin?'

'These Russian messages are so infrequent that although we've broken the code, we've no idea where they are sent from,' Raiko said.

'My company is constructing a modern direction-finding and radio-interception station outside of Tokyo,' Kenji said. 'Although it will be some time before completion. Only then will we be able to trace the locations of the senders.'

'In the meantime the Soviets have an eye on our secrets,' Hashimoto grumbled.

'The Whittefield message indicated Russia's biggest fear is that Japan will join Italy and Germany in the Axis

Alliance,' Raiko said. 'Whittefield confirmed Borodin's claim that Stalin's purge of army officers has flawed the fighting capability of Russian troops on the Mongolian border. To relieve that weakness, Borodin requested that the United States supply weapons to Chiang and Mao so their armies could pose a threat to ours. That would prevent the Kwangtung army from turning on the Russians and sweeping through Mongolia. Whittefield recommended the US State Department's support for Chiang's Nationalists, but not Mao's Communists.'

Tojo leaned back in his seat and steepled his fingers, looking over them at Raiko. 'Anything else?' His eyebrows raised in surprise when she spoke again.

'Yes sir, one last item. The Flying Tigers. They are a group of American mercenary pilots working for Chiang Kai-shek. Retired US General Claire Chenault, an American agent controlled by John Whittefield, leads them. They'll be supplied with the new Spitfire.'

Tojo stood. He was the same height as Raiko. He smiled and bowed to her. 'We little people often are full of surprises. Please wait outside with Captain Ishikawa.'

The door closed behind the couple and Tojo turned to Hashimoto. 'Do not harm either of them! They may be against Koda-ha's concept of a Greater Asia, but both are patriots. The young man is brave, the girl brilliant.'

Hashimoto's brow furrowed and he grunted. 'You are correct. I never thought I could respect a liberal, especially two who work for the Cherry Blossom Society. But they both have earned my approval. That girl may have given us Mongolia. And if Ishikawa can produce that fighter plane, we will rule all Asia. Can you imagine the children those two might breed if they were married?'

'There is a possibility of a connection between them,' Ando said. 'They display a strong affection for each other.'

'I believe in Darwin's theory of natural selection and

176

would like to help it along,' Tojo said. 'Give them adjoining rooms. Hitler's ideas about racial superiority have merit too. That is why Japan will rule Asia, and in time control world commerce.'

Kenji and Raiko looked up expectantly when Ando appeared. 'You'll both be given access to our Black Chamber,' Ando said. 'Kenji, you're to produce the positive slides of the Spitfire, read them and help Raiko encode the most important information needed by your factories in Japan. Raiko, you'll work with our people to break the new American brown code. Now you'll want to see your rooms. They were once part of the most famous bordello in all Asia.'

21

Raiko and Kenji each had tried the door between their rooms and found it unlocked. Both fell asleep wishing they had the courage to open it.

The following morning, Ando led them to a large square building located behind the Fifth Moon Inn. Guards, double-strand concertina barbed wire and land mines protected the building. On each corner of the roof was a concrete machine-gun bunker.

'This is Kwangtung army intelligence headquarters,' Ando said.

'Where are the aerials and antennae?' Raiko asked.

'In the roof and chimneys of the inn. Underground cables lead from there to here. Actually, more mail sorting and processing of field agents' reports than radio-communication interception is done here.' Ando led them past the guards and through a double-door security entrance.

Raiko and Kenji looked around the large, well-lit room. A hundred or more people were working – sorting envelopes from mail bags, translating and transcribing letters.

'This intelligence unit was founded by Colonel Honjo in 1900,' Ando said. 'It first saw service during the Russo–Japanese war. They hadn't one-quarter of the mail traffic you see now. In the thirty years of Japanese occupation of Manchuko, the literacy level of the native population has quadrupled. Accordingly, we expanded the size of the building to censor the additional mail.'

'You open people's letters without their consent or knowledge?' Raiko said.

'And the mail delivery is never late,' Ando said. 'The letter sacks arrive here every morning from the Mukden Central Post Office. The mail is sorted, opened at these steaming tables, then passed to translators and evaluated. We have scribes who record pertinent information. Forgers readdress ruined envelopes. They sometimes rewrite entire letters having to do with construction, contract bids, prices of raw materials or rerouting supplies destined for the Chinese army.'

Kenji stood near a clerk handling an official envelope. 'They'll know if he breaks the wax seal of the British Embassy, and the taped flap.'

The clerk looked up and smiled. Pleased at the opportunity to show his skill, he motioned Kenji and Raiko closer. 'I can remove the letter without disturbing the seal or flap.'

They watched him steam the lower right rear corner of the envelope. He worked a razor under the glued fold until there was a half-inch opening. He then switched on a powerful overhead light and positioned the envelope so the letter inside was clearly outlined. Inserting a well-worn stick of split bamboo, he worked it over the edge of the letter, then twirled the stick between thumb and forefinger. The letter rolled around the bamboo and he slipped it out of the small opening.

'I'll put the letter back the same way,' the clerk said. 'If you read English look at this.'

Kenji unrolled the letter and read it. 'Nothing here,' he said. 'A third secretary named Birns in Mukden is trying to impress his Chinese girlfriend with the official envelope. He's scheduled for a week's vacation and suggests they meet secretly in Peking to spend it together.'

The clerk thumbed through a file marked British Consulate Mukden. He pulled a card and smiled as he read it. 'This is better than usual.'

'What can be so important in a man going away for a vacation with his girlfriend?' Kenji asked.

179

Ando took the card from the clerk. 'This Englishman has a wife and two children in London. We might blackmail him on that account. He writes in English to a Chinese girl, which usually means she was taught by Christian missionaries and comes from a wealthy family. We could blackmail her to spy on her white lover. If we photograph the two together in bed, that could be enough to convince the Englishman to work for us.'

Raiko shivered. 'I prefer decoding. It's cleaner than reading people's mail.'

'I see no difference between opening envelopes and listening to radio messages,' Ando said.

'People don't send their mail to this room,' Kenji said, attempting to defend Raiko. 'Once a radio message is put in the air, it's accessible to anyone.'

'When people code their messages, they are in effect putting envelopes around them,' Ando said. 'Raiko's expertise is opening that envelope without the sender knowing.'

The look of dismay on Raiko's face as the truth of Ando's logic struck home dismayed Kenji. 'The morality of either method of obtaining information is not in question,' he said. 'Both are justified by the necessity of knowing our enemy's secrets.'

'Who is the enemy?' Raiko asked. 'The people in this room are opening British and American mail as well as Chinese.'

'And you broke the Dutch and French codes as well as the American cipher,' Ando said.

Kenji flashed Raiko a warning glance. Ando knew who she was. He had confirmed Kenji's suspicion that someone in the Cherry Blossom Society was spying for Koda-ha. The two followed Ando into another room filled with typewriters, telegraph and radio receivers. He took them to the desk at the head of the room and introduced them to the chief of the radio code section.

'Miss Minobe, feel free to ask whatever questions you wish,' the chief said. 'My staff and our equipment are at your service. I would like to know how you broke our army code.'

'It wasn't me who broke it,' Raiko said.

'General Tojo wishes Miss Minobe to concentrate on the new American brown code after she has enciphered and sent to Japan certain information for Captain Ishikawa,' Ando said.

'If there is a desk available, Raiko should begin immediately,' Kenji said. 'I must inform my engineers about certain new aeronautic devices used by the British.' He handed Ando several rolls of negatives. 'If you could have these made into positives and arrange for a projector and screen, I'll be able to read all the drawings.'

'We have a film laboratory in the building,' Ando said. 'Everything will be developed and printed by noon.'

After a few hours' work, Kenji and Raiko lunched in the officers' dining room. 'I'm on edge from watching my every word with Ando and the chief,' she said. 'They're polite, but they evaluate whatever I say.' She hesitated for a moment. 'And you also seem to be watching me most of the time.'

'You're beautiful,' Kenji said.

Raiko beamed. 'So are you.' Their eyes met and held.

Ando came to their table, looked at them and coughed. 'I hope I'm not interrupting but the slides are prepared and the projector in place.'

Raiko and Kenji followed Ando without exchanging a word. They set to work but, for both, the remainder of the afternoon dragged on. The door separating their rooms was on their minds. Every movement of their bodies initiated sexual sensations and awareness of each other.

At the dinner table with Ando, the meal seemed endless. They picked at their food, avoided meeting each other's eyes, and vaguely heard Ando's chatter as he ate his only meal of the day with gusto.

Finally, they could go to their rooms. Kenji took a steaming hot bath, then lay on top of the covers in his robe, watching the connecting door, praying it would open. What is wrong with you, he thought. You're acting like a child. She thinks you're beautiful. Go to her. Round and round went his thoughts.

The sound of the doorknob turning woke Kenji. His body stiffened. He watched the door slowly swing open. Light from Raiko's room outlined her body through her silk robe. She took a step into the room and hesitated. Fearing she would flee, he held his breath.

Raiko took a second step. 'Kenji,' she whispered 'I cannot wait any longer.'

He tried to speak, but his throat had closed to hold his heart down in his chest. He slipped off the bed and went to her. They stood close together, silent, not touching. He heard the sound of his own breathing, the pounding of blood in his head. Her face raised to his with parted lips. He lowered his head, gently touching her lips. He felt her hands moving, opening his robe, then hers. She pressed her body to his and they both gasped. Her hand reached down and touched his erection. She shuddered and swayed. 'I want you to make love to me, but I'm afraid.'

Kenji kissed her lips, her eyes, her neck. 'I won't hurt you, my beloved. Never, never. I will never hurt you.' Gently he lifted her in his arms and carried her to his bed. He hovered over her, kissing, caressing her soft, smooth body. He fondled her breasts, nibbled and sucked the nipples. Feeling her respond to him, he shuddered with happiness.

Raiko's grip tightened on Kenji's shoulders. Her eyes remained open as she drank in the wonder of being with him. Her body began to move of its own accord, pressing up to him. She spread her legs around his knees and took his face in her hands, kissing him over and over. 'Don't hurt me,' she cried.

Kenji's blood raged. He wanted to drive into her, to let her feel his love and know its depth. But he held himself back for her sake. He trembled as he pressed the head of his penis into the lips of her vagina. Raiko lowered her head and kissed his nipples as he had done hers. He moaned and grasped her thighs, pushing steadily downward. Something blocked his way and he pressed harder.

Raiko moaned deep in her throat and he hesitated, but she clasped him behind the head. 'Don't stop,' she whispered in his ear. 'Please don't stop.'

Kenji raised slightly and she dug her nails into his shoulders, holding him to her. He moved forward again, with greater strength, and she pulled his hips forward. Falling back on the bed, she threw her arms over her head. He kissed her mouth, her breasts, and pressed deeper, ignoring her cry, driving forward until there was no more of him to give. She lay with her mouth open, her back arched, her eyes wide. He saw her fists clenching and unclenching. Her body quivered and she moaned with pleasure. He thrust into her with great shuddering lunges and she began to rise to meet him, weeping tears of joy, crying out in exultation. He muffled the sound with his mouth, covering her body with his. He heard himself grunting, then shouting, engulfed in a tide of glorious pleasure. Realizing he was crushing the breath from her body, he rolled to the side, pulling her with him.

Raiko stroked his smooth black hair and handsome face. 'The gods are good to have given us this,' she said.

They lay entwined, speaking with their eyes, enjoying the waves of unexpected convulsions of pleasure that passed through their bodies.

Raiko pushed Kenji back and rolled on top of him. 'I

was afraid to let you inside me, but now I never want to let you out.'

'I don't want to leave.'

'This room is perfect for lovemaking,' Raiko said. 'Can you imagine how many people have been seduced in the Fifth Moon Inn.'

'That was sex in a house of professional pleasure,' Kenji said. 'It's not the same thing. I love you. I adore you.' He began to stroke her.

Raiko sighed. 'I read my mother's pillow books, you know.'

She began to explore Kenji's body, to experiment. Kenji had years of experience to share. They gave each other pleasure into the early hours of the morning.

For three weeks Raiko and Kenji worked every morning, toured in the Dusenberg and picnicked in the surrounding forest during the afternoons, and made love every night.

At the beginning of July the pace at Kwangtung army headquarters quickened. Ando was ordered into China. Kenji was kept busy evaluating field agents' reports. Although unsuccessful, Raiko's efforts to break the American brown code were applauded by the chief, who adopted many of her deciphering procedures into his daily routines.

Mid-morning of the next day, Kenji came into the radio section and went directly to Raiko's desk. 'My cousins have come for me. They'd like to see you before we leave.'

The concern in Raiko's eyes caused him to reach out to her in public. Their hands met and he squeezed hers. 'It isn't war yet,' he said. 'I'm ordered on a series of reconnaissance and photography missions.'

'The fighting will begin soon,' Raiko said. 'The flow of radio messages has doubled. Agents' reports are more detailed. Two days ago General Hashimoto activated

184

secret units in north China. I believe they're sabotage teams. Ando is in charge of a particularly large force operating between Peking and the Marco Polo bridge.'

Kenji nodded. 'It appears Tojo won't wait out the year ordered by the Emperor. The new army conscripts have been put directly into line companies. Hashimoto is holding full-scale manoeuvres near the Chinese border. I've sent a letter giving these details to Hiroki, via one of my ship captains.'

Raiko stood. 'Your cousins are waiting.'

She led Kenji outside. Hino and Genda bowed to her. 'How long will you be gone on your photography trip?' she asked.

'We can't take good photos at night,' Hino said. 'We'll bring him back every evening.'

Seeing Raiko's face brighten, Genda said, 'If Kenji will give you the keys to his car, I'll arrange for a special pass on to the air base so you can be there to meet us when we land. We've heard what a good driver you are.' He grinned.

The two cousins saw the unguarded look of affection pass between the lovers. 'We'll wait by the army car,' Hino said.

'Everyone at the air base will know we're lovers if you meet me there,' Kenji said to Raiko.

'Everyone here knows,' Raiko said. She smiled at Kenji's surprised expression.

'I didn't mean to ruin your reputation.'

'I came to your room,' Raiko said.

'Only because I dozed off while trying to get up the courage to open that door.'

Raiko sighed. 'These last weeks have been the most wonderful in my life.'

'Let's make it a permanent arrangement,' Kenji said.

Raiko's brow furrowed. 'What do you mean?'

'Marriage, of course.'

185

'You and me married?' Raiko whispered, her eyes so wide Kenji thought he would tumble into them.

'It's not such a terrible thing.' Kenji laughed. 'We could try it for 100 years or so. If you don't like it after that, we can separate.'

'It's the most wonderful thing to contemplate,' Raiko whispered.

'You mean you must think about it?'

'I've enjoyed thinking about it for some time. I would like very much to be married to you. When?'

Kenji knitted his brow. 'You know that Noriko and Hiroki lost their two sons and raised me. They're my parents. I want to give them the pleasure of a formal, traditional wedding. On the first leave I can arrange, we'll fly to Japan. Will you wait?'

'On the condition I can remain your mistress until I become your wife. But don't we need permission from the Cherry Blossom Society to marry?'

'If they don't agree, I'll cut off their funds.'

Raiko laughed. 'You're ruthless.'

'I'm in love,' Kenji said.

22

Noriko was concerned about her husband. In thirty-six years, Hiroki had never failed to mark their wedding anniversary with a gift at lunch. He had always ordered evening theatre tickets and made reservations for dinner. Today, if she presented her gift when they reached home, he would feel hurt for having forgotten. She glanced at him, still handsome, with strong features, clear skin and eyes bright with a touch of mischief. Yet, she thought, we are both getting old and forgetful.

At home, they changed into comfortable kimonos. Noriko served tea. She always performed an abbreviated version of the tea ceremony, which pleased Hiroki.

He sipped his tea, raised his thick eyebrows and peered over the cup at his wife. 'You are the most beautiful woman I have ever known.' Seeing her cheeks crimson, he laughed. 'And you still blush at compliments.' Hiroki replaced his teacup on the lacquer tray. 'It is time for a variation of our yearly anniversary ritual.'

'Modification sometimes disrupts the harmony of life,' Noriko said.

'Westerners say variety is the spice of life.'

'Occidentals see change as beneficial. Orientals view it as intrusive.'

Hiroki shrugged. 'Starting this year and for the next thirty-six years, let us exchange anniversary gifts in the evenings. And you must make the presentation first.'

Noriko bowed. 'I thought you had forgotten.'

Hiroki waved his finger and clicked his tongue. 'Never.'

Noriko reached under the table and withdrew a rose-wood cane with silver-encrusted head. She presented it as a samurai would present a sword, on the backs of her hands.

Hiroki bowed to his wife. He accepted the highly polished cane and admired the fine lines of deep-hued grain running from the steel tip to the silver head. 'I shall march into the Emperor's presence with this tomorrow. I expect his imperial majesty will take notice of such an exceptional walking stick. Lately the Emperor has engaged me in many private conversations. He appears to be lonely. His brother is of no help to him. The prince spends his time at nightclubs in the Roppongi when he is not travelling abroad.'

'His majesty has the Empress to confide in,' Noriko said.

'There are certain things men find easier to discuss with other men,' Hiroki said. 'By the same token, there are subjects more enjoyable to discuss with women. Or rather a woman. The woman. You.' From each of his large sleeves he produced a wooden box, and opened them on the table before Noriko.

'Ohino matsuri dolls,' she exclaimed, and bowed. 'Forgive me for thinking you had forgotten our anniversary.'

'These are original sixteenth-century Emperor and Empress dolls. They fill the vacancy in your collection.'

Nariko examined each doll. 'They are perfect in every detail,' she declared.

'But one,' Hiroki said.

'I will be proud to display them in my palace doll-house. And at the next Festival of the Dolls.'

'They have not yet brought you a message of joy,' Hiroki said. He placed an envelope across the laps of both dolls.

Noriko opened the telegram. It was from Kenji.

'Since the death of my honourable parents, I have thought of Noriko and Hiroki Koin as Mother and Father. I spent happy years in your home. Now the time has come for me to establish my own home. Would I be presumptuous in asking my aunt and uncle to act as my parents in negotiating a marriage contract, the exchange of wedding gifts and a traditional wedding ceremony for me and my bride-to-be, Miss Raiko Minobe?'

Noriko looked up at her husband with tears in her eyes.

'You have made a wonderful match,' Hiroki said.

Tears coursed down Noriko's cheeks. A great sob wracked her body and Hiroki moved to her side. 'Would that the message had been from one of our sons,' he said.

Noriko felt her husband tremble and saw tears in his eyes.

'There is not a day passes that I do not think of our boys,' he muttered.

'The worst curse of the gods is for parents to bury their children,' Noriko said, and sighed. 'But our boys are gone and Kenji is here. He is our son.' She dried her tears and read the remainder of the telegram. 'How can I consult the family astrologer to set an auspicious date if we don't know exactly when Kenji and Raiko will come home?' she complained to Hiroki.

'It will have to be after the invasion of China. That much is certain.'

'Another six months?'

'It could be six weeks,' Hiroki said. 'Kenji sent other messages from Manchuria. Hashimoto and Tojo will not wait the full year. Tomorrow I meet the Emperor to discuss this matter.'

A knock at the front door caused Hiroki and Noriko to exchange worried glances. There had recently been a spate of political assassinations of Hiroki's colleagues in the liberal party.

'It is late for someone to be calling,' Noriko said.

With a smile that belied his concern for having left his

189

pistol in his tuxedo, Hiroki said, 'If it was trouble, they would not warn us by knocking.'

He went to the front door, followed closely by Noriko, and greeted Admiral Yamamoto.

Noriko bowed. 'We are pleased to see you. We are celebrating our anniversary. Please have some tea.'

Leading the admiral into the living room, Hiroki asked, 'What brings you out so late at night?'

Yamamoto's face was grim. 'War! The Emperor has signed marching orders for the Kwangtung army. Tojo has imperial permission to invade China!'

Hiroki paled and leaned heavily on his new cane.

Yamamoto turned to Noriko. 'Perhaps saké rather than tea.'

'I never thought the Emperor would take this decision without consulting me,' Hiroki said. 'What caused him to issue such a hasty order?'

'Two of our naval officers drank too much and attempted to take over Shanghai International Airport. They killed a Chinese guard and were later shot down by the local police. There was a minor riot in downtown Shanghai between our marines and the Chinese army. The marines have been reinforced by our fleet in Shanghai harbour. There are now 10,000 of our men in Shanghai, surrounded by seven million Chinese! I have ordered the marines to remain in camp.'

Hiroki gulped the saké poured by Noriko and colour returned to his cheeks. 'Can our men be withdrawn without a fight?' he asked.

'Possibly,' Yamamoto said. 'My naval commanders report that the Chinese army has been restricted to barracks also. They do not wish trouble. But our general staff refuses to order the marines out of Shanghai.'

'Because of a drunken brawl, the Emperor ordered the army to march?' Hiroki shook his head in disbelief.

'Tojo will arrange for more legitimate reasons,' Yamamoto

190

said. 'At the same meeting with the Emperor, Prime Minister Konoe also sought imperial approval to invade Russian Mongolia in late 1938.'

'On what pretext?' Hiroki demanded.

'To stop the spread of communism in the Far East.'

'What was the Emperor's response?'

'He sanctioned studies of the possibilities for an aggressive probe into Russia. For political and racial reasons, our military would rather fight the Russians than the Chinese. They see communism as a greater threat to Asia than Chinese nationalism.'

Noriko saw her husband's shoulders slump as he repeated, 'I never thought the Emperor would take such a decision without consulting me.'

'It appears the Emperor has been involved in military affairs without our knowledge,' Yamamoto said. 'When the Black Dragon Society was incorporated into Koda-ha, it was assumed the imperial secret service was disbanded. It now appears that the Emperor secretly controls Koda-ha. This I pieced together from my naval intelligence service, and from Wantabe's and Kenji's reports. Yesterday a Koda-ha man carrying secret documents from the imperial palace had a heart attack on the street. One of my agents picked up his briefcase. The documents confirm the Emperor's involvement with the Kwangtung army.'

'Didn't Kenji write that Major Ando has dropped out of sight in Manchuria?' Noriko said. 'He is Tojo's senior intelligence field officer and certain to be involved in any false incident to start the war.'

'Dr Tsubota is senior,' Hiroki said. 'He has set up headquarters in Saigon. He controls all Koda-ha agents in French Indochina and the Dutch East Indies. I don't know where Ando is.'

'Kenji places him just the other side of the Marco Polo bridge with a 200-strong commando force,' Yamamoto said. 'He'll have to act soon, or risk being discovered.'

'But I thought the Emperor was against military expansion,' Noriko said. 'Didn't he postpone the invasion for a year?'

'The Emperor did not believe Tojo had enough men to defeat the Chinese,' Yamamoto said. 'But his majesty secretly allowed Prime Minister Konoe to press for a national conscription bill. The army thought it needed a year to train, transport and integrate the new recruits. Hashimoto did it in six months.'

'In John Whittefield's decoded message, Borodin claimed the Emperor was involved,' Hiroki said. 'How could Borodin know? I have been close to the Emperor for so many years. I would have known.'

Yamamoto shook his head. 'I too should have been more observant. But you must remember that you and I are from the old school. Blinded by tradition. Think of who recommended Konoe to be prime minister.'

'The Koda-ha faction did,' Hiroki said.

'Every schoolboy knows the army wants to dominate Asia,' Yamamoto said. 'Even though Konoe leads Koda-ha, the Emperor did not hesitate to confirm the appointment.'

'The Emperor put down the Koda-ha rebellion,' Noriko said.

'Because it did not succeed in winning over both the army and navy,' Yamamoto said.

'But his imperial majesty has always been publicly for peace,' Noriko said.

'And it seems, privately for war,' Yamamoto answered. 'He appointed Tojo commander of the Kwangtung army.'

'That was years ago,' Hiroki said.

'Yes.' Yamamoto nodded. 'Think back to other appointments of military expansionists. The Emperor could have stopped any of them with a nod of his head. He signed the national conscription bill. And through intermediaries approved the release from prison of Kingoro Hashimoto.'

'Are you condemning the Emperor?' Noriko asked.

'Not at all. His personal tactic of appearing uninvolved is to be applauded. He remains the faultless, infallible, god-king. I simply question his military strategy.'

'Do not do so in public,' Hiroki said. 'We need you alive.'

'Japan should move south to control the rubber, oil and tungsten there,' Yamamoto said. 'Those materials are necessary for our war industry.'

'But what of China's natural resources?' Noriko asked.

'Recent studies show it will take five years to develop them for our expanded needs,' Yamamoto said. 'The size of our army has trebled. The use of motorized vehicles instead of horses and mules, the increased power of ship engines, our rapidly expanding air force, have more than quintupled the immediate need for imported raw petroleum-related materials. Without those supplies, our entire military structure will collapse in on itself. That is Roosevelt's aim, via his policy of Ring Fence.'

Hiroki stood before Rodin's sketch of 'The Gates of Hell' and gazed at the twisted, tortured figures. 'A war with China would be a grave mistake. Their 500 million people represent the greatest market in the world. They could field the largest army in history. If Tojo goes to war with China, our nation may eventually stand at "The Gates of Hell".'

Yamamoto looked up at Rodin's picture. 'The question is not whether there will be war with China. Ask when.'

'The affair at the Temple of Heaven is arranged for 2 p.m. this afternoon,' the voice on the telephone said. The old adage, 'You receive what you pay for', popped into Ando's head. His forged orders had gone into effect. Six hundred men of the Nationalist Chinese Twenty-first Infantry Division would leave their barracks unarmed and on foot, for a non-existent ceremony in the ancient Forbidden City of Peking.

'It is proper to have the remainder of the gift delivered before their departure,' the voice said.

'It is on the way,' Ando replied, and hung up the receiver. He threw a packet to his aide. 'Deliver this $1,000 to that Chinese traitor at Twenty-first Division headquarters!'

Ando dialled the telephone, then spoke into the receiver. 'The number is three.' He hung up and went to the window.

Three blue smoke rockets zoomed into the summer sky. Somewhere in the surrounding hills, 200 Japanese imperial marines saw the rockets and checked their watches. They loaded their weapons and set out for the ambush point on the road to Peking.

Ando summoned a motorcycle messenger. 'It should take you ten minutes from here to the Marco Polo bridge, and five more to General Hashimoto's headquarters! Tell the general it's tonight!'

Ando dialled again and completed the negotiations with a local Chinese warlord. 'That's right. Have the trucks there at sunset. 5:30 p.m.!' He hung up and looked down at the bulge in his trousers. 'I pity the first woman I see after this war begins,' he said aloud. 'I've been deprived of sex for too many months!' He heard his stomach rumble and he shouted, 'Aide, pack me an extra-large picnic basket! After dark tonight I'm going to eat like one of those Chinese pigs, and then screw like a rabbit! We're going to war!'

The August sun was hot, the road to the Temple of Heaven dry and dusty. Alongside a veteran marine machine-gunner, Ando stood on a knoll overlooking the ambush area. The commandos had camouflaged themselves among the rocks and shrubs on both sides of the road, and Ando could not pick them out. He and the gunner lay down behind a bush. Ando checked the angle of the sun to be certain it would not reflect off his binoculars.

The Chinese infantrymen sang a Buddhist temple song as they approached, straggling forward in a loose column of fours. Ando put the binoculars away when he could make out the wispy chin whiskers of the Chinese colonel leading the column.

'They should be killed for pretending to be soldiers,' Ando whispered. 'Look how sloppily they march.'

The marine patted his Nambu machine gun. 'I don't need an excuse to shoot slope-heads. You want them dead, they're dead.'

'It won't be easy to gun down 600 frightened Chinamen,' Ando said. 'Wait for my signal!' He counted to himself, checked his watch, then pulled the machine-gunner down behind the hill. 'They're moving at ninety steps per minute.' Ando watched the minute hand on his watch jerk forward. 'That's it! They're in the trap!' He stood up and walked down on to the road.

The Chinese commander saw a lone Japanese officer striding towards him, and ordered his men to halt.

Ando continued walking until he reached the white wooden aiming stake his gunner had pounded into the ground. He stood twenty feet away from the Chinese commander. 'Colonel,' Ando shouted, 'tell your men to place their hands behind their heads and line up in a column of fours on the right side of the road!'

The commander sneered. 'Kiss my arse, you Japanese fart!'

Ando pulled his Luger, stretched his arm full-length and shot the colonel twice in the chest. The man looked down at the holes in his uniform. He staggered back, and fell dead.

'Drag his body to the side of the road,' Ando ordered. No one moved. The Chinese officers at the head of the column looked down at their commander, killed before their eyes. Although unarmed, they charged Ando.

The flat, rattling crack of the Nambu tore up the road between Ando and the Chinese. Five officers went down before the others stopped. All around the Chinese infantrymen, Japanese marines appeared to grow out of the rocky soil with submachine-guns levelled.

'Pick your officers up,' Ando ordered. 'The dead and the wounded! If you obey my orders, no one else will be injured! Line up in a column of fours! And do it like soldiers!'

The Chinese infantrymen shuffled into ranks.

'Dress right dress,' Ando ordered. 'Maintain proper distance and interval between ranks!' He walked the length of the four columns, stopping to reprimand men for not standing straight, for unbuttoned tunics. His attention to detail relaxed them.

Ando reached the last row and moved to the rear rank. He pointed his gun at the back of the head of the last man in line, and pulled the trigger. His marines opened fire, gunning down the unarmed Chinese. For twenty minutes blood poured; dead men sprawled. Here and there a soldier tried to crawl out from under his dead comrades, and was shot.

'One bullet through the back of every Chinaman's head,' Ando ordered.

'Sir,' a marine officer said. 'It won't look like combat wounds to the newspapermen if every corpse has a hole in his head.'

'Most of them are shot in the back anyway,' Ando said. 'I don't care how you finish the job! Make certain every one of them is dead! Stack the bodies on the side of the road! The trucks are due in forty minutes.' Ando sat next to his picnic basket and watched the sun go down. Soon he could eat. The invasion would take place tonight and then his sexual orgy would begin.

He imagined all the women he would grind himself into.

It grew dark and Ando gorged himself. He finished eating, and still the trucks had not come. Sweat poured from his body yet he felt cold, and was glad the marines could not see the nervous twitch of his eyes. The hands on his watch passed 6 p.m. and still the trucks had not appeared. He feared disaster.

Ando heard the sound of a motorcycle and expected to hear a shot killing the driver. Instead, the motorcycle with empty sidecar was directed to him.

'Sir, the warlord's trucks have been detained by a Chinese roadblock five miles south.'

'How many Chinese are manning the roadblock?' Ando asked.

'Fifteen. But there's an infantry company camped there. About fifty men.'

Ando cracked his knuckles. He sucked wind through his teeth. He stalked up the road, then rushed back and shouted at the marine commander. 'Run all your men the five miles and remove the roadblock! Finish that Chinese company! Bring their bodies back here in the trucks and load all these bodies!'

'By the great Buddha's balls,' the cyclist gasped. 'In the dark I thought that was firewood stacked along the road.'

'You'll take me and this machine-gunner to the Marco Polo bridge about seven miles further on!' Ando climbed into the sidecar and motioned the marine commander closer. 'You know what to do with the bodies. Make a good show of it!'

'Aye aye, sir.' The marine officer saluted and the motorcycle roared off.

The sound of gunfire from the opposite side of the river overcame the noise of the motorcycle as they approached the bridge.

'Has the invasion started?' the machine-gunner shouted.

'Those are Hashimoto's troops on manoeuvres with blanks,' the cyclist said. 'They've been trying to get the Chinese to fire at them for weeks.'

'Take us to the crest of that hill,' Ando ordered.

Moonlight reflected off the river flowing through the thirty graceful arches of the Marco Polo bridge. Ando stood up in the sidecar for a better view. He knew that 20,000 men of the Sixteenth Imperial Infantry Division waited on the other side behind those troops on manoeuvres. The First Motorized Cavalry Division was poised on the roads leading to China, ready to dash across the underwater bridges secretly laid brick by brick by the Second Combat Engineers Division. The Eleventh and Twelfth Artillery Divisions were in close support for the dash across the river and the twelve-mile race to Peking. Ando chewed his lip. Out there in the dark, over 100,000 men waited for him to start the war. He tasted blood in his mouth and spat. 'No trucks, no bodies, no marines, no damned anything! Gunner,' he shouted, 'will that Nambu of yours reach across the river?'

'Not from here, sir. Do you want me to shoot at our men?'

'Those stupid Chinese won't!' Kenji pointed at the Chinese army camp spread around the near side of the bridge. 'We have to cause an incident! We have to get our men across the river to shoot over here!'

The marine-gunner handed two ammunition boxes to the driver. He picked up the Nambu and more ammunition. 'Sir, I'll take a position up-river from the bridge and shoot from there.'

'I'll be watching from here,' Ando said. 'I want to meet the trucks.'

Ando waited, reviewing his scheme to place the Chinese bodies and weapons to look as if they had initiated an artillery duel with Japanese forces. The marines would set up the Chinese weapons supplied by the warlord, and fire a few rounds from the guns. The imperial artillery would be signalled to blanket the area with high-explosive shells.

The flat crack of the Nambu took Ando's attention to the river. He saw the gun-flash, but where were the tracer bullets? He slammed his fist into his hand. Damn! The marines are trained for night fighting. The tracers have been taken out to avoid detection in the dark.

There was no answering fire from the other side of the river, and still no sign of the trucks. Neither were the Chinese reacting to the Kwangtung troops on manoeuvres near the river bank. Ando had to admire the Chinese fire discipline, and curse the Japanese soldiers who did not even realize they were being fired upon. His bowels reacted to fear of failure and disgrace. He dropped his trousers to defecate in the grass, thinking as he squatted. There was only one thing to do.

Ando buckled his trousers. He hopped on the motor-cycle and rode to the Marco Polo bridge, where he was halted by a squad of Chinese soldiers. A young lieutenant came out of his tent in response to Ando's furious shouts.

The officer saluted and gave a sly smile. 'Major, you are free to go. We do not wish to inconvenience a Japanese cousin.'

Ando returned the salute. Although he wanted to race across the ancient cobblestone bridge, he moved in low gear.

On the other side, he shouted to the Japanese officer. 'Where's the nearest commander of manoeuvres?'

'Up-river a quarter-mile is headquarters company.'

Without bothering to return the salute, Ando barrelled down the dirt road. He skidded into the compound and up to the first officer he saw.

'You're under fire from the enemy,' Ando screamed.

The captain appeared bewildered. 'I don't think so, sir.'

Ando swung off the cycle. He grabbed the captain by the lapels and shook him. 'Don't you see that gun-flash across the river!' He pointed. 'You are being fired upon!'

The captain politely removed Ando's hands from his uniform. 'Major, that's a Nambu. Anyone can tell from the sound it's ours.'

'You're damned right it's one of ours!' Ando's voice cracked. 'He's firing at you because I told him to!'

'Sir?'

Soldiers crowded around. Ando was beside himself with frustration and fear. 'Everybody is waiting for an excuse to start the goddamned war! You have it! That gun across the river!'

'None of my men has been hit.'

'Idiot! Line them up and call the roll! That's an order!'

The captain saluted and repeated the order. He and Ando waited, Ando taking deep breaths to calm himself.

The officer received the results of the roll call and saluted. 'Sir, all present and accounted for but one man. He has diarrhoea.'

'Take me to him,' Ando ordered.

The captain looked flustered. Then he shrugged. 'Follow me to the company latrine.'

On the path behind the tents they approached a soldier buckling his trousers. Seeing the two officers, he snapped to attention and saluted.

'Private, what is the meaning of the word banzai?' Ando asked.

'Ten thousand years to the Emperor, sir.'

'About-face and give three banzais to his imperial majesty!'

The private turned smartly and followed orders. 'Banzai! Banzai!' Ando pulled his pistol and shot the man in the back of his head.

'The Chinese have just killed one of your men!' Ando said to the captain. 'Report it, and return fire!'

200

'Yes, sir.' The captain saluted.

Ando squatted, and waited. Japanese mortars and artillery began shooting across the river, lighting the skyline with the muzzle blasts of hundreds of heavy guns. Ando watched angry red balls of fire erupt amid the Chinese positions. His erection throbbed and he thought about where he would satisfy it. He had marked the finest whorehouse outside Peking. With the war on, his restrictions were off. He clutched his throbbing penis, squeezing until it pained him. He chuckled in the eerie light of the muzzle blasts and innovated the old samurai ditty,

'I'll come down from the hills through snow and sleet,
With eighteen feet of swinging meat.
I'll throw my balls on the Seven Sisters bar,
I swear it'll stretch from here to there.
I'll make my bet, put my money down.
The ground will be ploughed for miles around,
Where the Seven Sisters' arses will beat the ground.'

Ando stood and raised both fists over his head. 'Bless the gods of war,' he shouted. 'Banzai! Banzai! Banzai!'

23

Peking was under Japanese martial law and the outer courtyard of the Forbidden City had become Kwangtung army headquarters. A Japanese-led convoy of civilian cars waited in front of the Temple of Heaven. The drivers stood near their cars.

'What's holding things up?' an American correspondent shouted.

John Whittefield pointed to the tall, ramrod-stiff figure in a dusty trooper's uniform who strode along the line of press and consular cars. 'Here comes Vinegar Joe. We'll probably leave soon.'

'Jesus H. Christ,' the reporter said. 'He didn't return the Jap officer's salute!'

John opened his car door and saluted the approaching figure. 'Here's your transportation, General Stilwell.'

The dour-faced American commander stepped into the car and motioned John behind the wheel. 'Is it true the little bastards captured Peking in less than two days?'

'Yes, sir. There was some stiff resistance by the Chinese at the Marco Polo bridge, but after that the Japanese armour rolled through, or over, everything in their way. Our ambassador in Nanking and naval intelligence in Hawaii have been trying to locate you.'

'Yeah,' Stilwell said. 'Roosevelt wants to know if Chiang Kai-shek can put up serious resistance north of the Yangtze. I went from Hsuchon to Kaifeng, from Loyang to Honan to find out. Hopped a freighter on the Grand Canal. Sat on the bridge with the captain and identified military units along the way.'

'Is the Nationalist army prepared?' John asked.

'No signs of defensive preparations, troop training or reinforcements. Chiang's best units are in Shanghai.'

'Do you want me to send that message to our intelligence services?'

'Already did,' General Stilwell said.

'Sir, what code did you use?'

'Grey.'

John cleared his throat. 'Sir, the Japanese have broken that cipher. We've discontinued its use.' He watched for Vinegar Joe Stilwell's reaction. There was none.

The convoy of cars began to move and John concentrated on driving. They neared the Marco Polo bridge.

'If the Japs have read my report,' Stilwell said, 'Chiang Kai-shek has got to be notified to prepare for a lightning strike by Tojo against Shanghai.'

'My intelligence people claim the Japanese high command's only interest is in the five northern provinces,' John said. 'Central and southern China are ruled out.'

'Chinese intelligence informed me Jap T-97 single-wing fighters have been flying reconnaissance missions over Shanghai,' Stilwell said. 'The Third Imperial Fleet has anchored in Hangchow harbour forty miles from Shanghai. Yesterday the flagship *Izumo* joined them with forty seaplanes.'

'The Chinese have 300 fighter planes at Nanking,' John said. 'That's too far away for the Japanese seaplanes to reach, and close enough for the Chinese planes to protect Shanghai.'

'Since the Jap invasion two days ago, the Nationalist army has surrounded 10,000 Japanese marines based in Shanghai. The marines are outnumbered fifty to one. It's the excuse Tojo needs to save them. If he read my message about the state of Chinese unpreparedness between Peking and Shanghai, he'll move soon.'

John followed the cars ahead, and parked on the side of the road when they did.

'Tell me what the hell we're here to see,' General Stilwell said.

'The Chinese artillery unit that started the fighting is supposed to have opened fire from here on the Kwangtung army across the river.'

The two Americans joined the group of reporters, military observers and foreign government representatives.

'This tour is to be conducted strictly according to my instructions,' the Japanese military guide said in heavily accented English. 'Visitors to this historic battlefield are warned not to stray from the group.' He bowed and smiled. 'There are many unexploded shells in the area. Follow me, please.'

Several minutes later, General Stilwell wandered away from the group, out among the stiff, bloated corpses strewn about the open field. John followed him, both men using their handkerchiefs to blot out the putrid smell.

'You two,' the Japanese officer shouted in Japanese. 'Come back here immediately!'

John translated the officer's words and the grey-haired American general trained his fierce, dark eyes on the young Japanese, addressing him in Chinese.

'He says he doesn't understand Chinese,' John said.

Vinegar Joe Stilwell waved at the rotting bodies surrounding them. 'Tell the little bastard I know this whole thing is a poorly planned sham! No artillery officer in his right mind would choose this position to fight from! Half the weapons here couldn't be fired because the ammunition is wrong for the guns' bore size. These poor bastards weren't killed by artillery shells. They were shot with small-calibre bullets. And their uniform insignias are Chinese infantry, not artillery!' The American general stalked past the stunned Japanese officer.

John watched the young man's eyes examine the battlefield. He looked dumbfounded. 'Your superiors lied to you,' John said.

Back in the car, Stilwell turned to John. 'You tell Ambassador Grew those Chinese soldiers were unarmed when they were slaughtered! There were no personal weapons on that battlefield. Most of them were shot in the back. Those field guns were Russian, the ammunition German-made. The bodies were laid out after the shelling took place. There were no signs of high-impact injuries on the dead!'

'Will you report to President Roosevelt?'

'Directly.'

'I've advised the State Department to support Chiang Kai-shek and ignore Mao,' John said.

'Of course. Mao is leader of the socialist plague in the Far East. Communism must be stopped!' Vinegar Joe looked out the car window at Japanese reinforcements moving towards Peking. 'I'm an old China hand, but you're the Jap expert. Explain to me where these bowlegged little buggers got the nerve to take Formosa, Korea, Manchuria, and now want to conquer an additional one-third of the world's population in China.'

'Their desire comes from necessity,' John said. 'Japan needs to secure overseas supplies for its domestic needs. That's what shapes her foreign policy. Her military policy is dictated by the threat of her two largest neighbours, China and Russia. The energetic personality of the people comes from their never-ending fight against nature. Centuries of year-round, dawn-to-dusk, backbreaking work of growing enough rice on not enough land, has produced a population of indefatigable, uncomplaining workers.'

'All the peoples of South-East Asia are rice producers,' General Stilwell said. 'They're passive. Their economies are centuries behind ours. Industrially Japan has surpassed most Western countries. How did they do it?'

'When the Emperor eliminated all hereditary rank, an unusual and powerful alliance developed between the aristocracy and the formerly despised merchant class. The ex-samurai became capable administrators with imagination and daring. The businessmen were prepared to take orders as well as risks. That, coupled with the most honest, dedicated workforce in history, has created a national human dynamo. The invasion of China is just the beginning. They have agents in Malaysia, Indochina and India.'

'But they don't seem to have an original thought in their combined heads,' Stilwell said. 'They copy everything.'

'Copying saves time. They've always been great imitators. Their religion, language and traditions are borrowed from the Chinese and Koreans. They'll steal plans, formulas and patents from foreign countries without hesitation. Then improve on them with unbelievable speed.'

'So why didn't they copy Christianity?'

'Christianity challenges the supremacy of the Emperor and violates social status. It teaches individuality and loyalty to God before all others. Marxism is closer to Japanese thought. Both philosophies subordinate the individual to the group. Japan's leaders fear communism could easily sweep up the Japanese masses. Many members of Japan's political and military hierarchy would rather fight Russia and socialism than their Chinese cousins.'

'In the words of a Chinese philosopher, "Know your enemy and in 100 battles you will win 100 victories",' General Stilwell said. 'Tell me what you know about Tojo.'

'He's called The Razor by his colleagues because of his sharp mind. His father was a career army officer of mediocre ability who passed on his biased views of life to his son. Foremost of those was the belief in the inherent superiority of the Japanese people, and their god-given right to rule Asia. At Tojo's wedding the father presented his son with a detailed bill for the cost of raising him. Tojo paid without protest.'

'Now it appears the son is in competition with Mr Hitler,'

Stilwell said. 'Both want to rule the world.' He pointed out the car window. 'What does that sign say?'

'The Seven Sisters' Brothel.'

'I meant the Japanese sign.'

'Officers only.'

The two Japanese guards outside the brothel entrance watched the limousine with the American flag go by. Major Shira Ando had given them orders not to allow entrance to anyone below the rank of major.

Inside, Ando lay on a feather quilt with the four youngest of the seven sisters. Two lay cradled in his arms. The other two massaged his body with sweet oil, using their hands and lips to stimulate yet another erection.

Ando scrunched his chin down on his chest and looked at his limp penis. 'Get up, you lazy bastard. Six is an unlucky number.' He suckled the breast of one sister and played with the nipples of the other.

The two girls below used the technique called Feathery Wind. All touched Ando with delicate fingers, gentle and demanding mouths, taking it as a personal challenge to excite their client into a lucky seventh ejaculation. Finally, with the aid of an aphrodisiac, the Japanese major began to react.

Three sisters held him down on his back and continued their caresses. It was the youngest's turn to bring this climax. She lowered herself on to his engorged penis, using the muscles of her vagina to massage, to squeeze, to tantalize him to a frenzy. Ando let out a roar and flung the other three away. He grasped the girl sitting on him and rolled over on to her, pinning her shoulders to the quilt, ramming into her like a wild man. His body stiffened, he howled and began to shake violently.

The girl under him screamed. 'He's having a fit!'

'No,' the oldest sister said. 'He's overdone it. Seven

takes an unusual amount of stamina. Now maybe we can all sleep.'

'Major, get dressed!'

Ando's right eye opened and blinked in the morning sun, but it would not focus on the man standing before him. He pried open his left eye with his fingers. 'What do you want?'

'General Hashimoto has come to see you.'

Ando scraped the fuzz off his tongue with the edge of his front teeth. He closed his eyes and fell back on the quilt, then sensed the man leaning over him. Hands touched the hair on his temples and jerked hard. A shock wave passed through Ando's brain, electrifying his entire body. He found himself standing but could not remember getting up.

'Do I have your attention, Major? I am a colonel! It makes no difference to me how good you are at sabotage. I dislike all spies! Get your trousers on and snap to!'

Ando pushed one leg into his trousers and tried to force the second. He lost his balance and fell against the wall, upsetting a table.

The door opened and Kingoro Hashimoto entered. He looked down at Ando. 'I thought someone was being murdered in here.'

Ando pulled on his trousers and jumped up to salute.

Hashimoto pointed. 'Put your pecker in your pants, and listen to me. That little Raiko Minobe you brought to the Fifth Moon Inn has decoded a message from the American General Stilwell. The Chinese army is unprepared to fight between Peking and Shanghai. We are going to take Shanghai!'

Ando tucked in his shirt and rubbed his eyes. 'Our general staff has always warned not to become involved in central or southern China.'

'Shanghai is the jewel of the Orient,' Hashimoto said.

'It is home to the richest international trading community in the world.'

'It also has seven million people, and is 700 miles overland from Peking,' Ando said.

'No choice,' Hashimoto said. 'The Chinks have 10,000 of our marines surrounded at their base near the city.'

'I can negotiate an evacuation,' Ando said. 'Chiang Kai-shek and his German advisers want us to fight the Russians. They've approached me twice. Field Marshal Theodore Heidrich in Peking will make the arrangements.'

'Imperial headquarters has ordered us to take Shanghai.'

'They would sacrifice 10,000 of our best fighting men for that city?'

'The marines are not in such a terrible position as it may seem. We fed the foreign press that propaganda. Our men are supported by the Third Imperial Fleet in Hangchow harbour. Yamamoto is sending additional aircraft carriers. Hino Arai will lead the first transoceanic bomber raid from Formosa. Genda Arai and Kenji Ishikawa will lead our new T-97 fighters from the carriers.'

'What is my assignment?' Ando asked.

'Gather all your agents, saboteurs and the 200-man marine commando force! Go behind enemy lines and keep the roads and rail-lines open from Peking to Shanghai!'

'We can cover the water bridges, land trestles and some of the mountain gorges, but there are bound to be delays. The Chinese in Shanghai will have time to dig in.'

'On the twenty-third of August, 35,000 of our men will land in Hangchow harbour and march the forty miles to Shanghai. They'll take that city as we've taken Peking!'

'We outnumbered the Chinese army here,' Ando said. 'Chiang has half a million troops in Shanghai.'

'We have three times their firepower. Your assignment, after making a purchase for me in Shanghai, will be

Nanking. First you will buy the Necklace, a string of blockhouses, small forts and pillboxes strung across the Yangtze delta like a pearl necklace protecting Nanking's throat. German military engineers built those fortifications and claim they can't be taken. Buy them! I'll give you the name of the Chinese commander and enough gold to pay for his early retirement! If our navy can bypass the Necklace, we'll encircle Nanking by land and sea. I'll teach those Chinamen a lesson!'

'Are we going to take the capital city of China?'

'Yes,' Hashimoto said. 'Shanghai is a resting place. The Emperor wants to break the Chinese people's will to resist. Your agents in Nanking are to spread stories of a million-man Japanese army of death-dealing samurai descending on their capital city. The Ringo News Agency there is secretly owned by the Ishikawa zaibatsu. Use it! Strike fear in the Chinamen's hearts! Get them to flee the city!'

'I hope you won't be held back at Shanghai,' Ando said. 'Chiang has his best troops stationed there.'

'Since we signed the Anti-Comintern Pact with Italy and Germany, both countries have reduced weapons sales to China. Most of Chiang's artillery in Shanghai was made fifty years ago. Some of his men carry muskets, others only swords. Madam Chiang Kai-shek commands the Chinese air force. What can a woman do against the imperial Japanese air force?'

24

Raiko had not seen Kenji for three months. At the army air base a show of affection would have been out of order, but even in the car he made no move towards her, and seemed relieved when she started the engine. She watched him out of the corner of her eye. He had lost twenty pounds. His face was drawn and tight, like that of a fighting hawk. His eyes were too bright, constantly moving. His hands rested in his lap, but he repeatedly clicked his thumbnails. Raiko drove out of the main gate and turned left.

'Aren't we going to the apartment at the Fifth Moon Inn?' Kenji asked.

'I've rented a villa while you're on leave.'

He sighed. 'It will be good to bathe and get these clothes off. I've been sleeping in them. Madam Chiang Kai-shek gave us a hard time. At our first briefing General Kingoro Hashimoto laughed at her. He ridiculed the idea of a woman commanding the Chinese air force. That was before our attack on Shanghai. He didn't laugh after that.'

'Everyone here at headquarters thought Shanghai would fall as quickly as Peking.'

'It went wrong from the beginning,' Kenji said. 'Our amphibious troop landing was supposed to be a surprise. Ha! In late August General Matsui put 35,000 men ashore in Hangchow harbour under cover of a morning fog. The Chinese were waiting with a crack artillery regiment. They killed hundreds of our men before the fleet's big guns came into action. Hino was navigator for the bomber raid from

Formosa. They were supposed to blast the Chinese army units protecting the approaches to Shanghai, but Madam Chiang's fighter planes tore our bombers apart. Out of eleven planes in Hino's group, his was the only one that returned to base. We don't know how the Chinese could have intercepted that raiding party.'

'I do,' Raiko said.

'The bombers flew from Formosa over the Pacific and the Chinese fighter planes were waiting. It was an ambush!'

Raiko took one hand off the steering wheel and gently rested it on Kenji's. He stopped clicking his nails and looked at her. 'How did they do it?'

'Major Ando is again behind enemy lines,' Raiko said. 'He reported a primitive but effective aircraft warning system set up by General Claire Chenault of the Flying Tigers. The general has civilian plane spotters all along the coast to Shanghai, and inland to Nanking. They flash light signals, set bonfires and use local telephones to relay the information to Madam Chiang. She sticks pins in her map until the direction of the planes becomes clear. Then she sets up an intercept point for her fighters.'

'Our bombers zigzag towards their target so as not to give it away.'

'But they continue in a general direction,' Raiko said. 'I recently deciphered the American army weather code. General Stilwell provides Chenault with it twice a day. The winter cloud formations restrict your targets. Chenault and Madam Chiang use the combination of direction, weather reports and experience to predict your destination. Then she sends up her planes.'

'She certainly does,' Kenji said. 'We had to change our tactics because of her. All bomber missions that miss their rendezvous with our carrier-based fighters are aborted. Why didn't our intelligence tell us of this Chinese spotter system?'

212

'I personally gave Major Ando's message to army-air-force intelligence.'

'Well no-one told the navy.'

Raiko sighed. 'There's fierce inter-service rivalry among the bureaucrats of both services. I see it every day.'

'I know there's pride in both the army and the navy, but it's hard to believe someone would withhold information like that. Our bombers don't have a chance against the Russian I-14 Yak fighter planes. Our T-97s are superior to the Yaks in a dogfight, but the bombers aren't.'

'We had no T-97s at Taierchung,' Raiko said. 'There, Russian pilots flying I-15s ruled the sky and proved your theory that superior air power determines the outcome of land battles. Mao Tse-tung's Eighth Route Army cut off three of our armoured divisions sent north to capture the Lunghai rail-line. With the support of the Yak fighters, the Communist troops surrounded our units. They destroyed forty of our tanks, seventy armoured cars, 100 trucks, and caused us 16,000 casualties.'

Kenji pulled his hand from Raiko's and slapped the dashboard. 'We never heard about that!'

'Tojo doesn't publicize his mistakes here or at home.'

'He should have warned us about the Russians flying for Mao. They fight differently than the Italian-trained Chinese pilots.'

Kenji and Raiko rode in silence over the snow-covered road.

'What is happening in Japan?' Kenji asked.

'The government raised the conscription age to forty. The price of rice has doubled and the yen devalued by fifty per cent.'

'It sounds grim. Have you heard from Ruth Kuhn?'

'She's settled in her house overlooking Pearl Harbor,' Raiko said. 'Her father stays with a woman at a bungalow near Hickam field. Their reports have been confirmed as accurate by other agents. One piece of information Wantabe considers important from Ruth is that the Pacific fleet peaks in training during June and August and reaches its lowest point of efficiency from November to February.'

'Did she mention why that is?' Kenji asked.

'Because the fleet docks at Pearl Harbor for repairs in November. It's a tradition to spend Thanksgiving and Christmas holidays in Hawaii. I wouldn't mind spending a vacation there.'

'What have you been doing while I've been away?'

'I've been listening to the latest battle reports from Shanghai and praying you were safe.' Raiko wanted to stop the car and throw herself into Kenji's arms, but she could see that he was still far away from her. She braced herself once more, and asked, 'Have you seen any American Spitfires?'

'No Flying Tigers yet.'

'Why did it take so long to capture Shanghai?'

'The Chinese were unbelievably brave. They attacked with human waves in mass formations. Our men fired until their machine-gun barrels melted. They cut the Chinese down in rows, and the rows grew to hills. The Chinese climbed over their dead, until no-one was left. Then the next unit attacked.' Kenji shuddered. 'In the city they fought from house to house, despite their primitive weapons. Camel muskets. Nineteenth-century muzzle-loading cannon. Long, two-handed Manchu swords. Can you believe it? Our men collected the antiques. But until their final surrender, the Chinese didn't give an inch without a battle.'

Raiko pulled the car up to a small villa on the outskirts of Mukden. She turned and kissed Kenji gently on his cheek. 'I saw the reports detailing your negotiations that saved a quarter of a million Chinese soldiers and civilians.'

Kenji snorted. 'I was only an errand boy. John Whitte-field deserves the credit. He thought up the idea and

214

arranged for the other foreign consuls to guarantee the cease-fire.'

Raiko put her hand on Kenji's arm. 'I decoded General Hashimoto's request to slaughter those unarmed people.'

'Tojo couldn't allow him to do that. Shanghai is the largest international city in the world. Each foreign embassy there has a large marine contingent of its own. If Hashimoto had killed the refugees, Japan would now be at war with half a dozen Western countries, including the United States. Our troops were wonderfully disciplined. General Matsui saw to that.'

Raiko led Kenji to the villa's door. This was not the time to tell him about the Emperor's appointment of Prince Higashikuni over General Matsui. 'Come,' she said. 'There's a hot bath, a good meal and a warm bed waiting.'

Kenji looked at Raiko as if for the first time. 'I forgot to kiss you.' He took her in his arms and held her tight. 'I dreamed about holding you again. I prefer the warm bed first, please.'

Raiko laughed. 'We're going to spend a long time in that bed. But,' she wrinkled her nose, 'you smell like an old goat. And you feel like a skinny goat. You'd better wash and eat. You'll need all your strength. I've waited too long for you.'

The days in the snow-covered villa passed quickly for the lovers. While they whispered and caressed, the imperial task force moved closer to the Yangtze delta and the Necklace. When the aircraft carriers were in position offshore, Kenji and other pilots would be recalled to duty. The attack on the Nationalist capital of Nanking was swiftly approaching.

Kenji said nothing of his departure. Raiko remained silent about Prince Higashikuni's special orders to Generals Hashimoto and Nakajima, fearing that if she told Kenji and he objected publicly, Tojo would have him

215

killed. Others who learned of the orders and protested had been assassinated.

Raiko sipped champagne from a glass Kenji held for her. They listened to a recording of Amaryllis by Yeast and she saw that the hard lines of his face had softened. They always did after sex. She was proud of her ability to do that for him.

'You promised to tell me the story of Genda and the flying bear,' Raiko said, and rested her head in his lap.

He laughed. 'So you want the bear facts.'

'I hope this story is better than your jokes.'

'Bearly.' He tickled her, then stared into space for a few minutes. Raiko waited.

'We were flying from a makeshift airfield in close support of an infantry battalion,' Kenji said. 'They were stymied by a tough Chinese unit at a key position outside of Shanghai. The battalion commander drove back to the airfield and told us our divebombing and machine-gunning were ineffective because the Chinese trenches were ten to fifteen feet deep. When they heard his artillery fire or our planes approaching, they simply jumped off the parapets and huddled in their bunkers. Then, when our infantry attacked, the enemy would pop up and cut them to pieces. This was one of the few Chinese units with modern weapons and enough ammunition. Genda told the battalion commander he had heard of a dead bear in the area. He had an idea to solve the problem if the infantrymen would bring the bear to the airfield.'

'If this is going to be a gruesome story, I can't bear it.' Raiko giggled and curled up on Kenji's lap.

He kissed her, and continued, 'The animal belonged to a travelling circus and had been frightened to death by the noise of the guns and bombs. We helped Genda strap the bear into the front seat of a two-winged spotter plane. Genda dressed the bear in his aviator helmet, goggles

216

and long silk scarf. He stuck a big cigar in its mouth, gave us our instructions, then took off. Flying low and slow over the Chinese lines, he scrunched down in the rear cockpit. It looked like the bear was flying the plane. The Chinese fired a few shots until they caught sight of the aviator bear. Genda, still huddled down out of sight, flew back and forth until the entire Chinese unit stood on top of the parapets waving at the flying bear. Genda pulled on a rope tied to the bear's paw and it seemed to wave back. Then he trailed a smoke grenade over the trenches and the Chinese must have thought it was part of the show. Actually he was marking the trenches for us. We were flying with oxygen at 35,000 feet several miles away. We cut our engines, glided down, and our bombs caught those Chinese still waving at the bear. Then our infantry moved across the field without casualties and took the position.'

Raiko applauded. 'What happened to the bear?'

'Some of our men wanted to eat him, but the infantry commander convinced us we couldn't eat a comrade in arms. He said the bear deserved a party. We stood him in the corner with his aviator's uniform on, pinned medals to his chest, and toasted him until we were all drunk. At morning formation we promoted him to sergeant. He was buried with full military honours and a three-gun salute.'

The sound of a motorcycle engine stopping outside the villa brought Kenji to his feet. At the door he spoke to a messenger and returned to Raiko.

'I'm to meet with General Tojo, then lead a squadron to rendezvous with our aircraft carriers. The navy is going to fight its way up the Yangtze river to Nanking. The army will move overland from Shanghai. We'll fly cover.'

Raiko tried not to show her distress. 'I'll drive you to the Fifth Moon Inn and then to the airfield.'

* * *

217

Raiko waited for Kenji outside Kwangtung army head-quarters. She had inquired about a Shinto shrine to pray for his safe return. He came towards her, tall and handsome in his uniform, and she held back her tears. 'Was it important?' she asked.

'Tojo thanked me for allowing Major Ando the use of my Ringo News Agency in Nanking. Chinese civilians are already jittery from the propaganda.'

'They should be. They're all going to be killed.'

'Not civilians,' Kenji said. 'General Matsui's troops are well-disciplined. Their conduct in Shanghai was praised by the foreign press.'

'The Emperor has placed his uncle, Prince Higashikuni, in overall command of the attack on Nanking. I encoded the message. Matsui will be held responsible for whatever happens, although he doesn't know the plan.'

'What plan?'

'To break the will of the Chinese people by punishing the inhabitants of Nanking in such a way that in the future all Chinese will flee rather than fight the Japanese imperial army. I saw secret orders from the prince to Generals Hashimoto and Nakajima. They're to make an example of the inhabitants of Nanking that will never be forgotten.'

'Why would such an order be given?' Kenji asked.

'Everyone knows we can't rule the vast area of China or the multitude of its people by force. Prince Higashikuni has decided the way to do it is by fear. Our defeat by the Communists at Taierchung, and the determined defence by the Nationalists of Shanghai, have convinced imperial headquarters in Tokyo that the Chinese capital of Nanking must be destroyed. Only that will bring Chiang to the peace table.' Raiko took Kenji's hand. 'There is nothing you can do to stop them. If you try, Hashimoto, Tojo or someone else will order your death. Please come and pray with me at the nearby Shinto shrine.'

Kenji squeezed Raiko's hand. 'Let's also light joysticks

at the Buddhist temple on the way to the airport, in honour of our wedding. I received permission from the Cherry Blossom Society. And General Tojo has agreed to a special leave for you, me, Genda and Hino after the capture of Nanking.'

25

8 December 1937, Nanking

An aide to General Wu opened the office door. 'Sir, time for your 2 p.m. appointment with Mr Takeshita of the Ringo News Agency.'

'Send the reporter in and be certain we are not disturbed!'

The door closed behind the visitor. 'Major Ando, where is my gold?' General Wu asked.

'How soon is it possible to evacuate your men?'

'Immediately.'

'Excellent,' Ando said. 'Do it! Move your troops far from Nanking! The Third Imperial Fleet is moving up the Yangtze, 150 miles away. If your men are in their bunkers when our ships arrive, the River of Sorrow will live up to its name!'

General Wu unholstered his pistol and pointed it at Ando. 'Where is the gold?'

'At Barclays Bank,' Ando said. 'Two hundred thousand sterling was accredited to your account this morning.'

The general dialled with one hand while covering Ando with his pistol. He spoke rapidly, and waited. Then nodded and put down the receiver. 'The deposit is confirmed. Now, what prevents me from killing you and keeping the money?'

Ando smiled. 'The continued well-being of your wife, three children, your mother and father.' He threw a slip of paper on the desk. 'Call this number and speak to them.'

The general dialled again, this time with a shaky hand. He spoke and his ashen face confirmed the kidnapping. He put both the telephone and pistol down. 'Major Ando, there are rules, even in wartime.'

'Doesn't that phrase sound foolish?'

'Have you no scruples?'

'Not when it concerns my country,' Ando said, and placed a small box on the desk. 'Your father's little finger. You'll recognize the ring.'

With trembling hands the Chinese general opened the box, and gasped. He glared at Ando. 'I should kill you.'

'Tens of thousands will die in Nanking. I've saved your family by holding them. That is, if you co-operate.'

'You chopped off my father's finger.'

'A surgeon used anaesthetic. The lives of your loved ones, a million dollars in gold, all for a little finger. It's a bargain.'

'You want the Necklace too,' General Wu said.

'Without your co-operation, our fleet might be held up for several hours.'

'We could blow your navy out of the water.'

'A million dollars is a lot of money to sacrifice for a son of a bitch like the generalissimo,' Ando said. 'I learned the finger trick from his secret service. Think of your family.'

General Wu summoned his aide. 'Issue orders to evacuate the Necklace!'

'Sir?'

The general pointed his pistol at the aide. 'I want all our units out of their positions and aboard trucks with full equipment and five days' food! In four hours! They're going to defend the gorges of the Upper Yangtze.'

'Yes, sir!' The aide saluted, did an about-face and left the office.

'Where will you go?' Ando asked.

General Wu collapsed in his chair and put his hands over his face. 'Chinese is spoken in Singapore. A British crown colony has to be the safest place from you bowlegged bastards!'

'I've memorized the maps,' General Stilwell said. 'Tell me.'

'The Necklace has been abandoned,' John Whittefield replied. 'My agents report General Wu's men are moving up the Yangtze river and the general has flown south to Singapore with his family.'

'Where are the Japs?'

'Encircling Nanking. General Matsui sailed by the Necklace and landed two infantry divisions for a frontal assault on the city wall. Hashimoto is attacking from the west to the Yangtze. Nakajima came from Shanghai with his Black Division by railroad. They're closing the trap from the east to the river. Nanking will soon be cut off.'

'What about the Chinese army?' Stilwell asked.

'The retreat from Shanghai became a full-scale rout,' John said. 'Japanese agents propagandized the soldiers; saboteurs terrorized them. Only Chinese irregulars with primitive weapons have resisted. Their villages are being burned and their towns razed. Chiang Kai-shek is prepared to flee Nanking. He'll defend the Upper Yangtze and make Chungking his new capital.'

'The generalissimo has ordered his men in Nanking to fight to the death,' Stilwell said. 'He asked me to direct them. I told him the city is indefensible, that he should set up an in-depth line of bunkers, trenches and pillboxes behind the city. Chiang refused. I refused to direct his army and now his people will suffer.'

'Chiang's aim is to engage the world's attention,' John said. 'He wants Western nations to stop the Japanese while he crushes the Communists.'

'Would he sacrifice thousands of people and allow the destruction of his capital city?'

'I've heard Chiang brag he's prepared to lose fifty million dead before he would consider negotiating with the Japanese,' John said. 'And I know he'll never stop until the Communists are crushed. He accepts the fall of Nanking. Chinese civilians have begun evacuating the city. Those who remain are too poor or too rich to leave. Looting has begun. There are rumours of a million-man Japanese army descending on Nanking.'

'Propaganda,' Stilwell huffed. 'The Japs were outnumbered two to one when they took Shanghai. The odds will be about even in Nanking.'

'I received a personal message from Kenji Ishikawa,' John said. 'Prince Higashikuni was appointed commander of all Japanese forces in China. Nakajima and his Black Division are with the prince.'

'Nakajima was chief of the Japanese National Secret Police. Do you know the prince's background?'

'He's the Emperor's uncle and has been out of favour at the imperial court for some time. Hirohito sent Higashikuni here to redeem himself. He's a professional soldier whose speciality is thought control. He believes Japan's destiny is to dominate Asia and wage eternal war with other races. There's a cryptic sentence in Kenji's message that I don't understand. "The Black Division of Nakajima may be the Black Tent of Tamerlane." Does that make sense to you?'

Vinegar Joe Stilwell pursed his lips and hummed several bars of 'The Skaters' Waltz'. 'We've got to evacuate all Americans,' he declared. 'Civilians, military, embassy personnel! Get everyone out of Nanking immediately!'

'Do you know the meaning of Kenji's message?'

'Most military men have heard of the Black Tent of Tamerlane,' Stilwell said. 'It explains why the Japanese are trying to surround Nanking. They want to make it an example for all Chinese. Tamerlane's Mongols encircled many cities in the fourteenth century. He would camp in front of the city gates in a white tent. That was called the Siege of Mercy. All who surrendered were spared. When Tamerlane used a red tent, it meant that only women and children who surrendered would be spared. The Black Tent of Tamerlane meant that everyone would die. My God, I understand the Jap plan! Peking was the white tent, Shanghai the red tent. Nanking will be death to all!'

'The Japanese wouldn't dare kill foreign nationals too!' John said.

'From what you tell me, Chiang Kai-shek would give his eye teeth to have that happen. He wants the Western powers involved.'

'I doubt we'd fight, even if Americans are killed,' John said. 'It's why the State Department calls what's happening the China Incident. According to the US Neutrality Act, if we labelled this a war we'd have to cut off weapons supplies to both China and Japan. China would suffer more than Japan and the American economy would suffer worse than both. Our government's policy places the American economy before world peace.'

'We could avenge American deaths through groups like your Flying Tigers. Where is Chenault now?'

'Hamstrung by the British. They sent the Spitfires back to England. Hitler's invasion of the Sudetenland and Italy's annexation of Ethiopia has the British Foreign Office worried. Secretary of State Hull approved the transfer of two dozen P-40s from our bases in Manila to Chenault here in China. Chenault has been training his men day and night.'

'Chiang will need all the planes he can get in this war,' Stilwell said. 'If Kenji Ishikawa's comparison between Nakajima and Tamerlane is correct, thousands of Chinese are going to die. Possibly foreign nationals too. Order the gunboat *Panay* and the three Socony oil tankers it

224

was escorting to come back down-river! Take our people out of the city and on to those boats. Tell the other embassies! The British can bring the gunboat *Ladybird* to evacuate their people. Be certain all barges and boats are clearly marked with flags flying and painted on the decks! Evacuate immediately!'

'Kiioootz-kai! Attention!'

Five hundred officers and men of the First Imperial Air Wing snapped to attention as General Hashimoto and his staff marched out on to the parade field. The general stopped before a microphone.

'Warriors of the Wind, I salute you! Since the fall of Peking and Shanghai, the government of Nationalist China has embarked on a vicious anti-Japanese campaign throughout Asia. Japanese store owners can no longer do business. Japanese women are accosted on the streets in full view of Chinese police! Our children are beaten in Chinese schools! This must cease!'

Kenji, Genda and the men in ranks had read and reread the headlined stories of atrocities committed against Japanese civilians in China. Asahi newspapers detailed the horrors of each event, accompanied by photographs. Kenji did not care for Kingoro Hashimoto, but was moved by the man's words.

'The Chinese people shall be taught a lesson,' Hashimoto declared. 'Nanking will be destroyed! You pilots of the imperial air force have the honour to strike the first blow against the capital city of the warmonger Chiang Kai-shek! China's leaders will learn to act peacefully and live in harmony with their neighbours! No longer will the British and Dutch rule over Asians! It is time for the people of Asia to feel the benevolent rays of the Rising Sun! We have come to illuminate China with the radiant light of his imperial majesty's wisdom and goodness! Each man here is an eternal spark emanating from the Emperor, the direct descendant of the Sun Goddess Amaterasu! The gods created Japan and you are their heavenly messengers!'

Kenji recognized the general's speech as illogical, yet a fierce pride swelled his heart. He balled his fists and raised them to the sky, shouting with the others, 'Banzai! Banzai! Banzai!'

Hashimoto lowered his voice and cooed, 'I call on the memories of your blood. I call on the memories of your ancestors.' His voice grew stronger with each word. 'We are the product of 2,500 years of inbreeding. We are a warrior race meant to rule! With one voice,' he shouted.

'One voice,' the airmen echoed.

'One blood,' Hashimoto cried.

'One blood,' the airmen roared.

Tears of pride filled Kenji's eyes. He looked to Genda, whose cheeks were wet. They both threw their fists in the air again. 'Banzai! Banzai! Banzai!'

'Ground crews prepare for take-off,' Hashimoto ordered. 'Let no man disgrace the Emperor! Pilots, man your aircraft!'

The cabin of his plane was a world of its own for Kenji. A world he had designed and help build. He slid the canopy closed, adjusted the scarf Raiko had given him and led his squadron out. General Hashimoto, his staff and the ground crews lined up along the runway. They bowed to the planes. A red smoke rocket whooshed up into the winter sky.

Kenji gunned his engine and roared down the tarmac, feeling perfect bliss when the wheels left the ground. His body and mind were in tune with his machine. Below, the landscape was bathed in golden sunlight, a sign the goddess Amaterasu was giving her blessing. The doubts Kenji had harboured about the morality of his orders to destroy Nanking were gone. He would avenge insults to the Emperor and his people.

Kenji thumbed up the cover on his control stick and

pressed the button to test-fire his machine guns. He formed up his squadron to the right of Genda's, and led them over the Yangtze. Radio silence would be maintained until they reached the Chinese capital. Kenji's target was the Nanking railroad yards. Genda's objective was to support the army. Squadrons three and four were flying cover.

Five minutes to Nanking, fifteen Yaks flew out to engage the T-97s. Kenji laughed when they turned tail. 'They probably never saw eighty Japanese fighter planes at one time,' he said aloud. He sight-checked his squadron. Their discipline was good. No one chased the fleeing Chinese planes. Looking down, he saw black puffs below, but could neither feel the concussion of the shells nor hear the air bursts. The Chinese anti-aircraft guns lacked accuracy.

Kenji could see the confluence of the Grand Canal and the Yangtze river. He switched on his radio. Genda was already transmitting, and pulling his squadron away to support the infantry. Squadrons three and four began a climb to 30,000 feet.

'First Squadron, prepare to attack,' Kenji said into his microphone. 'I have the Nanking railroad yard in sight. There are enough targets for all. Be selective! The order of priorities are moving trains, oil and ammunition dumps and repair shops. If you miss your target on the first run, fire your machine guns to get the feel of your gun range and speed! Prepare to attack in line! Form a step formation to my left!'

The nineteen planes lined up in the air. 'Banzai,' Kenji shouted, and peeled off into a power dive, followed, one after the other, by the T-97s of the First Squadron.

Kenji spotted a steam engine snaking through the Nanking storage-yard. It trailed smoke over a long line of fuel tankers. His eyes never left the train as he swooped down and lined his sights on the caboose. He thumbed the fire button and his machine-gun bullets tore up dirt and track to the right of the train. Kenji let his plane slide to the left so he was directly behind the caboose, and pressed the button. Neither the roar of his engine nor the pounding machine-guns entered his consciousness. He concentrated his entire being on bringing his tracer bullets to bear on the line of fuel tankers.

Suddenly a hole appeared in Kenji's instrument panel and a spray of wood splinters brushed his face. He heard a sharp whap-whap of bullets hitting his fuselage. He saw the muzzle flashes of several machine-guns firing from in between the fuel tankers. He sent a long burst of tracer bullets walking up the train into the car behind the steam engine. The high-octane fuel ignited and the car exploded into a huge fireball. Other cars piled into the burning wreckage.

The force of the explosion bounced Kenji's plane 200 feet up and over on its back. For a moment, flying upside-down, he lost his bearings. He pulled hard on his control stick and the T-97 rolled right-side up. About to climb for a better view of his men and the railroad yards, a voice shouted in his earphones from the Third Squadron. 'Yaks! Yaks at ten o'clock high!'

'Escape tactic one,' Kenji shouted into his microphone. 'Escape tactic one! Evasive action! Bandits at ten o'clock high!'

Like a flock of frightened starlings, the men of the First Squadron dived, climbed and wheeled their planes as if to run. Kenji reduced his speed so he was last leaving the air space over the railroad yards. Behind him, the Yaks were coming up fast. Have I misjudged, he wondered. The single-seat T-97s had no rear guns. He and his men appeared vulnerable. Kenji pushed his throttle forward to the limit. Tracer bullets whizzed by his cockpit and the hair on the back of his neck stood up. Then, suddenly, aeroplanes with the orange fireball of the rising sun were whizzing by him. He looked back and saw Yaks spinning out of the sky. The trap had worked. The Third Squadron had caught the enemy from above.

'First Squadron, turn and attack,' Kenji ordered. 'Attack! Attack!'

26

Kenji's crew chief scrambled up on to the aeroplane's wing and pulled back the cockpit canopy. 'Didn't see any new bullet holes.'

'It's been quiet the past few days,' Kenji said. 'No Chinese interceptor planes. I keep busy shooting up ground targets and supporting the infantry. The Chinese pilots turn tail when they see our T-97s.'

The chief helped Kenji from the plane. 'Flying Tigers knocked down eleven of our bombers and five T-95 escort fighters. Your cousin Hino had to jump.'

Kenji's stomach rolled over and he swallowed the bile in his throat. 'Did he make it?'

'Chinese farmers found him and treated him like a hero. They thought he was a Chinese pilot from another province who spoke a different dialect.'

'They must have seen the plane's markings.'

'Those yokels never saw an aeroplane, or even a car up close. They think all enemies have white skin and round eyes. They also believe all Asians are Chinese. They showed Hino the body of an American pilot they killed after he parachuted. Hino said the man was wearing a leather flight jacket with the Nationalist flag on it. But the farmers didn't recognize it, or any other flag.

'Where's Hino now?'

'On his way back to Formosa. The Chinese helped him return to our lines. He caught a ride here and Genda gave him a party in the mess hall. We stuffed him with food and whisky and had to carry him on to the plane, he was so drunk.' The crew chief pulled an envelope from his coverall pocket. 'This was hand-delivered by a pilot from Manchuko.'

Kenji's heart leapt. The handwriting was Raiko's. He sniffed the perfumed letter, but waited until he was alone in his room to open it.

My dearest Kenji,

I will send this letter via a member of the Cherry Blossom Society because I don't want the censors to read my personal thoughts. It is also to protect your uncle and Wantabe, who have relayed certain information you should know. The Kempetai has begun to censor internal mail. Even letters of men in positions as high as Uncle Hiroki are being read by the secret police. Wantabe has made additional enemies by openly opposing this. He says the patriotic fervour sweeping Japan has convinced parliamentarians that consolidation of the secret societies will result in more efficient intelligence gathering. Wantabe claims the flood of information, unless properly directed, will cause chaos in the National Intelligence Service. He requests that you use your influence to keep the Cherry Blossom Society independent. Uncle Hiroki is unable to help as he is out of favour at the imperial palace. He attends cabinet meetings but since national military headquarters was relocated on palace ground, has not been invited to any planning sessions. He is quite sad and cannot understand the reason for this situation. I am certain he would enjoy hearing from you. I would too. I listen to the daily flight plans and know your combat assignments before you leave the ground. We have a large floor map with wooden blocks indicating our planes in action. I watch their movement, do much praying, and cry when one is taken off the board. Then we all watch the casualty list. I constantly think of bear jokes to tell you but know you couldn't *bear* my humour. It has only been two weeks since you left but seems much longer. I miss you in bed beside me in the morning when I awake, and especially at night. After work, I drive to the airfield and watch the planes landing. They remind me of you. I drive home and hold imaginary conversations with you. My work here has taken on more importance since I know it can help you. My colleagues at the Fifth Moon Inn do

231

not appreciate the sign I have placed over my desk. 'There is no man-made code a woman cannot break.'

There are several professional pleasure girls whom I lunch with. They are very nice and have given me some pointers which I am waiting to try on you. Ruth Kuhn had one of our people deliver a letter to me. She describes Hawaii as paradise. The fleet is in for the winter holiday. Lawn parties every day, cocktail parties in the evenings, formal balls and ambassadorial receptions at night. She supplies us with good information about the Pacific fleet, and has contact with the German Embassy there. The Nazi advisers to Chiang Kai-shek have been ordered to influence him to make peace with Japan, in order to allow the Kwangtung army to attack Russia through Mongolia. Ruth sends you a special message about German aeroplanes. The Luftwaffe has developed a series of superior fighter planes built by Messerschmitt. Junker produced the Stuka divebomber. That's being used in training with ground forces in a tactic called *blitzkrieg* – a swift, sudden, overwhelming attack. Ruth reports rumours that the Heinkel company is testing an aeroplane engine that doesn't need a propeller. It supposedly shoots air out the rear in jets strong enough to propel a plane at speeds close to that of sound. The aviation experts here at headquarters have discounted the information as fantasy. I wrote my father and asked him to question the scientists at Tokyo University.

Kenji stopped reading and searched his memory for information of a propellerless plane. He was reminded of the Buck Rogers movies he had seen. He read on.

More important to you and me, after our adventure at the British Embassy in Peking, is Otto Kuhn's report. Ruth's father keeps an open house for American pilots from Hickam field. He learned that the British have withdrawn the Spitfires from China. Secretary of State Hull rushed twenty-four P-40 fighters from Hawaii to Manila and on to General Chenault in China. Otto saw the P-40s. They have heavy metal bodies, are equipped with new self-sealing fuel tanks, and have tiger-teeth painted on both sides of the nose section under the propellers.

Kenji scribbled a note to himself. He would ask his American agents to uncover the secret of self-sealing fuel tanks. Raiko continued:

The P-40 carries four fifty-caliber machine-guns, two on each wing and two small, rapid-fire cannons in its nose. These planes sound very formidable to me and I pray you will not meet them in battle. Uncle Hiroki reports strong opposition in the cabinet and National Diet to any proposals of restraint on the army. The Emperor, he says, spends less time in his laboratory and more at military headquarters.

Here at the Fifth Moon Inn, the few of us who know the contents of Prince Higashikuni's orders to Hashimoto and Nakajima are sworn to secrecy. The people of Nanking will be slaughtered. In preparation for the news of that event, Kempetai has ordered all foreign magazines, journals and newspapers coming into Japan, Korea and Manchuria to be stripped of offensive articles. Radio stations and newspapers here and at home must clear everything with a government censor. I recently heard that all those soldiers imprisoned for the coup attempt last year were released. The public hasn't been informed of this. In the past two weeks, Prince Higashikuni has begun circumventing General Matsui. Matsui complained to Tojo, but nothing has changed. Only today I encoded important orders to Generals Nakajima and Hashimoto and no copies were sent to Matsui. The Year of the Bull appears to be raging its way out. I hear the ferocious roar of the Year of the Tiger preparing to enter, and I fear Japan will be disgraced in the eyes of the world by our army's actions in Nanking.

My most important message is to tell you how much I miss you, how much I long for you. Your tender touch and soft warm words are absent. I constantly relive our horseback rides, the picnics, the thrill of watching you land your plane, our time in that marvellous villa. I think of you and me in that villa most of all. When Noriko telephones me, we speak mainly about the wedding arrangements. She always asks when you will get leave and I must keep repeating it will be after the fall of Nanking. Then we are both silent. I dream of the two of us on the China

Clipper heading for Tokyo and then I worry about the pitiful Chinese people in that forsaken city of Nanking.

Kenji wondered how he could send Raiko an uncensored letter. If the Cherry Blossom Society was about to be taken over by Kempetai, he dared not trust any of the agents. When he had reread Raiko's letter, he put a match to it. He would warn her not to take such a chance again. He took up his writing kit, and laughed as he thought of a bear joke to include. But first he would give her positive news of Nanking.

10 December 1937
Dearest Raiko,
The Year of the Bull will march out with honour and the Year of the Tiger roar in with pride. The twenty-eight-mile-long, sixty-foot-high wall protecting Nanking was breached yesterday by our men. The Chinese army has all but disintegrated. Three-quarters of the Nationalist forces and the civilian population of Nanking have fled. Many of the remaining Chinese soldiers have discarded their weapons and uniforms.

General Matsui withdrew our troops for the night and issued orders to all officers and men to respect the rights and interests of all peoples when they enter Nanking tomorrow morning. There will be no plunder. Violators shall be severely punished. The most promising note is that General Matsui outranks both Nakajima and Hashimoto. Best of all, Nakajima was hit with a bullet in the buttocks by a Chinese sharpshooter. I doubt he will resume his seat of command very soon. Can you *bear* my seat joke?

'If either of you grins, smirks or even thinks this wound of mine is funny, I will kill you,' General Nakajima said. 'We shall talk standing!'

'We are not here to discuss your arse,' Hashimoto said. 'I invited Major Ando to join us in planning the destruction of Nanking.'

'That cannot take place while Matsui is here,' Nakajima said.

234

'Sir, Prince Higashikuni has requested General Matsui's presence in Shanghai,' Ando replied. 'General Hashimoto now commands the navy and air force. You, sir, are to send your Black Division into Nanking.' Ando handed both men their orders. 'The objective of this operation is to break the will of the Chinese people. They must learn never to resist the Japanese army. You are to spread fear through China by your actions here.'

'Good riddance to that lily-livered Matsui,' Nakajima said, rubbing his hands together. 'Foreign correspondents must be free to take pictures and report uncensored news.'

'I expect that would bring harsh reactions from the West,' Ando said.

'To hell with the West,' Hashimoto said. 'Hitler is right. Foreign diplomats will cry foul, ring their hands, and do nothing. They sat by for three months in Shanghai watching the street fighting as if it was a tennis match. They'll do nothing! Look at this feeble attempt to coerce Japan.' Hashimoto thrust an Asahi newspaper towards Nakajima and Ando. 'This is a translation of Roosevelt's speech in Chicago last week. He's calling for other nations to quarantine Japan. Even his own American industrialists are against it. The great Henry Ford for one.'

Nakajima tapped the article. 'This is a continuation of Roosevelt's policy of Ring Fence.' He turned to Ando. 'Major, I think we should kill that crippled bastard.'

Ando choked. 'The president of the United States?'

'Why not? He's the commander in chief of their armed forces.' Nakajima pointed to his rear end. 'If I can take a bullet in the arse, that round-eyed American devil can take one in the head.'

Ando looked at both generals, expecting them to laugh, but neither did. 'I'll inquire into the possibility,' he said, thinking to send a request to Tsubota in Saigon, then forget it. He stifled a sigh of relief when Hashimoto changed the subject.

'The reign of terror inside the walled city of Nanking will be initiated by men of the Black Division,' Hashimoto said. 'Looting should appear spontaneous and uncontrollable. However, all loot will be left at one of the seven gates of the city each night. The quartermaster corps will have storage areas, trucks and men to catalogue and handle the goods. Military police will be there to see that no one lines his pockets. Saleable items will be shipped abroad to pay for Kwangtung army expenses. Food will go to our commissary for use here and in Manchuko. Military equipment to be evaluated and packed for shipment to India. Tsubota has agents in Calcutta working with revolutionaries against the British.'

'The killing might take longer than you think,' Ando said. 'I found shooting 600 unarmed men a complicated task. People don't die so easily, and there are a quarter of a million soldiers and civilians inside the walls of Nanking. Some will still have weapons.'

'I've pulled the navy back from the river to make it appear the easiest escape route,' Hashimoto said. 'At the right moment, I'll turn our planes and motorized river launches loose. The small boats have been fitted with machine-guns and light artillery. The air force will burn out sections of the city, using incendiary bombs on the wooden houses. My artillery-men will cover both the river and the city.'

'In the Black Division, we trained our men in fear tactics,' Nakajima said. 'Also in the use of bayonets, knives and clubs. There is fierce rivalry between our units. We don't have to kill everyone. The best method of spreading fear is through eye witnesses. Half the population remaining in Nanking are women. We can kill the very old, the infants, and rape the rest. The survivors will be driven out of the city. They'll wander the countryside and spread the tale of Nakajima's Black Division.'

'Sir, there are still remnants of the Nationalist army

within the walls who are armed and under orders of capable commanders,' Ando said. 'We took 40,000 casualties in the Shanghai street fighting.'

'Our air force will drop these leaflets,' Hashimoto said, picking up a package from his desk. 'They promise amnesty to all who discard their weapons and go to the neutral zone located in the foreign quarter.'

'Most Westerners have left Nanking,' Ando said. 'My agents report only twenty or so teachers from the missionary college and as many doctors and nurses from the Christian hospital have remained behind. No neutral zone has been set.'

Hashimoto handed the package to Ando. 'These leaflets have maps denoting a half-mile square around the missionary complex. Chiang Kai-shek left sixty tons of grain and rice with his Christian friends before he ran. They can feed the people and promise them safety. That's what Christians love to do.'

Nakajima limped forward, grinning. 'Show those leaflets to John Whittefield on the US gunboat *Panay*. He negotiated the neutral zone in Shanghai. The Chinese will respect his word.'

'I've met this Whittefield,' Ando said. 'He's no fool. I would like permission to bring in Captain Kenji Ishikawa. He negotiated with the American for the zone in Shanghai.'

'Issue the orders for Ishikawa, the neutral zone and anything else you may need,' Hashimoto said.

'I'll bring them for your signature,' Ando said.

'Not necessary.'

'Who will sign?' Ando asked.

With the grin still plastered on his face, Nakajima said, 'General Matsui will sign.'

'But he's on his way to Shanghai.'

'Use a forger to duplicate Matsui's signature. We did just that on those amnesty leaflets you are holding.'

27

Pilots of the First Imperial Air Wing filed into the lecture hall. They bowed to the general on the stage and remained standing. General Hashimoto stared at his watch. When the sweep hand reached its peak at exactly 5 a.m., he stepped to the podium.

'Be seated!' The general waited until all the young faces looked up at him. Then, in a strong, deep voice trained on the parade grounds of Japan, Korea and Manchuria, he spoke to the hearts of the fliers.

'Fellow warriors! Samurai of the modern era! The moment of truth is at hand! Hear now the story of two brothers, China and Japan, who were bequeathed a rich and fertile valley. When hard times came upon the land, the older, stronger brother, China, ignored reality and lost himself in opium dreams. He stole from his workers, disregarded his children and allowed his land to lay fallow. Japan, the younger brother, worked a small corner of the valley. From sunup to sundown he and his family, day after day, year after backbreaking year, tilled the soil. For centuries they irrigated the land and enriched the earth. And they prospered. The younger brother was blessed with many children. But, like a potted plant without enough room for its roots, he saw starvation ahead for his large family. The small plot of land was no longer enough to support them. The younger brother approached his older brother. "Allow me to help you," Japan said. "Together we will return this valley to what it once was so that your people will prosper and mine will live." China sucked his opium pipe, pointed to his white Christian advisers and answered, "I have brought them in to repair the damage." "Have you no shame?" the younger brother cried. "They are of different blood. For 200 years these white barbarians have kept you drugged. They have stolen the treasures of this great land." The older brother smoked his pipe and began to doze. "The inheritance of this valley was yours by right of birth," the younger brother said. "Now I have come to claim it by moral right!'"

Hashimoto slammed the podium. 'Warriors of the Wind. Japan, the younger brother, has come to take his inheritance which has been so badly abused for so many centuries! We will return the fertile valley to its former glory! The Chinese people will benefit from our guidance. The battle for Nanking is a fight for survival of Japan and all China. If we succeed in instilling enough fear into our older brother, we can wean him from his opium. We will cleanse his body of the foul drug and purge his mind of foreign influences. We will show older brother how to live in the modern world and prosper. Older brother is too big to be forced, his family too numerous. He can only be controlled by fear! That, my warriors, is your mission! Strike terror into China's heart! Cause panic to rain down from the skies!' Hashimoto bowed and stepped back. 'Major Ando will now brief you on the most crucial battle of our campaign!'

'Gentlemen,' Ando said. 'There are a quarter of a million Chinese soldiers and civilians remaining in Nanking. Yesterday the great wall around the city was breached. Today, at 7 a.m., General Nakajima's men will enter Nanking and drive the enemy towards the Yangtze river. In order to avoid costly street battles, such as took place in Shanghai, it was decided to withdraw our navy down-river, leaving the Yangtze open as a means of escape for both Chinese civilians and Nationalist army deserters.' Ando did not mention that his agents and contingents of marines were stationed far up-river to block the escape. Nor that General Hashimoto was positioning artillery along the banks of the river to seal the city. 'For this operation, squadrons one and two will be incorporated into squadrons three and four.'

Genda turned to Kenji. 'Why are we relieved of duty?' Kenji shrugged. 'Listen.'

'All four squadrons will rendezvous with our bombers from Formosa and escort them over the target!'

'Why so many fighters?' a squadron leader asked.

'The Flying Tigers have taken a heavy toll on our aircraft,' Ando said. 'Until we can devise a winning tactic against their formations, we must maintain air superiority.'

Kenji wondered why the Japanese pilots were being defeated. Even the T-97s, which were faster than the American P-40s, had been downed in aerial dogfights.

'Our bombers will be carrying incendiaries tonight,' Ando said. 'Guide them to the Sun Yat-sen tomb, the Peace Gate and the Gate of Tranquillity. The bombs will be dropped in a line inside the wall. The evening wind should drive the fire and the people in that part of the city towards the river.' Ando bowed. 'I wish you good fortune. Your flight leaders will give you more detailed instructions. Captains Genda Arai and Kenji Ishikawa, please join General Hashimoto and me in the office.'

'You two have special and separate assignments,' Hashimoto said. 'Captain Genda, Sir Hugh Huggesen and the British Ambassador will be travelling from Nanking to Shanghai in about three hours. They have requested permission to pass through Nakajima's front line at nine this morning. When they do, Ando's agents will notify the control tower. Take a wing man from your squadron and destroy their automobile!'

'How can we recognize the car?' Genda asked.

'It's a Rolls-Royce,' Ando said. 'It will have two English flags flying from the front fenders and one lashed to the boot. Nakajima's men will make certain it's the only car on that stretch of road. Shoot the hell out of it!'

'Why?' Kenji asked.

'Sir Hugh and the ambassador have been negotiating with the Soviets in Mongolia,' Hashimoto said. 'They want the Russians to create an incident on the Mongolian border to take the pressure off China, and protect British holdings in Canton.'

'But we're not going as far south as Canton,' Kenji said.

Hashimoto ignored Kenji's comment and addressed Genda. 'Your strafing attack on the ambassador's car will be labelled an accident of aerial identification. It will send Tojo's message to the West. Stop meddling in Asian affairs!'

'What is my assignment?' Kenji asked.

'Accompany Major Ando,' Hashimoto said. 'You'll contact John Whittefield aboard the USS *Panay*. Arrange a neutral zone for the safety of civilians and unarmed Chinese soldiers, as you did in Shanghai.'

A great weight lifted from Kenji's heart. Raiko was wrong. Japan would not be shamed. The slaughter she predicted would not take place. 'Is it possible to inform the Chinese people of the neutral zone before the fire-bombing this evening?' he asked.

Hashimoto's and Ando's eyes met. 'We've prepared leaflets,' the general said. 'I'll see they are air-dropped this afternoon.'

Aboard the USS *Panay*, the radio operator handed John Whittefield the microphone. 'It's General Stilwell for you.'

'Sir, how is Chungking?' John asked.

'Like a Chinese fire drill. Everyone's blowing bugles and banging pots and pans, but no one is doing a damned thing. The generalissimo has established this city as his new capital. He's determined not to negotiate with the Japs. What's happening in Nanking?'

'Most of our nationals are safe aboard the *Panay* and the Socony oil tankers. A few remain in the missionary compound.'

'Is there any sign of the Black Tent of Tamerlane?'

'There's been no slaughter,' John said. 'We're receiving confusing signals from Japanese actions inside and outside the city. General Matsui withdrew his troops last night after routing the Chinese from the city wall. Except for a few rapes and killings, which is normal in Asian warfare, nothing exceptional has happened. Today at noon leaflets, bearing maps indicating a neutral zone around the missionary complex, were dropped from the air. I'm meeting Kenji Ishikawa at 2 p.m. to formalize the zone with an inspection of the area.'

'That sounds positive,' Stilwell said.

'There are rumours that Nakajima's Black Division took 10,000 Chinese prisoners outside the city gates last night. They're supposed to have driven the prisoners to the river's edge and shot them.'

'All 10,000?'

'My informants say the Japanese ran out of ammunition and 4,000 escaped. We heard shooting all night, and saw hundreds of bodies float by this morning.'

'When you reach the missionary complex, ask the people there to document any misconduct by Japanese troops,' Stilwell said. 'Photographs would be best.'

'One of the confusing things about this situation is that the Japanese, who are always hostile to the Western press, have issued passes to reporters and provided guards to protect them. The press people have freedom to move around.'

'Sounds as if the Japs have nothing to hide.'

'I've personally witnessed instances of Japanese soldiers humiliating white men and performing unnecessary body searches on white women in front of a camera,' John said. 'It's as if they want their gross actions to be recorded.'

'You're the Jap expert.'

'Excuse me, sir, there's an urgent message being received from the HMS *Ladybird*. I'll read it as it comes in. "11 December 1937. Sir Hugh Knatchbull-Huggesen and the British Ambassador to China have been gravely wounded. While travelling on the Nanking–Shanghai road, the ambassador's automobile was machine-gunned by Japanese fighter planes."' John paused. 'Second part of the message coming through. "For greater safety of British civilians aboard the HMS *Ladybird*, the ship is proceeding down-river to an anchorage near the USS *Panay*."'

'Tell the Brits to fly their flags and keep all ships lit at night. You have forty minutes before you meet Ishikawa. Draw him a map indicating the exact location of the *Panay* and the tankers so the Jap air force can't claim an identification error. Watch Ishikawa closely when he accepts the map. Listen to everything he says for a hint of betrayal.'

'Not Kenji,' John said.

'Listen to me,' the general said. 'Ishikawa may be your friend! He may have studied in the good old US of A! But he's still a Jap! His country comes first! Just as yours does for you!'

John took the launch ashore rather than meet Kenji on the USS *Panay*. Some Americans aboard had witnessed atrocities. Their women had suffered at the hands of Japanese soldiers. There were several men who swore to kill any Japanese they saw.

At exactly 2 p.m., a Japanese staff car pulled up to the Nanking dock. John joined Ando and Kenji in the rear seat.

'It's good to see you again,' Ando said. 'I hope we three will be as successful today as we were the night we stole the Spitfire plans.'

'And I hope the machine-gunning of the British Ambassador and Lord Huggesen was a mistake,' John said. 'To be certain no errors of identification occur on the river, I've drawn this map. It indicates the exact location of the USS *Panay* and three Socony tankers, all carrying American citizens who fled the fighting.' John handed the map to Kenji, but Ando reached over and took it.

'I'll give this to my driver,' Ando said. 'When he leaves us off, he'll rush the map to General Hashimoto.'

The staff car moved from the dock to the sixty foot city wall, and made a circle around the city.

'Although that wall was built in medieval times,' Ando said, 'its twenty foot thickness and notched brick ramparts presented problems for our modern artillery.'

'We're passing the Flower Gate,' John said. 'Isn't it the closest entrance to the missionary complex?'

'Yes. But there was heavy fighting here last night. General Matsui's troops are cleaning up. The black smoke is coming from the burning bodies of Chinese and Japanese soldiers.' Ando pointed at two Buddhist priests walking towards the gate. 'We allow them to work with the Chinese dead as well as ours. We'll enter through the Great Peace Gate. It's fitting for a mission such as ours to pass Sun Yat-sen's tomb. Most people don't know that Japan helped him overthrow the Manchus. Now we're fighting Sun Yat-sen's protégés, Chiang and Mao.'

Kenji saw the battle flag of Nakajima's Black Division as the car passed through the big gate. Suddenly the stench of burnt flesh caused him and John to gag. They covered their noses and mouths with handkerchiefs. Kenji studied the area, thinking it would look different after the fire-bomb raid. He saw only dead Chinese civilians lying in the street, and many live Japanese soldiers stalking the alleys. He sensed that behind the bullet-pocked walls of houses and shuttered stores, many people hid.

The driver slowed to pick a path around rubble and

more dead civilians. He stopped several times to allow armoured cars and light tanks to pass.

Ando seemed oblivious to the smell, and spoke as if he was a tour guide. 'This is the old Ming palace. Here is Government House and the central railroad terminal. We'll soon be at the Christian Staff College. I've asked for Westerners to meet us there, but first we'll have to change cars. We've halted our advance to allow the Chinese to reach the neutral zone or leave the city.'

A mile from the missionary complex, the car was stopped at a barricade. 'We go the rest of the way in a Red Cross vehicle,' Ando said. 'It's been arranged under a flag of truce. The Chinese commander of this area is aware of our mission.'

On the other side of the barricade, Kenji saw people crouching in doorways, running from house to house in the direction of the missionary grounds. The broad street was littered with bodies and leaflets. A line of Japanese soldiers stood along the barricade, methodically working the bolts of their Murato rifles as they picked off moving targets. They shot at wounded lying in the street.

'They're even shooting at children!' Kenji pointed to a group of youngsters. Screaming in terror, they stumbled from one side of the street to the other, tripping over bodies.

The Japanese infantry officer at the barricade looked at his watch. 'Two minutes before the cease-fire goes into effect.'

John counted seven more people killed. He grabbed the officer by the lapels of his uniform jacket and lifted him off the ground. 'Stop this senseless killing! Those are not soldiers out there!'

'Mr Whittefield, do not move,' Ando said. 'The lieutenant has a pistol pointed at your stomach.'

Kenji saw white spittle at the corner of the officer's mouth. His eyes were glazed with hate. 'John, release this man,' Kenji said softly. 'Lieutenant, put away your pistol. There is no honour to be gained in killing an official of the American government.'

The officer stepped back and spat on John's shoes. He leaned forward and sneered in John's face. Whistles screeched and, still holding his loaded pistol, the lieutenant shouted, 'Three p.m. Cease fire! Cease fire!'

Ando and Kenji hustled John around the barricade towards a Red Cross car. 'What is happening?' John asked. 'Are they mad? I've never seen Japanese act in such a manner.'

'I have no answer,' Kenji said. 'Only another question has occurred to me. If the people are free to leave via the river, why are they being shot? Why is it necessary to set up a neutral zone?'

Ando avoided Kenji's eyes.

28

'There's been no word from our embassy or you in three days,' General Stilwell said to John Whittefield. 'And why did a German-speaking radio operator contact me for you?'

'I'm under the protection of the swastika. The German Embassy is the only safe place in Nanking with a radio transmitter powerful enough to reach you in Chungking. The German Ambassador has been kind enough to make this equipment available.' John cleared his throat and Stilwell cleared his, an unrehearsed signal by both men acknowledging the monitoring of their conversation by the Gestapo.

'The ambassador and what is left of his staff are on their way to Chungking,' John said.

'What happened?'

John's hand gripped the radio microphone and began to shake. 'The Jap bastards sank the *Panay*, burned the Socony tankers, shelled the *Ladybird* and then machine-gunned us in the water.'

Stilwell heard the agony in the younger man's voice, but he needed accurate information. 'Tell me what occurred from the time you left the *Panay* to arrange the neutral zone!' the general said.

'Never thought I would hold the Japanese in contempt.' John gulped. 'My family was involved with Japan before Perry opened up their country 100 years ago.'

'Mr Whittefield,' Stilwell snapped. 'Your report! Make it now!'

John rubbed his forehead and knuckled the tears from his eyes. 'It's more than contempt. The Japs are

247

a disgusting, dishonourable, filthy, murdering bunch of lying bastards!'

'Man, get hold of yourself! Remember who you are and where you're at! What happened when you went to set up the neutral zone?'

John looked around the radio room. His eyes settled on the swastika under Adolf Hitler's photograph. In a monotone he began describing the trip into the walled city of Nanking – the shooting of innocent civilians, the dead bodies in the streets. 'There was a sign posted on the Japanese barricade. THE BIRTH PLACE OF PEACE IN ASIA. We went by it on the way to the missionary compound. What a joke.

'Sixteen Americans and six Germans with swastika armbands remained there. The Japs allowed us to move freely. They were helpful in setting up the zone. We used coolies to mark off the half-mile square with white flags. Kenji Ishikawa took me aside and asked that I leave and use my agents to warn the Chinese. He told me there would be a fire-bomb raid that evening from Sun Yat-sen's tomb to the Gate of Tranquillity. One of my agents informed me that Nakajima's men were pulling out of that area, which confirmed Kenji's information. I did as he requested. At 9 p.m. I returned to the *Panay*, in time to see a large force of Japanese bombers set fire to the northern part of Nanking. The night breeze drove the fire and the people fled towards the two river gates, the only escape routes from the city.

'I climbed up into the crow's-nest with binoculars. At 10 p.m. Hashimoto's heavy artillery opened up on the Lower River Gate. With the fire illuminating the scene, it was like watching a living portrait of Dante's Inferno. The high-explosive shells rained down on the crowd at the gate and the survivors panicked. They rushed back through the streets to the Upper River Gate. The collision of people fleeing the fire and those running from the shelling caused pandemonium. Cars, trucks and rickshaws jammed up.

Some overturned and caught fire. People trampled each other to reach the river. I saw the pile of dead at the city gate grow to a height of fifteen feet. People rushed to the city wall overlooking the river. Some jumped, and died. Some were pushed to their deaths on the rocks below. I saw Chinese soldiers try to lower people down to what they thought was safety. They made ropes of their belts, their leggings. They tore clothing into strips.'

John sobbed for a few moments, then continued. 'At the river's edge a fleet of junks and sampans waited to take the refugees, but there weren't enough boats. The fear-crazed mob swarmed over them. The Chinese boat captains shot at the mob trying to board, but the captains were overwhelmed. Many boats capsized. Thousands drowned. Some junks got away and started upstream, leaving tens of thousands stranded at the river's edge. Then Hashimoto's big guns opened up. A devastating, accurate artillery barrage that walked up the mud banks, driving people back, trapping them against the high city wall. I saw people climb back up over the pile of dead, through the city gate, into the oncoming fire.

'Then Japanese motor launches roared by the *Panay*. By the glow of Hashimoto's artillery flares, I could see the launches were fitted with heavy machine guns and light cannon. I watched those bastards slaughter the people in the unarmed boats. We monitored the Jap radio messages ordering the launches upstream to catch those refugees who had fled days before. I learned that Japanese commandos had blocked a narrow passage upstream. It would be another slaughter on the river when the launches caught up with the fleeing refugees.' John sobbed. 'I took a bottle of Scotch to bed with me.'

'Take a drink now before you continue,' Stilwell said over the radio.

'No, sir. I want to tell this stone sober. I hope you're taking notes. My report must be forwarded to Washington.'

249

'I am,' Stilwell said.

'I woke late Sunday, after morning church services. Eight of the *Panay*'s officers and all the civilians had gone to visit friends aboard the three tankers. It was a sunny 12 December. Except for the corpses floating by, muffled small-arms fire and black smoke drifting over Nanking, it could have been a beautiful winter's day. The *Panay* had two large American flags painted on her decks fore and aft. Three big ceremonial flags flew front, back and centre. Because I had a luncheon appointment with the captain at two, I checked my watch. It was 1:38 p.m. I saw three Jap planes flying up-river. They were two-winged bombers with the orange ball markings. I watched them dive at us and saw the bombs detach from their undercarriages. The first bomb was a complete miss. The second hit close to the starboard side and knocked a hole in the hull. The third was a direct hit on the bow. It blew our three-inch gun into the water. The radio shack, sick bay and pilot house were demolished. I woke up draped over the port rail with minor injuries. The captain was down with a side full of shrapnel. The first officer had a piece of metal in his throat, but he took command by writing out his orders.'

'Had you given Ishikawa a map of the location of the *Panay*?'

'Major Ando took the map from me and sent it directly to General Hashimoto. This attack was no case of mistaken identity. It was deliberate. Before we recovered from the bombing, six slow-flying Jap biplanes wheeled over the *Panay*, dove and strafed us for twenty minutes. Every one of the line officers aboard was wounded. The first officer wrote the abandon-ship order at 2 p.m. We manned the lifeboats and the planes began strafing the tankers. I saw two burning. The third ran aground to avoid sinking. As we pulled towards shore in the lifeboats, three Japanese launches approached the *Panay*. Her decks were awash but they boarded her, set demolition charges, then stood off. The explosion broke her back and she sank. Then the launches fired on the *Ladybird*. She was hit but fled up-river. The launches came after us. We were transferring wounded to the bank of the river when they began machine-gunning us. They caught a boatload of the *Panay*'s Chinese staff in the water and cut them to pieces. I heard a Japanese officer calling it a duck hunt as he shot at the heads of Chinese bobbing in the water. We hid in the reeds along the river bank for two days. I made it here to the German Embassy and arranged for the USS *Oahu* to rescue the remainder of the crew.'

'How many casualties?' Stilwell asked.

'Twenty-two Chinese dead, four navy officers killed and fifteen critically wounded. Sir, we've got to pay them back! This attack on Americans should be the start of a war with Japan!'

'I doubt that. Roosevelt will express his concern and shock, but he won't declare war. The German-American lobby and the anti-war movement in America are too strong. The AF of L and the other labour unions helped them collect twenty-five million signatures.' The general paused and John heard a swift intake of breath. Both realized that the Gestapo had just heard a senior officer in the United States army give a first-hand evaluation of American foreign policy. 'We'd best end this conversation,' Stilwell said. 'Are you alright?'

'I've got two broken ribs and a bullet hole through the calf of my leg, but I can get around.'

'Not in China. I want you out of there now! Ambassador Grew needs your advice in Tokyo. That's an order!'

'I have the snapshots you requested of the party,' John said, hoping the general would understand. 'Where do you want them sent?'

'Show them to Grew. They'll be my Christmas present to him. Tell the ambassador the Japs are making a tactical mistake in China. They've swallowed their own propaganda of being invulnerable and unbeatable. Tell the ambassador the sun that rises must also set.'

Bitter tears stained the letter under Kenji's pen

Dear Uncle,

I am sending this letter by a trusted friend who is flying our wounded back to Tokyo. I have just returned from three days inside the walled city of Nanking. A sign there reads THE BIRTHPLACE OF PEACE IN ASIA. But what I saw resembled Rodin's sketch of his door sculpture 'The Gates Of Hell'. The four black crows of death – the Emperor's uncle Prince Higashikuni and Generals Hashimoto, Nakajima and Tojo – have cast their shadows on the city. The map given Major Shira Ando in my presence by John Whittefield, which designated the locations of four US ships carrying American civilian refugees, was used by General Hashimoto to locate and bomb those ships. Our fanatic general may have started a war with America. Certainly he violated Bushido, our military code of honour. I confronted him and his reply was, 'Let the Americans, the British and any other round-eyed bastards challenge Japan and see what they get.' It was useless to argue with him. 'Honour,' he said, 'is between Japanese. Not to be wasted on foreigners.' When I questioned the economic implications of the bombings, Hashimoto answered, 'Roosevelt has already influenced other foreigners to implement his policy of Ring Fence. As for Japan, overpopulation in time of war is an advantage. Soldiers get paid the same in the barracks as on the battlefield. The army speaks with guns, not dollars.' Then he had me escorted out of his office. His aide told me that the combination of Roosevelt's 'Quarantine Speech' in Chicago, and Britain's agreement in Europe with Soviet Foreign Minister Litvinov to boycott Japanese products, sent Hashimoto into a rage. If a Russian gunboat had been on the Yangtze, he would have sunk that too.

In your last letter you mentioned army headquarters being relocated in the palace. And that the Emperor has taken to wearing a uniform. I did not believe those rumours that his majesty is directing this war until I

252

had time to think it over. The Emperor supposedly postponed the invasion of China, but he agreed to national conscription. He jailed the rebels last year but quietly let them go so they could lead the conscripts who were rushed to China. Our army crossed the Chinese border, presumably against the Emperor's wishes, but he did nothing, nor reprimanded anyone involved in the shooting of the British Ambassador. He relieved men like yourself and General Matsui, placing Prince Higashikuni in charge of taking Nanking. All general orders still carry Matsui's name, although the prince issues them. I recognized the prince at the barricade inside the walled city, wearing a gauze mask as if he had a cold. I believe it was to conceal his identity as well as keep out the smell of rotting bodies. The tactics used by our men in the taking of Peking, Shanghai and the drive to Nanking were masterpieces of military strategy, equal to the accomplishments of the greatest armies in history. But what is taking place in Nanking now makes me want to burn my uniform. The strategy of the four crows is to be so ferocious that fear will freeze the hearts of the Chinese people everywhere. Hashimoto claims such a policy worked for the Mongols. I asked if he equates Japanese with Mongolians. That was when he threw me out the second time.

I personally witnessed atrocities committed in Nanking in the past three days. On Saturday, John Whittefield, Major Ando, members of the missionary group here and I arranged a neutral zone where any unarmed person could enter and be safe. Outside the zone, our soldiers killed Chinese men, women and children without reason. There was no lack of Western photographers to record those scenes, and no restrictions by our army on the press. Ando disappeared and I took John Whittefield to safety from Nanking. At the railroad station he photographed dead bodies. One scene of a lone crying child sitting between the rails, remains with me. I feel as if that child is me. My heart weeps.

My squadron led the fire-bombing raid. I told John it would come in the evening and he warned the civilian population of that area. But there was really nowhere for them to run. Nakajima withdrew his men from the target area and 4,000 Chinese rushed into an unfinished tunnel near the railroad station – a quarter-of-a-mile-long tunnel with only a few air vents. The bombs didn't hit them but the heat from burning buildings, the fuel depot and nearby warehouses was so intense, oxygen was sucked out of the tunnel. Everyone in there was asphyxiated. Four thousand innocent people. After the flames died down, Nakajima's men re-entered the city and used 'dozer-tanks to seal the quarter-mile-long tomb.

The Black Division had orders to rape, loot and kill. At first the commands were implemented with military discipline. Squad leaders selected several women and tied them down. The streets of the city not levelled by the fire-bombing were filled with people fleeing in every direction. The men waiting in line to use the women were encouraged to shoot into the crowds. On the second day, Nakajima's officers instituted bayonet practice. The soldiers rounded up groups of people and stabbed, slashed and hacked them to death. They raped and degraded the young women, then let them wander off to spread fear. I saw our troops throwing little Chinese babies into the air and spitting them on bayonets. Even Nakajima's men couldn't continue the slaughter while sober. Their officers encouraged them to drink.

All that while, the neutral zone was respected. More and more Chinese soldiers threw away their weapons and entered the zone with the civilians. Outside, Nakajima's men turned to drunken sport with thousands of samurai swords that suddenly appeared. The availability of those swords took forethought and planning. Contests were held to see who could split a live Chinese from head to bellybutton. Competitions were held between units and the scores were published. Under the guidance of their officers, Nakajima's men drove captives, like cattle, down to the river. The soldiers doused the people with kerosene, set them afire and bet on which ones would reach the water alive.

Early on the morning of the third day, despite my protests, Nakajima's men entered the neutral zone. They systematically searched the thousands of refugees for money and valuables. At noon, all Chinese males, no matter their age, were bound hand to hand with communication wire and led down to the river. All afternoon we heard the banzai cry before each bayonet charge into the helpless captives. I forced my way down there with the German military attaché. 'Dozer-tanks were pushing piles of dead and wounded into the river. Machine-guns raked the thousands of men and boys until no one was left standing. I protested and was driven back to the air base in handcuffs. My escort told me that Nakajima's 80,000 men would surround the neutral zone that night and be allowed a week-long party with the women. Then Hashimoto's division would be brought in for a rape party. The escort pointed out truck loads of whisky entering the city. 'To help the men lose any inhibitions they might have,' he said. I asked him how he, a schoolmaster from Osaka, could participate in such actions. 'Orders,' he said. 'I receive my orders from a senior officer who is a representative of the Emperor. I taught my students to obey his imperial majesty. How could I disobey?'

Must I obey, Uncle Hiroki? Must I commit these terrible deeds? I don't believe in the gods. I thought I believed in the Emperor, although not as a god. Actually I don't know what to believe any more. Please inform the Emperor that Prince Higashikuni has ordered the 'Rape of Nanking' to continue for thirty days. My last memory of that city is the fat dogs wandering the streets – bloated from feeding on so many corpses. Do something, please, Uncle Hiroki. For the honour of Japan, please do something!'

Outside Kenji's building the alert bell sounded. 'Squadrons one and two, fall out immediately!' the loudspeakers blared. 'Escort duty! Fly cover for the First Imperial Bomber Squadron from Formosa!'

'Hino's squadron,' Kenji mumbled. He snatched his flight jacket, put the letter in the writing kit, then froze in place. 'Am I going out to continue the butchery in Nanking? Or do I leave my cousin and his bombers unprotected against the Chinese fighter planes?' Kenji looked into the mirror fastened to the back of the door. For a moment he saw his own haggard face. Then his reflection blurred and he heard John Whittefield's last harsh words ringing in his ears like a death knell. 'You'll do as ordered. A Japanese shows his courage by conforming, not rebelling.'

29

'You look like a turd.' Genda laughed and slapped Kenji's shoulder. 'When did you sleep last?'

'If our mission is to Nanking, I'm not going.'

'Your temperament matches your looks.'

'No jokes,' Kenji snapped. 'Where's the target?'

'Chungking. Our first raid on the new Nationalist capital. Hino is leading the bombers from Formosa. I'll guide them with the T-95s to the departure point and you'll take over from there.' Genda examined his cousin's face. 'You don't have to go. You have more flight time than anyone in the squadron. Get some sleep instead.'

Kenji brushed Genda's hand away. 'No sleep. I might dream. I couldn't survive that.'

'To survive this mission you'd better listen to what Hino told me about the Flying Tigers that shot him down. The P-40s are slower than our T-97s, but their guns and armour are heavier. They can take lots of hits and still fly. They're sluggish in the turns, but can blow our planes out of the air with a few short bursts of their machine-guns or repeating cannons. He said their tactics resemble von Richthofen's Flying Circus.'

'What does that mean?' Kenji asked.

'We were drunk and I forget. It didn't make sense to me either.'

'Nothing makes sense,' Kenji said. He turned and walked to his plane, climbed into the cockpit and took his lunch sack from the crew chief. He tucked Raiko's scarf around his neck and twirled his finger in the air. The engine cranked, backfired, then roared to life. The chocks were pulled from under his plane's wheels. Kenji led the First Imperial Fighter Squadron out on to the runway.

'*Ding how!* Work together!' The motto of Chenault's civilian Chinese aircraft spotters had sounded several times in as many minutes at Nationalist air-force headquarters in Chungking. Madam Chiang Kai-shek's thin, willowy body leaned over the topographical map of China. Senior military officers crowded around the beautiful leader of China's air force as she studied the latest US army meteorological report. She touched the map with an elegantly tapered fingernail and said, 'Enemy fighters proceeding south from Foochow. Enemy bombers reported moving in from the west over the island of Quemoy.' She turned towards the radio operators. 'Alert all available interceptor aircraft, our anti-aircraft batteries and Chenault's Flying Tigers! Prepare for battle! I know exactly where the enemy bombers will strike! There is only one opening in the cloud cover within the fuel limit of the Japanese bombers from Formosa. Chungking is their target! We'll be waiting!'

The Fifth Moon Inn

'General, Miss Raiko Minobe says it is imperative she speak with you.'

Tojo nodded, and his aide motioned to Raiko. She entered the office and bowed to the general. 'Sir, I beg your pardon for the interruption. Only you can issue orders to break radio silence and recall our bombers from the flight to Chungking.'

'Why should I do that?'

'Some time ago I deciphered the US army meteorological code. Today's US weather report to Madam Chiang indicates that Chinese interceptors and anti-aircraft guns will be waiting for our planes.'

'How could they know?' Tojo asked.

Raiko pointed to a wall map. 'Chungking is the only target in a westerly direction over mainland China that isn't closed in by clouds.'

Tojo came out from behind the desk and studied the map. 'You are certain of this?'

Raiko nodded and Tojo took her by the arm, leading her from his office to the communications centre. With a snap of his fingers, he caught the senior officer's attention. 'Colonel, contact the commander of the raid on Chungking!'

'Break radio silence?'

'Do it!' Tojo said. 'This is top priority! Order them to abort their mission and return to base!'

The colonel took up a microphone and switched radio bands. 'Flying Dragon, Flying Dragon. This is Golden Lion calling Flying Dragon. Answer please.'

Over and over, the colonel sent out the abort signal, but there was no response.

'Come with me,' Tojo said to Raiko. She followed him into the planning room. They stood to one side and watched.

The floor was covered by a large map of China. People stood around its perimeter using long sticks to push blocks of wood. Each block represented one of the forty fighter planes and thirty bombers moving towards the city of Chungking.

The communications-section chief entered and passed a message to the planning section's commander. At the commander's order the long sticks reached out, sweeping half the fighter escort blocks back, north towards Nanking.

'What is happening?' Raiko asked.

'Genda Arai's squadron is using the older planes,' the commander said. 'They don't have the range for Chungking and are returning to Nanking.'

'Kenji will be trapped,' Raiko cried. 'Why doesn't he answer your call?' She choked back a sob.

The commander pointed to a red line on the floor map. 'Captain Ishikawa and the bombers have gone beyond the power of our transmitters.'

'Why didn't he answer?' Raiko cried.

The thirty Mitsubishi bombers and forty fighter-plane escorts moved steadily across the heartland of China under grey snow clouds, maintaining strict radio silence. Only Genda, at the head of the formation, heard the Flying Dragon call, and assumed it was Madam Chiang's radio operators trying to confuse the formation. Kenji, as flight commander, had forgotten to inform him of the code word to abort.

They approached the Li river and Genda rechecked his map co-ordinates. From the departure line the second squadron would return to Nanking. He slid his cockpit window open and fired a red smoke rocket. He waggled his wings to Kenji, then flew past Hino's plane at the head of the bombers and waved goodbye. He re-formed the second squadron for the return flight to Nanking.

Kenji waggled his wings in response to Genda. He throttled forward into the lead, and watched his twenty planes take their new positions around the bomber squadron. It was another thirty minutes to Chungking and they were now flying above the low clouds. He ate part of the lunch packed by the crew chief and drank some miso soup from the thermos.

'I'm tired in the heart as well as the body,' Kenji said aloud. Then he laughed. 'I always talk to myself before an action. I'll be fine when the fighting starts.' He checked his instruments for the thousandth time. Against the colder air of the high altitude, he tucked the white silk scarf Raiko had given him around his neck.

Through thinning clouds, Kenji looked down at the

patchwork landscape of central China. There was a river below and he examined his knee map. It was the Jiang river, near the town of Baxia just outside Chungking. As he reached for his microphone to order a formation change in preparation for the bombing run, tracer bullets streaked by the front of his plane. Seven British Gloucester fighter planes, with the multi-pointed Chinese sun painted on their wings, dived past him. Kenji saw three of his planes peel off in pursuit. 'Good boys! Go get them!' Swivelling his head, he saw ten Yaks attacking the right flank of his formation, and was more surprised than concerned. His T-97s with their experienced pilots could out-fly and out-fight the older I-14s.

Kenji switched on his radio. 'Squadron leader to odd-numbered planes, chase those Chinese pests away!' He saw one of the Gloucesters cartwheeling through the air. Another trailed smoke. 'Bomber squadron, prepare to attack!'

'Reading you loud and clear,' Hino said. 'Keep your eyes peeled for those P-40s. They're slow in level flying but fast in power dives.'

'Bandits! Bandits!' a pilot shouted over the radio. 'Twelve o'clock high!'

'It's them,' Hino cried. 'Ten P-40s coming out of the sun! They're going after our planes chasing the Yaks!'

'I see them now!' Kenji said. 'Odd men, break off your attack and scatter! Take evasive action! Even-numbered, follow me! Attack! We've got our first crack at Flying Tigers! Banzai! Banzai!'

Kenji pushed his T-97 to full throttle and it swiftly closed on the nearest Flying Tiger. He fired two short bursts, then throttled down and flew alongside the P-40. Kenji, fully confident of his plane's superior speed and ability, waved at the American mercenary pilot. He reached for his camera and snapped a photograph of the shocked face in the all-metal plane with the tiger teeth painted under the bullet nose. This would be an excellent addition to his in-flight collection of new enemy models.

The P-40 dropped into a power dive and Kenji snapped another photo for aircraft-identification training. He returned the camera to its place and followed the Flying Tiger down, noting that it widened the gap between them in the dive.

'You've only got so far you can go down, then you've got to come up,' Kenji said. 'Then you're mine!' He pressed his radio transmit button. 'Men, get ready to call these Americans the Fleeing Tigers. Our airspeed is superior and we'll outmanoeuvre them!'

The sky seemed filled with diving, swooping planes. A dirty black cloud hung in the sky where a plane had exploded. Kenji caressed the machine-gun button on the control stick with his thumb as he watched the P-40 pull out of the dive and start to climb. Flying in behind, Kenji pressed his trigger button and his 7.7mm tracers poured into the metal plane. He kept firing, expecting to see the P-40 blow up, burn or break apart, but it kept climbing. Kenji forgot to throttle back and flew past the Flying Tiger. The pilot now waved at him, and fired a burst into the T-97's tail. Kenji raced ahead and veered off, with full confidence in his plane's ability to turn back on to the American's tail. There was another P-40 to his right. He rolled left and fired, but missed. Enemy tracers missed his plane. He pulled all the way back on the control stick, into a steep climb, feeling the tiger teeth behind him but certain of his escape. He could see Hino's bomber squadron being attacked by ten more Flying Tigers.

'Where the hell did they come from?' Kenji called into his radio. 'Squadron leader to odds and evens. Break off your combat and re-form around the bombers! I repeat, protect the bombers on the way to the target!'

'Too late,' Hino said. 'I recommend we abort this

mission! I've lost two planes! Three more have been hit! You've already lost several fighters!'

'How can that be?' Kenji asked. 'Only minutes have passed.'

'Bandits! Bandits!' Hino shouted. 'Out of the clouds from the west! Ten more Yaks! New model T-16s led by four Flying Tigers! We're outnumbered three to one! Time to go home!'

The cold chill that passed through Kenji's body came from the realization that he had led his squadron into a trap. Many more of his men would die if he did not get them out. 'Squadron leader to all pilots. This mission is aborted! Protect the bombers! Abort! Abort!'

Kenji pushed his plane to maximum speed, followed by four of his pilots. They flew towards the new formation of ten Yaks heading for Hino's bombers. The Yaks appeared oblivious to the five T-97s gaining on them from behind.

Kenji called off the narrowing gap. 'Two thousand yards, 1,000, 500 . . .' Suddenly a hole the size of a fist appeared in the cockpit canopy behind his head. Tracer bullets whizzed by. He saw six Flying Tigers diving on his formation and realized the Yaks had been a decoy. 'Trap,' he shouted. 'Trap! To the winds break!' Feeling a thrill of pride in his pilots at their execution of his escape order, Kenji held his position closing on the Yaks. The situation was dangerous, but still he was confident in his plane and his men.

The six Flying Tigers chased Kenji and his men in pairs, and two came diving on him. As if unaware of them, he fired a long burst into the formation of Yaks. He counted to three, then rolled his plane left and began to climb. Tracer bullets sprayed the place where he had been, and Kenji cheered. He looked around for Hino and the bombers.

Suddenly, Kenji's world exploded. The plane shuddered. It rolled and pitched. The front windscreen was blown away by machine-gun bullets. He lost consciousness and the plane dived. Cold air rushing through the shattered cockpit windows pushed Kenji's head back, driving cold air into his mouth, reviving him. Everything appeared in a haze of red. Realizing the roaring in his ears was the wind, he pulled back on the control stick to point the plane's nose up, but there was no response. He pulled harder on the stick and the T-97 shook as if it would break apart. He pulled with all his strength. Through the red haze he read the altimeter. Four thousand feet. He had dropped 16,000 feet! The plane stopped shaking. Its nose came up and levelled off at 2,000 feet.

Kenji listened to the engine. 'Still sturdy,' he said. 'I helped build you. If we've got to die, let's take one of those bastards with us.' He looked up, hoping to see a P-40 diving for him, hoping to try for a head-on crash. And for the first time realized he was wounded. 'I can't see,' he cried. 'I'm blind!' He tried to raise his left hand and pass it before his eyes, but could not. 'I saw the altimeter. I must have sight.'

Kenji touched his eyes with his right hand. The left eye mushy and sticky. He concentrated on the right, wetting his fingers in his mouth and cleaning. The instrument panel became clear. Then he saw his propeller. The end of the right wing was shot away. He looked again at the instruments. 'The altitude gyro must be broken.' He looked for the sky and saw earth. 'Damn it, I'm upside-down!' He tried to roll the plane over but his left leg would not work the rudder control. Pressing with his right hand on the bad leg, he straightened the aircraft and a searing pain shot through his head. He probed the left side of his forehead with the fingers of his right hand. There was an indentation in his skull. He could feel bits of bone and glass in the wound. The plane bucked and began to roll. Two more holes appeared in the right wing. Dirty puffs of smoke surrounded him. 'Anti-aircraft fire!'

He instinctively pulled back on the control stick and the plane climbed, but its response was sluggish. It's not fast enough to crash an enemy plane, he thought. I'll dive into the anti-aircraft guns, and he passed out again.

Kenji awoke a few moments later and looked around with one eye. This time everything was milky grey. I'm blind again, he thought. I'm dead. Then he laughed. 'I'm in the clouds. But where?' His altimeter read 15,000 feet. The engine was performing well. His head wound felt as if it was oozing, not bleeding heavily as before. 'Thank the gods the cold air rushing in has slowed the bleeding,' he said. 'Raiko, what a mess I'm in.' And the mention of her name made him realize he wanted to live. He tugged the scarf she had given him from his neck and unbuttoned the chin strap of his aviator's cap. He stuffed one end of the scarf into the cap, letting it hang over his wound. He pulled the cap down and tucked the other end of the scarf into the neck of his jacket, covering his injured eye and the side of his face. He fought the dizziness that threatened to engulf him.

'Where to go?' Kenji said. 'Where the hell am I? Best take a look.' He pressed the control stick forward, watching his altimeter and the rate of descent indicator. From 18,000 feet, it descended to 1,000 as he broke from the clouds. It took several minutes for him to recognize the Jiang river and Baxia. A direct line to Nanking was closer than the sea rescue teams off the coast of Foochow. 'I'm never going back to Nanking,' Kenji said, and pointed the T-97 towards the coast. 'I'm going further from you, my darling Raiko, but I don't want you to see me like this.'

Waves of nausea and weakness swept over Kenji as he flew. He attempted to concentrate on the key features of the land below. Black puffs of anti-aircraft shells exploded around him, rocking the plane. He preferred the chance of being hit again just to keep the ground in view, but knew he needed the colder air in the upper atmosphere to keep him conscious, to keep the wound from bleeding. He drove the plane above the clouds, and remembered his half-eaten lunch. He ate, drank the soup and regained some strength.

Kenji flew on, constantly checking his compass and his watch. From time to time, he dived under the clouds to see if he was on course.

He looked once more at his watch and saw that ten minutes had elapsed from the last time he looked. 'Either I passed out or I forgot the last time check. Must be losing blood from my wounds. Can't feel my left hand and leg. If I had more pain, I could stay awake.' He slapped his head wound and the streak of fire that shot through his brain caused him to scream. Tears filled his good eye. He gasped, passing in and out of consciousness.

Kenji awoke once more. He was flying upside-down only 500 feet above the ground. He righted the plane, then checked his compass and map against the rivers and roads below. 'Damn! I'm going in the wrong direction!' He did a mental calculation of his fuel reserve and the distance to Foochow. 'I'll never make that.' He swung the plane to the south east, heading for Nanking.

Nanking

'How did you get here?' Genda asked Raiko.

'General Tojo ordered a special plane to fly me in.'

'You know they were ambushed?'

'Is Kenji safe?' Raiko asked.

'Nothing definite,' Genda said. 'Hino called in on his way back to Formosa. He reported half our fighter planes had been lost when he left the formation. He saw Kenji's plane hit but it was still flying.'

'How many planes from the first squadron returned?'

'Six out of twenty,' Genda said. 'The rest have only

forty minutes of fuel left.' He saw Raiko's knees buckle and steadied her.

'Captain Genda Arai to the control tower immediately,' the base loudspeaker blared.

'Are you all right?' Genda asked Raiko.

'Yes. I'm going with you.'

They hurried across the tarmac, passed the hangars and went up the tower stairs.

'What is it?' Genda asked the tower chief.

'We may have something.'

'Tell me,' Raiko said.

'And who are you?' the chief asked.

'This is General Tojo's personal aide and intelligence adviser. She is also engaged to marry Captain Kenji Ishikawa. Stop the bullshit and tell us what's happening!'

'We have a garbled message from him. We've been tracking his plane by monitoring the reports of Chinese air-spotters. He's been all over the sky. Diving in and out of clouds, flying upside down and sideways. I think half of central China have come out of their farmhouses to report him.'

'Why didn't you tell me until now?' Genda growled.

'Because at least fifty enemy planes were up there looking for him. They've run out of gas now.'

'Kenji is almost out of gas too,' Genda said, pointing at the clock. 'Only thirty minutes left.'

'The Chinese could be setting another trap,' the tower chief said. 'General Hashimoto will allow only one volunteer to go out for Kenji.'

'Where should I look?'

'We'll relay the Chinese air-spotter reports to you. There's a plane warming up on the runway.'

Raiko grasped Genda's arm. 'Find him for me!'

'For me also,' Hashimoto said as he came through the tower door. 'Japan needs a samurai son like Kenji

Ishikawa. He shot down two Yaks before the Tigers got him.'

'They didn't get him yet,' Genda said, and ran out to his plane.

Raiko checked the tower clock as Genda lifted off. Kenji had only twenty-four minutes of fuel remaining. She and Hashimoto listened intently to the instructions given by the tower chief, and to Genda's terse replies. 'No sighting.'

'No sighting.'

'He's down out of the clouds again,' the tower chief said. 'The Chinese spotters place him over the Yangtze at Hexian. He must be trying to follow the river back to Nanking. That's only eighty miles from here. He's heading our way!'

'I'm in that area now,' Genda said.

Raiko stared at the radio receiver, willing Genda's voice to report he had seen Kenji.

And then Genda shouted, 'I've got him! Damn it to hell, I see him!'

There was silence on the radio. Raiko stopped breathing.

'By Buddha's red arse, that plane is shot to hell!' Genda reported. 'His tail and part of the right wing are gone! I'm pulling up along his right side. I can see him nodding off. His head is bobbing. It's covered with a big bloody bandage.'

'Keep him away from the river!' the tower chief said. 'The Chinese are readying anti-aircraft guns!'

Hashimoto grabbed the microphone. 'Genda, switch to channel five on your radio. That is the band Kenji was picked up on. We'll monitor your conversation from here.'

Hashimoto twirled the frequency dial and shouted into the radio. 'Captain Ishikawa, can you hear me? Come in! This is General Kingoro Hashimoto. Look to your right! Follow Captain Arai! Follow him! Do you read me?'

Raiko leaned close to the microphone. 'Kenji, don't give up. Stay awake.'

'I . . . I hear you,' Kenji murmured. 'Where's Genda?'

'I'm off your right wing, Cousin. Take a look.' Genda sang a verse of the American Negro spiritual, 'I'm comin' for to carry you home.'

'I see you, but I can't see well enough to land. I . . . I'm tired.'

Genda flew alongside Kenji's plane, talking to him, guiding him around the anti-aircraft batteries, keeping him headed towards the airfield.

In the tower, Raiko glanced away from the radio and down at the field. Every man on the base, including walking wounded, was out in front of the hangars staring up at the sky. The conversation between Kenji, Genda and the tower chief blasted out of the loudspeakers.

The chief dropped his binoculars and slammed the desk. 'I have your planes in sight,' he shouted into the radio. 'Keep coming!' He called into the loudspeaker microphone. 'Crash crews and ambulances, prepare for emergency landing and wounded pilot! He's coming in!'

'Give me the radio microphone,' Hashimoto said. 'Captain Ishikawa, what blood type are you?' he said into the radio.

'O,' the fading voice said.

Hashimoto snatched the loudspeaker microphone. 'This is General Kingoro Hashimoto. Every flight surgeon on this base will meet that plane with the crash crews! If this pilot dies, no doctor gets home leave for six months! Ten volunteers are needed with type-O blood. Prepare for immediate transfusions!'

Raiko saw hundreds of men rush forward to volunteer. She turned to go out but the bull-necked general gently placed a large hand on her shoulder. 'Remain here with me. We would only be in the way down there.'

Genda's voice shouted over the radio, 'Kenji, stay

269

awake! Do anything to keep alert! This landing has to be your best ever! Your right wheel is shot off and the left tyre is flat. I want you to begin to throttle back and reduce speed. Do you hear?'

'Batteries going dead. Your voice getting weaker.'

'Damn it, Kenji,' Genda shouted. 'You have no batteries in there! You're falling asleep! Stay awake! You're almost home! Throttle back! Throttle back!'

Everyone at the base waited. Finally Genda said, 'That's the way.'

Kenji realized what Genda was trying to do. He turned towards the plane off his right wing tip. 'Genda, I can't see. How can I land? Blood is flowing into my good eye again. It's the warmer air.'

'Can you cut your engine and drop the flaps when I tell you?'

'I think so.'

'You're nodding off again! Don't pass out on me now! When I tell you, pancake the plane belly-down! Got that?'

'I don't want to burn,' Kenji whispered.

'You haven't got enough fuel left to boil tea! Get ready!'

Everyone on the ground watched the two low-flying planes approach the far end of the runway side by side.

Kenji's plane wobbled and Genda shouted, 'Put your hand on the magneto switch! Get ready to cut your engine! Cut it! Cut it! Cut, cut, damn it! Kenji, cut the engine and drop the flaps or we're both going to die!'

Genda's plane zoomed up into the air. Kenji's plane slammed down on the runway. The one remaining landing strut collapsed. The plane skidded, screeching a rooster tail of sparks behind. The emergency vehicles took up the chase of the spinning plane. It careened from one runway to another. The right wing and tail section sheared off. The left wing broke away. The emergency trucks dodged flying

270

debris. What remained of the T-97 screeched to a stop in a cloud of smoke and dust 100 yards from the tower.

Raiko watched a crash crew ease Kenji from the wreckage. A hundred outstretched hands waited to put him on the stretcher. 'Is he alive?' she whispered.

'You may go to him now,' Hashimoto said.

The Year of the Hare
1939

30

13 May 1939

The big grey Dusenberg pulled away from the crowd in Yokohama port. Guards saluted; people waved.

'Driver, do you know the home of Lord Hiroki Koin?' Raiko asked.

'Yes, Miss Minobe. The lord keeper of the privy seal gave me specific instructions. He bids you and Captain Ishikawa a warm welcome on your return from Europe. All of Tokyo does.'

'Thank you,' Raiko said. She turned to Kenji and straightened his uniform jacket. 'Soon you'll be home. What a wonderful present for your aunt and uncle if you would speak to them.'

Kenji did not respond.

'Hiroki and Noriko will be sad enough. Please answer them.'

Raiko saw Kenji's eye flicker and was encouraged. She chattered on. 'Hiroki and Noriko know about your progress. I wrote them every week. The scar on your forehead is hardly noticeable. And the eye patch gives you a handsome, debonair look.'

Kenji's good eye blinked, and fixed once more on that distant point he had watched for most of the past eighteen months. Raiko was never certain if he was fully aware when he lapsed into this trancelike state. He could speak, but rarely did. Never in direct response to a question. If she left him standing somewhere, he would be there when she returned. He ate, made his toilet and went to sleep when told to.

275

To the Japanese public, Kenji was a living legend and Raiko his nurse. He was Japan's first air ace. His trip to Europe had been publicized as an official request from the German government to honour the Japanese war hero. Japan's newspapers featured photos of Kenji with Foreign Minister Matsuoka and high Nazi officials. There were articles about his travels throughout Germany. It had all been staged. With permission of German Minister of Propaganda Goebbels, pictures of Nazi officers were superimposed and distributed to the foreign press corps. Actually, Kenji and Raiko had spent the better part of a year in a private sanatorium outside Vienna, where he was treated by disciples of Sigmund Freud. Reporters were not allowed near the sanatorium.

Kenji had memories, although he had not shared them. He recalled Raiko shouting and stamping her foot at the Austrian doctors. She had taken him from the sanatorium to one of his own merchantships for their trip home. The doctors thought he did not understand. He had learned to focus on that distant point shortly after they took the bandages off his remaining eye and he saw his scarred face in the mirror. He became like one of the new cameras that made talking pictures – his eye the lens, his brain the film and his ears recording the sound.

Kenji had tried to talk, but was not understood. From the time he woke in the Nanking hospital, people no longer comprehended his speech. He had stopped trying to communicate. After the casts were taken from his arm and leg and he could use them, the Japanese physicians called his problem battle fatigue. The doctors in Germany claimed he had brain damage, and the Viennese doctors said it was a sexual problem. He remembered Raiko coming to bed naked. She had undressed him, but nothing happened. He remembered her crying herself to sleep many times. Sometimes he shook violently and wept with her, not knowing why he was crying. Raiko must have eventually agreed with the Viennese doctors. She stopped coming to his bed, and he stopped shaking.

Now, Raiko said to him, 'Kenji, do you recognize the house? We're here.' She reached over and opened his door. 'Your aunt and uncle are waiting on the front steps.'

When he made no move, Raiko stepped out of the car and came around to his door. She took Kenji's hand and led him up the front steps. He saw Noriko weeping. Hiroki's cheeks were puffed, his eyes misty. Noriko opened her mouth to speak, but could not. She reached out and touched the front of his jacket. The four people stood in silence. Tears formed in Kenji's eye and a thrill raced through Raiko's body. Perhaps coming home would draw him out.

'Come inside,' Hiroki said. 'Tea is waiting. Noriko made your favourite rice cakes.'

They entered the salon and Noriko indicated where they should sit. Raiko saw an unfamiliar look crease Kenji's face as his eyes searched the walls. She put her finger to her lips, alerting Hiroki and Noriko not to speak. They watched Kenji turn round and round.

Finally Raiko put her hand on his arm and stopped his circling. 'What are you looking for?'

'The Gates of Hell.'

Raiko's knees buckled and she grasped Kenji's arm for support. It was the first direct answer he had given to any question in a long time. She bit her lip. 'Ask your uncle.'

Kenji turned his head. He looked at Hiroki and wrinkled his brow. His lips started to move and stopped. Raiko's hopes faded.

'Where is Rodin's sketch?' Kenji asked.

'On the back porch,' Hiroki said. 'Since your injury I could not stand to look at it day in and day out.'

Kenji walked to the glass-enclosed porch. He stopped before the large picture, studying its twisted, tortured figures. For half an hour he stood without moving, without responding. His one eye continually roved back and forth over the canvas. Raiko's hopes rose again.

Kenji raised his hand and tapped the sketch. 'Rodin speaks my language, but he knows only the ABCs of cruelty.' He began to shake and Raiko went to him. He ignored her. 'I've seen the entire alphabet of barbarism. Our soldiers acted it out in real life.' Kenji tapped the sketch again. 'Rodin didn't see Japanese soldiers burning people alive, raping little boys and girls in front of their parents.' He turned to Raiko and looked down at her. 'They threw the babies into the air. The little babies. They caught them on bayonets and kicked the bodies into the river.' Heaving with sobs, Kenji lost his balance and collapsed to the floor.

Raiko knelt by his side. She put his head on her lap and soothed him. Noriko fled the room to call their physician. Kenji continued to pour out the story of Nanking, and that of his last flight. He spoke for two hours. Tears rolled down his cheek and Raiko cried with him.

Finally the catharsis ended. Raiko and the doctor helped Kenji to bed. The doctor administered a sedative.

Back in the salon, the doctor handed Raiko a sachet. 'Mrs Ishikawa, you also need a good rest.'

'I'm not his wife,' Raiko said sadly.

'The way you care for that man, you should marry him.'

Raiko blushed. The physician bowed and left.

'This is the most positive thing that's happened since he was hospitalized,' Raiko said. 'In Manchuria, Japanese doctors tried acupuncture and herbal medicines. In Germany it was shock treatments. The Viennese physicians used hypnosis and psychotherapy. I had Kenji sign a chit for a special plane to fly Hino and Genda from China to Europe. He spoke only a few words to them that didn't make sense.'

'That fantasy about Nanking and our soldiers,' Noriko said. 'It can't be true.'

Hiroki grunted. 'There were some gruesome stories told by the men on leave from China. Then Prime Minister Konoe gave orders to the military police and Kempetai to punish any soldier who talked about the battle for Nanking.'

'Excuse me,' Raiko said. She went to the front hall, took Kenji's writing case from the luggage and brought it to Hiroki. 'In here is the letter Kenji wrote before his plane was hit. I was afraid to send it through the mail for fear the censors would see it. I had nightmares after reading it. What Kenji told me today confirms what he wrote before his injury.' Raiko drank the herbal sedative Noriko prepared, and retired to her room.

Late the next morning, Noriko led Raiko to the rear porch. 'Hiroki was called out early this morning. I found Kenji here.'

He was seated cross-legged on the porch mats, staring up at Rodin's sketch. Raiko walked behind him and placed her fingertips on the sides of his head. She massaged his temples. Kenji's head lolled gently with the soothing motion of Raiko's hands. His face relaxed.

'Kenji, what do you see?' Raiko asked.

He did not respond. Raiko waited several minutes, then asked again.

Kenji's jaw moved. He pursed his lips and said, 'I see what is not there.'

Raiko's heart skipped, fearing he was again talking in disconnected words.

'I believe if Rodin had seen what I saw, he could not have drawn this,' Kenji said. 'Or anything else ever after.'

'Do you want to draw what you saw?' Raiko asked.

'No,' Kenji said, reaching up to touch her hands. 'I realize that by remembering, I can forget the horrors. But John Whittefield's words will not leave me. He said a

279

Japanese shows his courage by conforming. I should have defied the Emperor's orders.'

Noriko could no longer remain silent. She went to Kenji and knelt before him. 'The Emperor did not order the atrocities in Nanking. General Matsui did. He was stripped of all rank and privileges. He has since built a shrine of apology.'

'Matsui and his troops took the responsibility, but they never entered Nanking,' Kenji said. 'It was Nakajima's men. They were purposely turned loose on that city. Hashimoto's men helped. They were all commanded by the Emperor's uncle, Prince Higashikuni.'

'General Hashimoto has the greatest respect for you,' Noriko said. 'He gave glowing reports to the newspapers. I saved the articles. He personally recommended you for the Award of the Golden Kite.'

'I don't want a thing from his bloody hand!'

'What do you want?' Raiko asked, looking down at Kenji. She saw that distant look return to his eye and was afraid.

'I want bacon and eggs with pickled vegetables,' Kenji said.

Raiko's knees gave out and he caught her in his arms. She was crying and laughing.

'What should I have said?' Kenji asked.

'I've been waiting a year and a half for you to say you love me.' She turned her face into his shoulders and sobbed. 'I want to be your wife.'

Noriko saw the fright on Kenji's face. He trembled and Raiko soothed him into a chair.

Two weeks of bed rest, light exercise and lots of conversation was the beginning of Kenji's recovery. On the first of June he began a series of calisthenics with the master of the Imperial Hall of Martial Arts as his personal instructor.

After one particularly rigorous session, Kenji pointed

at the master as he went out of the door. 'It pays to get the best,' he said to Noriko.

'So why don't you marry Raiko?'

'Has she gone to the Black Chamber again?' Kenji asked.

'They need her to work on the Russian code that appeared several times before our attempted invasion of Mongolia. It has come through again.'

'I'm coming through, or I should say out of my mental fog. I have so much to catch up on. How did we get involved with the Russians when we haven't finished the Chinese?'

'Something to do with Germany supplying us with weapons,' Noriko said. 'It is not called a war, just another incident.'

'It was the Russian code that Raiko broke which gave me the idea to build the radio interception station. Has there been any progress?'

'The building is completed and the equipment is being assembled. But neither you nor the Cherry Blossom Society will manage it. All civilian intelligence organizations have been incorporated into the Imperial Rule Association. Government control. Their motto is, "A New Order in Asia".'

'Sounds like the Third Reich. Wantabe must be upset.'

Noriko looked at Kenji's pale face, at his scarred forehead and one eye. 'Wantabe is dead,' she said, watching his reaction. 'He and Raiko's father were attacked. Mini was lightly wounded, but immediately afterwards he was dismissed from the university. His books were banned and he is forbidden to give public lectures.'

'How can the government allow the banning of books? It's against the constitution.'

Noriko sat down next to Kenji and put her hand on his. 'You've been asleep for a long time. We've become a militaristic state. The China war and now the fighting with

Russia have been used as a pretext to ban public protests and parliamentary opposition to the army. Japan is now in a holy war for the leadership of Asia.'

'How has the government defined Asia geographically?' Kenji asked.

'They haven't. There are Kempetai agents in India, Burma and Malaysia. They have men in Panama, Mexico and the United States. The cabinet hasn't been called into session for six months, and Hiroki hasn't been invited to a cabinet meeting for two years. The National Diet is no more than a debating club.'

'Then how does the government rule the country?'

'Through the newly-created Imperial Planning Board that is located on palace ground near Imperial Military Headquarters.'

'You're saying the Emperor governs?'

'No one says that,' Noriko said. 'But the Planning Board overruled Yamamoto and the navy when they were against the army's drive on Hankow, Canton, and the recent attack on Mongolia.'

'Our strategy has always been to keep away from an over-extended land war with China. How could this happen?'

'Pride,' Noriko said. 'Tojo promised his imperial majesty that the China war would be finished in two months. The joke among liberals is that he did not tell Chiang Kaishek. The generalissimo refuses to surrender. Your Uncle Hiroki and others, who tried to counsel the Emperor differently, are out of favour at court.'

'Yamamoto and Hiroki have powerful followings in both the army and the navy,' Kenji said.

'That is past. They lost face when Yamamoto's prediction of war with America over our taking of Shanghai and Nanking did not come true. The army's successes in Hankow, Canton and other major Chinese cities created a taste for Mongolia.'

'Didn't Chiang Kai-shek make any overtures for peace?'

'The generalissimo is safely tucked into his mountain capital of Chungking, and swears he will never surrender. He stopped our army at Nanking for two months by blowing up a big dam on the Yangtze. It flooded 1,000 square miles of lowland. Two hundred thousand Chinese died from the flood waters, the starvation and disease that followed. Chiang is still holding out, even though Foreign Minister Matsuoka convinced the Germans to cut off all military aid to China.'

'What price did we pay for that?' Kenji asked.

'The invasion of Mongolia. Hitler wants the Russians kept busy with us in the east. He is supplying our Kwangtung army with ammunition, food and fuel.'

'Do you know the financial situation of the Ishikawa zaibatsu?'

'I don't, but I'm certain you have enough money to marry Raiko,' Noriko said. 'Her father agreed, and our families exchanged the traditional gifts long ago.' She pulled a slip of paper from her obi. 'This is a list of favourable dates chosen by our family astrologer.' She saw that same look of fear on Kenji's face as when Raiko had raised the subject of marriage a month before.

Kenji stood. 'I must go out now.'

'I'll go with you.'

'I will do this alone.'

'You have not been out by yourself yet,' Noriko said.

'Then it's time I was. Where's the Dusenberg?'

'Please wait for Raiko to go with you.'

'No.'

'Kenji, you listen to me. In the last year and a half that little woman has done more for you than a mother, wife and nurse.'

'That is the problem.'

283

'Kenji, I love you as my own son, but I also love Raiko. Don't you hurt her!'

'Where's my jacket?'

Kenji parked the Dusenberg on the Ginza. He used a public telephone, then drove to an apartment house in Tokyo's Roppongi district. He walked upstairs and rang the bell.

'I never expected to hear from you again,' Natasha said. 'Come in.'

31

The Black Chamber

'Miss Minobe, your work habits are admirable,' Toshio
Ogino said. 'Are conditions satisfactory? If you need
more people, typewriters, anything, please ask. Generals Hashimoto and Tojo wrote glowing letters of your
service in Manchuko and China. They urged me to watch
over you.'

Raiko forced a smile. She would never again feel
comfortable in the long windowless room Wantabe had
ruled. 'Every code expert needs a colleague to confide
in,' he had said. She missed him.

'You have been most kind to me, Mr Ogino,' Raiko
said to Wantabe's replacement. 'Everything is satisfactory. When will the new communications centre be
completed?'

'In about a month, possibly two. Do you have the
clear-text of the Russian messages?'

'I've prepared a synopsis for the meeting.'

'I cannot understand why Wantabe didn't leave the key
to this Russian code in his notes. We searched his house,
his safety-deposit box, even his car.'

Raiko felt certain Koda-ha had killed Wantabe and the
section chief knew it. 'Wantabe may have thought the
key to the Russian code was a form of life insurance,'
she said.

'He was wrong! You, I hope, are duplicating all your
material on the Russian code for me!'

'Yes, of course,' Raiko said, knowing it did not matter
whether she did or not. Whenever she left her desk,

285

someone copied everything she had written. Kempetai men followed her everywhere. The landlady straightened her books and pictures every day. Her telephone line was monitored and all her mail opened.

'You'll be speaking to a select group of the most senior military-men,' Ogino said. 'Are you prepared?'

'I would like to review my notes.'

'Miss Minobe, telephone call for you,' a secretary said.

'Raiko, this is Noriko. Kenji left the house on his own. I asked him to wait for you, but he would not listen.'

'It could be a positive sign.'

'But he is driving with one eye and a bad leg.'

'The injuries to his arm and leg are healed,' Raiko said. 'Driving with one eye is safe.'

'It is more than that. He did not look well when he left. He could suffer a relapse.'

As she talked, Raiko watched people going in and out of the section chief's office carrying folders marked SECRET.

'You'll be called soon,' someone whispered to her.

'I have a meeting now,' Raiko said to Noriko. 'If you haven't heard from Kenji by the time we're through, I'll ask my section chief to help locate him. I'll call you back.'

Raiko reviewed her notes until Ogino emerged from his office and came to her side. 'I want you to be at ease when you go in,' he said. 'Kempetai is already looking for Captain Ishikawa.'

'How do you know he's gone?' Raiko asked.

'Even during Wantabe's time, all telephone calls to and from the Black Chamber were monitored. I told you General Tojo ordered me to watch over you, and he is sitting in my office right now.'

'Does he know about Kenji going off?'

'No, and the Kempetai report will come directly to me. It is practically impossible for a stranger to visit any street or village, day or night, without it being reported by one of our patriotic societies. Someone as famous and easily distinguishable as Captain Ishikawa will be recognized. By the time you complete your report, I'll know where he is.'

'Won't you be with me at the meeting?'

'I am not privy to foreign-policy discussions. Please go in.'

Wantabe's old office had been enlarged to three times its former size. Raiko noticed that all the shelves, filing cabinets and furniture were new, and expensive. At the end of a long conference table sat Prince Higashikuni, flanked by Generals Hashimoto and Tojo. Major Ando and Dr Tsubota stood behind the three officers.

'Miss Minobe, take a seat at your end of the table,' Ando said.

Raiko was glad that someone had thought to place a pillow on the chair. It would raise her up to read her notes in comfort. She bowed to the officers.

'Miss Minobe.' General Tojo nodded. 'How is Captain Ishikawa?'

'He has improved dramatically since his return to Japan.'

'Ah, the Kingdom of True Men,' Hashimoto said. 'That is what Japan was called in ancient times. The air in Japan influences champions like Kenji Ishikawa. He is a true samurai.'

Prince Higashikuni grunted the general into silence, then nodded at Dr Tsubota.

'My dear young lady,' the doctor said. 'Information you decoded has led to this meeting. Japan's foreign policy is influenced by these gentlemen – his highness the prince and two of our country's most eminent strategists, Generals Tojo and Hashimoto. Choose your words with care.'

'Sirs.' Raiko bowed again. 'I have recently decoded a number of messages in the Russian cipher that were picked up by our radio operators last April and May.

More messages were addressed to General Zukhov in Mongolia. They detailed our army's plans for the invasion of Mongolia. Zukhov and his armoured divisions were waiting for your attack at Nohoman.'

Hashimoto slammed the table. 'I knew we could have beaten those pasty-faced scum! How did they know we were coming?'

'I have no answer to that,' Raiko said. 'But the messages I decoded are extremely detailed. You can determine their accuracy.' She passed several documents to Ando, who distributed them.

The men read quietly. After some time, Tojo looked up. 'This information on our troop strength, deployment and plan of attack is all correct. There seems to be a Japanese traitor.'

'At least one,' Raiko replied. 'He must be highly placed in the military planning section of the army.'

'Why do you say the army?' Hashimoto demanded.

'In all the messages to Stalin, Borodin and Zukhov, there was no mention of troop movements by sea. Or about the deployment of our warships and aircraft carriers.'

'Why do you assume the traitor is a man?' Tsubota asked.

'Women are not privy to such information.'

'You are,' Tsubota said.

The doctor's dark eyes, magnified behind his thick lenses, seemed to threaten Raiko. She was the only member of the Cherry Blossom Society who still worked in the Black Chamber.

'Miss Minobe, it was your decoding of the Russian message from Borodin which convinced us the Soviet army on the Mongolian border was weakened by Stalin's purge of his officers,' Tsubota said. 'That led us to believe an easy victory was achievable.'

Raiko's face flushed with anger. Her credibility was

being challenged. She disliked Tsubota and his attack on her. 'Information I pass on to the intelligence section is for your evaluation. If there is a mistake, it is yours. The material I gave you about Mongolia was not from the Russians. It was a decode of an American message sent by John Whittefield in China to Ambassador Grew here in Tokyo. Whittefield received his information from Borodin. The Russian spy could have been deceiving the American. We often send incorrect reports on the radio, with the knowledge it is being intercepted and deciphered by foreign agents. In this instance, I believe the information was correct.' Raiko felt like a bulldog after Tsubota and was not about to let go. 'Your knowledge of Stalin's purge was two years old by the time you acted on it. General Zukhov had plenty of time to retrain a new officers' corps for his northern army.'

Tsubota smiled. 'You assume the traitor is a man because only males are privy to such sensitive information. How is it you have risen so quickly in the intelligence service?'

Raiko was thrown off balance by Tsubota's nimble mind. He had focused attention back on her without responding to her accusations. She balled her small fists and stood. 'I have risen to a position of authority because of a vacuum of qualified personnel in Japan's intelligence service. Good military officers stay away from this branch because it is a career dead-end. We are so concerned with security that most of Japan's senior military officers have never heard of Tsushim Choho – Communications Intelligence. If the listening and tracking station being built by the Ishikawa zaibatsu at Owada had been in operation when these messages were sent, we would already have identified the traitor.'

'Miss Minobe, please sit down,' Tojo said. 'Dr Tsubota is doing his job as chief of foreign intelligence. He means you no harm nor disrespect.'

Raiko had not realized she was standing. She bowed deeply. 'I apologize for my breach of etiquette.'

Tojo motioned to her with his little finger. 'Please, join us at this end of the table.'

Raiko gathered her papers, took the pillow and walked to a chair held by Ando. She sat opposite Tojo and next to Hashimoto.

'Miss Minobe,' Hashimoto said. 'Your section chief informed us that some of the information you have decoded is extremely sensitive. So much so that he would not communicate it himself for fear of misrepresenting the facts.'

So that was Ogino's reason for remaining outside the room, Raiko thought. She understood the bald-headed general with the bull-neck was politely warning her that the section chief did not want responsibility for her report.

Raiko took a deep breath before speaking. 'Gentlemen, there are two sources other than the Russian code for what I am about to tell you. One is the trash bins of the US consulate in Tokyo. The other is Miss Ruth Kuhn, an agent of ours in Hawaii. We have known for eighteen months that the Germans wanted us involved with Russia on the Mongolian border to keep the Soviet army looking east while the Nazi army moved west. Hitler's recent takeover of Czechoslovakia was the first test of European democratic governments. They backed down, and only Stalin strengthened his armed forces. According to US Intelligence Chief John Whittefield's evaluation, which was confirmed at a recent meeting in Tokyo by Ambassador Grew with Generals Douglas MacArthur and Joseph Stilwell, Germany will invade Poland. To do so, the Americans say, Hitler must be certain of three conditions. A secure eastern border to protect Germany's rear from Russia, a blockade-proof Germany, and a short, conclusive war. The Rome–Berlin Axis Alliance does not satisfy those requirements. Ruth Kuhn reports that von

Ribbentrop suggested to our Foreign Minister Matsuoka that we join the Axis Alliance. Our prime minister rejected the idea.' Raiko looked at the men around the table for confirmation, but they remained silent, their faces studiously blank. 'Hitler is said to be furious over Prime Minister Konoe's rebuff,' she added.

'This Miss Kuhn supplies more information about her mother country than the American fleet,' Tsubota said. 'Are you certain you can trust her?'

'Ruth Kuhn is not German but Austrian. She hates Goebbels for her own personal reasons, and feels no disloyalty for her actions. She is performing very well for us. Because of her, we have many reports on War Plan Orange.'

Tsubota leaned closer to the table. 'I have had over 100 agents trying to get that information.'

'What is War Plan Orange?' Hashimoto asked.

'A joint US army and navy exercise to protect Hawaii from a hypothetical enemy in the Pacific,' Tsubota said.

'We are the only possible enemy in the Pacific, hypothetical or otherwise,' Hashimoto said.

'Precisely why the results are so important,' Tsubota said. 'Please tell us about War Plan Orange, Miss Minobe.'

'The Pacific fleet was divided equally,' Raiko said. 'Blue forces on defence, white forces attacking. The white forces' aircraft carriers approached, undetected, to within seventy miles of Hawaii. They launched their bombers from that position and theoretically destroyed Pearl Harbor, America's largest naval base in the Pacific.'

Tojo read the note slipped to him by Prince Higashikuni, then asked Raiko, 'How was it possible for the white forces to approach undetected?'

'They used rain squalls for cover,' Raiko said.

'By the gods, that is how Yamamoto claimed it could be done,' Hashimoto exclaimed.

Prince Higashikuni swivelled in his chair and fixed

Hashimoto with a cold, hard stare. Raiko saw the big general lower his eyes, bow his shaven skull and stare at the table top. A heavy silence pervaded the room.

It dawned on Raiko that the leaders of Japan had considered the possibility of an attack on Pearl Harbor. She continued talking to cover her shock. 'According to Ruth Kuhn's report, the war games' referees disallowed the white forces' aerial torpedoing of blue warships docked in Pearl Harbor.'

'That would be because of anti-torpedo nets,' Ando said.

'There are no nets,' Raiko replied, and saw Tojo's eyes blaze. For a hair-raising instant she had an insight into his mind, and understood why he was called The Razor.

'Every first-class naval base has anti-torpedo nets,' Tojo said. 'Why not Pearl Harbor?'

Raiko took a deep breath, then said, 'A lieutenant from the USS Arizona told Ruth Kuhn the referees disallowed the aerial torpedo hits because Pearl Harbor's depth is only thirty-four feet. American torpedoes dive a minimum of fifty feet when dropped from a plane. Only then do they level off and rise to the surface.' She saw that Hashimoto was bursting to speak but was held in check by the cold, hard eyes of Prince Higashikuni.

'When will we receive the translation of Miss Kuhn's report?' Tsubota asked.

'Tomorrow,' Raiko said.

'Whatever we are paying Miss Kuhn, double it,' Tsubota said. 'Please continue with your original report.'

Raiko referred to her notes, then said, 'The German high command's assessment of Italy as an ally parallels that of the Americans. Mussolini is more of a liability than an asset to Hitler. The Germans and Americans believe the only military allies of real value to Hitler would be Japan and the Soviets. This information came to Ruth Kuhn via an aide of von Ribbentrop, an old friend of hers, who visited Hawaii. Surprisingly enough, one of our decodes of the Russian messages to Joseph Stalin almost duplicates that information.'

'Are you saying the spy here in Tokyo is recommending an alliance with Germany to Stalin?'

'Yes, sir,' Raiko said. 'In his latest communiqué he refers to a meeting between von Ribbentrop and the new Soviet foreign minister, Molotov. The American evaluation of Molotov replacing Litvinov as foreign minister indicates there will soon be a radical change in Soviet policy.'

'Have the Americans said what this new policy might be?' Tojo asked.

'No, sir. But the Russian spy here in Tokyo is convinced that the European abandonment of Czechoslovakia to Hitler will be duplicated in Poland if Germany signs a non-aggression pact with Russia.'

'Miss Minobe, I am a physician by profession,' Tsubota said. 'You have been under a great strain for a long time in nursing Captain Ishikawa. We called upon you to return to the Black Chamber because of your exceptional talent. But I think we have placed an enormous burden upon those frail shoulders. Your conclusion that Germany and Russia are preparing to make an alliance is absurd. Hitler signed an Anti-Comintern Pact with us to stop communism. Stalin's International Socialist Party is politically mobilized around the world against fascism. In Spain, German planes are fighting Russian guns for the ideological leadership of that country.'

Raiko was tired. 'I have drawn no conclusions. I present information. My deciphering of messages in the American brown code indicates that John Whittefield, Generals Stilwell and MacArthur also believe Hitler must secure his border with Russia before he can move west. They are certain he will attack Poland.'

'I must agree with Dr Tsubota,' Hashimoto said. 'If Hitler signed a military pact with Russia, it would negate our Anti-Comintern Pact with him. The 38,000 casualties we suffered in Mongolia will have been for nothing.'

'Miss Minobe, you need a rest,' Tsubota said.

Raiko passed her hand over her eyes. She failed to brush a wisp of hair back into place. 'My theory that Germany and Russia are considering rapprochement is based on the documents here for your evaluation.' She turned to Tsubota. 'Doctor, in the future I request that you not attack me as you have today. You failed to fault my work, so you question my state of health. No one could pay me enough money to allow my brain to be twisted by the codes, ciphers and cryptograms. My health is excellent!'

'My dear lady, I beg your pardon,' Tsubota said. 'I am truly concerned for your well-being. Your eyes are red. They flit from one point to another. Under the table you continually cross and uncross your legs. Look at the bits of paper in front of you. You have shredded the edges of several sheets of your report. These are typical signs of stress.'

Raiko uncrossed her legs and looked down at the pile of torn paper before her.

'One more question,' Tojo said. 'Could it be that the Russian spy in Tokyo is a German? You did say the Russian message from Tokyo paralleled that information which came from von Ribbentrop's aide.'

'It is possible,' Raiko said. 'But I feel there must be a Japanese spy also.'

Tojo motioned to Tsubota and Ando. 'We need a German to smell out a German spy and a Japanese traitor. Whom do you suggest?'

'Sorge,' Ando said. 'He poses as a newspaperman, but I know him to be Gestapo. We've done some propaganda work with him. His office is in the German Embassy here in Tokyo.'

'Approach him!' Tojo said. He turned to Raiko. 'We are

most grateful for your efforts. Please take Dr Tsubota's advice and get some rest.'

Toshio Ogino awaited Raiko as she came out of the office. 'How was it?' he asked.

'They advised me to go home and sleep.'

'You can't do that just yet,' the section chief said. 'Another message has come through in that Russian code. I want you to work with my people and show them how to decipher it.'

'I'm tired,' Raiko said.

'This will cheer you.' Ogino handed her a sheet of paper. 'Kempetai located your Captain Ishikawa. This is the address and telephone number. He is visiting a white woman named Natasha Bronfman.'

32

October 1939, Imperial Military Headquarters, Tokyo

'Sixteen feet,' General Hashimoto said. 'Sixteen feet of water stands between the destruction of the US Pacific fleet and our domination of Asia.'

'An oversimplification,' Admiral Yamamoto said. 'I oppose any action which will bring Japan and America into military conflict.'

'Why?' Prince Higashikuni asked.

'We cannot win.'

'In the game of chess most people consider two alternatives,' General Tojo said. 'Win or lose. What if Japan plays for a stalemate? The Europeans have left Asia.' He pointed to the large wall map. 'If the admiral's naval aircraft can neutralize the American Pacific fleet, my army can take Malaysia, the Dutch East Indies, the Philippines, French Indochina and Burma. The smaller Pacific islands will fall to us like ripened fruit. If the United States is drawn into the European war against Germany, we keep everything. If not, we pay an indemnity and return certain territories for a negotiated peace.'

'What if the Americans insist on playing to win?' Yamamoto asked. 'They can out-produce us ten to one. Time is on their side.'

'It was until Miss Minobe's predictions came true,' Dr Tsubota said. 'Hitler's neutrality pact with Stalin, his taking of Poland in less than a month, the declaration of war by France and England against Germany, all change every concept of political or military time periods previously held. There is a secret agreement now being

296

implemented by Russia and Germany to divide up Poland and all of eastern Europe. Hitler's cry of, "Lebenstraum – Living Space", echoes Japan's, "Expand or die". There is no other choice for us.'

'But not expansion by war with America,' Yamamoto said. 'Attack their ships, kill their men and the United States will fight.'

'They did not fight when I ordered the *Panay* sunk,' Hashimoto said.

'They will fight if you attack Pearl Harbor,' Yamamoto said. 'Americans consider Hawaii part of the United States. On the other hand, we could take South-East Asia in small bites. Nibble away at the Dutch East Indies and Roosevelt could never convince a majority in Congress to declare war on us. The peace movement in America is too strong.'

'To kill a tree it is not necessary to chop it down,' Tojo said. 'A wire tightly bound around the outer bark cuts off the nutrients and the tree dies. Roosevelt's policy of Ring Fence is like that wire. Japan will choke to death if we do not cut the wire and expand southwards. To be certain Japan is not attacked by America, the Pacific fleet must be neutralized. Its existence is like a gun held to our heads.'

'Admiral Yamamoto, you sent me to Saigon to set up an intelligence network in South-East Asia,' Tsubota said. 'I have completed that mission. From the French colonial government in Saigon, I learned that Marshal Pétain and his generals in Paris expect Hitler to break out of the Siegfried line into the lowland countries in spring 1940. They predict an invasion of France in summer 1940. France and England are officially at war with Germany. Unofficially, so is America. Roosevelt's wife leads the Bundles for Britain campaign. In addition to food, clothing and medical supplies, her husband is secretly sending weapons. America cannot remain neutral in Europe, and it cannot fight a two-ocean war with a one-ocean navy. If Roosevelt does want war with us and the Germans and the Italians, we'll have a stronger hand to negotiate the stalemate General Tojo envisions. The Americans negotiated peace with the Germans in the Great War. The cost of demanding unconditional surrender was too high then. It will be more costly in modern warfare. Americans do not have the stomach for a fight to the finish.'

'We would be violating a basic military principle by opening a second front against the Americans in the Pacific before we have finished with China,' Yamamoto said.

'Sir, China is not a naval threat,' Ando said. 'The only danger to our islands can come from the sea.'

'China may not have a navy, but we would have to draw off troops from the mainland for the attack south,' Yamamoto said. 'The Nationalist and Communist forces could then drive our Kwangtung army from China, Korea and Manchuria.'

'If I have a solution to the mainland problems, will you consider a move into South-East Asia?' Tojo asked. 'Would you then participate in planning a military operation against the Americans?'

Yamamoto knew he was being drawn into a trap, but could not see where Tojo's tactical ambush would come from. 'I believe the move into South-East Asia is necessary,' the admiral said. 'Planning a strike against the Americans would be conditional. We cannot allow our Kwangtung army to be isolated on the mainland.'

'Wang Ching-wei is prepared to negotiate an unofficial truce for Japan with Chiang Kai-shek before we turn south,' Tojo said.

The Razor has struck, Yamamoto thought. 'How did you entice the vice-chairman of the Chinese Nationalist party to negotiate on our behalf?'

Tojo motioned Tsubota to explain. 'We would set up

Chairman Wang as leader of a puppet government in the Japanese-occupied territories of China,' Tsubota said. 'Wang was a disciple of Sun Yat-sen and his heir to lead the Nationalist party before Chiang Kai-shek pushed him aside. I sent Major Ando to Hankow where he planted rumours that Wang was about to overthrow the generalissimo and make peace with Japan.'

'I arranged two bogus assassination attempts on Chairman Wang in Hankow,' Ando said. 'He fled to Hanoi believing it was the Chinese secret service, under orders from Chiang Kai-shek, who were after him. Dr Tsubota offered Wang his protection and invited him to Saigon.'

'Wang was anxious to co-operate,' Tsubota said. 'He has already communicated with Chiang Kai-shek to stop the war between China and Japan.'

'Incredible,' Yamamoto said. 'Did Chiang Kai-shek agree?'

'In principle,' Tsubota said. 'He has three conditions. First we conduct a semblance of war so he will continue to receive aid from America. Second, we kill Chairman Wang. And third, the truce would only go into effect in areas where there are no Communist forces.'

Hashimoto grinned as he leaned towards Yamamoto. 'Chiang Kai-shek hates Mao Tse-tung more than us. He wants our Kwangtung army to eliminate the Communists for him. We'll make a good show of it but never quite succeed. That will ensure Chiang's neutrality.'

Tojo's trap was sprung and yet Yamamoto still sought a way out of war with America. 'If this brilliant but complicated scheme is successful, the Russians will still be at our rear. They are too powerful to ignore.'

'Again I say, if this question can be answered to your satisfaction, will you join us?' Tojo asked.

Yamamoto forced himself to keep his head erect and not bow before the pressure being put on him. 'I will certainly give the answer positive consideration.'

Tojo turned to Prince Higashikuni. 'Your highness, only you have the authority to reveal this information.'

The prince gazed at Yamamoto for several seconds. Then he said, 'Our operation in Mongolia against the Russians was an application of Realpolitik. Battles were fought to implement political decisions. People died but it was a fabricated war. The Emperor complied with a request from Hitler by ordering us to attack the Russians in Mongolia. The Germans needed the Russians neutralized in their rear so they could invade Poland.'

'There are not ten men in the empire who know what I am about to tell you,' Tojo said to Yamamoto. 'The instant our forces attacked at Nohoman, Stalin responded to German feelers for a mutual security pact. He sent General Zukhov to Mongolia with unlimited equipment and men. The Germans waited until Zukhov completed the massive military move, then sent troops to the Russian border and invited Molotov to Berlin to negotiate a neutrality pact. Stalin and Hitler do not trust each other. Nor do they wish to fight on two fronts. They have a secret agreement to divide up the Baltic states in addition to Poland. Hitler will break out from behind the Siegfried line next spring. The German timetable is to conquer all of western Europe and France before the winter of 1940. Then to invade England in the spring of 1941. That should draw America into the European war. If not, it will certainly keep her attention fixed on the west, not the east.'

'What if Hitler fails in Europe?' Yamamoto asked.

'We shall not consider a military commitment against the Pacific fleet until he succeeds,' Tojo said.

The admiral saw one last opportunity to fault Tojo's argument. He pointed at the map. 'Zukhov and his forces will still be on the Mongolian border. The Russian army is established all along the Tatar strait to the Sea of Japan. They are still in our rear if we move south.'

'Not as a threat,' Ando said. 'We had a Russian

300

general defect at Nohoman. He is a Mongol who claims strong kinship to the Asian people and our concept of a Greater Asia. He has shown us proof of Stalin's distrust of England, France and America. Those three nations purposely left the German army intact on the Russian border after the Great War, as a means to stop communism. The defector claims Stalin would look favourably on a neutrality pact with Japan.' Ando turned to Tsubota.

The doctor took off his thick glasses and blinked at the men around the table. 'I believe this Mongol general is a Soviet agent sent to sound us out regarding a non-aggression pact with Russia. If we can come to an agreement with Stalin, the way south is open.' Tsubota put on his glasses and peered through the thick lenses at Yamamoto. 'Admiral, all your conditions will have been met.'

There was silence around the table. Everyone looked at Isokoro Yamamoto.

The admiral had one more statement to make. 'Gentlemen, though trained for battle, I prefer peace. The Great War was good for Japan. Allied with the United States, Great Britain and France, we sustained minimum casualties and realized maximum monetary returns. Japan went from being a debtor to a creditor, from an agricultural to an industrial society, from a regional to an international military power. At the present time I would seek an alliance with the United States, at least a non-aggression treaty. Even with Roosevelt's policy of Ring Fence, the Americans sell us scrap iron for our war industries. They have placed orders for more silk than we can produce.'

Hashimoto slammed the table. 'The scrap iron they sell us is what the Americans consider garbage! They use our money to smelt new iron and steel for weapons against us! The silk they order is used for bandoleers, parachutes and machine-gun belts that will be turned on us! If we don't attack America, they will attack us! But

301

there is more to this than money, more than territory. There is a question of honour!' Hashimoto swivelled his big shaven skull towards Yamamoto. 'Admiral, have you forgotten the insults to our fathers when they were forced by the West to accept the unfair peace treaty with China in 1894? Remember how we won the Russo–Japanese war and Theodore Roosevelt stole the peace from us!' Beads of sweat grew on Hashimoto's face; muscles in his massive jaw twitched. He thrust himself closer to Yamamoto. 'You and I were young officers at Versailles when President Woodrow Wilson of the United States declared, before the leaders of the world, that we are an inferior race! Remember that private room off the corridor in the Palais D'Orsay. We wept tears of shame. We swore the oath of Bushido, a warrior's solemn pledge to avenge the slurs on the historical honour of Japan, on our ancestors and on the Emperor!'

Hashimoto's words rekindled the shame of Versailles in Yamamoto's heart. He owed loyalty to Japan, not to America. The injustices had to be righted, the fathers honoured. At the same time as his heart yearned to avenge Japan's disgrace, his mind still reasoned that war with the United States was the route to national disaster. There was only one possibility to reconcile his dilemma.

Admiral Isokoro Yamamoto stood to attention, he clicked his heels and bowed to Prince Higashikuni. 'Your highness, if the Emperor puts his seal on orders for preparations to invade South-East Asia and destroy the US Pacific fleet at Pearl Harbor, I hear and obey.'

33

'Gentlemen, you have each been chosen for a particular task,' Admiral Yamamoto said. 'From this moment, everything you hear is top-secret!'

Hino, Genda and Kenji bowed.

'The Emperor has affixed his seal to an order for preparations to begin the invasion of South-East Asia,' the admiral said. 'Our defeats at Taierchung and Nohoman, and Hitler's victory in Poland, have proved that air power determines the outcome of land battles. Mao Tse-tung's and Zukhov's successes against our army were the result of superior enemy air forces. In Poland, Goering's Luftwaffe had two priorities. One: destroy the Polish air force. Two: disrupt enemy communications and mobilization of reserves. They succeeded within six hours. Their heavy bombers were then free to demoralize the civilian population while their fighters and divebombers flew close support for the Wehrmacht's mobilized infantry. Those tactics will soon be taught in our military field schools.' He looked into each man's eyes. 'The three of you shall be involved in more sensitive assignments. Major Hino, your task is to find a port which resembles Pearl Harbor and practise high-level bombing runs!'

Kenji gasped. 'The Americans!'

Yamamoto silenced him with a deep grunt. Kenji saw that Hino and Genda were beaming with pride.

'I long to get back at those Flying Tigers who shot me down,' Hino said.

'You'll not find them in Hawaii,' Yamamoto said. 'The

second part of your assignment is to map the air currents to Honolulu during the months from November to February. I seek maximum range and minimum fuel consumption for our aircraft.'

'You are thinking of their Thanksgiving and Christmas holidays,' Hino said.

'I will plan the strategy. You will incorporate your technique of high-altitude flying with Kenji's variable-pitch propeller.' Yamamoto turned to Kenji. 'I understand you have made progress with the Zerosen.'

'Yes, sir. I may never fly again, but the Zero fighter plane will beat the Flying Tigers, P-40s, the Russian Yak 16s and British Spitfires all at once.'

Yamamoto grunted. 'Major Ishikawa, you were never given to exaggeration before your injury.'

'And I do not exaggerate now. The Zero is a modified T-97 with a new 1,000-horsepower engine. It carries two synchronized Mitsubishi repeating cannon in its nose and two 20mm machine guns on the wings. The folding landing gear and structural changes enable the Zero to fly faster, turn quicker and climb at steeper angles than any warplane in the world. If air power is the key to military success, Japan shall rule the skies!'

'Your T-97s were faster than the Flying Tigers, yet you and other experienced pilots were knocked out of the sky.'

Kenji shifted his weight and touched his eye patch. 'Hino supplied the answer. He should explain.'

'Sir,' Hino said. 'When my bomber was attacked by the Flying Tigers, I used every trick to evade them. But no matter which way I turned, one of them was on my tail. As I parachuted down I could not believe my eyes. Only six P-40s had attacked and destroyed our twelve-plane formation. Then I recalled the phenomenal success of Baron von Richthofen's squadron in the Great War. It was called the Flying Circus because to ground observers they flew what appeared to be aerial acrobatics in groups. Von Richthofen's pilots had the largest kill ratio and the lowest casualties of any squadron, including the allies. That is until Hermann Goering took charge.'

'Isn't he the present commander of the Luftwaffe?' Yamamoto said.

'Yes. And he is making the same mistake against the British with fighter planes as he did in the last war.' Hino used his hands to demonstrate. 'Goering has his pilots train for individual aerial combat. We call them dogfights. It resembles the samurai who went forward and challenged an enemy to single combat. Von Richthofen found the one-on-one situation inefficient. He trained his men to fight in pairs. Mathematically the odds appear two to one. In actual combat it becomes four to one. Von Richthofen proved his theory on paper, using geometry to show how to cut off an enemy's escape angles. The American, Chenault, is using von Richthofen's tactics. No matter which way our planes turned, there was always a Flying Tiger on their tail. Kenji's T-97 was faster, but the Americans used better tactics.'

'How will the new Zero fighter stand up against such team combat?' Yamamoto asked.

'I flew the Zero using von Richthofen's strategy against P-40s over Chungking,' Genda said. 'We were outnumbered seven to four, but downed two Flying Tigers. The others fled.'

'I assume these manoeuvres are being studied by all our pilots,' Yamamoto said.

'I recommended their implementation for all squadrons,' Genda said. 'The navy accepted my recommendation, but the army shelved the idea. Our intelligence claims the American air force also rejected Chenault's recommendations for the tactics to be taught. Their military bureaucracy is as bad as ours.'

'Write up a report on team flying and send a copy

to army headquarters,' Yamamoto said. 'I will endorse it.'

Genda cleared his throat. 'Sir, I have not yet been given an assignment.'

Yamamoto smiled. 'I am told you are one of the best fighter pilots in the world. You have downed even more enemy planes than Kenji.'

'I have had more time in the air. My cousin will always be Japan's first air ace.'

Yamamoto placed a large photograph on his desk. 'This is an aerial view of Battleship Row at Pearl Harbor. During the Christmas and New Year holidays, America's mightiest warships are anchored here by Ford Island. General Hashimoto says that if you can learn to drop a 1,000-pound torpedo from a plane under combat conditions, so that the torpedo does not sink lower than thirty-four feet, the Pacific Ocean belongs to Japan.'

Genda studied the photo. 'Torpedoes with net-cutting devices are heavier than 1,000 pounds.'

'There are no torpedo nets,' Yamamoto said. 'American naval experts claim it impossible to successfully launch a torpedo from a plane into the shallow waters of Pearl Harbor. They say it would plough down into the harbour bottom and explode harmlessly. Our naval experts concur that a fifty- to eighty-foot depth is indeed necessary.'

Genda bent over the desk and put his hands on both sides of the picture. He stared down, neither moving nor speaking. Then he growled deep in his throat, and purred. 'The Americans don't know about the Zero. Kenji could remodel it for two men and a load of 1,000 pounds. If the engine could be redesigned not to stall at 100 miles an hour, it would do the job!'

'I can alter the body, wings and armament for the extra weight,' Kenji said. 'With a changed propeller pitch and practice, a pilot should be able to remain aloft at reduced speed. I'm certain Mitsubishi can modify the engine.'

Genda put his finger on the photograph and traced a path. 'If I approach from the east and level off passing the navy dockyard at minimum speed, I can use this permanent crane to gauge my height. I could fly under it and make a soft drop at slow speed. Everything is possible!'

'At 100 miles an hour the combination of ship and shore anti-aircraft batteries would shoot you down before you got within half a mile of Battleship Row,' Hino said.

'Some of us would die,' Genda said. 'But if Kenji's Zeros are strafing the enemy positions and our divebombers are hitting those ships from above, there's the good chance of enough planes getting through.'

'Torpedoes are the only way we can be certain of destroying those big ships,' Yamamoto said. 'The force of an underwater explosion is seven times greater than an airburst. We need that extra power against their armour plate. The success or failure of the torpedo-carrying planes could mean victory. Or our hasty retreat.'

'I'll need Japan's best aviators, much practice, and the modified Zero,' Genda said.

'You'll have it!' Yamamoto said. 'As soon as your brother finds a place for manoeuvres.' He passed out three envelopes tied with red ribbons. 'None of you noticed or questioned it when I called you major. Congratulations on your promotions. Now I wish to speak to Major Ishikawa alone.'

After Hino and Genda had gone, Yamamoto said to Kenji, 'I see you have reservations about our move south.'

'It's the possibility of war with America that disturbs me, morally and tactically.'

'There are so many conditions that must exist before we ever move towards Pearl Harbor. I do not foresee it ever happening. Hitler has to conquer the rest of Europe in two years. The Americans must continue their Far East policy

307

of Ring Fence while helping their allies. We have to sign a non-aggression pact with Russia.'

'After our battle with the Soviets at Nohoman, they'll never sign with us,' Kenji said.

'Strangely enough, of the three conditions, that one could become a reality. Your bride-to-be recently decoded another Russian message from Tokyo. It was addressed to Joseph Stalin.' Yamamoto picked up a sheet of paper and read aloud. '"Have seen photocopies of Operation Barbarossa, Hitler's plan to invade Russia. No date for attack given."' The admiral looked at Kenji. 'Very soon after the warning was sent to Stalin, General Zukhov was recalled to Moscow from Mongolia with most of his armour and air force. If we wanted to take Mongolia now, there would be no problem. But we are committed to moving south.' He shrugged. 'Photocopies of the Barbarossa plan had been sent from Germany to the German security chief here in Tokyo, Colonel von Ott. He was urged to press Japan to join the Italian–German Axis Alliance against England and France, by assuring our leaders that Russia would not be a future threat because of Operation Barbarossa. Dr Tsubota and Foreign Minister Matsuoka are presently in India speaking to a communist revolutionary named Bose. They want him to approach Stalin with a proposal of neutrality between Japan and the Soviet Union. Motor-Mouth Matsuoka can be very convincing, especially since neither Stalin nor Hitler trust each other. The Soviets will want to assure a peaceful eastern border to protect themselves from Operation Barbarossa.'

'The spy in Tokyo must be German,' Kenji said. 'Orientals are never allowed inside the German Embassy. That message had to come from there.'

'Raiko believes there must be at least two spies, one of them Japanese. Your new Communications Intelligence Centre indicated the signal emanated from the foreign quarter where the embassies are located. The transmission wasn't long enough to triangulate a location. The next time they send, we'll pinpoint them!'

'I suggest you notify someone in the German Embassy,' Kenji said.

'Ando has already spoken to a newspaperman named Richard Sorge who is Gestapo.'

Kenji nodded. 'So at least one of the three conditions for war may actually come about.'

'There are many like myself and your uncle who are against war with America. We go ahead with the plans because it is our duty. The Emperor has ordered it.' Yamamoto pointed at Kenji. 'Your arm and leg appear fine. If you can drive a car with one eye, how do you know you can't fly a plane? You're needed.'

'I tried. A piece of shrapnel remains in my head and I've lost my sense of smell.'

'You're not going to sniff the enemy out at 20,000 feet.'

'No, sir.' Kenji laughed. 'But I did fly with Genda in a two-seater, which confirmed the flight surgeon's prediction. The moment we dived, climbed sharply or banked quickly, I either passed out or became disoriented. Under pressure, the bit of metal seems to touch some part of my brain.'

'Can't the surgeons operate?'

'They claim they would do as much damage to my brain as the shrapnel might do if it moves in deeper. They recommend leaving it alone. It just might work its way out.'

Yamamoto grunted and looked away. Then he said, 'I'm sorry to tell you that your request to have your uncle involved in affairs of state was denied.'

'By whom?'

'It comes from the highest level. But the rejection only regards military and political affairs.'

'What else remains for him?' Kenji asked.

'You and your uncle are to help finance the upcoming war in the south.'

'Are the high officials who asked, the same ones who rejected him?'

'They aren't asking.'

'Who can give orders to the lord keeper of the privy seal?' Kenji asked.

'Only his superior,' Yamamoto said, and Kenji understood he meant the Emperor. 'Hiroki is my friend,' the admiral said. 'I know he will be successful in whatever he undertakes. Japan needs money. Foreign currency. I'm speaking of millions, hundreds of millions of dollars, marks, sterling and francs. We're already paying exorbitant prices on the foreign markets for war-related materials. If the United States tightens its policy of Ring Fence, we'll have to go to war too soon, and unprepared.'

Kenji understood the older man to be saying that the second of the three major conditions for war with America would be met – the continuation of America's policy of strangling the Japanese economy. The only remaining condition was for Hitler to take Europe within two years. Kenji and Raiko had often discussed their positive feelings for the United States. He realized now they had always avoided discussing the possibility of war.

'My ships have nine months' fuel reserve,' Yamamoto said. 'And Japan does not produce a drop of oil. Eighty per cent of our petroleum imports come from the United States. Japan needs the Ishikawa zaibatsu to help finance the move south in order to secure a source of petroleum.'

Kenji turned to the Emperor's picture on the wall and bowed. 'So it is ordered, so it is done.'

'Good,' the admiral said. 'Now tell me how the amazing Miss Minobe is.'

'I don't know,' Kenji said. 'For weeks she has refused to see me.'

310

'That little woman is a most worthy person. You must not stand on ceremony. I recommend that you wait outside her house to catch her.'

'I have, but she doesn't come home. The chief at the Black Chamber must think me an idiot. I wait outside the new Communications Centre for her. She doesn't leave there. And the chief won't allow me into the building I built especially for her.'

'We shall see if he'll refuse me,' Yamamoto said, and dialled the telephone. 'Section Chief Ogino, this is Admiral Yamamoto. Please allow Major Kenji Ishikawa to visit Miss Raiko Minobe.'

Kenji watched Yamamoto's lips tighten, his eyes narrow and his knuckles whiten around the receiver. 'Silence,' the admiral growled. 'I do not care if Miss Minobe has broken the US brown code or anything else! My request for entrée has become an order! It does not concern me if Miss Minobe doesn't wish to see Major Ishikawa. I want him to see her! Let him in or I will send a contingent of marines to shoot you and break in!' Yamamoto slammed the receiver down and pointed at Kenji. 'Hurry, your woman is ill!'

34

From Tokyo the drive to Owada normally took an hour. Today, on the new road to the Communications Centre, Kenji caught sight of the aerials, antennae and machine-guns on the flat roof of the long, rectangular building in only thirty-five minutes. Guards recognized the Dusenberg and flung open the main gate. Kenji roared through, skidded to a stop in front of the entrance and jumped out of the car.

Section Chief Ogino stood on the bottom step. 'Before you go in, there are things we must discuss, Major Ishikawa.'

'We'll talk as we walk,' Kenji said.

'No. First you will hear me out. After my conversation with Admiral Yamamoto, I called General Tojo. Had he not granted permission, you would have needed marines to break in here. Miss Minobe's work has the highest security rating in the empire.'

'Say what you will and take me to her!'

'General Tojo cleared you for certain information,' Ogino said. 'We can now read all American diplomatic transmissions since Miss Minobe broke the US brown code. In addition, she was recently supplied with detailed blueprints of the new British M-138 cipher machine used for their diplomatic, military and maritime messages. Miss Minobe has been working on the contents of sixty packets filled with various British business codes, naval signals and the minutes of recent British secret military and cabinet meetings.'

Despite Kenji's desire to see Raiko, he could not help but ask, 'How did you come by all this material?'

'Miss Minobe decoded a radio message from the German merchant raider, *Atlantis*, to Berlin. It had captured, intact, the British steamer, *City of Baghdad*, in the South China sea. The contents of the ship were meant for the British governor generals of Singapore and India. Miss Minobe suggested we trade her solution of the Russian code to the Gestapo. Major Ando sounded out Sorge at the German Embassy in Tokyo and was introduced to Colonel von Ott. They met with Foreign Minister Matsuoka and completed the negotiations with Berlin via this centre. The *Atlantis* docked in Yokohama under cover of darkness, offloaded the crew and material from the *City of Baghdad*, and was gone by morning. Kempetai is holding the crew incognito outside Tokyo.'

'The British must know the Germans have the information,' Kenji said. 'They'll issue new code books.'

'The find was so important, Berlin ordered the *Atlantis* to report the *City of Baghdad* sunk with all hands.'

'Brilliant move. The value of the codes and cipher machine are clear. What do the envelopes contain?'

'More than you can imagine,' Ogino said. 'Since receiving this material, Miss Minobe has used the British codes to break the American brown code. She has been deciphering a two-year backlog of messages. She can now read the secret American communiqués like telegrams.' He handed Kenji an envelope. 'General Tojo ordered me to give you this. He said it is necessary for you to act soon on your financial scheme.'

'Very well. I want to see Miss Minobe now!'

'I must warn you that she is ill. For the sake of our country, I had to push her. Two weeks ago I saw how overworked she was. I tried to convince her to go home and rest, but she refused. She would not take a partner nor confide in anyone. In our business, that is dangerous.'

Kenji grabbed the section chief by the arm. He pulled

313

the man up the steps and past the guards. 'Show me where she is!'

Ogino led Kenji to a security door. 'Clear the chamber of all personnel except Miss Minobe,' the chief ordered the guard.

Several people came out, and Kenji entered. Raiko sat in a glass-enclosed cubicle at the far end of the room. Her hair was unkempt, her clothes looked slept-in. A cot with rumpled blankets was near her desk. Except for the occasional clatter of a teletype machine, the room was silent. Kenji watched her place some papers on the corner of her desk, stop, look at them, pick them up, examine them, put them back and stare at them. He entered the cubicle, but she did not notice him. She continued to stare at the papers.

'Raiko,' Kenji whispered. 'Raiko?' She looked up and he stepped back in shock. Her dark eyes were glazed and larger than ever before in her thin face. 'Why didn't they let me see you?' he asked. She just stared at him. 'Raiko, I'm here. It will be all right.'

She picked up the stack of papers in both hands and flung them in Kenji's face. 'You traitor,' Raiko screamed. She snatched a straight pen and raised it as if to stab him.

Raiko was half his size but Kenji fell back before her fury. He raised his arms to protect himself. 'How did I betray you?'

'With that big, white Russian woman! Natasha!'

Kenji's arms dropped. His shoulders slumped.

Raiko stood before him with the pen gripped in her small fist, shouting, 'Do you think I slept with you, nursed you like a baby for a year and a half so you could go off with your former mistress?' She trembled with fury. 'You betrayed me!' She threw the pen down and slapped his face – once, twice. Again she cried out. 'Why? Why? Why?'

Kenji stood motionless. 'Because,' he stammered.

Raiko punched his big shoulders with her little fists. 'You'd better explain or I'm going to hurt you! I'm going to hurt you worse than you hurt me!'

Tears filled Kenji's eye. 'I didn't betray you. I'd never want to hurt you.' He gulped. 'It's the wedding. I haven't agreed to a wedding date because I'm impotent.'

'How do you know that?'

'I remember what happened in Europe. I remember how you undressed me and came to bed with me and nothing happened. I pretended not to know or care, but I knew. The doctors said my mental problems are sex-related.'

'So you went to Natasha!' Raiko's cheeks puffed, her lower lip quivered. 'How was it with the white girl?'

Kenji lowered his head and shook it from side to side. 'I couldn't,' he whispered. 'I couldn't do it.' He began to weep. 'I'm permanently impotent.'

'You're stupid,' Raiko said. 'Of course you couldn't do it with her. You love me.' She began to weep, and moved into his arms.

'Yes, I love you,' Kenji said.

They held on to each other.

'When I was flying and lost consciousness, only the thought of you kept me from crashing my plane into the anti-aircraft guns,' Kenji whispered. 'I love you. Please don't hit me again.'

Raiko wept uncontrollably and Kenji cried with her.

'I'm not well,' Raiko whispered. 'I can't remember where I put things. I lost my eraser. I've been looking for it under so many papers. I had a pile on the corner of my desk.'

Kenji picked Raiko up in his arms like a child. 'Come home with me,' he said. 'I'll help you find everything you need for the rest of your life.'

Raiko had been in Kenji's care for three weeks before the

315

doctor allowed even her father to visit. Tatsukichi Minobe arrived at Kenji's house with Hiroki and Noriko.

Kenji greeted them at the front door. 'Raiko is sleeping,' he whispered. 'We'll talk in the salon.'

Minobe waited until the housekeeper had served tea and rice cakes before he spoke. 'Kenji, I appreciate your telephone call every day about Raiko. But I am most anxious to see my daughter.'

'And you will. The only medicine she needs now is rest. Today the doctor said she can go out for short walks, and in a few days do some shopping.'

'What course of treatment was used?' Noriko asked.

'Traditional,' Kenji said. 'The results were dramatic. When I brought Raiko here her pulse was 120, she had shortness of breath and trembled constantly. The doctor used acupuncture and within minutes her pulse was down and her body relaxed. She slept for twenty hours, woke, ate and slept again. The doctor has discontinued the acupuncture and liver pills. He prescribed herb tea, breathing exercises and a light diet.'

'What exactly caused Raiko's problem?' Hiroki asked.

'Overwork, and me. She thought I had picked up my affair with a Russian woman.'

'Did you?' Noriko demanded.

'No. I sent Natasha to America. Wantabe had warned Raiko to always work with a partner, someone to discuss her problems with, someone who would notice the danger signs of overwork. There was a recent flood of information into the new Black Chamber. Because she was angry at me, Raiko refused to go home and rest. She worked day and night. She has a recurring dream of walking a beach covered with numbered and lettered stones. Wantabe commands her to put them in order. She sorts them on her hands and knees, but when she is almost done the sea rushes in and tumbles the stones. She no longer becomes depressed after the dream, but is still anxious and weak.'

316

'I am indebted to you for taking care of my daughter,' Minobe said.

Kenji held up his hand and cocked his head. 'I think she's waking now.' He stood.

'I didn't hear anything,' Hiroki said.

'She rolled over,' Kenji said. 'I'll be right back.'

'Your nephew is more attentive to my daughter than I ever was to my wife,' Minobe said. 'Yet they are not married.'

'They soon will be,' Hiroki said.

Kenji returned to the salon. 'Aunt Noriko, Raiko asks that you help her dress and make up. She wishes to look her best.'

'That is a positive sign,' Hiroki said.

'I would be delighted,' Noriko said. 'Kenji, you stay here and help these two old buzzards solve the problems of state.'

'My wife is always right,' Hiroki said. 'It is good to be involved in national affairs again. I have drawn up plans for a coup on the world money markets.'

Kenji waited until Noriko closed the bedroom door before he spoke. 'I've learned that Major Shira Ando killed Wantabe. He and Dr Tsubota were also responsible for the riot at Tokyo University. Uncle, had you not taken charge of the operation to finance the war in South-East Asia, and Professor Minobe not retired from the university, you would both be dead.'

'What makes you say that?' Minobe asked.

'Mother of autumn, father of spring.'

'The same one who warned of my assassination?' Hiroki asked.

'Yes,' Kenji said. 'The same voice. My people traced his number to imperial military headquarters on the palace grounds. The last time it came from the army ministry building.'

'That and the fact the person calling must have been

317

an original Black Dragon, should narrow the number of people it could be,' Hiroki said.

'You cannot afford to make a mistake,' Minobe said. 'It could cost that someone his life.'

'You two gentlemen must also be careful,' Kenji said. 'Do or say nothing to anger the military. Koda-ha controls the government. Several assassinations of anti-war people haven't been reported in the newspapers. The army regulates the police, press and radio. They'll soon ban all public meetings not authorized by Kempetai.'

'We have become a country of fascists like Germany and Italy,' Hiroki said.

'There are differences,' Minobe said.

'Nuances, outside trappings,' Hiroki said. 'Our government leaders are acting just like Hitler and Mussolini.'

'The differences between Japan and Nazi Germany are basic,' Minobe said.

'This type of discussion solves nothing,' Kenji said. 'Professor Minobe, you must join us in seeking a financial solution to Japan's economic crisis.'

'I know nothing about finance,' Minobe said. 'My grocer is always threatening to dun me.'

'You have wealthy Japanese friends abroad,' Kenji said. 'We'll need their help. And I want Kempetai to learn of your support for the government's move into South-East Asia.'

'How?' Minobe asked.

'I'll tell them,' Kenji said.

'How can you be so positive we're going to take South-East Asia?' Hiroki asked.

'The last time I met with Admiral Yamamoto, it was to make plans. The chief of the Black Chamber gave me an envelope with the minutes of a meeting held by First Lord of the Admiralty Winston Churchill. The British are withdrawing their army from Asia to defend England. They can't spare a naval fleet here. Churchill instructed the governors of their Asian colonies to avoid any military confrontation with Japan until a mutual defence treaty is signed with the United States.'

'By the spirits,' Hiroki said. 'It means a secret agreement between Chamberlain and Roosevelt doesn't exist. That must have convinced Yamamoto that America will not go to war over British, Dutch or French possessions in the Pacific.'

'There's more,' Kenji said. 'Churchill recommends that the British buy us off with concessions and, if necessary, give up Singapore and Malaysia with only token resistance.'

The two older men stared in open-mouthed amazement at Kenji. 'Fortress Singapore,' Minobe said. 'If Britain is willing to give that up, the sun is about to set on their empire. There'll be no stopping Tojo.'

'I thought I had passed the age of goose bumps,' Hiroki said. 'But I see another sun about to rise in the world. The rays of the imperial flag will soon stretch over one-third of the earth's surface!'

Noriko called from the bedroom. 'Mini, your daughter wishes to see you.'

'Coming,' Minobe said.

'Is all this information confirmed?' Hiroki asked Kenji.

'Yes. But even if Roosevelt doesn't have a military pact with Britain, he's prepared to wage economic war on us. He'll help the English every way short of war. The American press accuses Roosevelt of promoting a war economy to end the American depression. Raiko deciphered a State Department message to Ambassador Grew. It says that if Japan continues her plans to invade South-East Asia, the United States will freeze all Japanese assets, break trade relations and implement a total embargo this coming May. We have six months to move our money.'

'War,' Hiroki said. 'Tojo may have been handed Malaysia and Indochina on a platter by the British, but if he

319

eats we end up fighting the Americans. Japan cannot afford war.'

'We must expand,' Kenji said. 'The ideal situation would be to move south, avoid a confrontation with the United States and supply the Europeans in their war.'

'Have you seen this anti-Japanese material from America?' Hiroki handed Kenji some pamphlets and fliers.

'This picture of the little girl sitting on the railroad tracks and crying was taken by John Whittefield in Nanking,' Kenji said. 'I was with him.'

'That picture and other stories about our actions in Nanking have raised millions of dollars for Chiang Kai-shek, and caused a nationwide boycott of Japanese products. People in America are checking labels. In the schools they are teaching their children not to buy anything made in Japan. There have been cancellations of orders by our US distributors. Some Ishikawa factories have had to close down. Thousands of workers are unemployed.'

'I've a solution to that.' Kenji printed three letters on a sheet of paper and showed it to Hiroki. 'Will the Americans buy products made in USA?'

'Certainly.'

'Think again. It doesn't mean United States of America. The city of Usa is located in Oita prefecture on our southern island of Kyushu. If the government would change the official Latin spelling of Usa to all capital letters and, on paper only, transfer the headquarters of our exporting companies to that city, they could stamp "MADE IN USA" on all our products.'

Hiroki laughed way down in his belly. 'This will give that bigot Henry Ford indigestion. And make William Randolph Hearst print his racist newspapers in purple ink. I still have friends in government who will enjoy pushing this through. Kenji, before those Wall Street manipulators freeze our country's assets, you and I are going to beat the pants off them.'

'Where did you learn a poker term like that?'

'From your great-grandfather.' Hiroki laughed again. 'Mung was a terrible poker player. Lost his clothes in a game with whalers. They let him go about naked for two days aboard ship. Now you and I are going to show the Americans how well we've learned their game. We'll need to use your Communications Centre at Owada. It will require the strictest secrecy and perfect timing.'

Noriko came up behind Hiroki. 'I think my timing is right. I want to speak with Kenji alone. You go see Raiko.'

'What have I done?' Kenji asked.

'It's what you haven't done. Marry Raiko.'

Kenji began to click his thumbnails. 'She's too weak.'

'The girl cannot stand another shock. She'll be disgraced if you don't either marry or leave her. If you go out walking and shopping and continue living with her, the Minobe family will be dishonoured. Set the wedding date!'

'Did Raiko say she wants that?'

'Yes.'

Kenji's head fell forward. He kept his eye on the floor. 'Aunt Noriko, I don't know how to tell you this. I'm not one hundred per cent healthy either. You're certain Raiko wants to be married?'

'Of course. What is it you don't know how to tell me?'

Kenji paused, then said, 'You set the date.'

'That's all you wanted to say?'

Kenji nodded. 'That's all.'

'Well I have something to tell you. Today you are moving out of this house. I will move in and care for Raiko until you two are married.'

'Where would I go?' Kenji asked. 'This is my house.'

'Stay with Hiroki. Invite Mini. You three bachelors should have fun planning to defraud the financial wizards of the world.'

The Year of the Dragon
1940

35

5 January 1940

Vinegar Joe Stilwell glared at the monkey wrench on Ambassador Grew's desk. 'Isn't there a law against Japs stamping stuff like that "MADE IN USA"?'

'No, sir,' John Whittefield replied. 'Japan's Geographical Survey and Post Office Departments made official requests to change the Latin lettering of Usa's name. The National Diet approved it.'

'My people in China have purchased Jap products believing they came from the States,' Stilwell said.

'Public awareness is the only answer,' Grew said. 'Since their raid on Wall Street, the slang to be Japped means to be duped.'

'The little bastards are tricking everyone,' Stilwell said. 'According to the London *Times*, they continue to milk the international money market.'

'The yen remains overvalued by twenty-three per cent,' Grew said. 'The Ishikawa zaibatsu is taking advantage of that to buy all the American scrap iron, oil and other petroleum products available. They're even involved in the American futures market.'

'Only until May,' John said.

'Are they reading our codes?' Stilwell asked.

'Either that or they've found a crystal ball,' John said. 'They know Roosevelt will cut off trade with Japan and freeze all Japanese assets in May. My agents report that Kempetai may have cracked our brown code.'

'Warn Washington that it's top priority to change the brown code,' Stilwell said. 'Ambassador, there's something

325

I'd like you to tell Secretary Hull. Chiang Kai-shek has to be pressured into offensive action against the Kwangtung army. Threaten to cut off his financial aid, or withdraw the Flying Tigers and stop shipment of arms to him. The generalissimo is laying back. Tojo has reduced his forces in Manchuria, Korea and China. Mao Tse-tung's Communists are doing most of the fighting and taking all the credit. The Reds are gaining popularity among the people. Washington has to know that without pressure from the Chinese Nationalists, there's nothing to stop Japan from moving south into the Pacific.'

'The Soviets can stop them,' Grew said. 'Japan has always been paranoid about Russia taking Manchuria, Korea and all of Sakhalin island.'

'Not lately,' John said. 'In fact, Tojo has withdrawn troops from the Mongolian border. The Russians have too. There's something strange about the whole Nohoman incident. It's taken months to piece together. There were only 60,000 Japanese troops used against Zukhov's army. They supposedly sustained 40,000 casualties, but weren't relieved until the truce was concluded. The replacements were new, untrained, forty-year-old conscripts.'

'Any second-year West Pointer would say it was a phony war,' Stilwell said. 'Does MacArthur know?'

'Yes,' John said. 'He reached the same conclusion and requested additional aircraft in anticipation of a Japanese move south. His advisers have begun to train the Filippino army.'

'We've got to break the Japanese codes,' Grew said. 'Our entire foreign policy is based on reaction. To take the initiative we need more information.'

'Our problem is the language,' John said. 'There's a lack of native Americans who speak Japanese.'

'What about the Nisei in California and Oregon?' Stilwell asked.

'Local prejudice and national distrust,' John said. 'After

326

the FBI caught two former American naval officers selling secrets to the Japs, and then the newspaper stories of Charlie Chaplin's valet being Kempetai, Americans of Japanese descent won't be trusted with sensitive military information. But I'm glad to say that naval intelligence is close to a breakthrough on one of Japan's high-level diplomatic codes.'

'I'll look forward to reading their radio mail,' Stilwell said. 'Let's get back to Wall Street. Tell us how the Japs took the big money boys.'

'They outfoxed the bourses of Paris, London and half of Europe too,' John said. 'First Yamamoto and Tojo blockaded Tientsin where England and France hold the silver bullion which backs China's currency. That devalued the yuan and strengthened the yen on foreign markets.'

'Yamamoto and Tojo aren't money men,' Stilwell said. 'Who are the manipulators?'

'Hiroki Koin and his nephew Kenji Ishikawa,' John said. 'Kenji used his zaibatsu's international connections to make a financial killing for his country. His uncle manipulated the Japanese government, its industry and banking system while Kenji orchestrated everything abroad. It took meticulous planning. The Ishikawa name inspired those involved to strict secrecy and unswerving faith in Kenji's word. Japanese abroad put up millions.

'Kenji waited until Friday night New York time when the major bourses in France and London were also closed for the weekend. He used the new Communications Centre at Owada to inform his agents and Japanese bankers of favourable opportunities in the short sale of foreign currency and purchase of commodities with yen. During the weekend, while the yen was still up in value because of the blockade in China, Kenji's agents and other Japanese abroad used the strong yen, just like these newfangled vacuum cleaners, to suck up foreign money and products. On Monday morning Hiroki Koin had the Japanese government devalue the yen by forty per cent. That freed 250 million dollars in the gold bullion that was being used to back the yen. Kenji had secretly shipped the quarter of a billion in gold abroad. Behind the scenes his people used the gold to buy up the previously cheap foreign money. On Monday morning the siege of Tientsin was lifted and the yen's devaluation announced. All foreign currencies shot up and the yen went down. The Japs held the more valuable foreign currency and the Western money markets held the devalued yen. Kenji Ishikawa and Hiroki Koin put Vanderbilt, J.P. Morgan and the rest of the stock-market sharks to shame.'

'Won't the international money people take revenge?' Grew asked.

'I doubt it,' John said. 'The Japanese are buying from these same men. Paying top price for Rockefeller's oil, Kaiser's steel and anything else they can lay their hands on.'

'I've never owned stock,' Stilwell said. 'Make it clear to me in dollars and cents how much they took in.'

'It's the largest coup in the history of money,' John said. 'My sources in the Ishikawa Specie bank claim they've already realized a 200-million-dollar profit.'

'You mean on the entire transaction?' Grew asked.

'No,' John said. 'Just that one bank. Estimates are of at least a billion-dollar return. The Japanese bought up most of America's cotton crop and are preparing to ship it back to Japan. If England can't purchase enough Egyptian cotton, her textile mills will have to close down.'

'Unthinkable,' Stilwell said. 'The British will soon be fighting for their lives against Hitler. They'll need that cotton.'

'Surely the French will stop the Germans at the Maginot line,' Grew said. 'They held the Boche in the Great War.'

'The French of today are not those who defended Paris in 1914,' Stilwell said. 'Observers in Paris say France has no strong leaders. Their army is equipped with old weapons, and the French people are tired from their losses in the last war. They're not marching to the recruiting stations like they did in 1914, but waiting to be called. They aren't hailing cabs to go out and stop the Germans, but dragging their feet and grumbling about having to fight again.'

'European intelligence confirms the general's information,' John said. 'France will probably surrender to a determined military effort by the Germans. Vichy France has already made overtures to Hitler. They'll co-operate if he doesn't invade their region.'

Ambassador Joseph Grew turned pale. 'My God, Man! You're talking about the fall of Europe. A Nazi conquest. Where's the French *élan vitale*? Their *esprit de corps*?'

'The Germans kicked it out of them twenty years ago,' Stilwell said. 'If not for the British, Australians and American armies, the French would have been goose-stepping two decades ago.'

Grew moved forward on the edge of his chair. 'John, you're telling us half of France is prepared to side with Hitler. What Frenchman would betray his country?'

'Laval,' John said, and poured a glass of water for the shaken ambassador. 'Pierre Laval, the former premier of France, is ready to play the role of Judas for political power.'

'He's the bastard who supported Mussolini's claim to Ethiopia,' Stilwell said.

'Don't either of you see the larger picture?' Grew asked. 'We're on the brink of a second world war that will dwarf the Great War. If France falls to the Nazis, nothing stands between Hitler and England except a few miles of water and the American navy. With our attention focused west, Japan will rule the east. I don't know if Roosevelt will

329

allow that.' He shook his head like a weary dog. 'I don't know if he can prevent it.'

'We have two years,' John said. 'That's how long before Japan's navy will have the ability to challenge our Pacific fleet. As for air power, our P-40 fighters have proved superior to the Japanese T-97s.'

'Chenault reports a new, faster Jap fighter plane,' Stilwell said.

'My sources give no indication of such an aircraft,' John said. 'I think Chenault's people are making excuses for recent losses. It's the same T-97 with folding landing gear.'

'I support John's argument,' Grew said. 'The last report from Chenault recommended that the US air force adopt what he called a new tactic of team flying. Our experts in Hawaii and Washington rejected the idea as an outdated tactic from the Great War. They also discount Chenault's claims of Japanese bombers flying missions from Formosa to Chungking. Air-force intelligence says the distance is too great.'

'That's it for Chenault's credibility,' Stilwell said. 'The validity of his reports will be forever questioned by army intelligence.'

'I've more bad news,' John said. 'Japan's foreign minister, the man we call Motor-Mouth Matsuoka, has again burst on to the international scene. He convinced Thailand to sign a non-aggression pact with Japan.'

'Thailand is no threat to the Japanese,' Grew said. 'What can Japan gain from the Thais?'

'The trust and respect of the Oriental people,' John said. 'The Japs are promoting the idea of a Greater Asia. Matusoka intends to champion Thailand's demand that the French return Laos and Cambodia to them.'

'I doubt the French will relinquish their colonies without a fight,' Grew said.

'The French colonists in Indochina supported Pierre

Laval several years ago when he was premier of France,' John said. 'Dr Tsubota, Japan's chief of foreign intelligence, has been speaking to them. He and Matsuoka have been in contact with the same German government officials working with Laval and his Vichy people. The Dutch, French and British have withdrawn their navies from the Far East. Admiral Yamamoto may not be able to defeat our Pacific fleet, but he's unopposed in Malaysia and Indochina by any European power.'

'I get the feeling of being swarmed over by a large pack of Japanese ants,' Stilwell said. 'The little bastards are everywhere.'

'Expect them in Burma too,' John said.

'How can there be so many of them on just four islands not even the size of Texas?' Stilwell asked.

'There were twenty million Japanese at the last census,' John said. 'Their level of education is higher than America's or any other country in the world. They're industrious, frugal and totally dedicated to the Emperor.'

'Maybe we should kill him,' Stilwell said.

'That idea has been rejected,' John said.

'Do you gentlemen realize the Japanese now have the manpower, money and are buying the materials to wage war against America?' Grew said.

'They're also building up a national psychological momentum towards war,' John said. 'Hitler's successes in Europe have awakened greed in many Japanese. They feel if Japan doesn't move soon to take the Pacific, Germany will.'

'I don't know if we can prevent hostilities between Japan and America, but it's our duty to try,' Joseph Grew said.

'They've recalled me to Louisiana,' Stilwell said. 'I'm to lead the invading force in the first large-scale training manoeuvres since the Great War.'

'Train them well,' the ambassador said. 'I'm afraid

331

they'll see action sooner than Washington expects. John and I will try to avoid that. We'll start by buttonholing Japanese and talking peace at the Ishikawa wedding. If they won't listen to sense, Japan, America and the rest of the world are moving towards global disaster!'

36

'It's as if we're preparing for a political convention,' Raiko said. 'Even today's presentation from the Emperor involves national politics.'

'I pronounce you fully recovered,' Noriko said. 'That old feistiness has returned to your voice. It shouldn't matter what you or Kenji think of imperial statecraft. It is an extraordinary honour to be presented with an award from his imperial majesty. Today's ceremony is the dream of Japanese children, the goal of every adult.'

'But I feel they're not rewarding me for my work, only using the ceremony as they are our wedding, to unite the anti-war and war factions.'

'Do you believe Kenji deserves his medal?'

'Yes, but he, Uncle Hiroki and my father are also guilty of manipulating the wedding-guest list like matchmakers. They have their heads together pairing this ambassador with that consul, those newspapermen with these industrialists, Yamamoto's navy people with Tojo's army officers.' Raiko pouted. 'I just want to get married.'

Noriko adjusted the ivory comb in Raiko's hair, gave a touch to her kimono and stepped back. 'I wish you had been born my daughter. No, on second thoughts, I prefer you as daughter-in-law. This way we shall be together more often. And I can teach you how to adjust to your newly-acquired social position. Your status as mother of the Ishikawa zaibatsu brings with it tremendous responsibilities. The prosperity of Ishikawa industries and their workers are in some way related to the welfare of half the people in the empire. Until his injury, Kenji was a playboy. He climbed mountains, designed planes, flew them and left business affairs to others.'

'He did well with the financial scheme,' Raiko said.

'His success was phenomenal. Hiroki described it as a fighter pilot's approach. Kenji swooped into the money markets, strafed the pound sterling, divebombed the dollar and then headed home. When you return from your honeymoon he must take control as managing director of the zaibatsu. No more wild parties, climbing buildings or doing figure-eights in the sky.'

'Unfortunately he's a different Kenji,' Raiko said. 'We're going by ship on our honeymoon rather than flying, because of the shrapnel in his head.'

'That is sensible. From now on everything in moderation. Your actions will always have economic and political implications. Your wedding is only the beginning.'

'Kenji and I have talked about our responsibilities. We understand and accept them, but also feel the year of our honeymoon belongs to us. The rest of our lives will be dedicated to Japan and the employees of Ishikawa industries. First Kenji and I are going to have fun.' Raiko thought of the cloud hanging over them. She and Kenji had talked of many things, but not about sex or children.

'Your last port of call before America is Hawaii,' Noriko said. 'If you wish to visit Ruth Kuhn, be sure to clear it first with Kempetai. Otherwise you could jeopardize her position there.'

The housekeeper entered the room and bowed. 'Ladies, the limousines shall arrive shortly. The gentlemen will be in the first car, you in the rear seat of the second car facing Princess Higashikuni and the wives of General Tojo and Admiral Yamamoto.'

'Why did Kenji have to buy two new Cadillacs?' Raiko asked.

'Actually Hiroki bought them for him after Roosevelt's threat to embargo Japan if we don't withdraw from China.

The second car is to be used for spare parts for the first. No one believes the Kwangtung army will leave the mainland.'

'It means war.'

'You know that your father, my husband and Kenji are trying to prevent war with America,' Noriko said. 'Your wedding provides an informal meeting place to exchange views between adversaries, without obligations or loss of face.'

'Our newspapers claim if we don't act in the Pacific, the Americans or Germans will. General MacArthur's war talk in the Filippino English weekly is not encouraging.'

'Ladies, the cars have arrived,' the housekeeper announced.

Noriko adjusted Raiko's obi. 'I am so proud of you. Hiroki and I are honoured we will have you in our family.'

Raiko bowed low. 'All these good things are happening and I am sad my mother isn't here to see them. But I am so very glad you are. I am honoured that I will become an Ishikawa.'

'Remember everything I told you about protocol while in the Emperor's presence,' Noriko said. 'The military have once again built him up as a living god. The common people can no longer even look upon his imperial majesty. It is like the old days. Last week a colonel was dismissed from the service because he moved his foot while standing in the imperial presence.'

The two beautiful women in traditional kimonos walked daintily down the gravel path to the second Cadillac. Before entering, they bowed to Princess Higashikuni, Mrs Tojo and Mrs Yamamoto. They took their seats with backs to the driver.

'In all the years I have been at court, this is the first time I have escorted anyone to receive an award from the Emperor,' the princess said.

335

'It is most exciting for us that a woman is to receive the Order of the Precious Crown,' Mrs Yamamoto said.

'Will you tell us what you did to deserve this honour?' Mrs Tojo asked.

'I am so sorry.' Raiko bowed. 'My instructions are not to discuss it.'

'Your work must be terribly important to receive the highest civilian award,' the princess said. 'I do not believe a woman was ever so honoured.'

'My husband recommended Miss Minobe for the award,' Mrs Yamamoto said.

'And my husband recommended Colonel Ishikawa,' Mrs Tojo said.

'Has Kenji been promoted?' Raiko asked.

'That was my husband's influence,' the princess said. 'It is the army's way of honouring their own before retirement. Today will be Colonel Ishikawa's last day in uniform.'

Raiko found it difficult to hide the relief she felt that Kenji's military career was officially over.

'It must be difficult for your future husband to accept his inability to fly again,' Mrs Yamamoto said. 'Have the doctors discerned any movement of the shrapnel in his head?'

'None,' Raiko said. 'But Kenji has kept busy designing a new version of the Zero torpedo-plane. He is in constant touch with the air force.'

'Kenji's cousins are with him, your father and the lord keeper of the privy seal in the first car,' the princess said. 'General Hashimoto personally arranged for Majors Hino and Genda Arai to accompany both of you into the Emperor's presence.'

'An honourable addition to this most happy day,' Raiko said.

Noriko patted Raiko's hand as the big automobile glided between the ancient trees, trimmed hedges and manicured lawns of the palace grounds.

Raiko looked out of the window. 'We have been so busy with preparations for the wedding, I wasn't excited about today. Until now. Entering the palace grounds has made it real. What are they building over there?' She pointed.

For a moment the three ladies opposite appeared uneasy. Then the princess said, 'That is Obunko, the imperial bunker. It is to protect his majesty in case of air attacks. This is not for public knowledge of course. It could lead people to question the need for it and . . .'

'And the wisdom of our military leaders,' Mrs Yamamoto said.

The princess and Mrs Tojo both frowned as the car stopped and the door was opened. The men, from the first car, preceded the women into the palace.

Mrs Yamamoto walked between Raiko and Noriko. 'The admiral arranged for Lord Koin and Professor Minobe to take part in this ceremony,' the admiral's wife said. 'Although this is a private affair, people in power will hear of their presence at court. It will gain them a degree of protection against further attacks by military fanatics.'

'Are you saying my father agrees with military expansion?' Raiko asked.

Mrs Yamamoto glanced at the princess and Mrs Tojo just ahead, and whispered, 'Both your father and Lord Koin agree with my husband that force may be necessary for Japan's move south.' She motioned with her little finger to the two other women. 'Their husbands want to fight America. Ours do not.'

The anteroom to the imperial reception hall was divided by a long table. The ladies sat down on one side, the men stood on the other.

'People from the physics and engineering departments of Tokyo University say a turbo engine that exhausts powerful jets of air is possible,' Professor Minobe said to the men in a semicircle around him.

'Could it be mounted on a plane?' Genda asked. 'How fast could it go?'

'Our scientists claim the only speed restrictions on such a craft depend on people like Kenji here. If my future son-in-law can design a plane to withstand the stress of one, two or three times the speed of sound, the jet air engine will propel it that fast.' The little professor smiled at the shocked pilots. 'Last year, 29 August to be exact, a Heinkel-178 flew a fifty-kilometre course with a jet air engine.'

'The country that can produce such a plane will rule the skies,' Kenji said. 'Are you certain of this information?'

'It came to me round about from Charles Lindbergh,' Minobe said. 'The American aviator is a frequent visitor to Berlin. I must add that the new aircraft is still faulty in performance and has caused the deaths of several test pilots.'

'We must have that engine,' Kenji said. 'I'll solve the aerodynamic problems. Such a plane would make the Zero obsolete.'

'I informed Foreign Minister Matsuoka in Berlin,' Hiroki said. 'He approached Air Marshal Goering, who denies the existence of a jet-propelled plane.'

'Oh, look at the light in Kenji's eye.' Minobe laughed. 'I never saw it there when you studied with me.'

'You never mentioned the possibility of flying faster than the speed of sound,' Kenji said.

'Since the authorities will not allow me to teach constitutional law, and I am going to have a pilot in the family, I've taken to reading American and British aviation magazines.'

'An ex-pilot,' Kenji said.

'An aeronautical engineer,' Hino chimed in.

'Whatever he is, as long as the marriage takes place in two days.' Minobe raised his glass to Kenji. 'I am following in the footsteps of my daughter. She reads other people's radio mail, I read their newspapers and magazines. You would be surprised at how much America's free press reveals. Igor Sikorsky has flown the S-300. The US marine corps is studying tactics for vertical envelopment by its infantry.'

'Sikorsky has been working on his eggbeater for twenty years,' Hino said. 'It has probably killed more test pilots than this German jet plane you mentioned.'

'He can make it go in any direction but forward,' Minobe said.

'You're joking,' Genda said.

'No. According to the article, vertical take-off and horizontal flight to either side or backwards are possible. The Mad Russian cannot make the machine go forward.'

'No problem,' Kenji said. 'Put the tail up front and the nose in the rear.'

The men laughed as they were served another round of drinks.

Hino took Kenji aside. 'I need your advice. I don't know how to map the air currents to the Philippines without being spotted by MacArthur's reconnaissance planes.'

'I thought you were mapping the air currents to the Hawaiian islands,' Kenji said.

'Those were Yamamoto's orders. Tojo changed them after I found a look-alike Pearl Harbor for Genda to practise on.'

'Does Yamamoto know?'

'Yes,' Hino said. 'He'll provide a small aircraft carrier, but not to go further than 100 miles from Formosa. Any closer to the Philippines, he says, the Americans may consider an act of war.'

'You can fly the weekly route from Formosa to Manila and back on our commercial airliner.'

'That will help, but I need more flight time at different altitudes to understand the effects of the sun's heat on the winds.'

339

'Is it necessary for you to fly the Zero for charting purposes?'

'No,' Hino said. 'Later on I can see if it's possible to fly the combat-loaded Zero non-stop from a land base in Formosa to the Philippines and return.'

'That's a 1,000-mile trip,' Kenji said. 'There's never been a mass military flight of such a distance.'

'And we would have to allow enough fuel for at least thirty minutes of air battles,' Hino said. 'If I can find consistent tail winds, train our men to use oxygen and the variable-pitch propeller, we might set another world distance record and surprise the hell out of MacArthur.'

'Do you realize we're talking of war with the United States?'

'They're the only ones left in the Pacific to fight,' Hino said.

'We can't beat them,' Kenji said.

'The Emperor wants to give it a try. He's building Obunko and who else could bomb Tokyo? Genda told me you were uneasy about General Billy Mitchell's complaint that our army had occupied and fortified islands in the north Pacific. Kenji, that was done in the 1920s. More recently, landing fields there have been lengthened for our new bombers.'

'Those islands are in the north Pacific,' Kenji said.

'Correct, dear cousin.' Hino grinned. 'For decades there have been men in high positions in our military who have seen America as the ultimate enemy of Japan. They have plans that would boggle your mind.'

'Why don't they listen to those who have lived and studied in the States? We can't defeat the American industrial machine! They could sink our islands just by dumping the output from their production lines on our shores. Japan has no natural resources. Oil, iron and rubber must be brought in by ship. If the Americans were to use submarine wolf packs to cut off our supplies, as the Germans are doing to the British, Japan would be finished!'

Hino put his hand on Kenji's arm. 'We can defeat the United States air force! Your Zero is the best military aeroplane in the world! Goering proved that whoever controls the skies wins the war. For the present, all we're doing is an exercise in long-distance flying to keep our brains from going stale. Help me figure how to stay out between Formosa and the Philippines without being spotted by American scout planes.'

Kenji shrugged. 'It's easy. I'll have our shipping company use the longest coal and cement barges we have on the route from Formosa to Manila. They'll be fitted with planking and plywood panels that can be assembled into a landing deck. Use the T-94 biplane. It's light and has a short landing and take-off range.'

'Brilliant!' Hino slapped Kenji's shoulder. 'You've given me a camouflaged baby aircraft carrier. I'll take along mechanics, load spare parts aboard and map the winds to hell and back!'

The big oak doors to the imperial reception room swung open and the master of protocol bowed. 'His imperial majesty will receive you. Ladies, please form a line on my left as we enter. Princess Higashikuni will lead. Gentlemen on my right. Lord Koin first. Please follow me into the presence of his most imperial majesty, the 124th sovereign of Japan who reigns in the era of enlightenment and harmony.'

Each of the men and women bowed as they crossed the threshold. They lined up in a row before the dais, as directed by the master of protocol, and remained bowed until he mounted the dais and said, 'Rise up!'

Raiko was surprised to see the Empress seated alongside her husband on a golden throne. She appeared to be a kindly, motherly figure. To Kenji the Emperor seemed uncomfortable in his stiff military uniform. To Hiroki and

Minobe the Emperor's uniform meant war, although with whom neither was certain.

The master of protocol unfolded a parchment and read aloud, 'In accordance with the fifty-fourth proclamation of the Great Council of State established in 1875, Miss Raiko Minobe is hereby awarded the Order of the Precious Crown. This decoration is bestowed in recognition of outstanding service to his imperial majesty and the people of Japan. By her diligence, perseverance and dedication, Miss Minobe saved thousands of Japanese lives. Her work will affect future foreign and national policies of our country. Miss Minobe, please step forward.' He held out a velvet pillow on which was draped a golden chain and pendant.

Raiko tried to move but her feet were rooted to the floor. Her caustic comments about the award had been her way of shielding herself from the great honour bestowed upon her. She looked up and her eyes met those of the Emperor peering through his wire-frame glasses. He smiled as if he understood her problem and nodded his head, pulling her forward with a movement of his right hand. Raiko melted. The spell was broken and another cast. The Emperor had won her heart. She stepped up to the dais, bowed and accepted the medal. She bowed again and backed to her place, vowing silently, 'I will serve your imperial majesty with all my heart and all my might.'

The Emperor adjusted his glasses and addressed Raiko. 'I have been aware of your talent for deciphering foreign codes. Your latest effort has given us here at imperial headquarters a significant advantage in planning the future. Your personal sacrifices were taken into account when Admiral Yamamoto recommended you for this honour. Because of the nature of your work, this award will remain a secret. But we here at the palace, and others high in government and the military, know of the service rendered by Miss Raiko Minobe to her country. Japan will soon call upon all her sons and daughters to make sacrifices. I expect that upon your return from abroad, you will take up your duties once again.'

Kenji wanted to protest. He wished to keep Raiko from twisting her mind on convoluted code patterns and ciphers. He heard the master of protocol begin the honorifics prior to his presentation. His achievements in aeronautical engineering were praised. The number of enemy planes he had downed were mentioned. A detailed account of his epic flight from Nanking was retold. Then he was called to the dais. He bowed, and received the Order of the Golden Kite. He bowed again and backed to his place.

'In times like these, Japan needs her heroes,' the Emperor said. 'Colonel Kenji Ishikawa has set a standard for all our men to measure themselves by. You are a modern-day Japanese warrior. Fearless courage combined with innovative intellectual achievements in the fields of aeronautics, and more recently in finance, have set you above your fellows. Moryiama Ishikawa, or John Mung as your great-grandfather was called, was honoured more than once by my grandfather, Emperor Meiji. Mung was given the title of Black Dragon eighty years ago, when the only wheeled vehicle in the empire was the imperial funeral coach. Now we stand at an important crossroad in our nation's history and you, Kenji Ishikawa, carry on for your great-grandfather. Your trip abroad will take you to Indonesia, Malaysia, Hawaii, Mexico and America. Your observations there will be of great interest to our military planners.'

Kenji was pleased by the Emperor's comparison of him to John Mung, and surprised by the mention of travels to Indonesia, Malaysia and Mexico. Those places had not been on the honeymoon itinerary.

Raiko had decoded enough messages from Kempetai agents in Mexico and southern California to understand the Emperor's meaning. Her honeymoon would also be a political trip with military implications.

Then the Empress began to speak. 'The Emperor and I wish the prospective bride and groom much happiness. May your wedding, two days hence, be the start of many years of joy and laughter. My presence here today is because of Miss Minobe and her award. It is unusual for a woman to be so honoured. However, the deeds of Kenji's great-aunt, Gin-ko Ishikawa, were recorded twice in the Book of Good Deeds. Gin-ko Ishikawa risked her own life to protect her mother-in-law from assassination. Then delivered a child to the dying woman. This child was Kenji's grandfather Shimatzu. A year later, while pregnant with her own child and caring for the orphaned baby, Gin-ko Ishikawa organized the women of Sapporo to defend that northern city against Vulcan pirates.' The Empress nodded at Raiko. 'You are cut from the same mould and will bring honour to the Ishikawa family. I understand yours is not an arranged marriage, but a love match.' She smiled at the young couple. 'I am a romantic and approve of such things. Most people do not know the Emperor chose me over the objections of his counsellors. We wish you well.'

The master of protocol backed off the dais and down the steps. 'Professor Minobe and Lord Koin will remain,' he said.

The others bowed and backed from the chamber. The anteroom table was set with food, drink and personal gifts from the Emperor. Noriko gave a short speech. Hino and Genda toasted the bridal couple.

'Miss Minobe, Colonel Ishikawa, please accompany me,' the master of protocol said. 'You are to meet with General Tojo's staff.'

37

Raiko and Kenji sat in the gazebo looking out at the ancestral tombstones. Past the cemetery they could see the imperial palace. Noriko stood in front of them, giving instructions.

'Kenji, tomorrow is your wedding day. Before the ceremony, shortly before sunrise, at the hour when it is neither night nor day, light nor dark, and spirits roam free, you, Hiroki and Minobe will be at the seashore. You three will fill small wicker boats with fruit, sweetmeats and lanterns. One basket for each of your departed parents, and for Raiko's mother. Those little boats will float upon the water and the tide will take them out to sea. The boats shall disappear into the spirit world, as gifts to those who dwell beyond the clouds.' Noriko pointed at the moss-covered tombstones. 'All my family, and several Ishikawas are buried here. We shall visit them and ask their blessings on your marriage. I have brought the two of you here to speak of our families' histories.'

'From the little I know of the subject, Kenji and I could be cousins,' Raiko said.

'In name, not in blood,' Noriko said. 'Adoptions of bright young men into upper-class families were, and still are, common. Mung was adopted into the Ishikawa family and given the rank of senior samurai. He later adopted Udo, who had three sons. My father adopted Hiroki, Udo's youngest son, in order to continue our family name. On paper it appears I married my brother.' Noriko giggled. 'Kenji's grandfather Shimatzu was born to Ukiko, Mung's second wife, and raised by Gin-ko. Gin-ko died of cancer and is buried over there with

345

her husband, Udo. He committed seppuku to join her in death.'

'Why speak of so much death before a wedding?' Kenji asked.

'I speak of our history,' Noriko said. 'Tomorrow you will both receive many gifts. I wish to present mine today. To Raiko I give the history of our families and our people, in the form of my ohino matsuri dolls. The collection is 450 years old, and comes from both the Ishikawa and Koin families. Both those names appear early on in the ancient Book of Chronicles.'

Raiko bowed. 'I shall treasure them always.'

'Dolls have been used from the beginning of time to teach our history,' Noriko said. 'Each family belongs to a society in which the members are responsible for certain historical periods. I shall teach you through the dolls, and you shall teach your children. As well as children of the neighbourhood.'

'Thank you, dear Aunt Noriko,' Kenji said.

'First let me say, Kenji, that since Hiroki and I have raised you as our son, we have the right to obligate you. Therefore, your present is an On.'

Kenji bowed. 'I am proud to accept the gift. Please tell me how I may perform Giri.'

'I did not think it possible for an On to be a gift,' Raiko said. 'It is an obligation that requires repayment.'

Noriko smiled and touched the young woman's hand. 'My husband received this same On from his mother, Gin-ko, and Hiroki claims it to be his most treasured gift. He has performed Giri to his mother by keeping his word and a faithful marriage. Kenji, your On is to sleep with no other woman than Raiko.'

'That's it?' Kenji found it difficult to stifle a laugh. 'I'm to have one wife and no concubines?'

'The concept of a one-partner marriage is Christian,' Raiko said.

346

'Grandfather Mung was converted to Christianity,' Noriko said. 'Although in later years he rejected it, he was influenced by the experience. Even when his first wife Saiyo arranged for another woman for him during her menstrual periods, he did not accept. Years later, Udo Ishikawa scoffed at all Christian beliefs except this one. Gin-ko's On to my husband Hiroki has made our lives so much richer that I now give this obligation to Kenji as my gift for a happy marriage.'

Kenji forced a smile and swallowed his bitterness. In my condition such an obligation means nothing, he thought. He bowed to Noriko. 'I will take no other woman to my bed, nor sleep with any other than my bride, Raiko Minobe.'

Noriko beamed at the young couple. 'Chaperones are supposed to watch their charges closely.' She bowed. 'But a few minutes alone cannot hurt. I wish to visit my father's grave and talk with him.' She walked away.

'I release you from this On and the Giri imposed on you,' Raiko said.

Kenji's cynical laugh startled Raiko. He looked away from her as he spoke. 'I would be afraid to sleep with another woman, even if I could. You were furious at me for having gone to Natasha before we were married. After our wedding you would probably beat me to a pulp. Besides, what can I do in bed?'

Raiko looked at Kenji's blind, patched eye as he looked out over the tombstones. 'It's not a tragedy,' she said. 'When we're away from here and alone together, everything will be fine.'

'The roof is the only original part of this gazebo,' Kenji said. 'Everything else was destroyed during the great earthquake.' He pointed to the bronze Buddha. 'That statue weighs one ton and it was thrown several feet by the upheaval. Mung and Noriko's father were seated in here and escaped unharmed when the 'quake struck, but

347

shortly after Iyeasu was burned to death on the main road. He had only one leg and couldn't outrun the firestorm. Mung saved an orphaned child and his own life by diving into a sewerage ditch. The child grew up and was adopted into Prince Saionji's family. We'll meet Iyeasu Saionji at our wedding.'

'You didn't answer me,' Raiko said.

Kenji turned so his one eye looked at her. 'Because this On is no real obligation. I might as well be a Chinese eunuch as a husband. I haven't had an erection since I was wounded.'

'Possibly the shrapnel is touching a part of your brain that controls your sex drive,' Raiko said. 'It could move and you'll be well again.'

'It isn't that I don't think about sex. I think about you and sex all the time. But nothing happens.'

'Do you love me?'

'Yes,' Kenji whispered. 'I daydream about the villa outside Mukden. I remember our lovemaking and my heart swells until I can't breathe. It has been difficult concentrating on the mechanical drawings for the aeroplane and shallow-draught torpedoes because of my memories. I want to make love to you. I want to enjoy it as we did in the villa. Just being your husband without bringing you the happiness we had can't begin to repay you for the time you nursed me.'

'You're talking of gratitude, not love.'

'Yes and no. I could rationalize having repaid my debt by nursing you through your illness. It's not that. I want to love you so you will have been loved by me. No one in the world can love you as I do.' A tear ran down Kenji's cheek and he sighed. 'I'm selfish. I want to hold you in my arms. Kiss you. Feel your body against mine. Run my hands up and down your back as you sit on me and move up and down with your head thrown back, mouth open, gasping. I want to reach up and touch your nipples, then roll on to you and crush you into the quilt.' He reached out for Raiko's hand but she was pointing down.

They both stared at the bulge in the crotch of his trousers. Raiko touched it, and squeezed gently. 'It's hard. I told you everything would be fine.' Their eyes met and she squeezed again.

Kenji moaned. He stood up and spread his arms. 'By the gods, I've got an erection,' he shouted. He embraced Raiko, lifting her from the floor. She clung to him and raised her face. Their lips met; their bodies swayed back and forth.

'It's alive,' Kenji murmured. 'It's alive. Can you feel it?'

'It's mine,' Raiko said. 'I feel your life pressing into me and it's mine.'

'Put that girl down this instant,' Noriko called as she hurried towards them. 'What will people think of you? What will they think of me as a chaperone? Here you are in the middle of a graveyard shouting about your erection and starting to make love in broad daylight. I should not have left you. Control yourselves!'

Kenji put Raiko down and both looked at the bulge in his trousers, laughing, crying.

'Have you two no shame?' Noriko demanded. 'Two utter fools! Where are your manners? Come with me!' She placed herself between them.

The young couple tried to appear dignified as they followed Noriko to visit the family graves, but they giggled every time they looked at each other.

On their way out of the cemetery, Kenji reached behind Noriko's back and patted Raiko's arm.

'Do not touch that girl,' Noriko ordered. 'Not until tomorrow!' She took Raiko by the hand and led her away. 'You are worse than he is. Teasing him with those big beautiful eyes and the sway of your hips. Where did you learn to walk like that?'

'From the girls at the Fifth Moon Inn,' Raiko said.

'Tomorrow please wait until the wedding guests have left before you jump into bed with him. And I'll be watching tonight. He's got more lust in that one eye than he ever had when there were two.'

'I love you,' Raiko called back to Kenji.

38

'This wedding is Tokyo's most important social event,' Joseph Grew said. 'Every foreign ambassador, consul and newspaperman is here.'

'Not to mention the bigwigs of Japanese industry, government and military,' John Whittefield said. 'It's an opportunity to hold out the olive branch. Yesterday's surrender of Finland to the Russians has to be worrying the head of the Kwangtung army.'

'Prime Minister Konoe and Foreign Minister Matsuoka don't appear concerned,' Grew said. 'Matsuoka hinted at Japan and Russia joining the Axis Alliance with Italy and Germany. I don't want to believe that.'

John frowned. 'Motor-Mouth Matsuoka put the German–Japanese Anti-Comintern Pact together. Nobody believed it possible. A four-power Axis treaty between Russia, Italy, Germany and Japan would end democracy in Europe and ensure the fall of China. Italy has already annexed a good part of Africa, and Russia would take Iran, Turkey and Saudi Arabia. The Pacific would be Tojo's!'

Grew hummed to himself. He ground his teeth. Then he said, 'Our ambassador in Germany reported that Matsuoka went from Berlin to Moscow, where he met with Molotov before returning home. Not good. Not good at all.'

'At this wedding we will encourage the peace-seekers of both sides,' Tojo said. 'We need a little more time to prepare for war.'

Hashimoto nodded his approval.

'Professor Minobe and Lord Koin both accept the necessity of invading South-East Asia,' Prime Minister Konoe said. 'The Emperor wishes them to allay America's fear of war with Japan. They will accompany our delegation to Washington.'

'They are fools,' Hashimoto said. 'Roosevelt will continue his policy of Ring Fence. If we do not face up to the Americans, we will be choked to death.'

'What would you do if the Americans abandoned the Ring Fence policy and accepted Japanese rule of South-East Asia?' Tojo asked.

'Attack them anyway,' Hashimoto said.

'War is a sign of political failure,' Konoe said.

'This fight is for the leadership of the Orient,' Hashimoto replied. 'We represent more than two-thirds of the earth's population. Why shouldn't we rule it?'

'I would prefer to dominate by political acumen rather than military might,' Konoe said.

'There will be war with the United States,' Tojo said. 'But not yet. It is foolish to disregard Yamamoto's assessment of American naval strength. They have moved their entire Pacific fleet from San Diego to Hawaii. Our navy is not ready.'

'We must show the whites of the world we are not only their equals, but their betters,' Hashimoto declared.

'Excuse me for eavesdropping,' John Whittefield said, slurring his words and sloshing the drink he held. 'Does your statement include humbling the Germans, General Hashimoto?'

There was much grunting from the three Japanese. 'Please join us, Mr Whittefield,' Prime Minister Konoe said. 'We are honoured to be attending this wedding with you and the American Ambassador.'

'Thank you, Mr Konoe,' Grew said. 'Please excuse John's brash question. But I wonder how General Hashimoto or any Japanese, for that matter, could consider Germany as a partner in the Axis Alliance. The Nazis call themselves the master race.'

Foreign Minister Matsuoka forced his way into the circle of men. He snuffed out a big Havana cigar and spoke in a rush of words. 'Japan unofficially supports Germany just as the United States does England and France. We will sign an agreement with Hitler just as Roosevelt will join his allies from the Great War. When Hitler takes France and makes his move across the channel to England, America will declare war on Germany.'

'That is an assumption,' John said. 'But if so, what would Japan do?'

There was tense silence. No one moved.

Ambassador Grew broke the uneasy quiet. 'John's original question was not directed to politics or military strategy. We Americans think the Nazi myth of Aryan superiority an insult to the Japanese people.'

'A German should answer the question,' Tojo said. He sent an aide to fetch a tall, handsome blond-haired man, who sauntered towards them in a custom-made white tuxedo.

'Sorge. Richard Sorge at your service.' He clicked his heels and bowed.

'Mr Sorge is the senior German newspaper correspondent in Tokyo,' Tojo said. 'Perhaps he can answer what appears to be a contradiction regarding the Nazi theory of racial superiority and a possible alliance between Germany and Japan.'

The tall German snapped open a gold cigarette case and offered it around. He composed his thoughts as he puffed a cloud of smoke above the heads of those near him. 'The principles of racial supremacy are proven by history,' Sorge said. 'Its present validity is apparent in Germany's recent victories in Poland and Japan's successes in China. Adolf Hitler has brought to the world an ideology compounded of racial imperialism which is justified by fundamental geopolitics. Racial superiority and the benefits derived therefrom determine Japan's and Germany's right of territorial expansion.'

John took another drink from a passing waiter and said, 'I'm impressed with your choice of words, but not their meaning. They make little sense, and certainly do not explain the contradiction in terms between Aryan supremacy and an alliance between Caucasian Germany and Oriental Japan.'

The Japanese shifted uncomfortably, but Richard Sorge remained unperturbed. He drew in on his cigarette, blew out the smoke, and said, 'Germany's Minister of Propaganda Joseph Goebbels refers to the Japanese as the Prussians of the East. Our Bureau of Race Investigation in Berlin has authorized marriages between Germans and Japanese. What more could you ask?'

'The truth,' John said, and downed his drink. He shrugged off Grew's restraining hand. 'Hitler's racial policies are stupid! How does the Führer's *Mein Kampf* justify, politically, racially or ideologically, Germany's recent alliance with Russia?'

Again there was much grunting from the Japanese. Sorge smiled and took a puff on his cigarette. Grew took John's arm and led him away from the group. 'John boy, that was rude and you are drunk!'

'No, sir, I'm not drunk. In Japanese society it's the drunk who can express himself without being held responsible. I downed half a bottle of olive oil prior to coming here so the booze wouldn't affect me. I got my point across.'

'Yes you did, but there was no olive branch hung on it,' Grew said.

'I didn't see theirs either.'

Kenji stood on the receiving line greeting guests as they

354

passed through the Torii gate into the grounds of the Kaneiji shrine. An impressive grey-haired man moved behind him and whispered in his ear, 'Mother of autumn.'

Kenji spun around. 'The telephone voice.'

'I am Iyeasu, Prince Saionji's adopted son, at your service.' The man bowed.

Kenji bowed lower, and longer. He stepped away from the reception line. 'It is I who am forever in your debt for the timely warnings,' he whispered.

'My On to the Ishikawa family is unrepayable,' Iyeasu Saionji said. 'Your great-grandfather saved me in the great earthquake. As Black Dragon, head of the imperial secret service, Mung was one of the most powerful men in the empire. But he took the time to establish the first orphanage in Japan. He put my adoptive father, Taro Kihei, in charge of the housing and education of more than 100 children. After Taro died, Mung singled me out for higher education. He recommended me to Prince Saionji. I was adopted into the prince's family and trained for government service.'

'What is your position now?' Kenji asked.

'I am a member of the advisory staff of the Imperial Military Planning Board at the palace. Dr Tsubota and Major Ando wish to recruit you as their agent. Listen carefully to their advice. You and your wife are expected to gather information while on your honeymoon. I know about Ruth Kuhn and her father, about the Yaqui Indians, the Southern Pacific Railroad and the fishing boats.'

'You mean the Ishikawa fishing fleet.' Kenji tapped his chest. 'I own those boats. The plan for using them is crazy.'

'Generals Tojo, Hashimoto and Prime Minister Konoe are extremely dangerous. How did you and your bride answer Tsubota and Ando?'

'We promised to consider their proposals.'

'Bless your father for not having sired a stupid son,'

Iyeasu Saionji said. 'But you must inform Hashimoto at the first opportunity that you and your bride accept. If not, Ando has orders to kill you.'

'Why?'

'Once you've left the country, the nationalization of all industries will begin with the Ishikawa zaibatsu. Your ships, planes, newspapers and industries will be put under government control. Prior to the invasion of South-East Asia, Prime Minister Konoe will appoint Tojo as Minister of War. Your agreement to spy means your compliance with the government takeover.'

'So,' Kenji said. 'What funds the Americans don't freeze, my countrymen will take.'

'Move your money to Switzerland, Sweden or some other neutral country before May. Do not try to fight the nationalization process. These men respect you as a warrior, but they fear your financial power. Strive secretly for a peaceful settlement between Japan and the United States, but work for your country. There is no dishonour in spying for Japan. And now I leave you with a reminder. Do not ever try to contact me. It would be dangerous for you and your family. The Kempetai are everywhere.'

Iyeasu Saionji's use of the Japanese term for extended family alarmed Kenji. Here was a powerful man, high in the military, yet he too felt threatened by the secret police. Saionji had disappeared in the crowd.

'You are wanted on the receiving line,' Hino said. He led Kenji back.

'Ambassador Grew and his cultural attaché wish to pay their respects,' Minobe said.

'It is my honour,' Kenji said, shaking hands with the Americans.

'I assume this wedding ceremony is as ancient as the shrine,' Grew said.

'I'm not certain.' Kenji laughed. 'This is my first time getting married.'

356

John Whittefield raised his glass. 'A toast to the groom. May he enjoy a lifetime with his bride and sire many bright, healthy, happy children.'

'Kenji may have received the highest medal of valour, but he would fail a test in cultural history,' Hiroki said. 'This type of wedding party is relatively new. Only family and close friends used to be invited. My wife is responsible for setting this trend of a large wedding at a local shrine. The first time was at the marriage of John Mung's son Shimatzu. Mung instructed Noriko to carry through the theme of modern and traditional.' Hiroki pointed. 'On each table you see two different flower arrangements, the old rikka style and the newer moribana. There are Japanese foods and Western-style meats. Look at the Japanese women. Half wear Western gowns, the others kimonos.'

'They appear more beautiful and at ease in traditional dress,' Grew said.

'I agree,' Minobe said. 'But one Western innovation I prefer over saké is whisky. Will you gentlemen join me?' He signalled a waiter.

John sipped his whisky. 'Where is the bride?' he asked.

'Changing into the white shroud of a corpse,' Hiroki said. 'When Raiko leaves her father's house she will be treated as dead. He will precede her on foot with presents for Kenji. When they reach here, the ceremony shall begin.'

'The bridal party will arrive soon,' Genda said. 'Kenji must change to traditional dress.'

Following relatives and friends, Raiko mounted the worn stone steps of the shrine. She was greeted at the top by the Ishikawa family. The gifts were accepted, food offered and Raiko led away by Noriko to a dressing room. Raiko exchanged her white gown for a silk kimono bearing delicate hand-painted bamboo and colourful birds. A large deep-brimmed white hat was pinned to her thick dark hair. An obi of the purest white silk was wound around her thin waist. Raiko's cheeks were rouged, her eyebrows pencilled and a delicate perfume applied to her wrists, neck and earlobes.

Kenji donned the brown silk kimono his grandfather had worn to his wedding. The short ebaori jacket was embroidered with good-luck symbols. Hino and Genda escorted Kenji between rows of people, over the great stone tiles towards the shrine's entrance. Halfway there they stopped. General Hashimoto stepped out from among the guests and stood at attention holding a blue velvet cushion on which rested a gold chain and medallion. General Tojo moved forward, picked up the medallion and handed it to Prime Minister Konoe, who slipped it over Kenji's bowed head.

'The Emperor officially awarded the Order of the Golden Kite in private,' the prime minister announced. 'It is my honour to present it in public.' The three high officials stepped back and bowed.

Kenji walked with his cousins to a long, low table set before the shrine. They sat down and were joined by Hiroki and Noriko, who sat on either side of Kenji.

Raiko made her entrance on her father's arm. She wore a single white lily on her breast as a symbol of her mother's spirit.

'Look at the military-men and government officials,' John whispered to the ambassador. 'I don't understand it. They're bowing as low to Raiko as to Kenji when he received the medal.'

Raiko and her father moved around the low table opposite Kenji. Her eyes stayed on him. His skin had a healthy sheen. The leather lacing of his eyepatch rested perfectly over an arrow-straight parting in his smooth dark hair.

Kenji's one eye caressed Raiko, drinking in the beauty that moved so gracefully before him. His heart banged

358

against his ribs and he had to breathe through his mouth. Her narrow waist, bosom and the long sweep of her neck were dominated by dark eyes that flashed like black crystals. He saw her look down at his waist, then into his eyes. She raised her eyebrows. For a moment he was at a loss. Then he glanced at his crotch and almost burst out laughing. With his lips he formed the unspoken words, 'Everything is fine.'

'You two have no shame,' Noriko whispered. 'Ogling each other before 1,000 guests.'

A Shinto priest appeared at the entrance to the shrine and intoned, 'Begin the san-san kudo – the three, three, nine.' Kenji and Raiko's eyes never left each other as they passed the ceremonial saké bowls back and forth between them.

They signed the government registration form put before them. Raiko accepted a sheathed dagger from Kenji, and solemnly recited, 'I shall use this against the enemies of my husband to defend the Ishikawa name, or upon myself to preserve the honour of my new family.'

The priest invited the bride and groom to the great bell of Kan-eiji. He chanted prayers and purified them by swinging an incense burner around and over their heads. Kenji and Raiko threw silver coins into the shrine and the priest swung the thick hemp rope. A deep rich sound echoed, alerting the gods to receive the bridal couple's prayers. They bowed in silent devotion until the resonant sound of the bell faded. They both clapped once to send their prayers to the gods, then faced each other, beaming. And turned to their families and guests as man and wife.

39

14 June 1940

Joseph Grew's private office on the third floor of the US Embassy overlooked the Sumida river, with a panoramic view of Tokyo and the imperial palace. The sombre grey sky and dismal rain matched the ambassador's mood. The radio played martial music and newspapers called for the liberation of Asians from Western colonial powers. The capital of Japan had become a tense city filled with uniforms.

John Whittefield was escorted into the office by a marine guard. 'Ambassador sir,' the guard said, 'the rooms above, below and on either side have been cleared. If you need me, I will be five paces from this door.'

Grew closed the door, locked it and returned to sit at his desk. 'John, have a seat. You look as if a good drink might help.'

'Very much, sir. I haven't touched a drop in three months.'

'Have you been away that long? No wonder Washington is anxious for a report. I also want a synopsis of what is happening in Asia.'

John drank the whisky. 'The latest bad news comes from the radio-room downstairs. The Germans have taken Paris.'

Grew shook his head as if trying to dislodge the information from his ears. 'We who fought in the Great War find these lightning advances of the Nazis incomprehensible. They conquered Denmark and Norway in April, the Netherlands and Belgium in May. They crushed the

360

English at Dunkirk the beginning of this month and have now taken Paris two weeks later. It's all unbelievable.'

'Marshal Pétain will surrender all of France in ten days,' John said. 'My agents report the Vichy government, in France and in Hanoi, co-operated with the Nazis before the invasion. Pierre Laval, through von Ribbentrop, is presently negotiating the handover of strategic airfields, harbours and military bases in north Indochina to the Japanese.'

'When Matsuoka signed the Anti-Comintern Pact with Germany, he merged the European and Asian conflicts,' Grew said. 'It seems like we're on the verge of another world war. How reliable are your sources?'

'Infallible and cross-checked. Admiral Darlan, France's Minister of Maritime, gave us the first report. Churchill says we can trust him. Our naval intelligence confirmed this. They've broken the senior Japanese diplomatic code and monitored corresponding messages to Dr Tsubota in Hanoi. The Vichy French traded off north Indochina to keep south Indochina and their Christian religious schools independent. When the Japanese mount an attack around Haiphong, the French will put up token resistance, then retire from the field of battle with honour. The Japanese will govern from Hanoi, using pro-Nazi Frenchmen and pro-Japanese Indochinese. In addition to handing over key military installations to the Japs, the Vichy French have agreed to teach concepts of Japanese moralism in the non-Christian schools thoughout the north. All French politics will be suspended there. Northern businesses and industries come under Japanese control.'

'There appear to be no restraints within either the German or Japanese governments,' Grew said. 'No one to hold back Hitler or Hirohito. Where are the inheritors of Japanese liberalism? What happened to those who wrote the constitution and built a democratic society out of a feudal society?'

361

'Many were assassinated,' John said. 'Others are cowed by fear. Some have lost patience with the West, but most succumbed to greed. They're caught up in the euphoria of German victories, and don't want to be left out of the territorial division of the geographical spoils.'

'With the liberals gone, the Japanese dragon will run wild,' Grew said. 'There must be some people left in power who will listen to reason.'

'Political parties are now forbidden in Japan. The press and radio are censored and pro-Americans, like Hiroki Koin and Professor Minobe, replaced.'

'But the professor and Lord Koin are in Washington discussing ways of improving relations.'

'My informants claim it's a smokescreen,' John said. 'Minobe and Koin have been tricked into talking peace to our State Department while Japan's military prepares for war. They're two of the most famous liberals to survive. Hiroki Koin is honestly attempting to head off a conflict between our countries, but he was quietly stripped of his title and office while in Washington. He and Minobe most probably will fail to end Roosevelt's policy of Ring Fence. Then the Japanese militarists will throw up their hands and claim they tried for peace. Their line is that either the Americans will starve Japan to death or there'll be a fight to the death. Japan, they say, has no alternative but war with America.'

'They can't win,' Grew said.

'They think they can't lose. We measure strength by numbers of men, equipment and money. The Japanese believe their spirit, the rightness of their cause and the sanctity of the Emperor, outweigh the numbers of men and weapons that might be sent against them.'

'They're wrong,' Grew said.

'I know it and you know it. Try to convince them.'

The American Ambassador took out a second glass.

He poured another drink for John and a double for himself. He downed the whisky neat and grimaced. 'There's little chance of success for the Japanese delegation in Washington. Secretary of State Hull doesn't trust them. He's looking for an excuse to go to war. Roosevelt is against war but if Japan sides with Vichy France and moves into north Indochina, the president must act. I imagine he'll institute a partial embargo.'

'The president made a grave mistake when he didn't impose the total freeze on Japanese assets in May as he had threatened,' John said.

'The president hoped his inaction on the matter would be taken by the Japanese as offer of an olive branch,' Grew said.

'Their military read it as a sign of weakness. Whoever blinks first, loses. The Japanese believe Hitler's successes have strengthened America's commitment to save England and that the Far East is low on America's order of priorities.'

'They must be informed such is not the case,' Grew said. 'I have a list of ranking American army and navy officers being transferred to the Pacific area. The fleet in Pearl Harbor has been reinforced, the Philippines have begun conscription and MacArthur is training their army with our soldiers.'

'There's no-one left to talk to in Japan,' John said, dropping his hands in exasperation. 'Most pro-American Japanese officers have been put on the retired list or transferred to China. Of the senior staff, only Yamamoto remains. Rumours are that Tojo saved the admiral from assassination. Tojo sees Yamamoto as the naval genius he needs to implement the planned invasion of South-East Asia.'

'Tojo appears not only to be running the military, but the government as well. While you were away he seemed to control Prime Minister Konoe.'

'Tojo will soon be Japan's first minister of war,' John said. 'If he ever becomes prime minister, God help Asia. The Razor wants it all.'

'I love my country, but I love Japan too,' Grew said. 'I don't want to fail either. We've got to show the Japanese they can gain more by supplying the Europeans against Hitler than by joining him.'

'Sir, no European country remains that is not either occupied, allied to or controlled by the Axis powers. If Japan wants to supply Europe, it's got to go through Germany, not America.'

'It's difficult for me to comprehend that the only thing standing between Germany and America is a weakened British army. Will they fight?'

'Churchill is now prime minister and has sworn never to surrender,' John said. 'A realistic assessment of the British situation is bleak. Roosevelt can't help Churchill now. The president's hands are tied by the American peace movement and the upcoming presidential elections. Most Americans don't want their sons fighting in another European war. The aid America gives Britain must be civilian and voluntary, at least until after the November elections. Goering has promised Hitler he'll bomb the English into submission before then. The German air force outnumbers the RAF at maybe 100 to one. We don't know exactly and won't know unless our intelligence-gathering services are dramatically expanded.'

'This isn't the time to prod Washington for extra money to establish new intelligence networks. Congress recently passed the largest military bill in history. Six billion dollars is more than the total expenditure for the army and navy in the last fifteen years.'

'Mr Ambassador, expensive can turn out to be economical. And cheap, costly. The price we may have to pay is thousands of American lives. Washington is information-blind about its enemies because our government considers spying immoral. We barely use $200,000 a year while England spends a million on espionage. The Japanese allocate twenty-four million dollars a year and have been doing so since 1936.'

'Where and how do they spend that kind of money?'

'They pay off people like ex-yeoman Harry Thompson in San Diego and former Commander Farnsworth, late of the US navy,' John said. 'Those two were caught by the FBI giving information about the firing systems, radar and range of the battleships *Colorado*, *Texas* and *Mississippi*. Those ships were recently sent to Pearl Harbor. Most barbers in Panama City are Japanese agents. Many dentists too. They buy information, maps and cargo lists of every ship that passes through the canal. Japanese fishermen ply their trade all over the world. They also chart bays, harbours and channels while monitoring our naval radio signals. Tijuana, Mexico is an hour's drive from our San Diego naval base. It's a wide-open town with drugs, sex and untaxed goods. Japanese agents there entrap our sailors and extract information. The Japanese own bars and beauty parlours on Sunset Boulevard in Los Angeles, the harbour area in San Francisco and downtown Honolulu. The history of Japanese espionage is as old as their country, and it's not frowned on. The study of Sun Tzu's 2,000-year-old *Principles of War* is mandatory for every Japanese officer. They're required to memorize the first paragraph.' John threw back his shoulders and recited, '"Hostile armies may face each other for years, battling over the same ground day in and day out. Then suddenly victory is won in a few hours because of critical information. This being the case, to remain unaware of the enemy's condition, because one grudges the outlay of 100 ounces of silver, is the height of inhumanity."'

Grew picked up his pen. 'A twenty-four-million-dollar yearly outlay by a country so business-oriented as Japan requires the expectation of a substantially higher return.

I doubt they'll settle for less than all of Indochina and Malaysia. If they want the Pacific too, it'll mean certain war with America.' He looked up at John. 'I have a special agreement with the president to write him personally on matters that might be delayed or misdirected in our bureaucracy. I will advise him of the Japanese expenditures for intelligence. I'll send an official request to Secretary of State Hull recommending that we drastically expand our civilian and military secret services.' He paused for a moment, then said, 'Even as I recommend that our country prepare for war, you and I must increase our efforts to avoid it.'

40

For the honeymoon couple, privacy aboard the newly-christened *Raiko Maru* was guaranteed. Kenji allocated the entire passenger deck of his newest merchantship for his and Raiko's enjoyment. Shuffleboard, badminton and tennis courts were set up. The big freighter zigzagged on what appeared to be an unhurried, unplanned course across the China Sea, stopping at ports along the way.

In the Gulf of Tonkin Raiko and Kenji stayed at the finest French hotel for two weeks, while Dr Tsubota and others went aboard the freighter to use the most powerful radio transmitter afloat. In the ports of Saigon and Bangkok, the ship was host to agents who went directly to the radio shack while Kenji and Raiko toured. Then on to Singapore and Brunei in the Malaysian Federation. In Manila the Ishikawa employees held a week-long festival in honour of the newlyweds. It provided time for agents from outlying islands to slip aboard and make their reports.

Neither Raiko nor Kenji met any of the silent people who came and went during dark hours of the night. It was part of their agreement with Ando and Tsubota. Until they arrived in America, nothing would be required of them.

From Manila, the *Raiko Maru* steamed past Guam, Wake and Midway islands, monitoring radio signals from the American army and navy forces stationed there. On 30 June 1940 the ship anchored outside of Honolulu harbour.

'This is the most beautiful of all the islands we've visited,' Raiko said. 'The water is so clear and blue, I can see into it for ever. I can't wait to go ashore.'

'Will you try belly-surfing with me?' Kenji asked.

They both noticed the speedboat flying an Ishikawa company flag racing out towards the ship, but neither mentioned it, each wanting to hold on to the beauty of the past three months.

'It's not safe for you to surf,' Raiko said. 'The shrapnel might move.'

It angered Kenji to be physically restricted, but Raiko was right. Lately he had been feeling a tingling sensation behind his wound.

'Grandfather Mung described this place in his diary,' Kenji said. 'The first time he came ashore was in an outrigger canoe. There were only grass shacks along the beach. Hawaiians paddled him and two other whalers, named Pistchiani and the Deacon, ashore. Mung tipped the canoe over on them as a joke.' Kenji expected a smile or laugh from Raiko, but her voice was flat.

'I hope you inherited Mung's sense of humour. That's Major Ando standing on the front of the speedboat. I believe our honeymoon has ended.'

Kenji moved to stand shoulder to shoulder with Raiko, and put his arm around her. 'Even your father advised us to co-operate,' he said. 'It was no coincidence that Ando and Tsubota were waiting for us after the award ceremony.'

'I know we agreed to allow their agents use of this ship's transmitter, but I wish it were otherwise.'

'It's not really our ship any more,' Kenji said. 'It now belongs to the Emperor.'

'It will be ours again one day,' Raiko said. 'Right now I'm looking forward to seeing Hawaii, but I'm sorry this part of our honeymoon ended so soon.'

'It's been wonderful,' Kenji said. 'The best time in my life.'

'Mine too.' They gazed into each other's eyes.

A cheer rose from the officers and men on the lower

deck as they crowded around Ando. 'Banzai! Banzai! Banzai!'

Ando looked up and waved. Kenji waved back but Raiko turned away from the rail.

'I don't like him,' Raiko said. 'He's responsible for Wantabe's death. I'll repay him for that.'

'I haven't forgotten Nanking either,' Kenji said. 'And as your husband, your Giri to Ando is my obligation.'

Raiko frowned and did not answer. Together with Kenji, she returned Ando's bow as he came on deck.

'I have wonderful news.' Ando beamed. 'Marshal Pétain has surrendered France to Germany.'

'We've kept abreast of current events,' Kenji said. 'It's anti-climactic after the fall of Paris.'

'Major, what does it all mean to Japan?' Raiko asked.

'Please call me Shira. It's easier than my present rank of Lieutenant Colonel. And we've known each other for some time now. To answer your question, the surrender of France means Indochina eventually becomes ours. You decoded the reports that the British have written off Singapore. We know the Dutch have ceased to be a power in the East Indies, and the American order of priorities is to save Europe. They've already pulled two battleships from the Pacific fleet and sent them into the Atlantic. There's nothing and no-one to stop us, from Hawaii to Tokyo.'

'The United States won't abandon the Philippines without a fight,' Kenji said.

'Many American Congressmen advise just that. They want their troops back in the United States to protect their east coast against Germany. Roosevelt will probably let MacArthur defend the Philippines with native troops, who will defect to us. I have spies from one end of the Philippine islands to the other.'

'Are you guessing about American policy or do you know for certain?' Raiko asked.

'My information comes from the best journalists in the world, Walter Winchell for one.' Ando flattened his lips against his teeth and spoke through his nose, imitating the American radio newscaster. 'Good evening, Mr and Mrs America and all our ships at sea. Here's the latest news hot off the wire from England. Prime Minister Winston Churchill has withdrawn his major fighting ships and most regular British troops from the Far and Near East. When asked who will defend the British colonies, the new prime minister of England replied, "Native soldiers led by the finest British officers." My question to Mr Churchill is, if he has no navy to transport weapons, ammunition and supplies to his colonials, how will they fight? It's a bit further from Dover to Singapore than to Dunkirk. Another question is, who will the British colonials fight? Mr Churchill has not replied. I say the Japanese.'

The intonation and dialogue were so cleverly done that neither Raiko nor Kenji could restrain from applauding. 'Bravo,' Kenji said.

Ando bowed. 'I've had much practice before Japanese-American businessmen in the States and here in Hawaii. That's how I open my recruiting speech for agents.'

'Are there many who agree to work for you?' Raiko asked.

Ando's eyes shifted. 'When they see our military successes against the French and Dutch, many will join. Right now they contribute large sums of money.'

From things overheard and messages seen in the Black Chamber, Raiko knew that often those donations were extorted by threats to the families still living in Japan. 'Did Walter Winchell really make that announcement?' she asked.

'Not in those exact words. But the uncensored American press is a gold-mine of information. Aviation magazine calls our pilots untrained, ill-equipped and incapable of standing against the American air force for more than a week.'

'That means our security is good,' Kenji said.

'It also means the American military isn't paying attention to Claire Chenault and his Flying Tigers. Confucius says, "The bigger the man, the more difficult it is for wisdom to penetrate." That fits the American military high command. In my opinion they can't believe a non-white nation could even conceive of attacking them. Security is unbelievably lax here at Pearl Harbor.'

'We're preparing to go ashore and enjoy Hawaii,' Kenji said. 'Our agreement is we're on our honeymoon until we reach the States.'

Ando frowned. 'Hawaii will soon become the forty-ninth state. You refused to meet Dr Tsubota in Haiphong and we respected your wishes. But now it's time for work! You'll travel from here to America with a large retinue of servants, as befits one of the richest couples in the world! Those people will all be my agents. They'll make the necessary contacts.'

'If that is to begin in America, why are you here now?' Raiko asked.

'Because I must return to Japan. My plane leaves tomorrow afternoon and there are some things only you two can do.' Ando opened his briefcase and handed Kenji a map. 'Come sit on the deck chairs and I'll explain.' Ando opened a similar map. 'Years before the nationalization of the Ishikawa fishing fleet, Kempetai began using your boats off the coast of southern California to scout the American coastline. When the *Raiko Maru* leaves Hawaii, in addition to your personal servants, there'll be eighty-five Japanese naval officers aboard. They'll relieve their counterparts in the fishing fleet. It's done every four months.'

'Are those officers being replaced to share the remainder of our honeymoon with us?' Raiko asked.

371

Ando laughed, ignoring the sarcasm in her voice. 'This ship will return to Japan with the eighty-five men. You and your entourage will transfer to the *Shinto Maru*. It's a passenger liner with graceful accommodations.'

'I own it,' Kenji snapped. 'What's our destination?'

'You did own it before the nationalization of Japan's industries,' Ando said. 'Guaymas is your port of call. It's a fishing village located on the eastern coast of the Gulf of California. Marked on your map by an asterisk.'

'What logical reason can be given for the head of the Ishikawa zaibatsu to visit such a small place?' Raiko asked.

'Guaymas is headquarters for the Ishikawa fishing fleet in that area of the Pacific. Our government established an experimental fishing station there in 1938. We sent scientists to aid the poor Mexican fishermen. Along with scientific examination of the waters, my men secretly took soundings of the gulf. We've learned that our largest warships could sail up the entire length of the gulf, almost to the Arizona–California border. You'll be visiting the station and your fleet captains.'

Kenji glanced at the map. 'Where do we sail from Guaymas?'

'You don't sail. I've taken the liberty of having your Dusenberg shipped on the *Shinto Maru*. You and your wife will drive around to visit the local sites, accompanied by our man at the experimental station. One of the attractions will be a visit to the Yaqui Indian tribe, where you'll meet Chiefs Urbalejo and Mattus. Ascertain their commitment to our cause, and the cost of the tribe's co-operation in the event we should invade.'

'Have you gone completely mad?' Raiko cried. 'Invading Mexico would be like attacking the sea. There's nothing there to fight, and little worth winning.'

'Not Mexico,' Ando said. 'No one wants that forsaken country. The people are cultural degenerates. They're inherently dirty and lazy. The plan is to invade America.'

'My wife is correct, you are mad,' Kenji said.

Ando moved forward on his deck chair, eyes burning. He pointed at the map. 'We already have a colony of over 100 Japanese living in San Gabriel Bay at the southern tip of the Gulf of California. And another colony across the way at Mazattan. Since 1937 Dr Tsubota has had Ishikawa purchasing agents buying surplus destroyers and cutters from the British, and converting them to fishing boats. The Black Dragon Society was involved in refitting those craft. The gun mounts remain in place. Most of your 500 ships can be converted into small gunboats within twenty-four hours. With our colonies in control of both sides of the bay, the converted fishing boats could block off the entrance to the gulf. Our troopships and warships would steam up to Guaymas.'

'And what will they do there? Bake tortillas?' Kenji laughed.

Ando stiffened and his eyelids drooped. 'Mr Ishikawa, you may be a civilian but you do serve the Emperor, don't you?'

Raiko and Kenji glanced at each other. The threat in Ando's voice was clear. 'All Japanese serve the Emperor,' Kenji replied.

Ando's voice softened. 'We've worked together before. I'm no fool. Look at your map. There's a rail-line and highway from Guaymas to the Arizona–California border. With Yaqui Indians as guides, our marines could control both the highway and the Southern Pacific Railroad. The naval base at San Diego is only a ten-hour ride.'

'You can't possibly consider capturing America's largest naval base,' Kenji said.

'The same way our troops took Weihaiwei naval base from the Chinese in 1894, they took Port Arthur from the Russians in 1904. And we'll take Singapore from the British. From behind. San Diego and all those bases have one thing in common; their weapons face seaward. We could take San Diego from the land side.'

'I can't believe your superiors even considered invading the United States,' Kenji said. 'It's impossible. The country is too large, the people too numerous. America is not China.'

'We have 1,000 operatives in Mexico ready to incite and enlist the peasants into a volunteer army. We expect help from all the oppressed Mexicans, Indians and coloured minorities in America. That's not counting the 500-boat fishing fleet, our troopships and fighting ships.'

'No matter how many fishing boats you could throw across the mouth of the gulf, they wouldn't stop the Pacific fleet. The American navy would catch our troopships before they could land our men.'

'The Pacific fleet is in Pearl Harbor, 6,000 miles from California. By the time they returned, our ships would be anchored in San Diego naval base under protection of the shore guns manned by our troops.'

Kenji chewed his lip as he examined the map again. 'The Atlantic fleet maintains a reinforced battle squadron at the Panama Canal,' he said. 'They might not prevent your landing the troops, but our ships would never get out of the Californian gulf before the American ships arrived.'

'They would if you and the Yaqui chiefs find a nice flat place near Guaymas for an airstrip. It's barren desert out there.'

'Flying ground support from such a temporary base would not be worth anything,' Kenji said. 'The number of planes needed, the refuellings required to fly the amount of missions necessary to be effective, cannot be done from a temporary field.'

Ando smiled. 'Three planes would only have to fly one mission. To the Panama Canal. If they sank one ship in that canal, it would block the American fleet in the Atlantic ocean. It would take that battle squadron a month to come

374

around the Horn and reach San Diego. Roosevelt has to worry about Hitler. He'll protect the east coast of America by helping England.'

'The idea of attacking the United States is absurd to begin with,' Raiko said. 'The invasion of America is ludicrous!'

'That's why it can succeed,' Ando said. 'The Caucasians can't believe Orientals would think of attacking them, no less invading their country. They're mentally and militarily unprepared. We're not foolish enough to think of taking all of America, not even all of California. San Diego and the Gulf of California down to our present colonies would be enough.' He smiled at Raiko and Kenji and tapped his watch. 'It's time for you two to leave. I must radio in a report. My speedboat driver will take you to see Ruth Kuhn. Raiko, your assignment is to renew your friendship with the German woman and get as much information as possible.' Ando handed Kenji a second map. 'This is of Pearl Harbor. Think like a combat pilot who would attack the ships anchored there. Genda is practising in Japan, but he requires more detailed information only someone with your experience can supply. When you're ready, have Ruth call my driver. He'll return you to the ship. Radio your report and then you're free for ten days before you move on to the Gulf of California.'

41

'It's terrible that Kenji lost an eye, but that leather patch gives him the appearance of a handsome, swashbuckling pirate,' Ruth Kuhn said.

'Your English is now better than mine,' Raiko said. 'And your imagination too.'

'It's those Errol Flynn movies and this island of Oahu. It's known for the three Ss – sex, screen and spirits. When the fleet's in for a holiday like this Fourth of July, there's enough whisky to float the whole American navy. Bar owners bring in women from as far away as the Philippines, and the movie houses stay open twenty-four hours a day.'

'It sounds seamy.'

'That's in Pearl City and downtown Honolulu,' Ruth said. 'I rarely go slumming. For me, it's usually tennis, swimming or dancing at one of the hotels or restaurants. Tomorrow night is a big pre-Independence Day luau for the officers of the battleship *Oklahoma*. They'll serve roast pig, yams, poi, chicken, rum punch, rice, steak, lobster and more rum punch. My escort will try to get me drunk and into bed, while I stay sober and ask questions about his ship. I'd invite you and Kenji, but Ando gave specific instructions we're not to be seen together.'

'I understand that Orientals, people of colour and even Hawaiians aren't received at the best restaurants and hotels in Hawaii.'

'That's right,' Ruth said. 'And the Americans call the Germans racist. Ha! When the Japanese move south, all that American prejudice will work to your country's advantage. Neither the Indochinese, Malaysians nor

Pacific islanders will forget the racial slurs. The coloured peoples will be important allies.'

'Why do you assume Japanese policy is to move south?' Raiko asked.

'My officer friends talk about it. The US army and navy are planning for it. They're reinforcing positions and stockpiling ammunition. Not only in Hawaii and the Philippines, but on Guam, Wake and Midway islands. There've been practice air raids here and in Manila. When I ask who could possibly bomb Oahu, they squint their eyes, bow and say, "Ah so, Yankee." That's supposed to be an imitation of a Japanese.' Ruth raised her eyebrows. 'I hope Japan doesn't go to war with America. I like the lifestyles of both countries. Japanese and Americans are in some ways alike. They're hard workers, proud and dedicated. And both relatively unpretentious because they're new in the community of nations. But neither can see past the colour of skin or the shape of eyes.'

'Are you saying Japanese are also racially prejudiced?'

'Are they ever!' Ruth laughed. 'More so than the Americans. Kenji's cousin Hino, Shira Ando and Dr Tsubota would each have me as a mistress, but never a wife. Japanese law forbids any foreigner from becoming a citizen. At least the American laws claim equality.'

'Kenji and I never saw it that way,' Raiko said.

'What didn't I see?' Kenji asked as he came down the attic stairs.

'The shrimps, clams and fish fillet that Ruth is making for dinner.'

'Sounds great. But wait until after the sun goes down. I need the light to fill in my map of the harbour.'

'Isn't it a perfect view from the attic window?' Ruth said. 'With the telescope I can even read the expiration date on the food and ammunition boxes. Some of their stuff is from the Great War. A gunnery officer off the *Mississippi* told me their white phosphorous shells are so old, half don't explode on impact.'

'I saw a ship I can't identify entering the harbour,' Kenji said.

'I'll have it in a minute.' Ruth opened a cupboard of canned goods next to the stove. She released a catch and the shelves swung out, revealing a radio receiver. She donned the headphones and adjusted the dials. 'I use this to monitor ship movements in and out of Pearl Harbor. There's another one upstairs with the transmitter.'

'But how can you identify the craft without seeing it?' Raiko asked.

'By its call letters. Don't forget I've been doing this for a couple of years now. When they change signals, I listen in on the ships' pursers ordering from the base commissary. They do that when they pass through the anti-submarine net at the harbour entrance. Shh, the purser is coming on now.' Ruth held up her hand and listened. 'BLT,' she repeated.

'Bacon, lettuce and tomato?' Kenji asked.

'No. Beef, legumes and toilet paper. Each purser has his personal list of priorities that rarely changes. I write the lists next to the names of the ships and their call numbers. The first time I heard it, I had to look up legumes in the dictionary. It means beans.' She ran her finger down the long list tacked to the inside of the false panel. 'BLT is the submarine tender *Curtiss*. Don't usually see them here. Must be a special Independence Day party for the crew.'

'How many fighting craft are there in Pearl Harbor?' Kenji asked.

'During holidays, 100 or more. Other times, about fifty.'

'Thanks,' Kenji said. 'I'm going upstairs. Call me for dinner.'

Kenji looked out of the attic window at the giant red sun sitting on the edge of the horizon. Its glaring rays painted the grey fighting ships on Battleship Row a deep gold. The water sparkled silver. Kenji felt the blood begin to race through his veins. He unconsciously reached out for a control stick. As if in the cockpit again, he swooped down on the anchored fighting ships from the south, raking the decks with machine-gun fire. From the west, Genda would lead his torpedo-planes in just above the water. The giant navy crane towered over the shipyard, just as in the photographs Yamamoto had shown Kenji. Hino's group of high-level bombers, led by divebombers, would split up to destroy the airfields. 'Later on the fuel-storage dumps can be levelled.' Kenji realized he was speaking aloud, as he did when in action. He yearned to feel an engine's vibration, hear the wind rushing over the wings, smell the old leather of his flight cap. He touched his scar and felt sweat on his forehead.

Kenji's feelings for America and against the war were forgotten as he filled in the map, making notations only a combat pilot could. The sun had settled behind the sea before he completed his work. He looked up in surprise at the darkness. His map depicted every docking place and fighting ship in the harbour. 'If Genda can launch a torpedo in thirty-four feet of water, the Pacific fleet can be seriously damaged!' He pictured the long low run Genda and his torpedo-planes would have to make before dropping their deadly half-ton missiles. Genda would lead his men under the long outstretched arm of the ship's crane in a head-on attack at a right-angle to the port sides of the ships anchored on Battleship Row. 'No room to manoeuvre or avoid the anti-aircraft fire,' Kenji said. 'Casualties will be high.'

In the kitchen, Raiko tore lettuce and sliced vegetables for a salad. Ruth checked the fish. 'American politicians don't want war,' Ruth said. 'Franklin Roosevelt and Wendell Willkie are trying to out-peace each other in the presidential campaign.'

379

'The first thing one learns about American politics is that no one holds politicians to their promises,' Raiko said. 'How do the military here in Hawaii feel about war?'

'I meet career-men. The professional's fastest way to promotion is in battle. Americans, Germans, Japanese, they're no different. Men all want to fight. The American army will even fight the American navy if they can't get a war with another country. The army–navy rivalry is so bad that enlisted men drink in different bars, fight when they meet, and officers belong to separate clubs. Their intelligence units are in competition and don't share information. Each wants to win approval from Washington to gain promotion. They rarely co-ordinate their efforts. For example, both services fly a daily dawn scouting patrol that overlaps every day. Except for Sunday, that is, when they both land at 7.30 a.m. for the late breakfast at eight. The day patrol comes to breakfast at 9 a.m. and takes off at ten.'

Raiko stopped slicing. 'You're saying there's a two-hour gap with no scout planes in the air on Sundays?'

'It's consistent,' Ruth said. 'Every Sunday like clockwork. My father has logged them coming and going for two years.'

Kenji came down the stairs. 'Wonderful view from the attic. I'll leave you my Zeiss binoculars, Ruth. They're better for tracking moving objects, and almost as good as your telescope.' He clapped his hands. 'I'm starving.'

'Sit down and be served,' Ruth said.

'Your work has been praised by our intelligence people,' Kenji said. 'But I'm curious as to why you spy for Japan.'

'Money,' Ruth said. 'I lost all sense of patriotism when I was Goebbels's mistress. I heard how the leaders of Nazi Germany lined their pockets. My father got rich on my body. Why shouldn't I?'

'There's $20,000 in a briefcase next to the telescope.'

'Your people are generous,' Ruth said as she served the food.

'Ruth, you must be careful,' Raiko said. 'They hang spies.'

'I've researched that,' Ruth said. 'Americans rarely kill spies in peacetime, although traitors are hanged. I'm Austrian. You're American.' From the shock on Raiko's face, Ruth realized her friend had not thought about her US citizenship. 'But you don't have to worry,' Ruth said. 'The Americans are very lax. They don't invade people's privacy like the Gestapo or Kempetai. There's not much chance of getting caught.'

Raiko made a mental note to tell Kenji her citizenship was the excuse they could use for not spying in America.

'I remember your fussbudget landlady and the secret police,' Ruth said.

'I misjudged her.' Raiko blushed. 'When Kenji was helping me move I told the landlady she would no longer have to put my books in place or straighten pictures and report to Kempetai. She shook her finger at me and said, "Shame on you. I did that so you would know I was there rather than the authorities."'

'An embarrassing moment,' Ruth said.

'But a very enlightening one,' Kenji replied. 'That simple old woman defied the secret police. There are many Japanese who reject the fascist mentality that dominates our country.'

'How do you two justify spying against America?' Ruth asked. 'You were both educated at America's best universities.'

'It's a choice between blood and intellect, heart and mind,' Kenji said. 'We're Japanese. Our people will starve if we're not allowed to settle in other countries. I once thought about farming the sea to increase Japan's food supply. I remember wondering if I shouldn't have studied marine biology instead of aeronautical engineering. The answer is no. Japan needs a powerful military in order to move into South-East Asia. My cousins, my friends and my country depend on the aeroplanes I build and the information I can supply.'

'But that doesn't answer the question of spying against the Americans,' Ruth said.

'Because I'm certain we won't go to war against them,' Kenji said.

Raiko had seen too many messages advocating and planning war with the United States. She felt Kenji's argument was weak, and tried to help him. 'I grew up in the States. I was always reminded of my Japanese heritage by places I couldn't go, parties I wasn't invited to, people who spoke down to me. They wouldn't let me forget my race. I remember learning about the Catholic mass. The wafer they eat and the wine they drink become the flesh and blood of Jesus. I believed then that I was Japanese in flesh and spirit, but I wasn't certain if returning to Japan was correct for me. Only recently, the simple act of a great man reassured me. I was in audience before the Emperor and Empress and the master of protocol called me forward. But my feelings of pride and awe had locked my joints. I found it impossible to move. The Emperor looked down from his throne, smiled and motioned to me. He smiled again and nodded his approval as I took the first step. That privilege, that honour, shall remain with me for ever.'

'I've been too close to the so-called great ones,' Ruth said. 'They're only people. I've been disappointed in them too often. Who can afford to be patriotic? Look at you two. They've nationalized the Ishikawa zaibatsu and you're paying for this trip by working for Kempetai.'

'We're serving the Emperor,' Kenji said. 'Every Japanese is obliged to do so.'

'I've heard about Chu,' Ruth said. 'Your unrepayable debt. Japanese owing their parents for being born.'

'That and more,' Raiko said. 'Our parents received life from the Emperor. His ancestors created the islands of Japan and all life on land and sea and in the air. On 10 November the nation will celebrate the 2,600th year of that creation and of the first Emperor's descent from Heaven to live on earth.'

'Do you really believe that fairy tale?' Ruth asked.

'It's easier to accept than the trinity and wonder tales about Jesus Christ,' Kenji said. 'The goal of a Japanese is to serve the Emperor. In every home throughout the empire there's a place set aside and always prepared just in case he should visit.'

'There are no gods,' Ruth said. 'If Jesus Christ was around today, the Nazis would throw the old Jew into a concentration camp.'

'At least we've agreed that war with America should be avoided,' Raiko said.

'One of your countrymen thinks differently. He published his plan for attacking those ships out there. John Whittefield translated it into English. The writer claims that during recent American war games the attacking force surprised the defenders of Pearl Harbor. And the referees allowed the theoretical destruction of the entire US naval base.'

'Who wrote that article and when?' Kenji asked.

'I don't remember the Japanese name. It was received here a month ago. The title is "Not If But When Japan Fights America". It envisions a fast moving force of aircraft carriers and cruisers approaching the Hawaiian islands and launching a long-range aerial attack on the ships anchored at Pearl Harbor.'

'The author is familiar with some very sensitive information I deciphered a while back,' Raiko said. 'Whittefield will know that their code is broken. This Japanese author mustn't be allowed to write things like that again.'

'It was never published in English,' Ruth said. 'The

383

California printer sent the translation to US army intelligence here in Hawaii for evaluation. They laughed it out of their office. That's how I got a copy.'

'What did US naval intelligence say?' Kenji asked.

'The army didn't show it to them. I told you they're in competition.'

'Bless the US army,' Kenji said. 'How about dessert? That cake smells wonderful.'

Raiko jumped up and gaped at Kenji. 'Repeat that!'

'I asked Ruth for the dessert.'

'You smelled the cake in the oven!'

Kenji's eye flashed and he sniffed. 'I do smell it! And the fish too!' He raised his fingers to the scar on his head, but Raiko caught his hand.

'Don't touch! It must be moving!'

'What are you two talking about?' Ruth asked.

'Shrapnel in Kenji's head. It's near his brain and was touching something that affected his sense of smell.'

'Does shrapnel move about in the body?' Ruth asked.

Raiko gave a grim laugh. 'I often wake up and find little metal or glass splinters on the sheet. You can see them working their way to the surface of his skin. I daub them with iodine until they fall out or we can pick them out. He still looks like a painted American Indian under those clothes.'

'Does the shrapnel always move to the surface?'

Raiko did not answer. She met Kenji's eyes, then stood and examined his scar.

'Anything?' he asked.

'No,' Raiko said. 'We must have x-rays taken.'

Kenji placed his face against Raiko's body. 'What are you doing?' she asked.

'I'm smelling you. Ahhh. I had forgotten what I was missing.'

'Well I don't want a missing husband,' Raiko said. 'We're returning to the ship. You'll make your report from bed and tomorrow morning you're going to see a doctor.'

'Will you come to bed with me?'

'No sex,' Raiko said. 'It could be dangerous.'

Ruth laughed. 'Kenji, you look like Peter Rabbit the way you're sniffing.'

'And I feel like a rabbit.' He reached for Raiko.

She eluded his grasp. 'Back to the ship, Bugs Bunny. Tomorrow we find the best neurologist in Hawaii.'

42

The well-dressed middle-aged Japanese man sat against a wall in the hotel kitchen. He held a large, flat, brown envelope and watched the Hawaiian waiters rushing in and out of double swinging doors leading to the dining room. The incoming flow stopped to allow a distinguished-looking Caucasian in a tuxedo to enter.

The Japanese jumped to his feet, overturning the chair. He attempted to pick it up and bow at the same time. 'Dr Abrahamson, please excuse me. So very sorry to interrupt your dinner.'

'That's quite all right, old chap.'

'I must apologize for having to meet you here.'

'That's not your fault. I understand the manager would not allow you into the dining room, Dr Itagaki. Have I pronounced your name correctly?'

'Yes, yes, quite so. Again I apologize. I come to you for a young, unconscious patient with a piece of metal lodged near his brain. I heard you were en route from Dublin to Australia and rushed to consult you. I have read your books and articles on brain surgery.' Itagaki bowed again. 'If you would be so kind as to advise me. There is no qualified brain surgeon prepared to examine my patient, Kenji Ishikawa.'

'I take it you are a surgeon,' Abrahamson said.

'I am an anaesthetist. The patient is Japanese. The only qualified surgeons in Hawaii at the moment, except you, are navy personnel. They will not touch him because, they claim, there are rules and regulations. Money isn't the problem.'

'Rules are influenced by things other than cash. I

must say the actions of your country in China have antagonized people the world over. The Nanking affair was atrocious.'

'I am Hawaiian of Japanese ancestry,' Itagaki said. 'If I needed help they would not operate on me.'

'I've seen British doctors act towards my Irish countrymen that way.'

'This patient has money.'

'Yes, so you informed me.' Abrahamson pointed at the large envelope. 'Is that for me?'

Itagaki pulled out several x-rays. 'These are a few months old, flown in from Tokyo. The rest were done here this morning.'

The neurosurgeon studied the sheets of film against the overhead lights. 'How is the patient's general health?'

'His wife said it has been excellent.'

Abrahamson returned all but two x-rays to Itagaki and looked around the busy kitchen. He motioned towards the swinging doors. 'You stand on this side and make certain no one comes barrelling through.'

Abrahamson went out of the door and held the films up to the square window, using the kitchen light to background the outline of Kenji's skull. He counted the fine teeth on his pocket comb to take measurements. For several minutes Mervyn Abrahamson compared the old and new prints against the door windows.

Coming back through the swinging doors, Abrahamson was surprised to find a line of waiters held up by Itagaki. 'I beg your pardon, gentlemen.' He bowed to the waiters and took the anaesthetist by the arm. 'Where can we talk?'

'Outside. The patient's wife is waiting.'

'Good, let's get on with this.'

Mervyn Abrahamson bowed to Raiko. 'Mrs Ishikawa, there is no sense in beating about the bush. It's your decision. Do we or don't we operate? The metal sliver has

387

shifted sideways. It will move again, but there's no way of predicting when, or in which direction. From experience, I would say from a week to a month.'

'If it goes in deeper, what effect will it have?' Raiko asked.

'I'll be frank. Permanent brain damage resulting in general paralysis, and possibly the need for one of those new iron lungs to maintain life.'

'You can't be certain,' Raiko said.

'Mrs Ishikawa, I see how distraught you are. Standing here in the parking lot doesn't make this easier.'

'Can you be certain?' Raiko's voice cracked.

'No, dear lady,' Abrahamson said. 'But neither, in good conscience, can I sugarcoat the facts.'

'Doctors sugarcoat anything they want,' Raiko said. 'My husband may be dying. He passed out in a taxicab and the navy doctors won't even look at him.' She sobbed.

'Madam, I am not a member of the American navy and I sympathize with you,' Abrahamson said. 'But I can also understand them. Some of those men had Chinese friends in Shanghai, Nanking and Canton. I've been told one of the medical staff lost a brother on the *Panay*. They see Tojo's recent appointment as Japan's minister of war to mean certain conflict with America. And there are rules against navy doctors attending civilians.'

'Rules are broken when it benefits the whites.'

'I'm Irish and some British think we're not white either. Let us discuss your husband's condition, not international politics. There is a piece of metal touching his brain. His present state of unconsciousness should indicate even to a layman that the situation is critical. You must decide.'

Raiko's hands came to her face and she stifled a sob. 'Will you operate?'

Mervyn Abrahamson reached out and gently took Raiko by the shoulders. 'Please listen closely, Mrs Ishikawa. The operation is dangerous. I cannot tell if permanent damage has already occurred. I cannot promise you that I wouldn't cause more damage during an operation.'

Raiko looked up with tear-filled eyes. 'Only the Presbyterian Hospital would treat him. But they don't have the facilities or the neurosurgeon.' She bit her lip, watching for some sign in the Irishman's eyes. 'If those x-rays were of your son, what would you do?'

'Operate. For my sake as well as his. I couldn't bear to see someone I love become a human vegetable.'

Raiko looked at Itagaki. He nodded and said, 'I agree.' She stepped back and inhaled deeply. She straightened her dress and said, 'I will pay $10,000 for the operation. If that is not enough, name your price.'

'The fee for my services, including that of my wife who acts as chief operating nurse, is $2,000,' Abrahamson said.

'That is for the operation,' Raiko said. 'I will pay $8,000 more for a guarantee that if my husband's brain is already seriously damaged, or if it becomes so during the operation, he will not leave the operating room alive. Long ago Japanese doctors warned us of such a possibility and Kenji and I discussed it. He wrote a letter to that effect. I can bring it to you.'

Mervyn Abrahamson shook his head. 'Not necessary. I see the pain of it written on your face.' His blue eyes hardened. 'I don't like to lose, Mrs Ishikawa. I shall fight for your husband's life.'

'If you win there will be another $10,000 deposited to your account.'

The surgeon coughed into his hand. 'I want you to know that whether I operate on a charwoman, a fishmonger or a Member of Parliament, I give the best that is in me. Now, there's the question of proper facilities.' He turned to the anaesthesiologist. 'Where?'

'The operating room at Pearl Harbor's naval base,' Itagaki said. 'All the equipment and people you need will be there.'

'How is it the navy doctors won't operate but they will allow use of their staff and facilities?'

'Not everyone in the navy is prejudiced,' Itagaki said. 'The administrator is a friend. Others will be paid under the table by Mrs Ishikawa. It must be done tomorrow morning early. It is 4 July and the medical staff will be on holiday until the afternoon when casualties start coming in from fireworks injuries and drunken brawls.'

'It's not my holiday,' Abrahamson said. 'My great-granddad lost to Andrew Jackson in New Orleans, and his grandfather retreated at Valley Forge. Let's twist the Yankees' tails. We'll need four hours to prep, operate and close. I assume you'll assist. Is it arranged to keep the patient in the hospital?'

'We've rented a bed in the recovery room for thirty-six hours,' Raiko said. 'Then he'll have to be transferred to the Presbyterian Hospital.'

'Transfer so soon could be dangerous,' Abrahamson said.

'There's no choice,' Raiko said. 'A car will call for you and your wife at 5 a.m.' She looked into the surgeon's eyes. 'Please save my husband!'

4 July, US Embassy, Tokyo

John Whittefield used a pair of opera glasses to scrutinize the guests in the garden below.

'Has everyone arrived?' Joseph Grew asked.

'Yes, sir. The German and British Ambassadors are standing north and south in the garden. The French and Italians are east and west. So far, no arguments.'

'Where's the Russian Ambassador?'

'Moving around to avoid Motor-Mouth Matsuoka,' John said. 'He and Prime Minister Konoe just arrived.'

'It's time to bring those two Japanese gentlemen up here,' Grew said.

John signalled a waiter below, who approached Konoe and then Matsuoka. The two were led into the building.

'Congratulations on this 164th year of your independence.' Prime Minister Konoe bowed. 'It looks to be a grand celebration.'

Matsuoka shook hands with the Americans. 'I came to see the fireworks. My first Fourth of July was in California when I studied at UCLA.'

'We've arranged for a gala display,' Grew said. 'Forgive me if I launch directly into the point of our meeting. The ceremonies downstairs will soon begin and we must put in an appearance. I did not want to miss the opportunity of this unofficial meeting. My cultural attaché will translate if necessary.'

The two Japanese nodded and smiled politely at John, fully aware he was the head of American intelligence in the Far East.

'A pleasure,' Konoe said. 'We shall dispense with the formalities. Please begin.'

'The swift German victories in Europe have taken everyone by surprise,' Grew said. 'Some predict the imminent fall of Great Britain. Many of your countrymen believe a Japanese alliance with Hitler would be advantageous. I doubt President Roosevelt will allow the Nazis to take England.'

'And I doubt he can stop them,' Matsuoka said.

'My colleague meant to convey an opinion held by several cabinet ministers,' Konoe said.

'If they are wrong and Japan was allied to the Third Reich, the consequences could be disastrous,' Grew said.

'But we already suffer the consequences of your unofficial trade embargo,' Konoe said.

'Roosevelt is a candidate for re-election in November,' Matsuoka said. 'As you well know, it is the first time in American history a president has sought a third term.

Many in the United States fear a Democratic Party dictatorship. Any move on Roosevelt's part to extend military aid to Churchill would lose him votes, and probably the election.'

Although the tall, suave Konoe made the better impression, John had reminded Grew that the stubby foreign minister hid a far more brilliant mind behind his erratic actions and brash talk.

'The appointment of General Hideki Tojo as Japan's first minister of war in the modern era has upset Washington,' Grew said. 'We hold him responsible for the invasion of China.'

'These are difficult times,' Konoe said. 'War is erupting all around the globe.'

'The greater the need for understanding between our countries,' Grew said. 'Until recently we've had a history of good relations.'

'When you treated us as children, things went smoothly,' Matsuoka said. 'Now that we've grown and act independently, it frightens your countrymen.'

Konoe bowed. 'My foreign minister's choice of words is inappropriate. Yet I must say that your government reacts harshly to our appointment of one man, while we see MacArthur and numerous other generals and admirals coming to Hawaii, the Philippines and those little islands in between. We resent your policy of Ring Fence. It chokes Japan's economy and causes our people to suffer.'

John realized that Konoe was trying to settle Matsuoka down by continuing to talk in a very soft tone.

'Neither England, France nor America seek alliance with Japan,' Konoe said. 'The recent pact between Germany, Russia and Italy isolates Japan from the Axis powers too. Japan stands alone. We have the only modern army in Asia. Whoever wins in Europe will turn on us.'

Grew wished for time. He believed a subtle indirect approach would accomplish more, but Secretary of State

Hull had instructed him to act. 'My government knows of your contacts with the Vichy French and their co-operation with von Ribbentrop for your move into Indochina. If this becomes a reality, it will result in America's freezing of all Japanese assets in the United States. Plus a formal embargo. In addition, the president shall demand Japanese withdrawal from China.'

'If we are good little boys and do not enter Indochina, may we please keep China?' Matsuoka said.

Konoe stepped forward, ignoring his foreign minister's sarcasm. 'America's threats, if carried out, will isolate us even further. You are pushing Japan into the Axis Alliance.'

'Sir,' Grew said. 'After Tojo's appointment as minister of war, Mr Matsuoka replaced thirty-nine pro-American diplomats with men who are outright Nazi supporters. It appears to Washington that you desire an accommodation with the Germans.'

John watched Matsuoka's reaction. The Americans both knew the foreign minister had personally selected the thirty-nine new emissaries with Tojo's approval. They were all either from Kempetai, the Black Dragon or White Wolf Societies.

'If we did everything you asked, America's attitude towards Japan would remain unchanged,' Matsuoka said. 'Your Open Door Policy has a whites-only sign over it. If Japan doesn't take Indochina, the Germans will. And if Hitler loses, the French will reclaim their colonies.' He spread his arms wide. 'In case both the Axis and the Allies are too exhausted after their war,' he pointed at Grew, 'then your country will take over those areas as it did Samoa, the Philippines and Hawaii. The choice facing Asians is between the Western ideologies of capitalism and communism, or Japanese moralism. We are the new spirit in the East!' Matsuoka's face reddened. He emphasized his words by stabbing them in the air with his index finger. 'We are closer in blood, thought and religion to more than two-thirds of the world's population.'

Konoe tried to interrupt, but was waved back.

'It's time they heard.' Matsuoka bent his head, hunched his shoulders like a bull preparing to charge, and fixed the two Americans with his angry black eyes. 'Japan's Monroe Doctrine began years ago in Korea and Manchuria! All of Asia is within Japan's sphere of influence! As South and Central America belong to the United States, China belongs to us!'

'Again a poor choice of words, Mr Matsuoka,' Grew said. 'South and Central America do not belong to anyone but themselves.'

'How would the United States react if the Panamanian people decided to expel American troops, administer their own affairs and operate the canal by themselves?'

For a moment the American ambassador and the Japanese foreign minister locked eyes. Joseph Grew lowered his first.

Konoe cleared his throat and tried to speak, but Matsuoka would not be silenced. 'I think it is time for the Americans to retreat to Hawaii and leave the Pacific to us,' Matsuoka said.

Grew tugged at his ear, a pre-arranged signal for John to look at his watch and say, 'Gentlemen, excuse me for interrupting, but Ambassador Grew must address the Independence Day party.'

Grew stood and smiled broadly. 'It would be an honour if the Japanese prime minister and foreign minister will join me in lighting the traditional fireworks display.' The four men left the office together.

John was taken aside by the embassy's security officer. 'Aren't you friendly with Kenji Ishikawa?'

'Yes. He's on his honeymoon in Hawaii.'

'He's in trouble at the Pearl Harbor naval hospital. He,

his wife and another Japanese are in the custody of naval intelligence.'

'On what charge?'

'Unauthorized entry into a restricted military area. Illegal payment of funds to American naval personnel for favours and information.'

John was reminded of Raiko's work in the Black Chamber and the break-in at the British Embassy. 'I'd like to talk with our people there.'

'I hoped you would. They're holding one of the richest men in the world. It could mean the end of a lot of careers. Hawaii called us for information on the Ishikawas. They're awaiting our response.'

In the embassy communications room a telephone operator pointed at John. 'You're on the line to Hawaii.'

'Time check,' John said into the phone.

'Seven a.m,' a voice said.

'You're three minutes fast,' John said. 'Put your scrambler on and report.'

There was a moment of hesitation on the other end of the line. In the short exchange of coded sentences, John Whittefield had identified himself as chief of America's Far East Intelligence Service. Lieutenant Joseph DeCarlo gave his report.

'Is Mr Ishikawa unconscious?' John asked.

'He appears to be. There are no naval neurosurgeons on the premises to check. It's a holiday.'

'Not for you, it isn't,' John said. 'Do you think the Japanese are faking or spying?'

'Not faking, sir. In my opinion the patient needs attention. His wife hired an Irish surgeon vacationing here to operate on him. Mrs Ishikawa had tried to pay navy people to operate, but they refused because they hate Japs.'

'Oh shit!' John pounded the table.

'Many of us here are embarrassed, sir. The Irish surgeon is standing by. What should I tell him?'

'OK Lieutenant, tell the Irishman to begin! Whatever he needs, make certain he gets! Round up every surgeon on the base and have them ready to assist! Pass this line through to Admiral Kimmel! He'll confirm my orders by the time you reach your car.'

43

Raiko's face floated above Kenji. 'I love you,' he whispered, and wondered why she was weeping. He felt himself drifting off to sleep and knew she would understand.

The Irish brogue was familiar. It had asked questions many times. Now the voice had a face, a friendly face with grey hair. A smiling Raiko stood by the man's side. Kenji knew he was a doctor.

'What is your name?' the Irishman asked.

Kenji struggled to sit up, but could not.

'Don't strain against the straps,' Raiko said. 'You shouldn't move until the sandbags around your head are taken away.'

'We'll have all the restraining devices off in a few days,' the doctor said. 'How do you feel?'

Kenji wondered how he felt. His head ached. He remembered a taxi driver slamming on the brakes to avoid a drunken sailor crossing the road.

Raiko moved into his view again. 'Kenji, if you can hear me, blink your eyes.'

'Why should I blink?' His slurred words surprised him but he could see they made Raiko and the doctor very happy. He drifted back to sleep.

The next time Kenji awoke he was resting on his side in a different room. The sandbags and straps were gone, but one arm was held straight by a board. A tube ran from his vein to a bottle above his head. Through the window he watched the giant ball of fire hanging over the edge of a sapphire-blue sea. The rising sun is a good omen, he thought. He shifted to see what had caused a sound behind him. Raiko was curled up in a chair. She reminded him of a beautiful cat and he wanted to reach out to stroke her, but there were rails at the sides of the bed. 'I love you,' he said aloud, surprised at the croaking sound of his voice.

Raiko's eyes snapped open and he gazed at her. She rose slowly from the chair and approached the bed, reaching out to wave her hand in front of his face.

'Why are you doing that?' Kenji asked.

Raiko jumped back in fright. 'I thought you might be . . . Your eye didn't move. Thank the gods you're . . . here.'

'Where else was I?'

Raiko rained fairy-light kisses on Kenji's face. 'I thought I'd lost you,' she cried. 'I thought you were gone.' She dipped a wad of gauze in a cup of water and wet his lips.

Kenji sucked greedily and asked for more. Raiko petted his face and put the wet gauze to his lips again. 'How do you feel?'

He thought about that. 'I feel like my head is detached from my body.'

Raiko shuddered. She touched his chest. 'Can you feel that?'

'Yes.'

She touched his hand and he nodded. She scratched his thigh with her fingernails.

'That tickles.' Kenji raised his eyebrows as he did when he wanted to make love to her. 'Could you reach a little further, please?'

'How can you think like that at a time like this?'

'When I stop thinking of that, then you'll know for certain that I'm stone dead. What happened to the old leprechaun?'

'He was the surgeon who operated on you,' Raiko said. 'He left for Australia.'

'Why did I have to be tied down?' Kenji asked.

'You had convulsions.'

'I'm thirsty.'

Raiko poured water into a plastic cup with a spout, but when she turned back Kenji was asleep. She bowed her head and wept, thanking the gods once again for returning him to her.

Another week passed. Kenji now remained awake more than he slept. Raiko wheeled his chair out on to the hospital balcony.

'Why was my arm sore?' Kenji asked.

'You threw it out to prevent me from falling forward when the cab driver put on his brakes. Your head just grazed the front seat, but you passed out.'

Kenji reached into his robe pocket and withdrew a small bottle. Inside, on a wad of cotton, rested a shiny sliver of metal. 'If I had hit that seat harder, this would have pierced my brain.'

'We were lucky Doctor Abrahamson was here.'

'I'd like to do something for him,' Kenji said.

'He wouldn't take the extra money I offered him. He suggested we use it to sponsor a Japanese doctor in Hawaii to study neurosurgery.'

'Let's sponsor two,' Kenji said. 'We'll set up a fund in Doctor Abrahamson's name. A permanent grant for Hawaiians of Japanese ancestry.'

'It's a wonderful idea.' Raiko leaned over and kissed her husband. 'After John Whittefield called from Tokyo, we received royal treatment. This room is reserved for admirals, generals and visiting dignitaries.'

'It has a perfect view of the harbour. Even better than Ruth's attic. I could improve those maps for Genda.'

'Don't even think of writing or drawing anything to do with gun emplacements or munitions storage buildings,' Raiko said. 'It was naval intelligence who stopped us, and they're still around.'

'I may be coming back here with Genda and Hino.'

Raiko came around to the front of the wheelchair and dug her fists into her hips. 'We'll see about you flying again

399

only after you're fully recovered. That will take another couple of months. Doctor Abrahamson left an outline of exercises for you to follow. Remember, we're still on our honeymoon.'

'Some honeymoon. You should have seen the look on the nurse's face when I asked if you could stay overnight with me. She said it's against regulations.'

'I heard you asked if it was against regulations for her to sleep with you.'

Kenji threw up his hands and ducked behind them. 'Joking, only joking. But it isn't much of a honeymoon being in a hospital.'

'You're getting out next week. The *Raiko Maru* will pass through on her return voyage to Japan. We'll take a slow trip back home.'

'What about our plans to tour the States? And the assignments in Mexico?'

'You and I aren't getting involved in that,' Raiko said. 'I radioed Ando and lied. I told him the doctor ordered you home. If we continued on our trip, that weasel would expect us to work. I no longer have qualms about spying on the United States, but I want you to be well and healthy first.'

Kenji leaned forward in the wheelchair and stood. Raiko put her arm around his waist and walked him to the balcony rail.

'Until you told me the story of what happened here at the hospital, I too had misgivings about spying against America,' Kenji said. 'No more. I still believe we shouldn't fight them, but if we must then we'd better win.'

'I've been watching the anti-submarine net at the left side of the harbour,' Raiko said. 'It's not always closed after each ship passes. In the morning when the first patrol boats go out, they leave it open for two or three hours, until the night patrol boats return.'

'Good observation,' Kenji said. 'I agree we shouldn't

400

put anything on paper. But we can sit here and soak up details about Pearl Harbor until we leave. Then we can write it all down aboard the ship.' He looked out at the naval crane across the bay, then at Battleship Row. Unconsciously his thumb began to move, lifting the cover off the firing button on the control stick. 'The next time I come here it could be in the cockpit of a Zero!'

Raiko, about to chastise him, saw the fire in his eye – the look of a hawk. The gods have returned you to me, she thought. If they want their warrior back, I won't stand in his way. Neither will I help.

Kenji knuckled sweat from his eye. It was worse now than at the start when he had asked the *Raiko Maru*'s captain for someone to get him back in shape. At 5 a.m. the following morning, he had been roused by pounding on the cabin door. He had patted Raiko's thigh, got up and stumbled to the door. A well-muscled grey-haired man, wearing tennis shoes, shiny red boxer's shorts and a tiny red beret, said, 'Time to exercise.'

'I'm still sleeping.' Kenji yawned.

'You know how to sleep,' the man said. 'I'll teach you how to remain awake while others rest!' He threw a bundle at Kenji, duplicates of his outfit. 'Put these on!'

'Who are you?' Kenji asked.

'Your teacher.'

Kenji was tempted to slam the door. Then it occurred to him he would need a tough personality to put him in shape to fly again. 'I'll dress and be out in a minute.'

'Drop that robe and follow me now! You can dress while you walk.'

'This beret will never fit me.'

The man spun around and held up a finger. 'First lesson. Balance is more important than strength. Put the beret on and keep it there during your exercises!'

Kenji hopped and wriggled down the ship's passageway,

trying to get into the shorts and not drop the shoes while balancing the small beret on his head. 'What's your name?' Kenji asked.

'You may call me Teacher.' He pointed at the deck. 'Start with push-ups! Will your brain burst if your blood pumps too hard?'

'My injury has nothing to do with the blood vessels in my brain.'

'Good. Do push-ups until you fall on your face!'

Muso, Japan's athletics coach at the 1936 Berlin Olympics, had driven Kenji to his limit every day since. At first it was ten sit-ups, push-ups and chin-ups. Kenji jogged, lifted small weights and duck-walked around the deck. As he gained strength, exercises were added and the older ones extended, until Kenji could do fifty, then 100 repetitions of each set. Running replaced jogging, duck-walking gave way to hopping up and down the ship's stairs on one foot, all without losing his little red beret.

'A fighter pilot with one eye must prove he is superior to those with two,' Muso said. 'You must be better co-ordinated, your timing and reflexes quicker. Give me the beret and roll your head 360 degrees from right to left! Get used to doing that while you run, exercise and eat! That movement will enable you, even with one eye, to see an enemy coming from any angle. You'll need strong neck muscles to keep it up during a long flight. Now hit the deck on your back!'

Kenji dropped to the floor with hands at his sides.

'Put your hands over your head! Reverse them so your palms are on the floor! Press the floor with arched body from hands to toes! It's a reverse push-up.'

Kenji arched his back and pushed with his feet and hands.

Muso shoved the beret under Kenji's head. 'You may use your head to help brace your body.'

Kenji sighed as he rested his head. 'My muscles were beginning to quiver.'

'Remove your hands and remain braced from head to heels!'

'What!' Kenji collapsed on his back. 'That's impossible!'

'American football players in California do this.' Muso dropped to the floor on his back. He folded his hands over his stomach, arched his body from feet to head and proceeded to walk around in a circle with only his feet and the back of his head touching the floor. 'If the Americans can do it, what's wrong with you?' Muso asked.

Kenji mastered the technique by nightfall.

Raiko could not bear to watch the physical punishment he subjected himself to. She found herself clenching her teeth and fists to help him do the last chin-up or climb the rope to the top of the mainmast. She had spent most of the first week in their cabin writing letters and reading, but then found herself drifting to the radio shack with its modern equipment. She watched for a while, then volunteered to help code and decode messages. Soon she was monitoring the British and American military transmissions.

At meals, Raiko told Kenji the latest news from the BBC and American broadcasters out of Hawaii and Manila. They both listened to Japanese news from the Osaka Nagoya station. She would have enjoyed cooking their meals, but Muso insisted on measuring and preparing all Kenji's food.

Kenji looked across the dinner table in their cabin with a mischievous grin. He handed her three small coins, then stood and rolled up his sleeves. Holding his right arm out, he said, 'Space the three coins along my arm, please.'

'What is this?' Raiko placed the coins four inches apart, and Kenji threw them up in the air. He snatched the first, caught the second and knocked the third to the cabin floor. Raiko clapped her hands.

'Muso can do five at once and catch them one at a time before they hit the floor,' Kenji said.

'Muso didn't have his brain tampered with two months ago.'

'I'm in better shape now than when I finished flight school.' Kenji tapped his head.

'Why must you go back into fighter planes?'

'It takes a certain personality to be a fighter pilot. I'm good at it. Japan needs me.'

'I need you,' Raiko said.

'There's going to be a war. Do you want me to hide from it?'

'I wish we could all find a place to hide.' Raiko shook her head. 'I know you can't run. It seems nobody will be able to dodge it. I sit by the radio and listen to the news and it seems as if the whole world is closing in on us. If only people could sit down and talk instead of fight.'

'Your father and my uncle are in Washington talking.' Kenji answered a knock at the door. He took a decoded radiogram from the steward and read it. 'Raiko, you're ordered immediately to the Black Chamber. A different Russian code has come through and they can't break it. This radiogram is signed by Hideki Tojo himself. The minister of war.'

'They should have been able to triangulate the sender's position with the new direction finders.'

Kenji tapped the radiogram. 'It says the transmitter was moved from its former location.'

Raiko's brow furrowed. 'If they changed the code and their position, they must know we're on to them.'

'I see that gleam in your big, beautiful eyes, but I swore you would never go back to that brain-twisting, windowless room.'

Raiko went to Kenji, put her arms around him and

rested her head on his chest. 'I love you,' she whispered. 'But if you're going to fly because it's what you do best, then I must return to the Black Chamber. Japan needs me too. I want to serve the Emperor.'

Kenji kissed the top of Raiko's head and spoke into her soft, sweet-smelling hair. 'I love you. My greatest fear is of losing you.'

'Soon all Japan will be in danger,' Raiko said. 'I must get to Tokyo.'

'This ship has a seaplane. If the ocean is calm tomorrow morning, I'll fly you back.' Kenji held Raiko at arm's length and looked into her face. He ran his hands inside her robe and felt her warm body, the curve of her hips, her breasts. 'On one condition,' he said in a voice thick with passion. 'You must have a partner who reports to Noriko or me every week!'

Raiko opened Kenji's robe and pressed her body against his. She lifted up her face and their lips met. Her tongue sought his. She felt him shiver as he picked her up and took her to the sleeping mat.

Raiko had felt Kenji's body hardening as a result of his training. Now she seemed to hold one large muscle in her arms. Yet he was gentle with her. The look of the hawk was replaced by that of an eagle who wanted to fly. Raiko knew the gods had saved Kenji for something special. It was impossible to hold him back. She prayed his spirit would not break if Hashimoto refused to allow him to return as a fighter pilot.

44

'Not much longer,' Kenji said. He banked the seaplane and swooped down. 'There's Tokyo bay. It feels great to be flying again.'

'I'd like to agree, but my stomach would call my mouth a liar,' Raiko said. 'Is this dipping and diving what you and your cousins call fun?'

Kenji levelled the plane into the familiar descent pattern to the harbour. 'There's nothing like it. You'd have to be in a fast plane to really experience the thrill. I haven't lost my touch.' He patted the control stick.

'You rolling your head around makes me dizzy.'

'I've got to practise. They'll only give me one test in a mock dogfight.'

'Try calling Owada centre, please. Ask the chief if I can come in tomorrow. If it's yes, let's stay at the Imperial Hotel and invite Noriko for dinner. She must be lonely with Hiroki in the States.'

Kenji spoke on the radio as he lined up the plane between the double row of white buoys marking the landing area. Fishermen waved as he glided in over their heads. He waggled his wings in greeting.

'The chief is glad to have you back,' he said to Raiko. 'He looks forward to seeing you in the morning and will give Noriko our message.'

Raiko gripped the dashboard with both hands. 'Please don't wave your wings any more. Remember my stomach. Is landing on water worse than on the earth?'

'You won't even feel it when we touch down.'

A tremendous whooshing sound filled the cabin as the single large pontoon sliced neatly into the water. 'You're right,' Raiko shouted. 'The noise frightened me so much, I didn't feel when we touched the water. I'll take wheels any day.'

Kenji grinned as he taxied the plane between the buoys to the Ishikawa landing slip. 'The last time I took off from here was when Genda and I dropped leaflets on the rebels. That was four years ago, 1936.'

Kenji lay his head back against the rim of the hot tub. Steaming water rose around him. Raiko watched him relax. 'Who did you speak to at the base?' she asked.

He rested his feet on hers under the water. 'A friend. I need to do some serious flying. Hashimoto will want to know if I can pilot a Zero in combat. If I can lead a squadron.'

'You're a colonel and should command an air group, not just a squadron.'

'A retired colonel,' Kenji said. 'I have to request reactivation also.'

'Not necessary. Hashimoto loves you. He thinks you're the reincarnation of some ancient samurai hero. He'll do what you want.' Raiko got out of the tub and towelled herself. 'We may not see each other for a while. Come to bed with me.'

'I thought we'd do that after dinner.'

Raiko stood framed in the bedroom door. She let the towel fall, tossed her glistening wet hair and looked back over her shoulder. 'We can do it again after dinner.'

Noriko knew in which of the seven restaurants at the hotel she would find Raiko and Kenji. All of them preferred French food. Kenji bowed to her and she beamed at him. 'You are the happiest thing I've seen in Tokyo for months. I expected to find an invalid. You look very fit.'

Raiko bowed to Noriko. 'Married life agrees with him.'

'It is obvious. I think he has lost his neck. Kenji Ishikawa is just one big muscle from his jawbones to his shoulders. And you are in bloom too. Positively handsome, the two of you.'

Kenji blushed as he held the chair for Noriko. 'I'm really hungry. I've had too much of training diets. I'm having Chateaubriand. Rare.'

The table had been cleared and Noriko looked about, to be certain no one could overhear. 'I regret to tell you we are on the verge of war with the United States. Hiroki is returning home against Prince Higashikuni's orders. Kenji, he used your name and Yamamoto's influence to gain an audience with the Emperor. Our invasion of north Indochina is set for 22 September.'

'How did Hiroki find out the date?' Kenji asked.

'I told him. I heard from the voice that says mother of autumn, father of spring. The same person who warned you of the assassination attempt.'

'What did he tell you?' Kenji asked.

'Matsuoka has returned with a special German envoy to sign an alliance between Japan, Italy and Germany,' Noriko said. 'He has brought assurances the Russians will not move into Manchuria or Korea if we head south. Hiroki will arrive tomorrow afternoon and meet with the Emperor tomorrow night. I would like you to be at the airport with me to greet him.'

'Do you expect trouble?' Raiko asked.

'A member of the National Diet, who is also anti-war and who pressed for Hiroki's meeting with the Emperor, was shot yesterday in Tokyo's main railroad terminal,' Noriko said. 'There were police and soldiers all around, but supposedly no one saw the killer.'

Kenji shook his head. 'I thought public assassinations were a thing of the past.'

'They still happen,' Noriko said. 'Except that the government has stopped publicizing them. War fever is high in the country. Communists are being sent to prison. Liberals are considered unpatriotic. Everyone belongs to the Alliance for the Mobilization of the National Spirit.' She pointed at Raiko's colourful kimono, at Kenji's tuxedo. 'Do not dress like that on the street.'

'But you're wearing an evening gown,' Raiko said.

'I am older, and I stepped from the car directly into the hotel lobby. Prime Minister Konoe addressed the nation on radio in July. He called for frugality in all things, total devotion to the Emperor and determination to make Japan strong to face our enemies. Everyone must work two hours overtime daily to make up for the men called to military service. The radio plays only martial music and the new national dress is an ugly green uniform. The women wear something that looks like coveralls on top and knickers on the bottom. Gangs of toughs roam the streets enforcing the dress code, and the police help them. The gaiety and fun is gone from life. People are stockpiling food and growing vegetables in every possible place and container. These patriotic gardens supposedly release more food to our soldiers abroad.'

'Life in Tokyo sounds drab compared to Hawaii,' Raiko said. 'The Americans talk about a war, but you'd never know it to see them play, party and lounge around the beaches.'

'Places like this hotel are the only havens in Tokyo,' Noriko said. 'Here one can still get a good meal, listen to Western music and laugh out loud.' She motioned at a young, stern-faced man in a double-breasted suit standing at the entrance to the restaurant. 'But even here Kempetai is watching.'

'I'll cancel an appointment at Haneda air base so I can go with you tomorrow.' Kenji stood.

'Be careful what you say on the telephone,' Noriko said. 'They are probably listening.'

Noriko waited until Kenji was out of hearing, then

409

turned to Raiko. 'How long will you be at the Black Chamber?'

'For the duration of the crisis.'

'If you don't have war essential work, they will draft you to listen in on English language telephone conversations. The government is always advertising for good English speakers.' Noriko smiled at Raiko. 'I said you are in bloom, I should have said radiant. Are you pregnant?'

A mischevious gleam crept into Raiko's big dark eyes. She leaned forward and whispered, 'I missed my monthly period and normally the Institute of Science could set their clocks by me.'

'Do you want me to arrange a test?'

'I feel so happy. Let the rabbit live a while longer. If the test was positive, Kenji might stop me from returning to the Black Chamber.'

At Tokyo's international airport, the manager personally guided Hiroki Ishikawa through customs. Kenji directed the porter towards his Cadillac. The manager bowed goodbye and a policeman followed them to the car.

Nearing the Cadillac, Kenji sensed that the policeman had dropped back. He turned, and saw a young man break from the crowd of passengers, running towards Hiroki, brandishing a newspaper.

'Traitor!' the young man shouted. 'Traitor!' His newspaper fell away. He raised a samurai short sword to hack at Hiroki.

The policeman watched, making no attempt to interfere. A second attacker broke from the crowd carrying a short sword. Kenji's fist shot out towards the first man, hitting him with a straight right cross from the shoulder. The man crumpled, dropping his weapon. Kenji whirled to face the second attacker and saw the sword descending on his uncle's head.

Hiroki whipped up his cane, deflecting the razor-sharp

blade, and drove his fist under his attacker's heart. He brought the point of his elbow up between the man's eyes, knocking him unconscious. 'Arrest this villain,' Hiroki shouted at the policeman.

The first attacker jumped up and stumbled past the policeman, disappearing into the crowd of onlookers.

'Stop him,' Kenji cried.

Not one of the many uniformed men in the crowd moved. The civilians who did were blocked, and threatened by fierce glares.

Kenji took Hiroki's arm. 'We'd best leave here.'

'Not until that police officer arrests this thug!' Hiroki bent down and picked up a sword. He handed it to the policeman. 'This is evidence!'

The policeman reluctantly accepted the sword. He took the stunned attacker by the arm and led him away. Gently but firmly, Kenji hurried Hiroki to the Cadillac, ushering him into the rear seat next to Noriko.

'I saw everything,' Noriko said as she embraced Hiroki, patting him everywhere to be certain he was unhurt. 'They were all in on it. The uniformed army men, Kempetai in the crowd and the airport police. They wouldn't help and prevented anyone else from intervening.'

Kenji gunned the Cadillac's engine and roared out of the airport terminal. He raced down the Tokyo highway. 'You're both staying with me. Raiko is sleeping at Owada for a day or two and my place is easier to protect. I'll call some friends from the air base to come and stand guard.'

After the first two guards had arrived, Kenji drove to the imperial palace in uniform. 'Tell General Hashimoto that Colonel Ishikawa is here to see him!' he told the secretary.

She looked at her appointment book. 'You are not scheduled.'

Kenji's jaw muscles twitched and his one eye blazed.

411

He spoke between clenched teeth. 'Tell the general if he doesn't open that door, I'll kick it in!'

The secretary rushed into the general's office. She rushed out again and ushered Kenji in.

'It is always a pleasure to see you,' Hashimoto said, and pointed to a chair in front of his desk. 'Have a seat.'

'I will stand on my feet and on my oath. If anything like the assassination attempt at the airport happens to my uncle again, I'll use my personal fortune, my influence and any power I have inside and outside this country to discredit this government's policies at home and abroad!'

Hashimoto stared at Kenji for some moments, trying to decide how to handle him. He leaned back in his chair. 'Are you against our policy of expansion into South-East Asia?'

'No. Neither is my uncle. He doesn't want war with America if it can be avoided.'

Hashimoto steepled his fingers under his chin. 'What if it can't be avoided?'

'Then we fight,' Kenji said.

'By we, you mean your uncle too?'

'Yes.'

'I did not order the attack on your uncle,' Hashimoto said.

'You have the power to prevent it happening again!'

'You have my word it will not.'

'One more thing,' Kenji said. 'I want to be reactivated and given command of my old squadron.'

'There is my samurai,' Hashimoto exclaimed. 'Tell me about the Japanese in Hawaii. Will they rise up against the Americans if we call on them?'

'No. They talk of themselves as Hawaiians of Japanese descent. Even Ando doesn't expect them to act. He said they represent thirty-five per cent of the island's population. In another ten years they'll control the government through their votes.'

'We do not have ten years,' Hashimoto said. 'Did you see Pearl Harbor before they operated on you?'

'Yes, and Genda is correct. If we make simultaneous attacks with fighters and divebombers, many of the torpedo-planes will get through. The problem is how to successfully launch a torpedo in thirty-six feet of water.'

'I thought it was thirty-four.'

'If we can time it for high tide, he'll have two more feet,' Kenji said.

'Genda is practising at Kagoshima. Go down there. Take some training flights before you leave. You will have to requalify. Hino will be there in a week. He is flying between Formosa and Manila, mapping air currents.'

'If the target is Pearl Harbor, why practise long-distance flights to Manila?'

'The America War Plan Orange for the defence of Hawaii requires fifty new Flying Fortresses to be stationed at Clark Field outside Manila. MacArthur claims he can annihilate any aircraft carriers trying to attack Hawaii with the big bombers.'

'He's correct,' Kenji said. 'The Flying Fortress is the largest and most powerful bomber in the world. With fifty of them stationed behind our aircraft carriers, Yamamoto could never send his planes forward to attack.'

'Yamamoto may be against war with America but since the end of the Great War, like most of us, he has thought about it. He has a solution. The Americans know we do not have enough aircraft carriers to launch simultaneous attacks on both Manila and Hawaii. If we hit Hawaii first, the Flying Fortresses would wipe out our carriers. We would lose our planes and our ships. If we hit Clark Field first, we cannot surprise them at Pearl Harbor. The American army-air-force high command doesn't believe a mass military long-distance flight can be made from

413

Formosa to Manila. If Hino can solve the distance problem, we can hit the Americans at Manila and Pearl Harbor simultaneously.'

'Will you give me back my squadron?'

'No,' Hashimoto said. 'If tomorrow's meeting with the Emperor goes well and you prove your flying ability with one eye, you'll take active command of an entire combat air wing.'

'What if I anger the Emperor?' Kenji asked.

'You would have to wear that dumb green civilian uniform and shovel shit for the duration of the war. If you don't requalify as a fighter pilot, I want you to command a new flight-training school.'

Kenji saluted and stepped back. 'Yes, sir!' Then he leaned forward and spoke softly. 'I remind you that if anything happens to my uncle, you are dead.'

'Ishikawa, I love war,' Hashimoto said. 'You are a natural killer and I want you up there flying for me.' The bald-headed general pulled his Luger and fired a round into the floor at Kenji's feet. 'The next time you show the least disrespect to me, I will kill you! Get yourself out of here!'

Kenji did an about-face and marched past the frightened secretary.

Hashimoto was dialling before the door closed behind Kenji. 'Kill those fools who botched the assassination!' he said into the phone. 'Have them commit suicide tonight! Tell our Koda-ha people to remove Hiroki Koin's name from the assassination list! Make a special note! If by chance someone does kill the bastard, make certain Kenji Ishikawa dies as soon after as possible! This is a no-second-thoughts order! Confirmation is not required!'

45

'Both men committed suicide by hanging,' John Whittefield said. 'One in his cell, the other from a tree near the Yasukune shrine. They left death poems condemning those traitors who are against military expansionism.'

'Your man at the airport reported the assassination attempt was arranged by the army,' Ambassador Grew said.

'That's been confirmed. There'll be more assassinations, anti-Western demonstrations and travel restrictions on foreign diplomats in Japan. Kempetai has accused me of spying.'

'Have they proof of anything?'

'No,' John said. 'They listened in on a phonecall to my house in which the caller identified himself as Mangiro. Few Japanese recognize the name that John Mung, the peasant fisherman, was born with. No one would realize its relevance to me.'

'What was said?'

'The voice did all the talking. He warned that Japanese ships would land troops in the Gulf of Haiphong on the twenty-second of this month. The Vichy French will put up token resistance, then lay down their arms.'

'That's consistent with your reports from Admiral Darlan,' Grew said.

'The rest also sounds true. Foreign Minister Matsuoka arrived from Berlin with a German official prepared to sign a mutual defence agreement with Japan. If we slap an embargo on Japan, the Emperor will join the Axis Alliance.'

'That's another step closer to war between Japan and the

United States,' Grew said. 'Hitler is preparing Operation Sea Lion – the invasion of England. In addition to Italy, he has Russia as a military ally.' The ambassador began to pace the office. 'I've got to inform Washington that Japan may join the Axis. If Roosevelt declares war on Germany, will it mean we're automatically at war with Russia, Italy and Japan?'

'I don't know,' John said. 'If Japan invades Indochina and the president doesn't react with a total embargo, he'll lose face in Asia. The caller also said that American aid to Chiang Kai-shek is misdirected. It should go to Mao Tse-tung because the Communists are the only ones fighting the Japanese.'

'Even a hint of helping the Communists before the presidential election would be disastrous for the Democratic ticket. I doubt the president would consider it.'

'The caller claims that Chiang Kai-shek met with General Hashimoto and the Japanese puppet president of occupied China. They agreed on an unofficial truce. The Japanese are to attack the Communists for Chiang and he'll keep his Nationalist army quiet while Japan moves south.'

'I feel like we're on the dark side of the moon choosing up teams, and former friends have become enemies,' Grew said. 'In the last war Japan, Italy, Russia and France were allies. Now Russia, half of France and all of Italy are with Germany. And if your caller is correct, Japan is preparing to sign with Hitler. Will we know in time if Japan is going to war with us?'

'Yes. I have agents at listening posts throughout the empire. When the Emperor removes his immediate family from positions of responsibility in the military, war will be imminent.'

'Did the caller say that?'

'I say it. My sources indicate that two members of the Privy Council have been ordered to keep false diaries of meetings that might implicate the Emperor in military decisions. It's to protect him from responsibility if Japan should lose a war.'

Grew stood with his back to John, looking out of the window at the imperial palace. 'If that's correct, they're definitely preparing for war with us. Can you give me the names of your sources for this information?'

'The former Lord Keeper of the Privy Seal Hiroki Koin and Professor Tatsukichi Minobe. Hiroki Koin, Admiral Yamamoto and Kenji Ishikawa are meeting right now with the Emperor and his senior advisers.'

Grew returned to his desk. 'In the event Kempetai wants to expel you because of the phonecall, I'll see that Secretary of State Hull evicts half the Japanese delegation from Washington. You and your people are our eyes and ears. Let me know what happens at today's meeting with the Emperor.'

The Anteroom to the Imperial Reception Chamber

'Those assassins at the airport never had a chance against your uncle,' Admiral Yamamoto said to Kenji. 'He learned karate in Korea where he grew up. At the age of twenty-one he returned to Japan and was invited to teach in the Imperial Hall of Martial Arts.'

'I would like to use some mental karate on those inside the imperial chamber,' Hiroki said. 'I learned in Washington that many Americans do not trust us. They want war. Whoever wins next month's presidential election will then be free of political restraints and repercussions.'

'Those Japanese who want war must believe you can sway the Emperor, or they wouldn't have tried to assassinate you,' Kenji said.

The doors to the imperial chamber opened. The master of protocol bowed and said, 'Gentlemen, please follow me.'

417

General Hashimoto, Prime Minister Konoe, Foreign Minister Matsuoka and Minister of War Major General Hideki Tojo stood near a long table running at a right-angle to the dais. Yamamoto, Hiroki and Kenji entered the chamber and bowed to them. The Emperor entered, wearing an army uniform. All turned to the dais and bowed low until he took his place on the single golden throne.

'Be seated,' the master of protocol said. 'This meeting is convened at the request of the honourable Hiroki Koin, former Lord Keeper of the Privy Seal. Sir, you are permitted to speak.'

'Your imperial majesty.' Hiroki bowed to the throne again. From that moment no-one looked at the Emperor. Hiroki bowed to the men seated opposite. 'Gentlemen, I have returned from Washington because I think you misjudge the Americans and the situation here in Japan. Being outside the country gives one a different perspective. Five years of war with China has strained our economy, taxed our military and burdened our people. Still, China has not collapsed as was predicted. Roosevelt promises to implement the monetary freeze and total embargo if we move on Indochina. If so, we face economic disaster. Secretary of State Hull stated that Japan has gobbled up Korea, Manchuria and large parts of China. He will not allow us to continue into South-East Asia. There is a desirable alternative to confrontation with the United States. Do as they ask. Withdraw our troops from China, put them into factories and enjoy the profits from Hitler's war, as we did in the Great War. The economic power of Europe is temporarily in limbo. Japan can take advantage of this to establish an economic empire in Asia and the West without going to war ourselves.'

'The Americans are so full of peace, brotherly love and political isolationist drivel because of their upcoming election,' Hashimoto said. 'Roosevelt's reaction will be mild if we move before November. He won't freeze our money and he won't go to war.'

'That can be a dangerous assumption,' Hiroki said. 'If you are wrong, we could be looking into the gun barrels of the Pacific fleet.'

Matsuoka scribbled a note to Tojo, and received an affirmative nod. 'General Hashimoto is correct,' Matsuoka said. 'Three years ago when I signed the Anti-Comintern Pact with Germany, you liberals asked what we could gain from Hitler. My answer was shared technology and intelligence. Now my answer would be to share the world. The Germans have taken Europe and will help us take Asia. They gave us the information that Great Britain would not defend Singapore, Malaysia or India. Von Ribbentrop negotiated with Vichy France on our behalf. He has used his influence with Germany's new ally Russia to keep the Mongolian border quiet so we can move south. He will arrange for me to meet with Molotov next year.'

'My uncle questions how you can be certain the US won't attack us if we enter Indochina,' Kenji said.

'We have the word of Churchill and Roosevelt,' Matsuoka said. 'One of the gifts I returned with from Berlin was the transcript of a conversation between them. The Germans perfected equipment to unscramble the radio-telephone conversations between the US president and the prime minister of Great Britain. Those two agreed to make a great deal of noise if we move on Indochina, but America's commitment is first to Europe.'

'I too dragged my feet on the move south,' Konoe said. 'But our choice now is either to move or miss a golden opportunity. France is done and England will soon fall. Holland is occupied by the Germans. The oil and tin of the Dutch East Indies, rubber and rice of Malaysia, coal and tungsten of Indochina, are abandoned treasures waiting to be plucked. Germany is willing to let us have them, but we must act!'

'Gentlemen,' Kenji said. 'England may appear on the brink of defeat according to Goering, but not according to the BBC or American reporters in London. The German air marshal's vow to bomb the English into submission or annihilation has not come about. Goering has asked Hitler to assemble an invasion force. The English are preparing to fight, not surrender. The Luftwaffe has not swept the RAF from the skies. Whoever controls the air, controls the ground. English night bombers cross the channel every evening on raids against the Germans. The Germans cross back in daylight. Goering's indiscriminate terror bombings have strengthened, not broken the will of the English people.' Kenji had previously requested and received Tojo's permission to mention Operation Barbarossa. 'If Hitler attacks Russia next spring, before he finishes with England, it will violate the basic military principles against dividing one's forces and fighting on two fronts.'

'You, a pilot, can be excused for making a tactical error regarding ground manoeuvres,' Hashimoto said. 'Hitler will have interior lines of communication and supply, which eliminates the negatives of a two-front war. The German army is completely mobilized, including its infantry. They have been consistently victorious. England will surrender this winter, Moscow next summer, and we shall take north Indochina in the coming week.'

'Lord Koin should return to Washington,' Konoe said. 'Explain to the Americans we are taking only north Indochina in deference to Roosevelt's objections. South Indochina will remain in French hands. We do not want war with the United States.'

'Signing with the Axis is almost a declaration of war on America,' Hiroki said. 'And that is suicide!'

'Seppuku has never been a disgrace in Japan,' Hashimoto retorted. 'We would suffer loss of face if we retreated because of unsubstantiated threats. Retreat would show a lack of courage and bad tactics. Let's see what the Americans are made of!'

The Emperor hitched his thumbs in his garrison belt and pointed both forefingers at Yamamoto.

'Our army's premise that Western democracies are corrupt and their people soft is without foundation,' the admiral said. 'American pacifism should not be mistaken for the lack of will to fight. Americans are slow to anger, tough in combat and unforgiving to those who betray them. If they were to cut all our oil supplies, we would have to fight. But an embargo of aircraft fuel and scrap iron is a small price to pay for north Indochina. Regular gasoline can be cracked by our refineries to make the octane rating required for aircraft engines. Scrap iron can be purchased through a third party. I support the move south, but not an alliance with Germany. It would bind us to their future, which is uncertain. Hitler's submarines have sunk several American merchant ships carrying supplies to England. Germany and America will soon be at war. If we were allied with Germany, then we would be at war with the United States. We must act, not react!'

'How could America possibly stand against Germany, Italy, Russia and Japan?' Matsuoka asked.

'Russia is not party to the Axis alliance,' Yamamoto replied. 'They have a separate agreement with Hitler. If he attacks the Soviets, as we are told he will, his ally shall become his enemy. England has not fallen yet, and will stand with America, Australia, New Zealand, South Africa and Canada against Germany. Those countries can muster formidable armies.'

'Do you agree the Americans underestimate our air power?' Hashimoto asked.

'Yes,' Yamamoto said. 'The Zero will control the skies.'

'Then we shall control the ground too,' Matsuoka replied.

'Hitler's tactic of *blitzkrieg* proved this. Colonel Ishikawa, our air expert, confirmed it a few minutes ago.'

'We shall control the air, sea and land for a while,' Yamamoto said. 'But you miss the meaning of total war. It no longer has to do with the number of men prepared to die. The fall of the shogun came about when the armourer replaced the samurai in importance. One bullet fired by a peasant ended years of aristocratic military training. Global conflict between modern nations requires the greatest co-operation and co-ordination in the history of mankind. America's ability to mobilize exceeds that of Japan. They have natural and human resources on a scale you cannot imagine. Their scientific, engineering and production skills will send unending waves of military equipment, materials and supplies to overwhelm the fighting spirit of our soldiers.'

Kenji saw The Razor's eyes blink behind his round horn-rimmed glasses. Tojo put his hand out and there was silence. Everyone leaned forward to hear Japan's minister of war.

'Admiral, for some years you have studied the military situation in the Pacific,' Tojo said. 'Can you cripple the Pacific fleet?'

'Yes.'

'If a decision is made to fight America, it will not be done in a frenzy of euphoric slogans and martial music,' Tojo said. 'We shall study the enemy's weak points and train our men to take advantage of them. Only if pushed by a total trade embargo shall we move against the Pacific fleet. It shall be a calm, calculated attack with more than a moderate chance to succeed.' Tojo paused and met the eyes of each man at the table. 'I am for an alliance with Germany only if Roosevelt takes economic or military action against Japan. America would never concentrate all its power in the Pacific while Germany is a threat to her east coast. If Germany defeats England, then we win.

If Hitler loses, he loses alone. In either case, we shall have time to consolidate our gains in South-East Asia and lay the foundation for the economic empire Lord Koin envisions. The difference being, we shall have the military might to defend the enormous natural resources there and put those millions of Asians to work for the Emperor, the empire and the Japanese people!'

The Emperor stood. All rose to their feet and bowed.

'Those in favour of occupying northern Indochina?' the master of protocol asked.

Everyone raised a hand.

'Those in favour of joining the Axis Alliance if America takes economic action against the empire?'

Everyone opposite Kenji voted in favour. Then Yamamoto raised his hand and Hiroki followed. Kenji put his hand up, becoming part of the collective decision that could lead to war with America. He bowed with the others and intoned, 'So it is ordered, so it is done.'

The Year of the Snake
1941

46

Kenji checked his knee map, airspeed and did a quick calculation. 'Not much longer to Kagoshima,' he said aloud. Below him the landscape of the southern island of Kyushu showed green and lush under the noonday sun. He looked at the picture of Raiko taped to the sleeve of his flight jacket. 'Everything is for beauty,' he said.

Raiko had broken the Russian code and been recommended for another citation. She had decoded a message to Stalin warning that Japan was planning to bomb Pearl Harbor. Kenji had assumed this would end the training exercises for the attack. Yamamoto had cautioned him to remain silent, continue preparing to attack Pearl Harbor and hope it never happened.

Kenji thought about how much had changed since his and Raiko's return to Japan. Political parties were now completely eliminated. The Emperor ruled with his new cabinet ministers, although some claimed the cabinet ministers ruled the Emperor. There was strict enforcement of laws forbidding public celebrations, sports or entertainment. Every day the press and radio announced additional restrictions regarding food, dress and behaviour. Japan was a solemn place.

Kenji looked again at Raiko's picture, thinking of his child inside her. He remembered how he learned he was to become a father.

'You've put on weight,' he had said to Raiko.

'Are you displeased?' she asked.

'You are more beautiful than ever.'

'I've killed a rabbit,' Raiko said.

Kenji had experienced a sense of pride, then overwhelming fear. Responsibility for the creation of another soul. His own flesh and blood. An extension of his parents and ancestors. The prospect of fatherhood made him view life differently.

The only condition remaining of Yamamoto's three prerequisites for war is an alliance with Russia, he thought, and Matsuoka has a meeting scheduled with von Ribbentrop and Molotov in March. Matsuoka's predictions about American reactions to Japan's occupation of Hanoi and takeover of north Indochina have come true. The United States didn't freeze Japanese funds. They only embargoed scrap iron and aviation fuel, and lost face even in the eyes of those Japanese most reluctant for war. The same day that Roosevelt announced the embargo, Tojo had the Emperor's seal on a mutual defence pact with Germany and Italy. Japan joined the Axis Alliance on 27 September 1940. Roosevelt won the presidential election in November and immediately signed a national conscription bill drafting men between twenty-one and thirty-five into military service. In December, Congress approved Roosevelt's massive six-billion-dollar defence budget. Included was the production figure of 50,000 war planes. Kenji sighed. 'The coming of war has a momentum of its own. I have no control of the future. The best I can do is try to keep our country safe for my wife and child.'

He rolled his head, scanning the sky above, the earth below. He checked the map co-ordinates, his watch, then switched on the radio.

'Kanoya, Kanoya,' Kenji called. 'This is flight 13–21–0 approaching. Request permission to land.'

'Kanoya air base to 13–21–0, permission denied.'

'Should I park this thing on those clouds outside the harbour and walk down?' Kenji asked.

There was a pause in transmission. Then Genda's voice came over the radio. 'Just hang up there a while, Cousin.

428

You've come to show us what you learned in combat flying at Haneda. We want you to take over this air group, but you'll have to earn it. Are you ready?'

'Come up and try me!'

'Someone might claim I took it easy on my cousin. We held a dogfight competition between the top pilots of every squadron in the air wing. The best of the best are standing by to take you on.'

Kenji checked his gauges. 'I have enough fuel for a half-hour of fun and games. Send them up!'

'The tower chief is the referee,' Genda said. 'Try and stay over Kagoshima. Every pilot in the area has been waiting to see this. Let the circus begin!'

Kenji switched radio channels until he found the one used for the two interceptor planes. He listened to their take-off instructions and silently thanked his cousin. Genda's use of the word circus meant they would employ von Richthofen's tactics against him. He heard the tower chief assign number-one runway. Below, on Kanoya field, he watched the two planes taxi to their take-off positions. Kenji looked once more at Raiko's picture. 'Wish me luck.'

He shoved the throttle forward and rammed the control stick ahead, going into a power dive that thrust him hard against his seat. From 10,000 feet the plane dropped to 1,000, and he levelled off over the runway, roaring head-on towards the two aeroplanes rising wing tip to wing tip from the field. Kenji seesawed his plane from left to right, covering both planes. He dipped down and zoomed over them.

'Two kills for Colonel Ishikawa,' the tower chief said over the radio.

'Not fair,' one of the attackers shouted.

'War isn't fair,' Kenji said. 'Winning is.'

As he roared past the tower, he saw hundreds of pilots and members of the ground crew waving. He brushed a tear from his eye and started to climb. Muso had put him in top physical condition, but if he was to lead these men into combat he would have to show them more than a surprise attack.

'Come and get me,' Kenji said into his radio microphone. 'That's an order!' He rolled his head in that same slow circle.

The two Zeros came into Kenji's view sooner than expected. They had not waited for his command. 'They must be good to have made that fast a turn,' he said. 'It had to be a half-inverted loop coming off the runway. I really am up against the best. Well I've got a surprise for you boys.'

Kenji knew Kagoshima from the ground as well as the air. Hiroki and Noriko had brought him here on vacations during winter recesses. It was the city of his great-grandfather, John Mung. Here Mung had met the Lord of Satsuma and became a samurai. In the harbour below he had built Japan's first whaling ships, armed them and trained samurai swordsmen to use rifles and overthrow the shogun. At 5,000 feet above that harbour, Kenji levelled off and headed for the peninsula that reached out into the ocean. He let the two Zeros gain on him, let them believe they had the advantage of speed. 'Nothing in war is fair,' he said, and laughed. He would not chance losing the opportunity of leading these men into combat. He personally had supervised Mitsubishi mechanics preparing his plane's special engine. They had milled the cylinder head down a fraction, which increased the compression, and bench-tested it with various carburettor jets until Kenji was satisfied. The standard Zero fighter plane was sluggish in the turns and steep climbs at high altitudes. He had compensated for that with different carburettor valves and adjustments. It reduced his speed at lower altitudes, but he had a contingency plan for that.

Behind him, the two Zeros had separated, one moving

430

below and to his left, the other up and to his right. 'Let them try to cut off my escape angles.' Kenji aimed his plane at the 10,000-foot Sakurajima volcano that spewed smoke another 1,000 feet in the air. He roared in so close to the side of the volcano that tourists on the trail dived for cover. He laid his plane over on its left wing and flew a circle around the middle, starting the second circle closer to the summit. Without reducing speed, the two fighters chased him. The first broke off and zoomed up into the smoke pouring out of the crater. Kenji came around the opposite side of the mountain. The second fighter was moving into position for a kill. Kenji dropped his flaps, stalled his engine and the second plane whizzed by. The first, coming over the top, almost crashed into his partner.

Kenji went to full throttle and came up behind the first of the shaken pilots. 'Gotcha,' he shouted.

'Kill,' the tower chief called over the radio.

'Catch me if you can,' Kenji called. He raced for the big cloud just outside the harbour.

With two furious fighter pilots after him, Kenji entered the cloud's belly at 15,000 feet, and came out of the head at 17,000. The two Zeros charged after him, again coming up faster than he expected, but he had designed their planes and knew their limitations. The higher they went the less power they had, and the more efficiently his fuel burned. He reduced his speed gradually, maintaining the distance between them so they would not suspect the extra horsepower he had left. At 30,000 feet he pulled his control stick left, hit the rudder pedal and gave full power. The two planes tried to follow, but their engines gasped while Kenji's roared. He flew full circle behind the rear plane. 'Gotcha,' he shouted again.

'Kill,' the tower chief shouted.

The first pilot put his plane into a full-power dive and Kenji went after him. In the dive, both planes were equal and Kenji knew he couldn't gain. He whispered

431

the familiar saying, 'There's only so far down you can go, my friend, then you've got to come to me.' The pilot kept diving. 'This man has courage,' Kenji said.

The roar of the approaching planes reached those on the ground. 'They'd better pull up or they're both finished!' the tower chief said.

'Kenji won't back off,' Genda said. 'When that Zero pulls out of the dive, Kenji has him.'

'It doesn't look like he's going to pull up!'

The two planes screamed towards earth, and emergency crews moved for their trucks. Pilots, maintenance men and ground crews started backing off the runway. Then, only fifty feet over the field, the first plane pulled up and screamed by, with Kenji right behind.

'Kill,' shouted the tower chief.

Kenji radioed his two opponents. 'Join me in a victory roll over the airfield.'

The two pilots lined up their planes on either side of Kenji's as they approached the field.

'Roll,' Kenji ordered. He rolled his Zero, alone over the cheering crowd. His opponents waggled their wings in salute.

'Colonel, it was your victory,' one of the pilots radioed. 'Teach us how to fly like that and we'll be invincible.'

Kenji landed his plane and climbed down from the cockpit. He was raised shoulder-high by cheering pilots, and carried to Hino and Genda, who each held a hat full of money.

'What are you doing with all that cash?' Kenji shouted.

'Put the new wing commander down!' Hino said. He saluted Kenji. 'This money came from bets that you would have three kills within ten minutes.'

Kenji gazed around at the eager faces crowding in for a close look at Japan's first air ace, the legendary, one-eyed Colonel Ishikawa. 'You mean to tell me these young squirts bet against their new commander!' His eye raked the men and they fell silent.

'I told them they should have seen you fly with two eyes,' Genda said.

'I told them how you used to shoot down Chinese planes blindfolded,' Hino said.

'Did you tell them both of you are paying for the celebration that's about to begin?' Kenji asked.

The pilots cheered, and lifted Genda, Hino and Kenji on their shoulders. Marching en masse to the dining hall, they sang an old samurai fighting song at the tops of their voices. Cases of saké were brought from the commissary. A telephone call to a nearby restaurant assured there would be an elegant buffet delivered.

Kenji was lifted on to a table. Toasts were made to the new wing commander and he was pressed to make a speech. He cleared his throat and said, 'We here in Kagoshima will rewrite the history of warfare! The fundamental rule of air battles is to contol the area over a target by eliminating the enemy's fighter planes. I'll teach you how to do that not only over land, but also at sea! Naval experts around the world believe their battleships rule the oceans. We'll show them it's our air force that rules! I'll sharpen your skills in training, then in actual combat, before we ever go after the big target. You're younger than me. Your reactions should be faster than mine.' Kenji took six coins from his pocket and placed three on the back of each arm. He held his arms out before the silent crowd of pilots, then threw the six coins into the air. Using both hands, he caught each of them, one after the other. He held out his fists, opened them and showed the coins. He closed his fists, made several passes with his hands, then opened them palms-up. The coins were gone. 'Yes, it's a trick,' Kenji said. 'I practised many hours to make a point taught by the ancient sword saint Musashi, the greatest warrior ever. Surprise your opponent and he's yours! We are going to surprise the world! All but thirty T-97s will be withdrawn from China. Those returning pilots will train here for the task that lies ahead in the Pacific. To give you combat experience, we'll send thirty pilots back to China every month. But you will run from the Flying Tigers! You will shadow-box the Russian Yaks and British Glosters!'

A disgruntled murmur swept the crowd. Kenji waited for silence, then said, 'There's a tactic in karate called monkey-fighting. The man dances about, hopping from one foot to the other, waving his arms like a fool. When his opponent relaxes, believing he is dealing with an idiot, the monkey becomes the Golden Haired Lion. He attacks, and wins! We've been ordered to keep the superior aspects of the Zero under wraps.' Kenji dropped his voice and the men crowded in closer. 'Western intelligence believes our air force is inferior in quality, quantity and determination. We must continue to promote that image by dancing like monkeys.' He pointed, turning as he spoke so his eye touched each of his men. He had caught their young minds. Now he wanted their hearts. He wanted them angry enough to push beyond what they believed themselves capable of. His voice was a whisper. 'I will train you to fight like the Golden Haired Lions, against the Americans who sing about us in Hawaii. Their song comes from the movie *Snow White and the Seven Dwarfs*. They refer to us as dwarfs!' He took a deep breath and sang the song, enunciating each word clearly,

> 'Whistle while you work.
> Hitler is a jerk.
> Mussolini is a meany
> And the Japs are even worse!'

There was absolute silence in the crowded dining hall. Kenji could hear the angry hiss of breath whistling in and out through clenched teeth. He sang the song again, slower, louder.

> 'Whistle while you work.
> Hitler is a jerk.
> Mussolini is a meany
> And the Japs are even worse!'

'No party,' someone shouted. 'Let's start the training to kill the American bastards!'

There was a mad rush to the door that would have emptied the hall had not Genda and Hino blocked the way.

'It's raining out there,' Hino shouted. 'That cloud Kenji punctured is telling us there is time for a party. Tomorrow we start training! Tomorrow!'

Hino raised a bottle of saké and bowed to the cloud. 'Here's to you, most honourable and glorious cloud.'

His humour was infectious. Pilots sought out bottles and soon everyone was drinking. They bowed to and toasted the honourable cloud. Kenji was asked time and again to teach the song. They wanted to sing it when they attacked the Americans.

Hino jumped on to a table and hung a large covered frame on the wall near the entrance. He shouted for quiet, then addressed the group. 'My brother and I were certain of winning your bets. What other pilot but Kenji Ishikawa would first photograph his enemy, then shoot him down.' Hino whipped the cover off the frame, revealing an enlarged photo of the startled American pilot in a P-40 with Flying Tiger teeth painted on the nose cowling.

'Here's to the new commander of the First Imperial Air Group who has come to train his Golden Lions,' Hino shouted. 'Colonel Kenji Ishikawa!'

'Banzai! Banzai! Banzai!'

47

'Everyone in this outfit has empty pockets,' Hino said. 'They've lost so much money trying to catch coins off the backs of their arms, they can't afford the pleasure girls in town.' He grinned.

'Maybe they'll pay attention to target identification and high-level bombing,' Kenji snapped, glaring from the podium at his squadron commanders. He pointed at the nearest man. 'You're back here from the mainland because you can't obey orders!'

'It's criminal to run from the Chinese interceptors. We can fly circles around them.'

'I know it, you know it, but damned if we want the British or Americans to find out until we're ready to show them!' Kenji jabbed his finger towards the offending squadron leader. 'You and anyone else who can't obey orders will fly a desk! Dismissed! Hino and Genda, remain!'

'You've been hard on them,' Hino said.

'Because I know the Americans!' Kenji said. 'They can fight! Don't believe our Ministry of Propaganda! The round-eyes aren't soft and they won't run!'

'Ando's intelligence reports say they're training in Louisiana with weapons from the Great War,' Genda said. 'They're using wooden rifles for conscripts and simulating artillery with TNT.'

'If we went to war now they'd be caught short on material,' Kenji said. 'But we're not ready either. Our first strike must be so devastating, it will take the Americans two years to recover. We need that time to secure and reinforce our positions in the Pacific. Admiral Yamamoto wants accurate high-level bombing to be used against the American fleet.' He nodded to Hino. 'Your bomber group had three different runs at moving naval targets and all ten planes missed each time.'

'Divebombers are best,' Hino said. 'On moving targets they're eighty per cent accurate.'

'That's what you'll have to achieve from above!' Kenji turned to Genda. 'Half your dummy torpedoes are stuck in the harbour bottom. We need a solution, and quick!'

'The British may have given us just that,' Genda said. 'Dr Tsubota reported on their successful torpedo attack against the Italian fleet in Taranto harbour. The British planes launched torpedoes with wooden boxes attached to the rear near the propeller. The box breaks off on impact and prevents the torpedo from diving too deep.'

'Test it immediately,' Kenji said, turning back to Hino. 'You've mapped the air currents from Formosa to Manila. Can our pilots make it?'

'The bombers, yes. The fighter escorts require more intensive training. We've increased the efficiency of formation flights to ten hours.'

'Very good,' Kenji said, making no comment that a ten-hour mass formation flight of battle-loaded fighter planes exceeded the world record. 'That's what's needed to reach Manila and back.'

'Yes,' Hino said. 'But fighter pilots must achieve twelve hours non-stop with a fuel consumption of only twenty-one gallons per hour. They'll use a minimum of forty gallons at high speed in thirty minutes of combat over the target. They must be able, after sitting five hours in a cramped cockpit, to best the American pilots fresh off the ground.'

'Our success or failure will be determined in that first half-hour of the war,' Kenji said.

'You're contradicting yourself,' Genda said. 'First you

talked about if we attack Pearl Harbor. Now you're predicting the success or failure of war with the Americans on the outcome of our initial attack.'

'In Tokyo, Raiko showed me children lined up for food at the garbage cans behind the Roppongi restaurants,' Kenji said. 'Old people beg on the streets. One of our subsidiary companies is testing the tanning of rat skins to replace leather. People here in Kagoshima are pickling, drying and preserving whatever food they can find, and we aren't even at war yet. The last population census showed we've increased a million a year for the last five years. There's not enough room or food in our country, and the Americans are the only ones who can stop us from expanding. War with them appears inevitable.'

'The answer is to neutralize the Pacific fleet so we can take what we need,' Genda said.

Kenji had not revealed, even to his cousins, the wild scheme to invade Mexico and southern California, or the more immediate plans Raiko had told him of to break the agreement with Vichy France and take south Indochina too.

'I know what's got your goat,' Genda said. 'Hitler and Mussolini.'

'You're right,' Kenji said. 'We're lumped with countries who are more racist than the Americans or British ever were. How do we convince the Asian world we want to free them from white colonial rule when we've joined forces with the fascists and their concept of the master race?'

'One can be either a soldier or a politician,' Genda said. 'Today Japanese politicians aren't worth a fart. The Razor tells them what to do and the Emperor slaps his seal on it. If it weren't for Yamamoto's objections to a move south, we'd already be on our way to Pearl Harbor right now.'

438

The Spanish guitars played strident chords for a flamenco dancer in a black-sequined dress clacking her heels on the wooden floor. Men in tuxedos stood around, talking, drinking and looking for an excuse to leave without insulting the Spanish Ambassador. Tradition required that each embassy have the opportunity to act as host. New Year's parties would continue well into February.

Joseph Grew and John Whittefield stood shoulder to shoulder watching the dancer. The ambassador had already bid farewell to their host. He waited for the music to end so he could leave.

A voice behind John whispered, 'I would like you to meet Mangiro.'

John whirled, and recognized Iyeasu Saionji. A tall, handsome blond-haired man staggered to Saionji's side and asked, 'Can you point me in the direction of the bar?'

'You'd best be getting home,' Saionji said. 'I'm certain the ambassador would give you a lift.'

'I'd have to ask about that,' John said.

'If Mangiro requests it, I'm certain the ambassador will listen,' Saionji said.

'Is there a problem?' Joseph Grew asked.

'None whatsoever,' John said. 'I hope you don't mind giving Richard Sorge a lift to the German Embassy.'

'We're not at war yet,' Sorge said, trading an empty whisky glass for a full one.

'Perhaps Mr Saionji wishes to accompany us?' Grew asked.

'Thank you, but I drove here myself.' Saionji bowed, and was gone.

Although grasping John's arm for support, Sorge's voice was sober and serious. 'I'll sit in the rear with the ambassador.'

John slipped his .45 Colt automatic from his shoulder holster and openly handed it to the ambassador. 'It's loaded,' John said. He got into the front seat of the car and palmed the snub-nosed .38 revolver from his leg brace.

The big, black limousine, American flags flying from both front fenders, pulled away from the Spanish Ambassador's residence. Sorge sat erect. 'Driver, take evasive action,' he ordered.

'Do it,' John ordered.

'The information transmitted to you by Mangiro, or Saionji, was to establish confidence in me as a reliable source of intelligence,' Sorge said. 'Mr Ambassador, would you include your driver in the highest-level security meeting at your consulate?'

'No,' Grew answered.

Sorge leaned forward. 'Driver, go to a nightclub of your choice and enjoy yourself.' He reached over the front seat and stuffed some bills in the driver's pocket. 'Cultural Attaché Whittefield will drive us from there.'

The driver caught Grew's eyes in the rear-view mirror and the ambassador nodded. The driver pulled over to the curb and left the car. John slipped behind the wheel, with the .38 stuck in his cummerbund. He drove slowly towards the German Embassy.

'What is it you wish to tell us?' Grew asked.

'The Japanese are planning and practising to bomb Pearl Harbor at dawn on Saturday, 6 December,' Sorge said.

'You're mad,' Grew said. 'Japan in her wildest dreams couldn't hope to defeat the United States.'

'You don't reason like a Japanese,' Sorge said. 'They believe their will, their fighting spirit and the rightness of their cause to lead Asia will negate all material, monetary or geographical advantages you have. Ask Mr Whittefield, your chief of Far Eastern intelligence, if Iyeasu Saionji, the man who arranged this meeting, is in a position to know or not.'

'Saionji is on the Imperial War Planning Board,' John said. 'Mr Sorge, why are you telling us this?'

'Because Joseph Stalin hasn't. I sent him this information several times, and asked him to inform you. He hasn't yet. My code has been broken by the Japanese and they'll break the new one soon. There isn't much time left for me.'

'Why do you, a German, spy for the Soviets?' John asked.

Sorge grimaced. 'I'm one of those stupid idealists who believes socialism is the answer to world peace. It's in my genes. My father was personal secretary to Karl Marx.'

'How is it the Gestapo doesn't know you're a communist?' John asked.

'Because I'm one of them. I hold the rank of captain in the SS, and I can tell you that their uniforms are brighter than their minds. I'm a personal friend of Goebbels and acquainted with Himmler. The SS wouldn't think of investigating me.'

'Documentation,' Grew said. 'Do you have any?'

'If I did, your chief of intelligence would think me an imbecile to carry it.' Sorge turned and faced Grew. The passing street lights lit his cold, blue eyes. 'Mr Ambassador, I'm good at what I do. The proof you seek can be found in Kagoshima. It's their training ground for Pearl Harbor.' He faced forward. 'You can make the last turn now, Mr Whittefield.'

John pulled the car up to the swastika on the embassy gate. 'No-one is allowed to travel to Kagoshima,' he said.

'That's your problem.' Sorge shrugged and stepped out of the car, playing the drunk. He waved good night, staggered to the sentry box and gave a stiff-armed salute. 'Heil Hitler,' he shouted.

John backed out of the driveway. 'I don't know whether to believe him or not.'

'We can't ignore it, that's for certain,' Grew said. 'I'll

441

send the information directly to the State Department via courier.'

'I'll inform Admiral Kimmel in Honolulu,' John said. 'MacArthur in Manila will be tickled pink to hear this. He just received the first twenty of fifty Flying Fortresses in accordance with War Plan Orange. Those Flying Fortresses can take out any carrier force that would launch planes against Honolulu. They negate a sea strike against Hawaii. That's what makes me doubt Sorge's word. The Japs have so many spies in the Philippines, they must know about those planes.'

'Possibly Tojo has figured a way to neutralize them,' Grew said.

'He can't. That's the beauty of War Plan Orange. If they attack Manila first, Hawaii will be warned. If they attack Hawaii first, then Manila will send the Flying Fortresses to wipe out the Jap planes on Formosa as well as the aircraft carriers that launched the planes for the first strike. Japan would be lost. She's an island nation and needs naval aircraft to defend herself.'

'Why couldn't they hit both fields at once?'

'Because they don't have enough aircraft carriers and their nearest airfields are too far away,' John said. 'Without fighters to protect them, the bombers would never get through. Sorge's story doesn't sound plausible. It seems impossible the Gestapo wouldn't have checked his background. I'll have to visit Kagoshima, but I doubt I'll find anything. There's something else to include in your report to Secretary Hull. If Sorge is telling the truth, there are Russian spies in our State Department at a high level. It's the only way he could be certain we weren't informed by Stalin.'

48

March 1941, the Imperial Palace

Aerial photographs, maps and papers were scattered over the long table, but Generals Hashimoto, Tojo and Dr Tsubota were looking at the empty chairs around them. 'The traitor in this War Room has not yet been identified, nor the foreign spy found,' Tsubota declared. 'This cannot go on!'

'Whoever the bastards are, they have informed the Russians,' Hashimoto said. 'Stalin will tell the Americans. We must revise the plans for Pearl Harbor.'

'It has been months since the first message was sent,' Tsubota said. 'Moscow has not yet informed Washington. We know Admiral Kimmel's request for anti-torpedo nets was denied by the American navy. The army anti-aircraft guns defending Pearl Harbor and the airfields are still not supplied with ammunition. Both the army and navy in Hawaii are understaffed and their morale is low. They expected promotions, pay raises, new recruits, and none have arrived. According to Ruth Kuhn, there were rumours of a December attack, but US naval intelligence discounted them.'

'I wonder why the Russians have not warned the Americans,' Tojo said.

'Our foreign minister is now in Moscow with Molotov,' Tsubota said. 'Matsuoka believes the Soviets may not want the Americans to know of our intentions because Stalin expects the Germans to attack Russia earlier than this December. He wants the United States supplying him with war materials and he wants our troops moving south, rather than attacking him through Mongolia.'

'Matsuoka should try to effect a four-power alliance between Russia, Italy, Germany and Japan,' Tojo said.

'He is trying,' Tsubota said. 'It was von Ribbentrop who arranged the meeting with Molotov, but the Germans seem to be playing a double game with us and the Soviets. They act as intermediaries for Matsuoka with the Russians, then invade Yugoslavia despite the neutrality pact Stalin signed with the Slavs. On the one hand it indicates Hitler wants a four-power Axis Alliance. On the other, he's going ahead with Operation Barbarossa to attack Russia.'

'We must move south,' Hashimoto said. 'But if the Americans are alerted, we should do it gradually. Forget Pearl Harbor. We can take Burma and south Indochina. We know Churchill has written off Singapore and Malaysia. The Dutch cannot defend the East Indies. That is where the oil is. We can only succeed against the Americans with a surprise attack. If they know our plans, we must cancel the Pearl Harbor operation.'

'I recommend Yamamoto's strategy,' Tsubota said. 'We continue attack preparations and keep a vigilant watch in Hawaii. I'll plant false information with the Americans. Bogus messages have already gone out from the Owada Communications Centre, which indicate Malaysia and the Philippines as our targets. All radio transmissions to and from Hawaii will be reduced by twenty per cent. Our ships in the Pacific will relay information through the Philippines. I have an operation in progress now. John Whittefield, Chief of US intelligence in the Far East, and two Japanese–Americans, posing as tourists, were taken to Kyushu by an American destroyer. They went ashore outside Kagoshima and set up an observation post near the peak of an active volcano. I've ordered half the military personnel in the area on vacation, and cancelled all special manoeuvres. The remaining forces will carry out routine training exercises. When we're ready, Colonel Ando will move in and capture the American. He and several of his agents will be expelled. They will report that nothing is happening in Kagoshima.'

'Whittefield's presence there indicates the Americans know of our plans,' Tojo said.

'Whittefield is trying to confirm a rumour,' Tsubota said.

'How can you be sure of that?' Hashimoto asked.

'One of my agents is travelling with him. Miyagi Yotsoku is extremely reliable. We have his parents in custody to ensure his loyalty.'

The army transport plane crowded with soldiers began its descent to Haneda air-force base outside of Tokyo.

'I don't know why we got leave,' Hino said. 'But geisha girls get ready, pleasure ladies take off your clothes, Roppongi, here I come!'

'I never thought I could be so lonesome,' Kenji said. 'I hope Raiko's advanced pregnancy didn't prevent her from coming.'

'I hope the cowboy flying this crate has good brakes,' Genda said. 'We're going in too fast.'

The pilot stuck his head into the passenger compartment and shouted, 'Sit down or fall down! We're landing!'

The plane hit the runway and everyone cheered. Men tumbled in the aisles, laughing. There was a rush to be first out of the door.

'There's your Cadillac,' Genda said. 'Raiko is here. Hino and I will catch a cab.'

Kenji moved like a sleepwalker towards the civilians waiting behind the fence. He searched for Raiko and saw her standing apart from the crowd, her tiny form in a bulky winter coat like a large ball. Her face lit up at sight of him. Her large eyes poured out love. Kenji ran to her, laughing, and she waddled towards him. They stopped just inches apart, wanting to reach out and touch but restrained by

445

tradition. Like the others, they bowed. Her cheeks were stained with tears.

'You walk like a duck, a beautiful pregnant duck,' Kenji said.

'You're making fun of me.' Raiko frowned.

'I love you,' Kenji said. 'Let's hurry to the car so I can hold you and kiss you and tell you how much I love you.'

Raiko handed him the car keys in silence. Kenji held the door for her, then slipped behind the wheel, reached over and embraced her. 'I missed you so much. Are you all right? Is the baby all right?'

Raiko grabbed Kenji and held on, weeping uncontrollably. 'I need you with me,' she sobbed.

He petted her and kissed her face. 'I didn't mean to hurt your feelings. I'll never call you a duck again. I love you. The child that makes you round, makes me proud. Please don't cry. When the baby comes out, you'll be thin again.'

Raiko leaned back and sniffled. 'It isn't that. Noriko has been taken into custody. Uncle Hiroki and my father will be arrested for treason when they return from Washington.'

'But how? Why?'

'They've been accused of passing information to the Americans. Not military secrets, but the negotiating positions of our delegation. They were suspected before. That was why Hashimoto and Tsubota ordered the attempted assassination at the airport.'

'How did you hear of this?' Kenji asked.

'I still go to the Black Chamber once a week. There are so many new people, they don't know my maiden name is Minobe or that I'm related to Hiroki by marriage. I saw the decode from Washington. Ando works with a Japanese-American double agent here in Tokyo. The man informed Ando, who ordered the arrest. He took Noriko into custody three days ago.'

Kenji put the key in the ignition and started the car. 'I'll go to Tojo. I'll take Genda and Hino with me. We'll do something. Don't worry. When are Uncle Hiroki and your father due back from Washington?'

'Tomorrow. But I don't think you can bargain with Tojo.'

'The accusations are false.'

'No,' Raiko said. 'Noriko confessed to sending information to Washington. But even her interrogators and the double agent agreed no military secrets were passed. The report says my father and Uncle Hiroki were trying to find common ground with the Americans for reconciliation after the US embargo and our invasion of north Indochina.'

'That's not spying.'

'Those people in the Black Chamber who know Ando say he wants to become a general.'

'First we must get Noriko out of prison.' Kenji slapped the steering wheel. 'I don't know what else to do. I can't let anything happen to them.'

'I may have an answer,' Raiko said. 'The problem is if anyone looks at me, I cry. I feel nauseous morning, noon and night. I might throw up if I went before the authorities alone.'

'What could you tell them?' Kenji asked.

'Who leads the Japanese spy ring in Tokyo. The chief was away, in hospital for a gallbladder operation. His replacement sent what he thought was an intercept of a new Russian code to me at home. Actually it was the cipher I had broken some time ago. It was addressed to Richard Sorge and Iyeasu Saionji.'

'Do they have any connection with your father and Uncle Hiroki?'

'No, but you miss the importance of this particular transmission,' Raiko said. 'Sorge sent repeated messages to Stalin in a different code about a 6 December attack on Pearl Harbor. The Russians didn't reply for some time.

When they finally did, it was in the old code. Don't you see? It was to be certain we'd decipher the contents. The Russians named their two agents. They want us to capture Sorge and Saionji. They may want us to attack the Americans.'

Kenji rubbed the scar on his forehead. 'You've had time to think about this.'

'Moscow may want their own spies caught to keep Japan moving south while Russia prepares to face the attack from the Germans,' Raiko said. 'I checked our intelligence reports from Mongolia. The Soviets withdrew most of their armour, almost all their aircraft and their best troops from the Mongolian–Manchurian border. Our old men are facing their old men.'

'I must see Tojo immediately. It's possible, just possible, this information is enough to free our family.' Kenji frowned. 'But I have an On to Iyeasu Saionji. If I honour it, they may all die.'

'We've talked about Ando paying for the atrocities at Nanking,' Raiko said.

'And now for imprisoning Noriko.'

'I owe him Giri for Wantabe's death,' Raiko said. 'There is a way to save Saionji and end Ando's career. We have to be willing to lie. I am.'

'Inform General Tojo that Colonel Ishikawa and his wife are here on the most urgent business!' Kenji said.

'The general is expecting you,' the aide said. 'Will you both follow me.'

Kenji and Raiko exchanged worried glances. They had only decided to come to imperial headquarters in the car from the airport.

Tojo looked up from his desk at the tall, handsome colonel with the eye patch and his short, round wife. He motioned to his aide. 'Get a chair for the lady and put it here in front of my desk!'

Except for the floor lamp behind Tojo, the room was dark. Kenji sensed someone in the shadows. He marched up to the desk and saluted. 'I respectfully request permission to speak.'

Dr Tsubota stepped out of the shadows and stood at Tojo's side. 'Again you have come to trade for the lives of Hiroki and Noriko Koin and Professor Minobe,' Tsubota said.

Kenji disregarded the doctor and looked directly at Tojo. 'Officers in the Japanese military do not bargain like shopkeepers.'

'You and your family have been under surveillance for months,' Tsubota said.

Tojo flicked his little finger and the chief of Japan's intelligence service was silenced.

'Colonel, you and your wife are not accused of being traitors,' Tojo said.

'Neither are Hiroki and Noriko Koin and Professor Minobe traitors!' Kenji said. 'Even the doctor's agents don't refer to betrayal in their reports. My uncle and Professor Minobe are patriots trying to save their country.'

'The difference between a patriot and a traitor depends on one's point of view,' Tojo said. He leaned over his desk and peered at Raiko. 'Are you feeling ill?'

'Excuse me,' Raiko said. 'I need the toilet.'

Kenji saw fear on Tojo's face. 'Are you preparing to give birth now?' the general asked.

'Not yet. But I'm going to be sick.'

With a look of relief, Tojo motioned Kenji to step back. 'Help Mrs Ishikawa,' Tojo ordered his aide. He turned to Kenji. 'Why do you bring your wife here in such condition?'

'Because she is the one who discovered the names of the spies who have been sending the Russian code. Those who informed Stalin of the attack on Pearl Harbor. If my uncle and father-in-law have made mistakes, so has

449

Dr Tsubota. Colonel Shira Ando is a communist,' Kenji lied. 'His contact and his senior in the Soviet intelligence service is Richard Sorge.'

Tsubota staggered. He lowered his head like a wounded bull. 'Colonel Ishikawa, you are trying to buy your uncle's life with false information.'

'I told you military men do not bargain! My relatives are not guilty of anything that doesn't normally take place in high-level negotiations! My wife saw the file.'

'How do you know Sorge and Ando work together?'

'My wife deciphered the message identifying them.'

'She was duty-bound to inform her superior,' Tsubota said.

'Raiko is not a soldier,' Kenji said. 'She wished to reveal the truth for her father's life. If she were in better condition, she would have done it before I arrived.' He looked at Tojo. 'The good doctor has missed what my little wife immediately understood from the Russian message. Stalin wants Sorge and Ando caught and the information about our attack on Pearl Harbor suppressed. That's why the old code was used and the names of the spies given in the message.'

Tojo pointed at Tsubota. 'Wasn't it Colonel Ando who suggested contacting Sorge to find out if someone in the German Embassy was spying against us?'

'Yes, sir,' Tsubota said.

'Where is Ando now?'

'About to finish an operation outside Kagoshima,' Tsubota said.

'Release Noriko Koin and cancel the detention orders for Professor Minobe and Lord Koin! Find out all Ando knows!' Tojo turned to Kenji. 'It may be that Ando is the traitor. Your uncle will not be arrested. He is too prominent a personality to be publicly accused of treason. Yet he, your aunt and the professor have erred. They can no longer be trusted.' Tojo thumbed through a folder on his desk and pulled out a letter. 'This is a request for a district administrator. It is as far south as I can send them. Your relatives will leave this week and remain there for the duration of the military emergency!'

'Thank you, sir.' Kenji bowed. 'In what city will they take residence?'

'Hiroshima.'

49

Miyagi Yotsoku longed for his palette and brush. The scene below was one he yearned to capture on canvas. Morning mist blanketed the city of Kagoshima. Here and there the peaks of temples and shrines poked through the velvety haze. Moving seaward on the outgoing tide, fishing boats emerged from the fog-shrouded harbour into the purple light of dawn.

Miyagi and his parents had emigrated from Okinawa to the United States. Upon graduation from art school at the height of the Depression, he was approached by the FBI to infiltrate the communist Workers Party of America, and accepted the job. The bureau, satisfied with his information, sent him to study art in Kyoto and spy for John Whittefield. Miyagi's success as a painter earned him an invitation to teach at Meiji University, where he befriended Tokyo's élite, among them Prince Higashikuni. The information he gleaned from his social contacts was passed on to John Whittefield.

Early in 1940, a member of the Workers Party in California returned to live in Japan. She reported to Kempetai that Miyagi was a communist. At first Shira Ando suspected the artist of being the source of the Russian code. Ando personally listened to recordings of every telephone conversation and read every letter Miyagi sent to his family in California. He learned that the Japanese-American worked for US intelligence.

Late in 1940, Ando's forgers in Section 10 sent a letter to Miyagi's parents containing boat tickets and money, inviting them to visit Japan and celebrate the Year of the Snake with their son. Miyagi's mother, father and sister arrived in Yokohama in December, and were jailed. Miyagi became a double agent.

The artist looked at his watch, then at the camouflaged pup tent behind him. The booted feet of John Whittefield and Ozaki Hotsumi stuck out of the tent. They were asleep. Miyagi blinked his flashlight twice, then once, and twice again. A hundred yards away, a bush moved and his signal was answered. Miyagi pulled his pistol, aimed it at the pup tent and flashed his light again. Several figures moved towards him.

Ando used arm and hand signals to direct his men. Two pounced on the tent, two tied Whittefield's and Hotsumi's feet. The last two covered them as they were dragged from the tent.

'You're under arrest for spying on Japanese military installations,' Ando declared.

John struggled to a sitting position. 'We were bird watching, Colonel Ando. These two gentlemen are my guides.'

'I'm honoured the cultural attaché of the American embassy recognizes me,' Ando said. He pointed to the maps and sketches held by one of his men. 'I also admire your wit. These diagrams depict the Kagoshima naval base and military airfields on either side of the harbour. No birds here. I'm certain if I examine the film in your cameras I'll find pictures of ships and planes, but not our feathered friends.'

'Mr Hotsumi and Mr Yotsoku are not involved,' John said. 'They didn't know.'

'Quite noble for a Caucasian, aren't you?' Ando pointed his pistol at Miyagi Yotsoku and pulled the trigger. Miyagi tumbled backward, a hole between his eyes. 'If he would work for the Americans and then for me, who can trust him? Get them on their knees next to this dead one,' Ando ordered his men.

John was dragged next to Hotsumi. He tried to reassure

453

his Japanese friend, but the man's face was a mask of fear. Someone moved behind them and John held his breath. A moment later Hotsumi's face exploded and he fell forward in the dirt.

John looked down on the city where his grandfather had helped Mung build whalers and train the Emperor's troops to fight the shogun. The sun had burnt off the mist and he could see the place where Lord Nariakira had made his grandfather a samurai of Satsuma. John straightened his back and raised his head. He felt the pistol muzzle behind his right ear and began to recite. 'Yea though I walk through the valley of the shadow of death, I shall fear no evil . . .'

Ando moved the gun muzzle a fraction to the right. He pulled the trigger and kicked John in the back. 'Look at the fool twitch and shake.' Ando giggled. 'Pick the round-eye up! Careful, he may have shit his pants.'

John used every bit of will-power to stop his body from quivering. It took several moments before he could form words. 'Why?' he cried. 'Why?'

'Why did I scare the shit out of you?'

'Why didn't you kill me too?'

'Orders from above,' Ando said. 'There's always someone else giving orders. With these maps and cameras as proof, we'll expel you and many of your agents from Japan. Our high command thinks that is more important than trying to explain one dead American cultural attaché. I'll take you back to Tokyo myself. You'll have the honour of travelling with the youngest general in the imperial Japanese army. I certainly earned a promotion for this.' He kicked John in the stomach.

Ando assumed there was to be a party in his honour when he was invited to the old Koda-ha headquarters in Tokyo. A celebration for his recent successes. He knew Tsubota had come especially to meet him. In preparation for the expected drinking bout, Ando swallowed half a pint of olive oil to line his stomach.

At headquarters, Ando was surprised to find only a few men in the recreation room. They're probably planning to surprise me, he thought. The others will show up soon. He was directed to a private office on the top floor.

He bowed to Tsubota. 'I am honoured to have a private meeting with my commander. I know you must be busy with preparations for the invasion of south Indochina.'

Tsubota poured two cups of saké and handed one to Ando. 'We must wait for Matsuoka to sign the non-aggression pact with Russia before we can take the rest of Indochina.'

'You cannot trust Stalin.'

'But we can trust each other.' Tsubota raised his cup. 'I came here especially to talk with you. Here's to your success.'

Ando drank, but Tsubota lowered his untouched cup. 'Was the American taken in by your plan?' Tsubota asked.

'Completely,' Ando said. 'He and ten of his agents posing as embassy personnel will quietly leave Japan tomorrow. We'll remain silent about the incident and so will the Americans. Everything that Whittefield saw in Kagoshima was routine. Nothing related to Pearl Harbor.' He pointed at Tsubota's cup. 'You didn't join me in the toast.'

'Because the saké is drugged. I suggest you sit down before you fall down.'

Ando smiled. 'You're joking. Why would you drug me?'

'Because you're a communist bastard, son-of-a-bitch spy who could have cost me my head!'

Men rushed in and pinned Ando's arms. Someone shoved a chair under him and he was slammed down. The room began to spin around him.

'Richard Sorge admitted you were part of his government's espionage ring,' Tsubota said. 'He tried not to give you away, but twenty-four hours of electric shocks loosened his tongue.'

Ando shook his head from side to side to fight off the effects of the drug. 'No! I didn't conspire with Sorge. I am loyal to the Emperor!' He wanted to explain that he had only met Sorge in the line of duty, but his tongue could not form the words.

Tsubota's voice came from far away. 'My electric toys will get at the truth.' He thrust his face close to Ando's; his eyes peered large and black from behind the thick lenses. 'I am going to light you up like those neon signs on the Roppongi.' He stepped back. 'Don't fight it. Get some rest. You'll need it for when the drug wears off in an hour.'

Ando felt his arms being tied behind him to the wooden chair. The last thing he saw before blacking out was the wall clock that read 8:15.

Ando woke with his tongue thick and fuzzy in his mouth, hearing voices behind him. He opened his eyes and saw no-one. It took several seconds for him to focus on the wall clock that read 8:35. Only twenty minutes have passed, he thought. Tsubota said I would wake in an hour. The olive oil I drank must have diluted the drug's effects. He turned his attention to the conversation behind him.

'Damn, the wires are tangled,' a voice said. 'Who was supposed to straighten them when we finished with Sorge?'

'Should we start with the colonel's ears or his balls?' There was laughter.

'Begin with his fingers and toes!' Tsubota said. 'The anticipation of worse to come always heightens the pain and adds a free flow of information.'

Ando had seen Tsubota use electric shock. He had learned from the doctor how to make men pray for death, or condemn their own families to stop the pain. It isn't fair, he thought, knowing that in time he would confess to whatever they asked. He moved his head only the slightest bit to his right, towards two large windows, and dug one thumbnail into the cuticle of the other to drive the fog from his brain. The bonds on his hands were tight, but his feet . . . His feet were free! He knew the building and grounds. They were on the third floor, above a concrete walk. He pulled his feet back inch by inch until they were under him. He would run with the chair, dive through the window and die quickly on the pavement below.

'Ancestors, know that I have served the Emperor and performed Chu,' Ando whispered. He bunched his muscles, took a deep breath and jumped up. Dragging the chair, he moved as fast as he could, ignoring shouts from behind. He dived at the window and smashed through the glass, gashing his head. He crashed into metal bars, and fell back into the room.

Hiroki shut the radio. 'Why would Colonel Ando kill himself?'

Raiko and Kenji looked at each other but remained silent.

'I am not sorry,' Noriko said. 'That man threatened me and everyone in our family with torture. He called us traitors.'

'That is over with,' Hiroki said. 'We are moving to Hiroshima. They say it is a happier place than Tokyo these days. There is public entertainment, food is available and the new dress code is not enforced.'

Two workmen came into the room and bowed. They carried the large Rodin sketch. 'Do you wish this sent to Kagoshima?'

'Leave it here,' Hiroki said. 'Your father made me look at the ugly thing, Raiko. It is coming too close to reality.'

'What am I being blamed for?' Minobe asked.

'The Gates of Hell.'

Minobe watched the picture carried out and replaced on the porch wall. 'We tried our best to prevent war,' he said. 'The trumped-up charges were to stop us from making peace.' He looked up and smiled. 'There is an American song that says, "Every cloud has a silver lining." Hiroshima is our silver lining. Raiko will come with us. We'll raise our grandchild there. It is only 250 air miles from Kenji's base.'

'Raiko, I expect that you and Kenji will return to Tokyo sooner or later,' Noriko said. 'That is why we're leaving the furniture. This house is yours.'

Kenji looked down at his wife. 'The moment the pains begin, call me. I'll have a plane warmed up and waiting at all times. I'll be there to see our child born!'

Raiko bowed to the others and took Kenji's arm. 'Excuse us. I must speak with the father-to-be before he leaves for Kagoshima.' She led him to another room.

Kenji patted Raiko's belly. 'Keep well. Tell the baby I love her or him. At every opportunity I'll fly up to see you.'

'Bend down and let me kiss you goodbye,' Raiko said. Kenji wanted to hold her tight but feared hurting her. She clung to him. They both stepped back and bowed.

Kenji moved to the door, then stopped and fished a piece of paper from his pocket. 'I received this message from Iyeasu Saionji in Moscow. Prince Higashikuni sent him to assist Matsuoka's negotiations with Molotov.'

'If Saionji is a communist, he could help arrange a neutrality pact between Russia and Japan. I'm glad he wasn't exposed. I feared Tsubota would see through our scheme.'

'Ando is dead and Tsubota doesn't know we tricked him.'

50

'Von Ribbentrop, Goering and Hitler showed me their sandtable mock-up of Singapore,' Matsuoka said. 'Too bad you were not there. But tomorrow we will have more fun with Stalin.'

'Why do the Nazis want us to take Singapore?' Saionji asked.

'To pressure the British into using part of their Atlantic fleet to evacuate their nationals from Malaysia. It would reduce the pressure on the German navy in the North Sea. I led Hitler on, but we have no need to antagonize the Americans by taking Singapore. Churchill has handed it to us on a platter. Only when Hitler moves against Russia will we move south.'

'Will the Germans attack the Soviets?'

'It appears so,' Matsuoka said. 'Hitler cancelled Operation Sea Lion. Germany will not invade England this year. He needs wheat from the Ukraine and Russia to feed his armies.' Matsuoka looked at his watch. 'I need some rest. Tomorrow we meet the Russian bear himself.'

Saionji stepped into a taxi outside the hotel and immediately ducked down in the rear seat. An Asiatic, dressed and built like Saionji, sat up in his place. The taxi took the passenger to a popular restaurant. It took Saionji to a meeting with Vyacheslav Milailovich Molotov, foreign minister of the Soviet Union.

'Commissar Molotov,' Saionji said. 'Richard Sorge was a hero. One of the most dedicated communists I have known. You betrayed him.'

Molotov's clean-shaven poker-face never twitched. His pale blue eyes did not waver. 'I would betray you, even myself for 1,000 tanks, 100 planes or even five warships. We need America on our side. I want Japan to bomb Pearl Harbor. Hitler has 160 combat-ready divisions on our border. His planes outnumber ours twenty to one. If Germany attacks us and Japan attacks America, Stalin and Roosevelt become allies. It's the only way Russia can be saved.'

'Then you've taken precautions against the German invasion?'

'The only thing we can do is wait,' Molotov said. 'If Stalin were to mobilize against Germany before Hitler attacks us, there would be a military mutiny and civilian revolt against our government. Hitler would walk into Moscow. The people are unhappy and the soldiers discontented with communism. We need outside pressure to bind the Soviet Union together. Hitler will provide that. We must have a peace treaty with Japan to ensure we are not overrun from the west and the east. Our situation is desperate.'

'Matsuoka won't sign a peace treaty, but he is interested in the alternative non-aggression pact you sent him?' Saionji said. 'Tojo has the Emperor's permission to move into South-East Asia if Russia is neutralized. By that they mean some written guarantee that Russia will not attack Manchuria and Korea. Even then, Tojo will wait before moving south, until either Germany attacks Russia or Russia joins Germany, Italy and Japan in a four-power Axis alliance.'

'Stalin meets Matsuoka tomorrow,' Molotov said. 'Let's see if that big mouth can out-talk Uncle Joe one on one.'

Joseph Stalin received Foreign Minister Molotov in his bed-sitting room. 'Matsuoka is on his way,' Molotov said. 'His aide, Saionji, is a loyal communist. He says the

Japanese will not participate in Operation Barbarossa. Hitler pressured them to attack through Mongolia when he crosses our border. They would not commit themselves.'

'Since when did the little yellow bastards give up their dream of taking Mongolia and Siberia?' Stalin asked.

'They've postponed it on recommendation of their engineers and geologists. It would take five years for them to develop the Siberian oil fields. Enough petroleum can be pumped immediately from the Dutch and British colonies in South-East Asia to supply Japan's needs.'

'We need the Japanese quiet on our northern border,' Stalin said. 'Would it pressure them if I have Mao Tse-tung's troops attack the Kwangtung army in China?'

'It's an option,' Molotov said. 'Spring is late in coming. The Nazi armour will move when the weather warms.'

'Is this character dossier on Matsuoka up-to-date?'

'Yes. The nickname Motor-Mouth is appropriate. He, like most Japanese, is overly proud and insecure. He claims to stand by his word, but will interpret any agreement to suit the Emperor.'

'What does Saionji think of our chances with the non-aggression pact?' Stalin asked.

'Matsuoka is under pressure. He must return with something that will allow Tojo to give marching orders for the takeover of all of Indochina.'

'When the foreign minister arrives, leave us alone.'

Matsuoka was surprised to see that Stalin was not much taller than he was. Photographs and newsreels of the Soviet leader give the impression he is taller, Matsuoka thought. Ego. That is his weak spot. I shall use the tactics of Musashi against him.

For over an hour, Matsuoka harangued the silent Russian leader sitting on the edge of his bed. Matsuoka related the history of Japan from the mythological creation in 7 BC to the present reign of Emperor Hirohito. 'Hakko

Ichui is the goal set by our gods for all Japanese. To have the eight corners of the world under imperial rule. Today it means that Japan wishes to bring the peoples of all countries together in mutual respect, under two or three superior governments working in harmony for the benefit of all.'

'Da!' Stalin said.

Matsuoka looked around. 'May I have a drink of water?'

Stalin chewed his thick moustache and pointed at the clock. 'Time is running out for both of us. I am from Georgia and I am an Asiatic. You are an Asiatic. You want a peace treaty with Russia. I want peace with Japan.'

'Peace is a complicated process,' Matsuoka said, licking his dry, cracked lips.

'No aggression,' Stalin said. 'It is unimportant how you describe it. We don't ask the Japanese to love us. Just do not fight us.'

'No one looks for war.'

'Japan is a land-hungry lion waiting to break out into the Pacific and tear the Caucasian lambs to pieces! Be assured if Japan moves against Russia, you will not be facing the corrupt soldiers of the czar, as happened in 1905! The people of the Soviet Socialist Republic will fight to the death!'

Matsuoka was exhausted, his throat dry. He was taken aback by the fierceness in Stalin's voice, by the dark, angry eyes and powerful hand motions of the wily moustachioed peasant who ruled 200 million people. 'Why talk of war when we seek each other's co-operation,' Matsuoka said.

'Sell me the Japanese half of Sakhalin island,' Stalin said. 'You took it from the little czar in 1905. We need that coal for our Siberian colonies and our naval fleet in the northern seas.'

Of all the things Matsuoka and his aides had prepared for, Sakhalin was not one of them. 'I cannot.'

Stalin threw up his hands. 'You cannot! If you cannot, then why did you come here? I can negotiate anything! I am a simple man. My father was a shoemaker. I am not familiar with sophisticated bargaining procedures.' He leaned forward and peered closely into the Japanese foreign minister's face. 'You were also born poor. My people say you worked with your hands and head to achieve your station in life. I respect that. I thought we could cut the dancing and talk like men.'

Matsuoka's face turned red. 'I am empowered to lease coal rights on Sakhalin to a friendly country.' He pointed his finger at Stalin. 'Do not waste your time trying to purchase the rest of that island. The further away from Japan Russia is, the more certainty there will be peace between us. If the Soviet Union wants to expand, do it in the direction of Turkey, Iran and Saudi Arabia. You have our blessings.'

'Agreed!' Stalin went to his desk and pulled out a copy of the non-aggression pact. 'Write in your stipulations. Japan will lease Russia coal rights on Sakhalin and Russia will not approach the Japanese mainland. I will initial the pact.' He looked into Matsuoka's eyes, challenging him. 'Do you have the authority?'

Matsuoka tried to draw saliva in his mouth, but his tongue stuck to his teeth. He saw the Russian's eyes crease in a scornful smile.

'Can you sign this or not?' Stalin mocked.

'I can, but there is a problem with China.'

'I verbally promise you that Mao Tse-tung shall keep Chiang Kai-shek's forces from attacking the Kwangtung army. I ask you to neutralize the Chinese air force. If you want to move south, you must do that anyway. Chiang cannot be trusted in your rear with his wife in charge of so many planes.'

Matsuoka looked at the document on the desk, then at Stalin seated on the bed. A cynical smile crossed the commissar's face, daring Matsuoka to assert his authority. The Japanese foreign minister walked to the desk. He picked up the pen, wet the nib and initialled the document. 'I will need forty-eight hours to study this and give my final decision.'

Stalin got up from the bed, walked to the desk and signed the document.

14 April 1941, the Kremlin

The formal confirmation of the non-aggression pact had taken place that afternoon. The gala celebration that evening was attended by every Japanese and Russian dignitary in Moscow. Stalin personally served food to the Japanese guests. Vodka flowed, champagne corks popped and caviar was spread on everything, including the pastry.

Stalin pulled Matsuoka on to the bandstand and waved for quiet. Both men raised their glasses and shouted, 'We are all Asiatics!'

The crowd roared back the toast in Russian and Japanese. More toasts were made, pledges sworn and vodka drunk. By the time Matsuoka and Stalin staggered into Moscow's central railroad station, the Trans-Siberian express had been held an hour beyond departure time.

Stalin embraced Matsuoka and kissed him on both cheeks. 'Even though our ideologies differ, what matters is that we are Asiatics. Honour is honour. A man's word is his bond. Diplomatic agreements between countries should not be broken.'

Matsuoka bowed, and staggered. 'I signed a treaty. It is made. Let us drink to the treaty.'

An aide handed Stalin a bottle, but it slipped out of his hand and crashed to the floor. Stalin, a teetotaller who always remained in control, had not touched a drop of alcohol throughout all the toasting. He looked down at the broken bottle with sad eyes and apologized profusely. He embraced the bleary-eyed Matsuoka once again and kissed him on both cheeks. 'Banzai to the Emperor,' Stalin cried. 'Let the treaty stand between men of honour!'

Matsuoka staggered free of Stalin's bear hug. 'I do not lie. This treaty shall be kept. If I lie, my head is yours. If you lie, I will surely come for your head.'

Stalin fixed Matsuoka with cold eyes. 'My head is important to Mother Russia. Yours is important to imperial Japan. Let us both take care to keep our heads on our shoulders.'

51

18 May 1941

The three pilots strode shoulder to shoulder through the corridors of Hiroshima General Hospital.

'Where is the maternity ward?' Kenji asked a nurse. He hardly waited for the answer and was off. Turning a corner, he saw Noriko, Hiroki and Raiko's father sitting on a bench. He ran to them. 'Am I in time?'

'Your wife has gone to sleep,' Noriko said.

'And our honourable grandchild seems very content inside the womb,' Hiroki said.

'But Raiko is two weeks, three and a half days late,' Kenji said.

'My daughter is good at puzzles, wonderful at statistics, but simple addition eludes her,' Minobe said.

Noriko saw Kenji's concern. 'Why don't you go in and see your wife? It will not speed things up but will make you feel better.' She stopped Hino and Genda from following Kenji into the room. 'You two remain with us.'

A moment later Kenji hurried out, pale and shaken. 'Where's the doctor? Aunt Noriko, please get the doctor!'

'Did the pains start again?'

'No. Raiko is sleeping. But we'd better have a doctor instead of a midwife.'

'Midwives are more experienced,' Noriko said. 'Raiko chose this one.'

Kenji leaned close to Noriko and whispered, 'The child is so large in her belly and her opening so small.'

Noriko patted Kenji's cheek. 'Do not concern yourself

466

about that. The doctor examined her and everything is fine.' She pushed Kenji back into the room.

Raiko lay on a mat covered by a light sheet. Her giant stomach moved with each breath. Kenji squatted at her side. 'I love you,' he said. 'I'm afraid of losing you.' He had never prayed for himself nor for his men, but now he silently addressed the gods. 'Don't take my wife from me. She's good. I need her. Let our child be born healthy with all the pieces and parts. Let it love its mother, honour its father and serve the Emperor. I admit I've not always been one hundred per cent behind preparations for war with the Americans. But I swear that if you give me this wish, I will not withhold one ounce of myself from any endeavour commanded by his imperial majesty. Oh gods who dwell beyond the clouds, bless my family! Protect my wife! Help me!'

'Open your eye,' Raiko said.

Kenji blinked at her. He kneeled to kiss and hug her. 'Are you all right?'

'What were you doing?'

'Praying for you and the child.'

Raiko reached up and touched his cheek. 'You haven't shaved.'

'Why is the birth taking so long?' Kenji asked.

Raiko smiled. She scrunched her chin down and looked at her big stomach. 'Baby isn't ready to come out yet.'

'How do you know?'

Raiko took Kenji's hand and placed it on her stomach. 'Whoever is in there is sleeping.'

Kenji's face lit up. 'No. The little bugger waited for his father to wake him. He kicked me.'

Raiko cried out.

'What's wrong?' Kenji asked.

'Finally.' Raiko smiled. 'The pains have begun again. I've been lying here waiting for twenty-four hours. Oh,' she cried. 'There's another. Look at your watch and time them.'

'Time it, hell,' Kenji said. 'I'm getting the doctor right now!'

Raiko held out her hand to stop him, but Kenji was out of the door. He returned, dragging a doctor and a midwife. The midwife's assistant trailed behind, urging Kenji to remain calm and wait outside.

'I'll stay here with my wife!' Kenji's tone brooked no objections.

Raiko cried out again and Kenji ordered, 'Help her!'

The midwife calmly prepared for the delivery, and Raiko raised her head. 'Kenji, you have to be quiet.'

He backed against the wall, feeling weak and useless. He used the wall for support as Raiko's moans and groans became louder and more frequent.

The midwife moved in front of Raiko; the assistant stood behind. 'Breathe deep and push, breathe deep and push,' they chorused.

The doctor standing off to the side looked at Kenji and raised his eyebrows. Kenji realized he was huffing, blowing and pushing down with his stomach muscles, following the midwife's instructions.

'Here it comes,' the midwife said. 'Head first, just like a good little child.' It seemed like hours to Kenji before she spoke again, then: 'The shoulders are through . . . there!' She held up the baby.

Kenji saw a wet, red blob with plastered-down black hair and a squished face. 'It's full of blood,' he gasped, and was mesmerized by the movements of the little human being. His child. He watched the tiny little legs and arms move like a tadpole. There were little fingernails at the ends of the tiny fingers.

The midwife wiped the mucus from the eyes, nose and mouth, examining the baby as she worked. She then knelt and solemnly placed the child on a towel on the floor. 'This

between army and navy intelligence. In the navy there's the contest between those at sea, those ashore and those in the Navy Department in DC. To confuse matters, the State Department doesn't share its information with our intelligence units. They send their information directly to the commanding officers here and in the Philippines.'

'How can we improve the situation?'

'Shoot the senior intelligence officers in the army and navy. Then hang the bastards in Washington.'

'Sarcasm won't help,' John said. 'I expect constructive criticism.'

'Shoot them all and start over!' DeCarlo stood. He was a powerfully-built block of a man with square jaw, piercing dark eyes and brown crew-cut hair that bristled. 'I believe we're going to war with Japan! The ass-kissers here and in the States are worrying about who gets credit for revealing the most valuable information at the correct time! Timing is important to them only for how it'll look on the record and affect promotions! It's not related to what's good for our country! One unit doesn't tell the other anything that might help gain praise or recognition!' DeCarlo pointed at his hair. 'I dye this because it's really grey. I'm the only grey-haired lieutenant on this goddamned island because I've got a big mouth! I'm on the verge of an ulcer! Send me back to watching the base hospital! This shit makes me sick!'

'Give me an example of the problem,' John said.

'Are you aware that radio traffic from Hawaii to Japan has decreased eighty per cent?'

'How did you find that out if your assignment is the hospital?'

DeCarlo shrugged. 'I make it my business to go into the Fourteenth Naval District Headquarters on my own time and examine reports. Were you informed that Japanese radio traffic from the Philippines increased by the same amount?'

'I've been recovering in the San Diego naval hospital, and then had my first stateside vacation in seven years,' John said. 'When did these changes in the flow of radio messages begin?'

'Washington knew two months ago, but we were only informed last week. Two goddamned months!' DeCarlo slammed the desk. 'It could mean the invasion of the Philippines! The minute they cabled the information to MacArthur, he put his people on maximum alert!'

'What's the reaction here in Pearl?' John asked.

'A great sigh of relief. Both army and navy intelligence now regard an attack on Hawaii as unlikely.'

'The report I submitted in March supports that view.'

'What report was that?' DeCarlo asked.

'I and two agents went to confirm rumours of Kagoshima harbour being used as a training ground by the Japs for an attack on Pearl Harbor. We were caught and my agents were killed. I was roughed up and expelled from Japan with several of my men.'

'What did you see at Kagoshima?'

'Nothing to indicate preparations for a large-scale attack,' John said. 'I sent my report to the State Department in April.'

'It hasn't been received here,' DeCarlo said. 'That information would take a lot of pressure off the men in Pearl Harbor. We're twenty per cent understaffed in both the army and the navy. With the high state of alert, men stand extra watches and liberty is cut. Morale stinks! The military police have a hard time controlling brawls on and off the bases. I saw a knife fight over a place in line to buy cigarettes.'

'We can't get bogged down with internal problems,' John said. 'Ambassador Grew used his pull with the White House to get me this position. We've got to increase the flow and sharing of information between here and the States!'

Sirens inside and outside the building began to whoop. 'Where do we go in case of an air raid?' John asked.

'That's a call to battle stations,' DeCarlo said. 'Watch the main gate from the window. You'll see buses and cars come roaring through. It's practice. Keeps everyone on their toes.'

The telephone rang and John picked it up. He listened to the voice at the other end, then said, 'Yes, sir, I'll be right there.' He put the receiver down and looked at DeCarlo. 'If you have a duty station, get to it! We're on one hundred per cent alert! Germany just invaded Russia! Admiral Kimmel believes the Japs might make a simultaneous strike in the Pacific!'

477

The Emperor has agreed to withdraw our troops from certain areas of China and all of Indochina to avoid war. If the Americans accept, war could be prevented. Kenji, when are you leaving for the imperial conference?'

'Tomorrow morning. Raiko and Mangiro will fly with me to Tokyo. She'll return to the Black Chamber.'

'Please guard my daughter's health,' Minobe said.

Kenji bowed to his father-in-law. 'I promise I will.' He bowed to Hiroki. 'My natural father gave me life and I shall always honour his memory. You have raised me, given me love and knowledge. You are my father too. I shall honour you until the day I die.'

Hiroki bowed. 'My sons were lost and the gods gave me another. I am thankful to them and to you.'

Yamamoto's private plane left Kagoshima air base with only Kenji, Raiko and Mangiro as passengers.

After take-off the pilot came back, saluted and bowed. 'I am honoured to have you as my guests. This trip will be more pleasant than our last, Colonel Ishikawa.'

'Please forgive me,' Kenji said. 'I don't recall having flown with you.'

'I was a cadet at the time. You borrowed my trousers after climbing naked through the cockpit window. Do you recall the incident?'

'I've heard stories of my husband climbing buildings, but not aeroplanes,' Raiko said.

'We were on a commando raid in China,' the pilot said. 'Colonel Ishikawa saved my life and all those aboard.'

Kenji smiled. 'I'm pleased to see you've earned your wings. This plane is luxurious compared to that other one.'

'I'll be making two more landings and taking on several passengers for the gathering of chiefs of staff at the imperial palace. Senior commanders from all over the empire are converging on the capital. Excuse me, I must return to the controls.' The pilot bowed.

'Are you ready with your report?' Raiko asked Kenji.

He took the baby in his arms and cradled him. 'Hiroki and your father believe the Nomura mission is Japan's last hope to avoid war with America. But I don't think there's a chance of gaining concessions. If the US embargo remains in effect, we'll have to fight.'

'Isn't Yamamoto against attacking Pearl Harbor?'

Although no one else was in the passenger cabin, Kenji looked around to be certain they weren't overheard. 'The imperial conference wasn't called on the spur of the moment. We've had war games duplicating the attack. Our ships and planes are in staging areas for the attack. When Roosevelt enforced a total embargo, Yamamoto went to the Emperor and told him the navy had only a few months of fuel remaining. That either Japan should bow to the Americans or fight them. He told the Emperor that if given the order to capitulate, he would commit seppuku rather than face another humiliation as he did at the hands of President Wilson in Versailles at the end of the Great War.'

'Then this conference isn't so much about whether we go to war as when we go to war,' Raiko said.

Kenji sighed and rocked the baby. 'I like to hold Mangiro, but when the other officers board I'll give him back to you.' He touched the baby's soft hair, smelled him and rubbed cheeks with his son. 'Tojo and Yamamoto want to know from me if we can control the air over the Pacific.'

'Can we?'

'For a year at least.' He made a face and passed Mangiro back to Raiko. 'That is if the babies of the world don't pee on their fathers. My trousers better dry quickly. I've been so busy I forgot to pack another pair. I wouldn't have believed a child so small could have such large kidneys.'

'You never knew a child with kidneys as beautiful as little Mung's.' Raiko laughed. 'I'll change and feed him. You

481

change yourself. I brought you extra trousers. They're in the bag under the seat.'

Kenji changed his trousers in the aisle. 'How much time will you have to spend at the Black Chamber?' he asked.

'The chief agreed I wouldn't monitor, decipher or decode. He wants me to concentrate on Ruth's reports from Hawaii. I taught her how to send and know her touch on the radio key. A nanny will care for Mangiro but it won't be for long, or often. Ruth has a set time for making her reports. I'll receive them and return directly home.' She examined her husband's face. 'Don't worry, Kenji.'

'I'm worrying about what your father and my uncle said. If there is going to be a war, it's going to be ugly!'

54

'Gentlemen, please follow me,' the master of protocol said.

Kenji was last in a long line of admirals and generals to enter the imperial reception room. As senior air-force representative, he was the youngest man in the room and the most junior officer to sit at the centre table.

General Tojo, minister of war and recently appointed prime minister, was supreme civil and military commander. Less than 100 years before he would have held the title of shogun. He sat opposite the supreme commander of the imperial fleet, Admiral Isokoro Yamamoto, closest to the dais. General Hashimoto, spokesman for the army in Japan, and General Nakajima for the army abroad, sat side by side. Kenji and Dr Tsubota, in their uniforms, faced the two generals.

Everyone stood and bowed as the master of protocol recited the honorifics and Michi no Miya Hirohito, supreme sovereign of Japan, entered wearing his army uniform.

With the formal ceremony completed, the commanders sat down, erect, eyes fixed straight ahead, arms stiff, hands on knees. Kenji glanced at the Emperor on his hand-crafted throne of gold, his booted feet resting on a red velvet carpet. Over Hirohito's head a gold embroidered canopy was supported by two silver lances.

The master of protocol intoned, 'This imperial conference is convened to discuss the national policies of our country in view of present developments. The Emperor has read the proposal to move south into the Pacific. Before his seal can be affixed to the orders, several questions will be answered. First. What are the possibilities of achieving our objectives by diplomacy rather than war?'

Having received the questions beforehand, Kenji and the others at the centre table had prepared their responses.

Hashimoto stood and bowed to the Emperor. 'Your imperial majesty. The opportunity for diplomatic reconciliation is no longer viable. America, Britain and China have frozen all Japanese assets and instituted a total embargo, which violates international law. Our occupation of Indochina was begun with the written consent of the Vichy governments in Hanoi, Saigon and France, all of whom are recognized by America. In Washington, Ambassador Nomura proposed to Secretary of State Hull that we withdraw from Indochina and certain areas of southern China, in return for a guaranteed oil supply, lifting of the economic embargo and release of Japan's assets abroad. Secretary Hull replied that the Japanese military must evacuate all of China, Indochina and Manchuko. In addition, they expect us to renounce our alliance with Germany and reduce our military forces. These outrageous, uncompromising demands indicate that the American government is determined to force us into war.

'Roosevelt seeks to justify war with Japan, which will take America into conflict with Germany and Italy. It would give him an excuse to side with Britain and Russia, and take over the entire Pacific and China markets. Secretary Hull and President Roosevelt believe a war will end America's economic depression. I remind his majesty that in 1854 the American Commodore Perry, in a first official visit ever by a Western ship to Japan, left many gifts on the shores of Tokyo bay. I quote the commodore's words, "These gifts from the people of America will be returned a hundredfold by the people of Japan." Among those presents was one cannon. Now I humbly suggest that we comply with the commodore's wishes. We should return that cannon a thousandfold on 8 December at Pearl Harbor!'

There was not a sound nor movement in the room as Hashimoto sat down.

'What are the prospects for success in a military confrontation?' the master of protocol asked.

Admiral Yamamoto stood and bowed. 'Your imperial majesty. We can inflict serious damage to the Pacific fleet if we act now. Secretary Hull's reply to the Nomura mission indicates an overconfidence in his military, and misjudgements by General MacArthur in the Philippines and Secretary of the Navy Stimson in Washington. They believe the fifty Flying Fortresses at Clark field near Manila will deter our air force from attacking the Philippines, Singapore or Hawaii. They intend to send another eighty B-17s to Manila. The American military view of our potential striking power is myopic. The magnitude of the plan General Tojo and I have created is beyond their ken. Never in the history of warfare have military operations been simultaneously co-ordinated over an area of 7,000 miles. We shall achieve dramatic success during the first year of war. During that year, it shall be the politicians' duty to make peace. In a prolonged confrontation with the United States we shall be hard pressed to maintain the advantage. The Americans are numerically superior and have the ability to outproduce us.'

The room remained silent as Yamamoto outlined the changing of the naval code to confuse American intelligence, the high state of readiness of his men, the low efficiency of the American forces during their holiday period.

Yamamoto's strategy is to win a great victory, then negotiate, Kenji thought. But there is not one politician present. Even Matsuoka is absent.

'The Americans are preparing for war,' Yamamoto said. 'Their productivity potential is ten times greater than ours.

Each day they gain strength and we become relatively weaker. Our operational plans are completed. They have been tested and retested. The recent war games proved the vulnerability of Pearl Harbor.'

'How is it possible for the major part of your fleet to cross 7,000 miles of ocean and approach Hawaii undetected?' the master of protocol asked.

'During the winter months all merchant and naval vessels stay clear of the stormy waters north and west of Hawaii,' Yamamoto said. 'Several of our merchantships have passed undetected on that route. Only yesterday the *Tairo Maru*, carrying twenty naval officers disguised as crewmen, arrived in Honolulu unreported. Our objective is to control the petroleum of the Dutch East Indies within four months, Singapore in three months, take Manila in two and Burma in five. Sire, it is well known I have been against war with the Americans. But Roosevelt's response to the Nomura initiative leaves us no choice.' He bowed and sat down.

'What effect have the warnings of a possible attack by our forces on Pearl Harbor had on the Americans?' the master of protocol asked.

Dr Tsubota stood and bowed. 'Sire, the initial high state of alert in Hawaii has been reduced to twenty-five per cent. The warnings have been disregarded. There are daily demonstrations outside the White House. The American president is virtually a captive to peace groups who want the compulsory conscription law cancelled. With all Roosevelt's popularity in last year's election, he only succeeded in continuing military conscription by one vote in Congress. The morale of those drafted into their army is low. There are many desertions. Requests to be excused from military service are so numerous that police protection is needed for those empowered to decide who will be drafted. Although Admiral Yamamoto is correct regarding the potential of American productivity, their

486

people lack the dedication and fighting spirit of the Japanese. The Americans may outnumber us overall, but will not on the battlefield. According to reports, it takes twelve Americans to support one soldier on the front line. By eliminating non-essential services such as the medical corps, our support system is only four to one. On the battlefield our twenty-five-calibre five-clip Murato rifle is less powerful than the thirty-calibre American 03, but one wounded American immediately removes six others from combat to try to save him. Our men fight to the death. Statistics are deceiving. Our soldiers and their officers are combat veterans. Even Jan Smuts, prime minister of South Africa, recognizes our superiority. He warned Churchill, but the British, like the Americans, are puffed with their own pride.'

Kenji had read the intelligence reports from German agents in Washington and South Africa. After the Germans cancelled Operation Sea Lion and attacked Russia, Churchill had acceded to Roosevelt's request and sent a naval task force to protect Singapore. En route, the aircraft carrier *Indomitable* had run aground off Bermuda. Admiral Sir Thomas Phillips left the carrier behind and pressed on, with two of the world's newest, most powerful battleships and three destroyers. In Cape Town the admiral had brushed off Jan Smuts's warning of a first-class disaster if he went up against the Japanese without air cover. Smuts cabled Churchill, to no avail. The British really believe themselves invincible, Kenji thought. He had already briefed his squadron leaders that the five-ship British task force was an important secondary target after Pearl Harbor and Manila.

General Nakajima's comments followed those of Dr Tsubota. The general concluded by saying, 'Since so much depends on the outcome of the initial air strike, it is for Colonel Ishikawa to address this issue.'

Kenji stood and bowed. 'Your majesty. The air force

487

is at peak efficiency. Operation Killer was a complete success. The Chinese Nationalist air force no longer exists as a viable fighting unit. We have flown diversionary reconnaissance flights over Port Moresby, Australia to give the impression it is one of our invasion sites. The problem of launching torpedoes in the shallow waters of Pearl Harbor is solved. High-level bombing has been perfected. Mass-formation long-distance flights from Formosa to Manila are now routine. We are prepared to strike simultaneously at all major targets on 8 December, Tokyo time.' Kenji bowed and sat down.

Hideki Tojo stood and bowed. 'Your majesty. I confirm the timetable for our conquests in the Pacific, as stated by Admiral Yamamoto. Our chances of success are optimal. However, each day that passes, our military consumes 15,000 tons of irreplaceable petroleum. We have less than six months' fuel reserves remaining. If we do not act immediately, there will not be enough petrol to power our tanks, ships and planes. We cannot hide our intentions indefinitely. The British have begun to evacuate their civilians from Malaysia. The ideal date to attack Singapore, the Philippines and Pearl Harbor is 8 December. It is a Sunday, the Christian sabbath. The fleet is in port for the holidays and at its lowest state of alert. The time of attack is set between 7 and 8 a.m. when the anti-submarine nets guarding the harbour's entrance are left open. The new enemy radar station closes at 7 a.m., and enemy air reconnaissance has a two-hour gap between seven and nine. High tide is at 7:55 a.m., giving greater depth into which to launch our aerial torpedoes.'

Tojo continued speaking but Kenji's thoughts wandered to Ruth Kuhn's last report. She had confirmed that in the Philippines and Hawaii, planes were still being parked wing tip to wing tip in the centre of the airfields, away from the perimeter fences for fear of sabotage. He wondered about the possibility of catching them on the ground. He

488

pictured his men strafing parked planes into a mass of flaming junk.

Tojo was answering Kenji's own question about Hitler. Kenji listened.

'Sire, the failure of Germany to invade England or defeat the Soviet army should not delay our plans,' Tojo said. 'I have never taken Nazi Germany into account when estimating the possibilities of our success. The history of warfare is rife with the failures, blunders and betrayals of military coalitions and divided commands. America's alliances with Canada, Great Britain and other countries is a weakness. Multiple alliances lead to inaction because of political differences, conflicting economic goals and diverse military objectives. We Japanese have one leader. One authority.' He bowed to the Emperor. 'I respectfully request your imperial seal on this battle order.' Tojo handed the document to the master of protocol and sat down.

From the corner of his eye, Kenji saw the Emperor raise his hand. Everyone in the room jumped to his feet and bowed. No one had expected that the Emperor would address the assembly.

'Commanders of the imperial forces,' Hirohito said. 'You speak of war with Great Britain and America, yet you have not succeeded in defeating the Chinese. I was promised Chiang Kai-shek's surrender within six months.' The Emperor paused, then said, 'Such an elaborate, grandiose scheme co-ordinated over thousands of miles of open sea is a dangerous gamble. Weather conditions could disrupt everything. Ship-to-shore landings in Malaysia and the Philippines are complicated procedures. A number of your landing craft capsized in the war games and hundreds of our men drowned. Five months is not much time in which to conquer the areas your plans encompass. The Pacific is more vast than China.'

Kenji saw the faces opposite him redden. Nakajima's

eyes bulged. Spittle appeared at the corners of Hashimoto's tight, pressed lips.

'How will you achieve surprise and honour Article I of the 1907 Hague Convention to which Japan is a signator?' Hirohito asked. 'I quote, "Explicit warning must be given in the form of a reasoned or conditional declaration of war."'

Tojo fumbled in his pocket and pulled out a document. 'Sire,' he said. 'My rejection of Secretary of State Hull's demands is our informal declaration of war. It reads as follows, "Our government regrets to inform the Secretary of State that in view of the attitude of the American government, it is no longer possible to reach an agreement through negotiations."' Tojo looked up. 'Sire. This letter is an ultimatum with a conditional declaration of war as agreed to in the Hague Convention. To be certain that history does not fault his imperial majesty, I have arranged for a formal declaration of hostilities to be presented to Secretary of State Hull shortly before our attack. The Hague Convention does not specify how long in advance the enemy must be notified.' The Razor did not say he had ordered Ambassador Nomura to deliver the message only minutes before the attack on Manila, Singapore and Pearl Harbor. 'Sire. President Roosevelt, Secretary Hull and other American politicians have made further negotiations impossible. We can capitulate and starve, or we can fight!'

'Poll the Council of War,' the Emperor ordered.

The master of protocol read out the names of Japan's military leaders according to rank. 'General Tojo.'

'War!'

'Admiral Yamamoto.'

'War!'

Again and again the word was repeated.

'Colonel Ishikawa.'

'War!' Kenji said, feeling elation and sadness. He had

planned, trained and fought for this decision. His feeling of pride overcame his doubts. He watched the Emperor take a sheet of paper from his uniform jacket and adjust his spectacles.

'This poem was written by my grandfather, Emperor Meiji,' Hirohito said.

> 'All the seas
> In all directions,
> Are birthed from the same womb.
> Why must the winds and the waves
> Clash so violently throughout the world?'

Hirohito looked out over the assembly. 'This poem reminds me of my grandfather's desire for peace between nations.' He stood and walked from the room, leaving the master of protocol holding an unsigned attack order.

'He lost his courage,' Nakajima gasped. 'He was not even supposed to speak.'

'It was agreed,' Hashimoto said. 'The Emperor agreed to put his seal on the attack orders. Everything is ready. He dismissed his family from responsible positions. Even Prince Higashikuni is not here. What has happened?'

'The Emperor could be registering this protest to further protect himself in the future should we lose the war,' Tsubota said. 'It is too late to turn back. My agents have begun sabotage activities in the Philippines and Singapore.'

'This meeting was a formality,' Yamamoto said to Tojo. 'My ships are moving towards Pearl Harbor and the Emperor knows it.'

'The army is not an instrument for taking orders,' Tojo said. 'We give them!' He flicked his little finger at the master of protocol.

'Yes, Mr Prime Minister.'

'Address me as general!' Tojo said. 'The people at this centre table will have a meeting with the Emperor when he returns from the Yasukune shrine tomorrow morning!'

55

Raiko, folding Mangiro's clothes, sat across from Kenji.

'Are you able to spend enough time with the baby?' he asked.

'Ruth only calls twice a week,' Raiko said. 'And my section of the Communications Centre will soon be moved to the imperial palace. It'll be even closer to home.'

'Has Ruth indicated the state of alert in Pearl Harbor?'

'Low-level. Their planes are still parked in the centre of the airfields.'

'Could you find out from her where the *Prince of Wales* and *Repulse* are?' Kenji asked. 'They report their positions to US navy headquarters in Hawaii. That British battle squadron has no air cover, but if they're in range of American land-based planes they might request air support.'

'I'll try,' Raiko said. 'We've purposely reduced our radio traffic from Hawaii and increased it to and from southern Japan and Malaysia to confuse British and American intelligence. I suggested to the chief he rebroadcast messages sent during the last naval manoeuvres to and from non-existent ships in and around Kyushu. The British and Americans will be monitoring the number, length and direction of our transmissions. We must make them believe our aircraft carriers are in southern Japan and our fleet is moving on Malaysia.'

'Won't that alert the British to the attack on Hong Kong and Singapore?' Kenji asked.

'Exactly, and they'll remain behind their fortress walls looking out to sea while our troops come ashore behind them and take Singapore from the land side. The chief believes if Nakajima's forces strike quickly enough, the commander of Singapore may adhere to Churchill's original order and surrender after a brief fight for honour's sake. Tojo has given Nakajima only half the number of men as there are British soldiers to take Singapore. He must know something. When does the Kido Butai – task force – move on Pearl Harbor?'

'The Emperor hasn't given his approval. He read an anti-war poem and walked out, leaving us with our mouths open. We meet again tomorrow. If he puts the imperial seal to the order, I must immediately fly out to the flagship *Kaga*.'

'I'll feed Mangiro, then we'll have some time together,' Raiko said. 'Read this.'

Kenji took the large leather-bound scrapbook. On its front was the picture of a Caucasian mother and child. The heading in English read MY BABY BOOK. Inside, Raiko had written about Mangiro from the moment of his birth at 6 p.m. on 18 May 1941. Kenji read that his son had gained eleven pounds in six months. Raiko had outlined Mangiro's little hands and feet at five months. She came into the room holding the child to her breast.

Kenji tapped the book. 'Did he really sing?'

Raiko smiled. 'I wrote that yesterday. I was feeding him as I am now and singing his lullaby. He stopped suckling, looked up at me and began to sing.'

'Try it again,' Kenji said.

Raiko hummed a few bars, then softly began to sing 'Lullaby of the Nightingales'. Mangiro's eyes opened. He looked up at his mother, then sideways at Kenji. His lips parted in a smile and slipped off the swollen nipple.

'He recognizes me,' Kenji whispered.

'You sing with me,' Raiko said.

Softly, Kenji and Raiko sang together. Mangiro's widening eyes never left his father.

'It's you,' Kenji said. 'He has your big, beautiful eyes. He's a little person.'

'Ga goaaa ga ga gooaaa.'

'He's singing,' Kenji shouted. He saw his son's eyes open wider, his little chin scrunch up. 'Don't be frightened of your daddy,' Kenji said. 'I'm your best friend. I wouldn't hurt you or anyone else.' His son's little chin quivered and tears filled the wide eyes. 'How could I say that?' Kenji whispered. 'I'm going to lead the attack on Pearl Harbor. Maybe the child has the ability to see the destruction and death I'll bring to the Americans.'

Raiko pressed her nipple to Mangiro's wet lips. He suckled, his eyelids fluttered closed and he settled into his mother's arms.

'Now that the attack plans are about to become reality, I'm examining the morality of my actions,' Kenji said.

'We've talked about morals before,' Raiko said. 'Your targets are military and protected by professional soldiers. It's not Nanking. Neither the Philippines nor Hawaii belong to America. The Americans are the foreign occupying military force. You, Uncle Hiroki and my father tried for peace. If we don't expand, there won't be enough food for your son, or for other Japanese children.'

'I voted for war against America and was saddened,' Kenji said. 'So much of what is good in Japan has come from the United States. They sent agricultural experts here to show us how to grow new strains of rice and use chemical fertilizers. They taught us modern medicine. They helped feed our people and make them healthier. Now, because of their generosity, we're overpopulated and must fight them. It doesn't make sense.'

With the suckling child between them, Raiko embraced Kenji. 'Whatever the Emperor decides, you and I will do.'

In the nineteenth century Emperor Meiji had dedicated

the Yasukune shrine to all Japanese soldiers who fell in combat. Their names were listed and their souls remembered in prayers by those who came to worship. It was from this place that Dr Tsubota had given the orders for the 1936 attempt to overthrow the political leaders of Japan. The shrine had become a place used by political and military leaders to make nationalistic announcements and proclamations.

Emperor Hirohito was preceded into the shrine by his security men. Alone, he walked to the centre of the hall, bowed his head and recited the ancient prayer by rote. 'Having succeeded through the benign influence of my imperial ancestors to the throne of lineal succession unbroken for ages eternal, and having assumed the power to reign over and govern the empire, I perform with solemnity the ritual of invoking the spirits and the gods on behalf of the people. I ask that the people of Japan be allowed to maintain the rules of correct conduct, allowed to cultivate inherited virtues and continue intact the glorious traditions set by their ancestors.' Hirohito added his own prayer to the ancient one. 'Spirits of my family who dwell beyond the clouds, bless the decision I have taken this morning. A million men await my command. This action will shape the future of our people for eternity.' He clapped once to send his prayer on its way, and a bell chimed. The security men closed in around the Emperor and escorted him to his limousine.

The throne on which the Emperor sat was the only furniture remaining in the imperial reception room. Tojo and Yamamoto led Hashimoto, Nakajima, Tsubota and Kenji to stand before the Emperor and bow.

Tojo bowed again. 'Your imperial majesty. For a year and a half the United States has supplied arms, ammunition and aircraft to Britain in its war with Germany. In September Roosevelt gave Britain fifty destroyers on condition Prime Minister Churchill send a battle fleet into the Pacific against us. Hitler's submarines have been sinking American cargo ships carrying war materials to Britain. Last month Roosevelt gave his navy orders to sink on sight any German submarine. The Germans have since sunk three American warships in addition to several merchantships. The Atlantic Charter allies Great Britain and the United States. The Tri-Partite Pact allies Italy, Germany and Japan. The war has already begun. The plan which the master of protocol has for your approval is only a formality to sanction a situation which exists. Roosevelt has said an attack on Singapore will result in an American declaration of war on Japan. We must take Singapore if we are to expand into Malaysia. Roosevelt's proclamation of an alliance with Britain makes an attack on Pearl Harbor a necessity! We will succeed! We will neutralize the principal enemy force in the Pacific! While the Americans recover from our lightning blow, we shall build impregnable defence positions in the Philippines, the Dutch East Indies and South-East Asia!'

'Bring the imperial seal,' the Emperor said.

The master of protocol carried forward a small table and withdrew the seal from the drawer. He inked the seal and spread the document on the table.

The Emperor took up the imperial seal, paused to look at the men standing before him, then pressed it to the rice paper.

'We tremble in awe before your highness,' Tojo said. 'I personally assure your majesty that on 8 December, we shall repay Chu and Giri for all those living and dead who were insulted by the Westerners in the unequal treaties and agreements forced on us during the past ninety years.'

'You are hereby commanded to fulfil your duties and conduct yourselves in an honourable manner,' the Emperor said.

'So it is ordered, so it is done,' the men echoed. 'Banzai! Banzai! Banzai!' They backed out of the Emperor's presence.

In the anteroom, the six officers raised saké cups. 'One blood! One voice! One command!' Tojo bellowed.

The others chorused the toast and drank.

'Admiral Yamamoto will remain in Tokyo with me,' Tojo ordered. 'General Hashimoto leaves for Formosa and the Philippines attacking force! General Nakajima to the Singapore attack group! Dr Tsubota to Shanghai! Colonel Ishikawa will fly out to the aircraft carrier *Kaga*! Gentlemen, man your battle stations!'

'Is it war?' Raiko asked.

'Yes,' Kenji said, and hugged his wife and son. 'There's a car waiting outside. I have to change and leave.'

'Your aunt and uncle called twice. I'll dial them while you dress.'

Mangiro Ishikawa's eyes opened wide when his father strode into the room in his leather flying suit and flight cap with goggles. Raiko handed Kenji the telephone. He spoke with Noriko for several minutes, then to Hiroki.

Kenji listened attentively to his uncle before he replaced the receiver. He went to a cabinet, took out a large packet wrapped in old, cracked oilskin and showed it to Raiko. 'Hiroki asked me to give this to Admiral Nagumo, commander of Kido Butai. Do you know what it is?'

'Yes,' Raiko said. 'It is only right that you present it to him before the attack. Now put out your left arm. It's closest to your heart. That is where your son and I shall always be.' She taped a photograph of herself and Mangiro to Kenji's sleeve. He embraced them both, smothering them with kisses.

Raiko and Kenji stepped back from each other and bowed. 'Go with the gods and return victorious,' she said, and began to sing the 'Lullaby of the Nightingales'.

Kenji thought his legs would buckle when he heard his son singing, 'Ga ga goaaa ga.' Kenji turned so Raiko would not see his tears.

Just as he entered the waiting car, Yamamoto's coded radio message was received in the Kurile islands north of Hokkaido. 'Kido Butai, forward!'

Four battleships, six aircraft carriers, nine destroyers and several supply ships weighed anchor at two-hour intervals and left their moorings. They sailed separate routes to a rendezvous in the north Pacific 1,000 miles from Pearl Harbor.

56

'Just my luck,' Joe DeCarlo said. 'This year Congress declares the fourth Thursday of November as America's official Thanksgiving Day and it's my turn to be duty officer.'

'What part of the turkey do you want?' John Whittefield asked. 'I'll bring it over.'

'Don't bother. My wife and the kids are coming on base to be with me. How did the big brass here react to the Japanese turndown of Secretary Hull's proposals?'

'General Short and Admiral Kimmel agree with the State Department that relations with Japan are at a critical stage and an attack is probable against the British in Malaysia and the Dutch East Indies. Even the Philippines are considered a target. There's no mention of Hawaii. I reminded them that rumours of preparations in Kagoshima to attack Pearl Harbor were false and we can breathe easy.'

'I've been thumbing through my tickler file on Jap naval radio traffic,' DeCarlo said. 'Their six big carriers are still located around southern Japan. They'd have to sprout wings to get here by 6 December as Ambassador Grew warned. Two Jap carriers are in the Gulf of Siam with a couple of battleships, a flock of cruisers, destroyers and troopships. A lot of radio messages to and from there. The British have an unconfirmed sighting of a large flotilla moving towards Singapore. Does the code word Raffles mean anything to you? The Brits are sending it out to all units every half-hour.'

'Raffles is their call to one hundred per cent alert,' John said. 'I'll inform General Short and Admiral Kimmel. I'm their guest for Thanksgiving dinner.'

'They'll be pleased to hear the main Japanese force is 7,000 miles away,' DeCarlo said.

'Call British intelligence. Recommend they send the *Prince of Wales* and *Repulse* out to sea, away from Singapore. In the harbour those battleships would be sitting ducks for Jap bombers.'

'The Brits have got some land-based Spitfires in Singapore. They'll knock the Nips for a loop. Chenault reports the Japs run at the sight of Western pilots.'

'I know three Japanese squadron commanders who won't run,' John said. 'They set the long-distance flight record a few years back and are as tough as any soldiers in the world.'

DeCarlo picked up a letter. 'Did you read this from Ambassador Grew in Tokyo?'

'He sent it to me,' John said.

DeCarlo lowered his head and gave a sheepish grin. 'I'm so snowed under with paper, I don't know whether I'm coming or going. Can you depend on Grew's evaluation?'

'No,' John said. 'His refusal to believe the Japanese would attack either Hong Kong or Singapore is based on the assumption that since Tojo is now leader of the civil government and supreme commander of the military, he'll control the extremists' desire for war. I believe Tojo leads the extremists. He's just quieter than Hashimoto and others. Grew's evaluation is coloured by his love for Japan and the Japanese people. No ambassador has held the same post as long as Grew. That can be dangerous. His opinion is coloured by wishful thinking.'

'What do you make of the reported unidentified aircraft around Manila?' DeCarlo asked.

'Has MacArthur sent out reconnaissance planes?'

'To the four points of the compass. Not an aircraft carrier

501

in sight and it's too far away from any Jap-held islands or land bases for them to fly from.'

'MacArthur's boys may be celebrating the holidays too early,' John said. 'You could use a vacation. If you want, fly there and check out what's happening.'

'You mean go to Manila?'

'I've got an invitation to what promises to be a great party at the Manila Hotel on 6 December. The Twenty-seventh Bomber Group is honouring General Bereton. He's the new commander of MacArthur's Far East Air Force.'

'I'd like to beg off this one,' DeCarlo said. 'The wife and kids expect me to take them on a picnic next Sunday.'

Aboard the aircraft carrier *Kaga* in the north Pacific, Kenji addressed his squadron leaders and navigators. 'Gentlemen, two days ago the first blow against the enemy was delivered by our military. On the first of December the Australian cruiser HMAS *Sydney* sank the German sea raider *Kormoran* somewhere south of the Philippines. Our reconnaissance planes flying missions over Manila heard the German call for help and radioed one of our submarines in the area. It fired two torpedoes at close range and the Australian cruiser sank within one minute.'

'When do we go into action?' a squadron leader asked.

'In five days,' Kenji said. 'These rough seas may not please our stomachs, but the storm hides our fleet. We take off at dawn 7 December, Hawaiian time. We have an agent in Pearl Harbor who reports ninety American ships in port this weekend. We expect there'll be more when we arrive next Sunday. Squadron Commander Arai will continue this briefing.'

Genda stepped to the podium. 'The enemy has insufficient aircraft to search the sea 360 degrees around the Hawaiian islands. They've sent many of their planes to

502

Guam, Wake and the Philippines. There has been no air search beyond 100 miles from Honolulu in our direction. The American navy believes the seas too rough in the north Pacific for us to launch planes. Pearl Harbor, its airfields and shore installations are unprotected by barrage balloons or anti-torpedo nets, and the anti-aircraft batteries ashore are without ammunition. This means that if we achieve surprise, we can expect fire from naval targets and a free run for several minutes at the army bases. Take advantage of this and attack with vigour. If we can destroy some of their planes on the ground, knock out one or two of their battleships and a couple of heavy cruisers, our navy will rule the eastern hemisphere. I've explained what radar is and how it works. The American army has a radar station guarding the approaches to Pearl Harbor. On Sunday it closes down at 7 a.m. We must not get within its range before that time! Squadron commanders, push your men on enemy ship identification! If I point to a picture or silhouette, I want to know more than the ship's classification! I want the names of those battleships – *Maryland*, *Tennessee*, *Arizona*! All pilots must not only be able to identify the American planes, but know their armament and weak points in combat! I've arranged around-the-clock periods for each squadron to study the sand-table mock-up of Pearl Harbor.' Genda stepped down and handed out the schedules.

Kenji returned to the podium. 'The Americans in Hawaii fear sabotage from the 130,000 Japanese living there. In Manila the US army is harassed by Filippino guerrillas who desire freedom from American rule. Therefore the American planes are still parked together in the middle of their airfields, away from fences. If we should catch those planes on the ground, don't hesitate to shoot! The Americans don't have wooden decoys as Chenault used in China. Shoot up everything that looks like it can fly! Study the aerial photographs of Battleship Row! Place

the pictures under your bombsights and look at them from
every angle! Whatever degree of surprise we achieve, take
advantage of it!'

5 December 1941, Formosa

'Our objective is to bomb Nichols, Iba and Clark fields,'
Hino said. 'Squadron leaders will key on me all the way to
Manila! As senior navigator, I'll lead you to your targets.
But in this flight, direction is not enough. Because of the
great distances to and from the targets, we must change
altitude several times to catch the tail winds. I've mapped
the air currents to Manila and back. The fighter-plane
escorts must conserve fuel. Without fighter escorts, even
the Chinese air force chopped our bomber formations to
pieces. The Americans are far better pilots than Madam
Chiang's little boys. Absolute radio silence is essential!
Your radio on-off switches will be handed to you by your
crew chiefs and taped to your right sleeves. You'll replace
them only when you see my green smoke rocket prior to
our attack. Until then we'll communicate by arm and hand
signals. I've given each of you a mimeographed copy of
my flight plan. The flight speed will be 170 miles per hour
for minimum fuel consumption. You must study the aerial
photographs of enemy airfields! There can be no mistakes!
If we fail, those Flying Fortresses in Manila will bomb our
bases here in Formosa! They'll return to Nichols, Clark
and Iba to refuel, rearm and attack General Nakajima's
troops landing behind Singapore! Then they'll reload and
catch Kido Butai on its way home from Pearl Harbor!
We've got to get them!' Hino stepped back and saluted
General Hashimoto.

The husky commander of the Formosa strike force
stepped to the podium. 'Practise, practise, practise using
your new German bombsights! Accuracy is a must! If you
catch enemy aircraft on the ground, destroy them! If not,

destroy their landing strips in and around Manila! The closest American landing field is Mindanao, 550 miles away. After a half-hour of combat with us, Mindanao will be beyond the range of their divebombers, fighters and torpedo-planes. They'll have to crash-land in the jungle or sea if you pockmark their runways!' Hashimoto pulled a magazine from his uniform pocket and held it over his head so everyone could see the headlines. 'If your English isn't as good as it should be, I'll tell you what this says. The lead article in *Aviation* magazine is entitled, "The Japanese Air Force".' He shook the magazine and shouted, 'This rag is considered to be the authority on military aircraft in use around the world! Listen to what they write about you!' He read aloud, accenting every word. '"The imperial Japanese air force has the worst accident record in the world! Japanese pilots are unable to co-ordinate and carry out large-scale manoeuvres! Japanese tactics are outdated and their strategies stolen from the Germans, British and Americans!"' Hashimoto watched the young faces before him redden with anger. 'Gentlemen,' he cooed, still passing the magazine slowly before their eyes, 'do not let this irritate you. Be thankful our tactics of monkey-fighting, initiated by Colonel Kenji Ishikawa, have produced an inaccurate impression of our capabilities.' His soft tone and manner led the men to relax, but seeing that he slammed the podium with the magazine. He leaned forward, his shaven skull gleaming in the overhead lights, and his eyes rolled up under his hairy eyebrows. His voice rumbled from deep in his chest. 'This is what we have been working for since that bastard Theodore Roosevelt stole our victory over the Russians in 1904! Since that racist Wilson told us we were not equal to whites in 1918! I cannot fly with you,' Hashimoto growled, throwing the magazine to the floor. He pointed at his men. 'Take me with you to Manila in your hearts! Let me be there when you swoop down on their airfields and zoom up in the chase to knock the enemy from the sky! Oh how I hate those pasty-faced sons of bitches! Give a Banzai for me and one for all those, dead and alive, who worked to bring you the opportunity to do battle for the Emperor and repay Chu!' Hashimoto snapped to attention. 'Warriors of the Wind, I love you! I salute you!' He threw both hands in the air and shouted, 'Banzai! Banzai! Banzai!'

57

'I thought you were off this weekend,' John said.

'I heard you received a special message from Washington and a telephone call from Vinegar Joe,' DeCarlo said. 'What's happening?'

'Washington now claims the three Jap aircraft carriers we thought were in southern Japan could be somewhere else. Our traffic analysis in DC shows those carriers may be heading towards the Philippines. They've also been reading the senior Japanese diplomatic code. The Japanese embassy staff in Bangkok burned their cipher machines and code books last week.'

'What's Washington's evaluation?'

'They're telling us in Hawaii not to worry. Joe Stilwell says we should watch our asses because the Nips could be rounding Diamond Point. He received a warning message by public telephone from Chiang Kai-shek.'

'What's the generalissimo got to do with the price of pineapples in Hawaii?' DeCarlo asked.

'One of Madam Chiang's planes supposedly shot down a Jap bomber near the Indochina border and salvaged documents from the wreck. Orders to the Japanese air-force commanders in Saigon and Hanoi to participate in bombing Hong Kong and Singapore. Orders to the Vichy French to protect their military installations from British and American retaliatory attacks on 8 December, Tokyo time.'

'That means an attack on Singapore, probably Sumatra, Siam, and maybe the Philippines!' DeCarlo said. 'Does MacArthur know?'

'I notified him. He cancelled all leaves and put his men on one hundred per cent alert. What troubles me is that we learned of it through Stilwell, not Washington. When Chiang Kai-shek spoke to the State Department and found out that Hawaii hadn't been informed, he called Stilwell to tell him that Pearl Harbor was also supposed to be hit by the Japs this Monday.'

'Sorry to tell you, but I don't trust that sly old Chinaman,' DeCarlo said. 'He and Madam Chiang want more aid from us. He's crying wolf again.'

'That's the State Department's attitude. But it troubles Admiral Kimmel and me that the information wasn't forwarded by naval intelligence. General Short told Kimmel about another intelligence mix-up. The army received a warning from Washington about Japanese submarine activity in Hawaiian waters. But the navy was never told.'

'This is getting to be like those Looney Tunes cartoon films,' DeCarlo said. 'Nobody is telling anyone else what the hell is going on. You brought me here to help straighten out the mess of non-sharing of intelligence between the armed services and Washington, but we haven't been able to accomplish a damned thing! I feel like the world is coming down around our ears!'

'It's coming down, but not that close to us,' John said. 'Manila is 5,000 miles away and Singapore 6,700 miles from Hawaii. There's where Dr Tsubota's sabotage teams have already gone into action. If even one Japanese civilian lit a match near Pearl Harbor, I would sound the call to general quarters. As it is, I'm staying on base today. Kimmel and Short want another intelligence evaluation after lunch.'

'I heard you've been in there twice this morning.'

'And we're meeting again at five this evening. They're on top of things. They know how hard-pressed their men are and don't want to cancel weekend leaves and liberty unnecessarily.'

508

'Tell you what,' DeCarlo said. 'When you complete the five o'clock briefing, go home, get some rest and I'll be here at seven tomorrow morning to help you clear up the backlog. I promised to take the family on a picnic at ten. I'll give you three solid hours.'

'Thanks anyway, but not necessary.' John sighed. 'I'm the fourth generation involved with Japan. My great-grandfather helped Perry open up that country. My grandfather was a personal friend of the great Lord Nariakira. And my father was ambassador to the imperial court. I speak perfect Japanese. But in the last two years, my love for Japan and its people has soured. The other night I dreamt about the Japanese sport of Kendo. It's fought with a bamboo sword. There's a tactic taught by the greatest samurai ever, Musashi the Sword Saint. When attacking an enemy of superior strength, strike one lightning, death-dealing blow, then disappear.'

'How can they hit us here without our knowing? There isn't a cloud in the sky for 100 miles. If MacArthur's spotter planes don't see them, one of ours will. They can't reach us unless they take the northern route and their aircraft carriers would be tossed around like corks this time of the year. If any American port is targeted, it's got to be Manila.'

'I'll repeat that to Kimmel and Short,' John said. 'It's time for another briefing.'

Headquarters Fourteenth Naval District, Pearl Harbor

'I've tried to put myself in the enemy's shoes and think like him,' John Whittefield said to General Short and Admiral Kimmel. 'But with Japanese that can be frustrating. Just when you believe you know what they'll do, you find they have logical reasons for deciding the opposite. Having said that, and having predicted most of their moves relatively

509

accurately, I'll now attempt to analyse what the Japanese people are thinking. They know Japan is going to war. The minute the Emperor removed his family from positions of responsibility, the people knew they would be liable for whatever actions occur, not Hirohito. They know the imperial army and navy are prepared for hostile action in Malaysia and the Dutch East Indies, possibly the Philippines too. They don't consider an attack on Manila as attacking America.'

'It's not clear if Roosevelt will either,' the general said. 'That's why he sent MacArthur to be employed by the Philippine government. But go on.'

'Japanese wives and mothers have stood in the streets for months asking passers-by to sew one stitch for good luck into 1,000-stitch belts, which their sons and husbands will wear into battle,' John said. 'Almost every Japanese soldier has one of those belts. The Japanese public doesn't expect war with America. Neither Japan's press nor its radio has publicized Roosevelt's commitment to support the British. Admiral Halsey is now on his way to Manila with three aircraft carriers to support MacArthur. When he arrives in Manila bay on 15 December, Yamamoto will know. Dr Tsubota's agents are all over that city. Any plans Tojo or Yamamoto had of hitting the Philippines will have to be abandoned. The combination of Bull Halsey's fighter planes and General Bereton's B-17s could wipe out any size fleet in the south Pacific. Yamamoto will have to worry about taking Singapore if we get into the act.'

'What about Hawaii?' Kimmel asked.

'There's no chance of an attack here,' John said. 'Naval intelligence and the State Department discount those rumours.'

'What does your radio traffic analysis indicate?' Short asked.

'A large Japanese fleet moving through the South China sea towards Hong Kong and Singapore.'

'Do you believe the major part of the Japanese fleet is there?' Kimmel asked.

'The Japanese naval build-up in the South China sea is so massive, I doubt they'd have enough left to bother the Philippines,' John said. 'The three aircraft carriers that Washington said are no longer in southern Japan couldn't possibly reach the Philippines before Halsey and his carriers arrive in Manila.'

'The last Washington memorandum regarding belligerence by Japan recommends delaying the outbreak of hostilities until spring 1942,' Short said.

'This isn't a ballgame we can put off on account of rain,' Kimmel replied. 'The Japs might want to play sooner. Roosevelt has issued conflicting orders that immobilize us. On the one hand he wants us to avoid war for the time being. Yet he has us committed to backing the British if they're attacked. When I questioned what to do if the Japanese invade Malaysia, Washington didn't answer.'

Kido Butai steamed undetected into the western hemisphere. Six Japanese aircraft carriers, two battleships, a formation of cruisers and destroyers rendezvoused in the stormy seas of the north Pacific. They crossed the international time zone where 1 a.m. December 8th became 1 a.m. December 7th. Blanketed by fog, they steamed at fourteen knots in strict radio silence. Two hundred miles ahead two submarines, with canopied seaplanes lashed to their decks, scouted for the main force.

Three hundred miles ahead of the scouts and ten miles from Pearl Harbor, five of Japan's largest submarines broke the surface of the dark waters. The crews swarmed out of the hatches and conning towers. They unlashed the two-man midget submarines fastened to their decks. Despite damage to one of the small subs in the rough-water launching, its crew vowed to undertake their mission. They would slip through Pearl Harbor's open torpedo net in the morning, or sink the sub and die.

The hangar deck of the flagship Kaga

'When the weather clears, we shall make history!' Kenji told his pilots, mechanics and armourers.

'Suppose it doesn't clear?'

'Admiral Yamamoto says it will,' Kenji said. 'The admiral is an old blue-water sailor.'

'Admiral Yamamoto is not here with us.'

'He is with General Tojo at the imperial palace to supervise the most brilliant, diverse and complicated military manoeuvre in the history of warfare!' Kenji said. 'Admiral Yamamoto, supreme commander of the Japanese navy, has given me permission to detail his plans: when we take off for Hawaii, Japanese aircraft will already have left Formosa to attack Manila. As we start our bombing run on the Pacific fleet at Pearl Harbor, General Nakajima's men will begin the invasion of Malaysia, the Dutch East Indies and Siam. Simultaneous air attacks will take place on the American-held islands of Wake, Guam and the Philippines.' Kenji touched his eye patch. 'I left an eye in China because I underestimated the enemy. Now it is the Americans who underestimate us. Their Wildcat and P-40 fighter planes are death traps against our Zeros. Their pilots fly suicide missions against us and they don't know it. I have one eye remaining. With it I want to see victory! A victory so perfect, historians throughout the ages will study it! They'll see that it wasn't created only by the pilots! But also that seamen and maintenance crews made our triumph possible!' He pointed at the men hunkered down on the hangar deck. 'Pilots, stand and face your maintenance crews and the seamen of the *Kaga*! In unison, repeat with me! I swear to render Chu to the Emperor!' The pilots echoed his words. 'I swear to repay Giri to the enemies

512

of Japan! I honour the men before me who have made it possible for me to fly in combat. I will do my duty in a military manner in the ancient tradition of Bushido!' The airmen bowed to the crewmen of the *Kaga*.

'Pilots,' Kenji said. 'It is time for you to place clippings of your fingernails and cuttings of your hair in the envelopes containing your photographs! Give them to your crew chiefs! In the event of your glorious death in battle, the envelope will be sent to your family! The shipboard shrine and temple are now open for pilots!' Kenji bowed.

A long shrill whistle froze everyone on the hangar deck. 'Now hear this,' the *Kaga's* chief bosun bellowed. 'Pilots, we salute you! Men of the *Kaga*, rise up and give honour to our Warriors of the Wind!'

The crew snapped to attention and bowed to the pilots.

The chief bosun's hoarse voice echoed through the hangar deck. 'My grandfather met the Russians in the straits of Tsu-shima with Admiral Togo. Before the battle, he and the men of the fleet took a solemn oath. It was a simple declaration of dedication to the Emperor and their commander. "To the death!" They painted those words on bands of cloth and bound them around their heads!' He whipped off his cap, revealing his headband. Eyes burning with fierce pride, every crewman took off his cap and showed his headband.

'We are with you to the death,' the chief bosun cried. 'We cannot be with you in body, but we shall be over Pearl Harbor in spirit! Each of us has taken a sacred vow! If a plane does not reach its destination because of mechanical failure, that crew chief and his men will commit seppuku! If you die in combat, we shall take responsibility for your family!' The crewmen bowed with the chief.

Kenji felt blood pumping through his veins as if on the final climb to the summit of a mountain. He whipped off his colonel's cap. 'Where is my headband!'

513

His crew chief reached into his coverall pocket and handed Kenji a headband. The chief's eyes gleamed. 'I know my commander!'

Kenji tied the band around his head. When he looked up, everyone on the deck wore TO THE DEATH emblazoned on their foreheads. He gazed out at the eager faces. 'We are about to do battle for the Emperor and Japan! To those who go into combat for the first time, I warn you that waiting is the most difficult part. We have three and a half hours to take-off. Pass it as best you can. I go first to the Shinto shrine.' He bowed.

Back in his cabin, Kenji thought to write Raiko, but decided they had said it all before his departure. He picked up the cracked oilskin packet from his seabag and went to the war room.

58

Pounding on the front door woke Raiko from an afternoon nap. She was up from the sleeping mat before her eyes opened, but Mangiro slept on. Raiko heard the housekeeper speak to someone at the front door.

Three young men and an older woman stood there. 'May I help you?' Raiko asked.

The woman bowed. 'Please, you are to come with us.'

'Where would you be taking me?'

'The child too,' the woman said, and held out an envelope bearing the imperial seal. Both the housekeeper and Raiko bowed. 'This letter is for you,' the woman said.

Careful to save as much of the seal as possible, Raiko opened the flap. She recognized Toshio Ogino's handwriting.

'Come to the palace immediately,' the chief of the Owada Communications Centre wrote. 'Follow the instructions of the one who delivers this letter.'

'These men are from the Emperor's personal bodyguard,' the woman said. 'I am Osan, a nanny in the imperial household. You and the child are to be quartered at the palace for several days. Put out what is necessary to pack. You and the baby will be escorted immediately to the palace. The imperial nursery is prepared.'

'Is it war?' Raiko asked.

'I am not permitted to answer. On the way here I stopped at a shrine and bought a prayer for my son who is with Kido Butai. You may wish to do the same for your husband.'

515

'Thank you,' Raiko said. 'I'll be ready in a short while.'

She returned to the bedroom and looked down at her son. He slept on his back, head turned to the side and tiny clenched fists held up over his shoulders. 'Little Mung, your father is going to war against America. Your namesake would never have believed it possible.'

The American Embassy, Tokyo

'Mr Ambassador, the president's message has finally arrived,' the marine sergeant said.

Joseph Grew took the envelope. 'Have my secretary arrange a meeting with the Emperor immediately!'

'Sir, it's almost midnight.'

'That's not important. I'm leaving for the palace in a few minutes.'

'Aye, aye, sir!'

Grew's hands trembled as he opened the envelope. He had heard of Roosevelt's message to the Emperor several hours before on a shortwave news broadcast from San Francisco. He looked down at the pile of decodes scattered across his desk. They were irrefutable proof that Japan was going to war against the Dutch and British. He had several messages from British intelligence warning of an attack on the Philippines. Those he had forwarded to MacArthur. Now he read a copy of the president's message to the Emperor and went pale. 'It was sent in the grey code!' he said aloud. 'Washington knows Kempetai broke that cipher some time ago!' Grew poured himself a jigger of Scotch and downed it. 'On second thoughts, maybe Washington isn't so stupid after all. They know Japanese intelligence will read this. Even if I don't reach the Emperor, he'll be informed in time to prevent war, if he wants to.'

* * *

Raiko, along with other code experts, was still at her desk in the imperial reception hall at midnight. Cable, telegraph and telephone lines crisscrossed the floor. She had been ordered to read aloud all communications as they were received from Ruth Kuhn in her attic overlooking Pearl Harbor. The dais behind Raiko was screened off by heavy curtains. Someone had said the Emperor was listening from behind the curtains.

Raiko left her desk and was stopped at the door by a guard. 'It is time to nurse my baby!' she said.

An officer checked his list, then escorted Raiko to the imperial nursery. Passing the anteroom, she saw the American Ambassador in rumpled clothing and dishevelled hair speaking with the master of protocol.

Joseph Grew opened the letter he was holding. 'If you won't allow me to deliver this personally to the Emperor, I insist you hear it and give it to his imperial majesty as soon as possible!'

'The Emperor sleeps,' the master of protocol said. 'When he wakes, I will take this to him.'

Grew opened the letter and read aloud, 'From the President of the United States to His Imperial Majesty, Emperor of Japan. Greetings . . .'

Grew read Roosevelt's historical account of the friendly relations that had existed between Japan and America since Commodore Perry landed almost 100 years before. And concluded, 'I, the President of the United States, address myself to Your Imperial Highness, Emperor of Japan, at this moment, in the fervent hope that Your Majesty may, as I am doing, give thought in this definite emergency to ways of dispelling the dark clouds that enshroud us. I am confident that both of us, for the sake of the peoples not only of our countries, but for the sake of humanity in neighbouring territories, have a sacred duty to restore traditional amity and prevent further death and destruction in the world. Respectfully,

Franklin Delano Roosevelt, President of the United States of America.'

Grew folded the letter, replaced it in its envelope and handed it to the master of protocol. 'You will see this delivered at the earliest possible moment!'

When Raiko returned to her desk the ambassador had gone, but the room buzzed with excitement. A message had been received and decoded two desks to her right.

'From Dr Tsubota, Shanghai,' the decoder read aloud. 'Our marines have advanced from their base into downtown Shanghai. British police remain passive. The waterfront property, including the foreign settlement and banking district, are now under our control. Roadblocks have stopped all traffic out of Shanghai. My agents are now in charge of civilian and government communications in the city. Ships in the port are under the guns of our artillery. The ships have been boarded by our marines and their radio sets rendered inoperable.'

Raiko realized that General Tojo and Admiral Yamamoto had entered the room and were standing behind her. The radio to her left came to life.

The decoder recorded the signals, then read aloud, 'From General Nakajima, Strike Force, Singapore. Bombardment begun against the Ninth Division of the Indian army. Landing craft ashore at Koto Bharu. Minimum casualties and beachhead secure. The march on Singapore has begun. Banzai!'

Raiko was startled by Tojo's voice. 'Banzai your arse! Nakajima started the attack an hour and a half too soon!'

'Mrs Ishikawa, have you heard anything from Hawaii?' Yamamoto asked.

'No, sir. I am not expecting contact unless there is an alert at Pearl Harbor prior to our planes' arrival there. Kido Butai planes are due to take off in ten minutes. Their target attack time is in two hours.'

'Thank you,' Yamamoto said. He turned to Tojo. 'It is out of our hands. If the British notify Hawaii, Pearl Harbor may go on one hundred per cent alert. Our planes could be flying into a trap.'

'Everything appears to be going wrong!' Tojo said. 'The airfields on Formosa are closed in by fog! Those bombers destined for the Philippines are already hours late! Can you imagine the mess over Manila when they arrive ten or twelve hours after MacArthur knows about the strike on Pearl Harbor? He will be waiting for them. And there is another problem. I sent out orders last week for our Washington embassy to destroy their records and code equipment. They have only one cipher machine and an old typewriter to decode and print our Declaration of War. It won't be delivered to Secretary Hull before our planes bomb Pearl Harbor!'

'What was the Emperor's reaction to the letter delivered by Ambassador Grew?' Yamamoto asked.

Tojo snorted. 'It was a flimsy last-minute attempt by Roosevelt for peace. The Emperor rejected it.'

'Colonel Ishikawa's take-off may also be delayed,' Yamamoto said. 'We monitored a US weather report indicating rough seas in the north Pacific. Our carriers will be listing ten to fifteen degrees. The rule is against take-off if there is more than a five-degree roll.'

Raiko felt pain in her hands and looked down. Her tight clenched fists had dug her nails into her palms. She prayed for Kenji. She prayed Ruth Kuhn would call, then retracted the second prayer. 'It's too early,' she whispered, and stared at her radio receiver, willing it to remain silent until 7:30 a.m.

Men of the Kido Butai drifted to their battle stations in silence. On the aircraft carrier *Kaga*, pilots sat in their cockpits while mechanics moved around the planes wiping imagined smudges from the wings and fuselage. The planes

519

were lashed and chocked against the weather. Now and then, pilots' and mechanics' eyes met, and looked away. No one spoke.

Kenji entered the flagship's war room, snapped to attention and saluted Admiral Nagumo. The commander ignored Kenji and hurried out on to the observation platform. Kenji followed the deck officers outside. Above them a solid ceiling of heavy grey clouds had risen to 1,000 feet. The rain had ceased but the ocean was still rough. Waves burst over the bow. The fleet was racing into attack position at twenty-two knots. Kenji saw several seamen slip and slide over the tilting flight deck. Although there had been an attempt to keep it quiet, everyone knew a lookout man had been washed overboard the night before.

'There it is,' the admiral shouted.

'Blow the Russian bastard out of the water,' the *Kaga*'s captain cried.

'What are they talking about?' Kenji asked the man next to him.

The naval officer pointed at a large, lumbering freighter several miles ahead of the flagship. She sat low in the water, barely visible amid the deep swells.

'Shouldn't we sink her?' Kenji whispered.

'If she gives one peep from her radio, we will.' The officer pointed at two battleships racing forward with guns aimed at the freighter. 'We received word from Dr Tsubota the day the *Uritsky* sailed from San Francisco that it would intersect our course prior to the attack.'

'How could Tsubota know?'

'I assume Russian intelligence informed him. We've received help from them before. Admiral Yamamoto instructed us not to sink the *Uritsky*.'

'Is Admiral Nagumo prepared to risk everything on the word of a Russian sea captain?' Kenji demanded. The big freighter was now in clear view of the entire task force.

'It's not the sea captain's word,' the naval officer said. 'It's Stalin's. According to Dr Tsubota that ship is loaded with lend-lease guns, tanks and planes bound for Vladivostok, and from there on the Trans-Siberian railroad to Moscow. The Nazis are trying to surround the Russian capital. This is the only sea route on which the Soviets can ferry supplies from America and avoid the German submarine wolf packs.'

'You mean the Russians are taking aid from the Americans but won't warn them we're going to attack Pearl Harbor? It's insane. Where is the honour between allies?'

'There is little honor among Caucasians, and none among allies.'

Admiral Nagumo marched back into the war room. 'Not much going right,' he said, and pointed to a civilian radio on the chart table. 'Only good thing is that music.'

Kenji heard soft American music coming from the radio.

'Never liked aeroplanes,' Nagumo said to Kenji. 'Our fighters shot down an Australian scout plane on their way to Singapore. The enemy pilot saw the whole fleet and radioed Nakajima's position and number of ships before your flyboys got him. Nakajima had to attack an hour and a half early.' Nagumo cocked his head. 'Isn't that music pleasant?' He hummed along with the radio. 'We can receive messages, but can't send. I can't ask about that damned Russian freighter. Aeroplanes make me nervous.' He pointed at Kenji. 'Colonel Ishikawa, if I send you and your men up, we're at war with the United States. If you can't destroy at least one of their battleships and two heavy cruisers, the Pacific fleet is going to come buzzing out of Pearl Harbor like a bunch of angry hornets and kick our arses all the way back to Yokohama.'

'We'll do the job,' Kenji said.

'You know why aeroplanes make me nervous? You can't depend on them. Your cousin Hino promised to do the job. He's hours behind schedule because of a little fog. Weather doesn't bother a good sea captain. We've made a rendezvous after a 6,000-mile trek in fog and rough seas. And we'll attack on time! Hino can't possibly stop MacArthur's B-17s from getting to us on the return voyage.' Nagumo moved close to Kenji, looked up and tapped him on the chest. 'Aeroplanes make me nervous. You can never tell where the hell they are.' The little commander of the Kido Butai waved his arms. 'Do you know that Admiral Halsey is sailing somewhere around here with three aircraft carriers and a couple of hundred planes? The scout planes launched from our submarines say there isn't an aircraft carrier in Pearl Harbor. Two battleships are also missing.'

'What's left?' Kenji asked.

'Don't worry! There'll be enough for you. Except for Halsey's ships, the entire Pacific fleet is anchored in Pearl Harbor. Ninety-four of them.'

Kenji breathed a sigh of relief and pointed at the radio. 'Sir, it's difficult to concentrate with that music.'

'Getting edgy?' Nagumo asked. 'Well my boy, you should be. I'm as nervous as a Christian whore in church. That music comes from Honolulu. If it stops and they announce an emergency, you know we've been spotted. Then our arse is for Davy Jones's locker. General Short, General MacArthur and Admirals Kimmel and Halsey will send every one of their planes looking for us. If they find us, they'll shit bombs and piss bullets on our heads.'

Kenji felt stinging in his empty eye socket and realized he was pouring sweat.

Nagumo pointed. 'What's that under your arm?'

Kenji had forgotten the oilskin packet. He held it out. 'Sir, this is the Z flag Admiral Togo hoisted off the Mokpo light on the southern tip of Korea in 1894. My Uncle Yaka stood on the quarterdeck when, with only a torpedo-boat squadron, they attacked three Chinese battleships. They sank those ships and the Chinese troopship *Kowshing*. In 1904 my Uncle Uraga stood with Admiral Togo and raised this same Z flag as the signal to attack the Russian fleet at Tsu-shima. My Uncle Hiroki commanded me to give the Z flag to you, with these words. "This flag has never known defeat or dishonour. All Japan is with you."' Kenji unwrapped the flag, handed it to Nagumo, stepped back and saluted. 'Sir, do we fight?'

For some moments Nagumo stared at the flag. Reverently he caressed the material. 'Yamamoto and I were there with both your uncles at Tsu-shima and the Mokpo light,' the admiral said. He looked up at Kenji with misty eyes. 'I am samurai!' he declared.

Kenji slammed his fist over his heart. 'I am samurai!'

'Which way blows the wind?' Nagumo asked.

'Easterly,' Kenji answered.

Without taking his eyes from Kenji, Nagumo shouted, 'Communications officer! Make light signals to the carriers *Akagi, Shokaku, Hiryu, Soryu* and *Zuikoku*! "Come about into the wind and prepare to launch planes!" Signal the fleet! "Man your battle stations!"'

For a moment the war room of the flagship *Kaga* remained silent. Then the chief bosun blew his whistle. He took the microphone and roared into it, 'Now hear this! Now hear this! Man your battle stations! Man your battle stations!'

Bells clanged and the ship's whistle sounded. Kenji felt the deck tilt under his feet as the *Kaga* turned into the wind. Huge ocean rollers burst in massive sprays over the bow. The sky lightened as the sun appeared over the horizon. Suddenly it was day.

'Why don't I see men running, hear hatches banging and officers encouraging their crews to battle stations?' Nagumo demanded.

The captain saluted. 'Sir, the men of the *Kaga* have been

523

at their battle stations for hours. They have trained years for this moment. They await your orders.'

Nagumo turned to Kenji. 'I have reduced speed. Can your men take off in a pitch and roll of ten to twelve degrees? It is over the safety limit.'

'We'll do it!' Kenji said.

'Then move quickly! We're a few minutes off schedule as it is!'

59

'General Hashimoto, how can you sleep at a time like this?' Hino asked. He plopped on to a chair and was up again in a moment, pacing the control tower. 'On the *Kaga* it's ten minutes past take-off.' Hino pointed out of the control-tower window. 'All we do is sit here and watch the fog roll in. We're already hours late.'

'If I could blow away the mist, I would,' Hashimoto said. 'Wishing or complaining will not help. This is our karma.'

'General, I've seen you pound podiums and make fighting men tremble by the tone of your voice. This is the most important day of our lives and in the history of Japan. Yet you're calm.'

'Confucius said, "Anger is a form of mental suicide."' The bald-headed general pointed to the control-tower window. 'That fog will lift. When it does, I will send you and your men into battle, no matter what warnings MacArthur has had. Whatever the outcome of Kenji's attack on Pearl Harbor, you and your men will fly. The odds no longer make a difference. Japan is like a terminally ill patient. Radical alternatives are necessary. Either we expand, or we die!'

'All the same, it would make me feel better if I heard you shouting,' Hino said. He peered into the swirling fog.

Tokyo

Raiko's eyes remained glued to her receiver while she

525

listened to other operators tell of Tsubota's successes in Shanghai and Nakajima's advance on Singapore.

'Time check,' Tojo ordered.

'Tokyo 2:30 a.m. Hawaii 5:30 a.m., Washington 11:30 a.m.'

'Our men should be taking off from Kido Butai,' Tojo said. 'They'll reach Pearl Harbor at 7:30 a.m.'

Raiko glanced at her watch. She felt a hand on her shoulder and looked up at Admiral Yamamoto. 'Your husband and I are going to make a prophet of the American General Billy Mitchell,' he said. 'Years ago Mitchell gave me the key to Pearl Harbor. Now your husband is about to unlock the gateway to victory. His men need only destroy three or four major ships and we shall control the Pacific.'

'Admiral Yamamoto,' the operator next to Raiko said. 'The battleships *Prince of Wales* and *Repulse* put to sea before our planes bombed Singapore. There have been no sightings of the British fleet.'

Yamamoto turned to Tojo. 'Those battleships are among the mightiest in the world. All our merchantships in the Far East are at risk with those two on the loose.'

'I'll notify Hashimoto in Formosa,' Tojo said. 'He'll send out search planes. Whatever is left of Hino's bombers after the Manila raid, we'll use to sink those ships.'

Raiko prayed for Kenji, Genda and Hino and their men. 'May the gods protect all of you.'

5:45 a.m., Aboard the Kaga

Kenji leaned into the wind as he made his way between the planes he had designed. He heard singing and stopped to listen, then laughed. His pilots and their crews gave him thumbs-up signs as he climbed into his cockpit, and went on singing.

Kenji sang along,

'Whistle while you work.
Hitler is a jerk.
Mussolini is a meany,
And the Japs are even
Worse, worse, worse!'

The ship's loudspeaker crackled to life. 'Now hear this! Admiral Nagumo will address the men of Kido Butai!'

Static preceded the admiral's voice. Then he spoke, loud and clear. 'At this moment our ambassador in Washington is on his way to the White House to deliver a declaration of war! I notify you that I also wear a headband. To the death! There is no turning back! The blow you strike today is not only for Japan, but for all peoples of colour throughout the world! Life on this planet will never be the same again! Today will show that the whites can be beaten!

'Following is General Tojo's message to all of us. "Fighting men of his majesty's imperial armed forces! America's political leaders have failed to negotiate with Japan in good faith. The solution to our country's problems is in your hands! On this one battle rests the fate of the empire, the Emperor and the future of our people! I have told the Emperor in your name that we shall be victorious! His imperial majesty replied: Let every man do his duty!"'

There was a pause on the loudspeaker. Wind whipped around the planes. Men stood etched against the ever-brightening sky. Nagumo's voice again echoed over the ship. 'Look to the main mast! There flies the original Z flag of Admiral Togo! It was used as the call to battle at the Mokpo light and Port Arthur! It last flew on 27 May 1904 in the straits of Tsu-shima! On that fateful day, outnumbered by the imperial Russian fleet, Admiral Togo won the most resounding sea victory in the history of the world! Look to the other ships of our fleet! They have responded with a replica of the Z flag! Warriors of the Wind, start your engines! Deckmaster, launch your planes!'

Kenji's crew bowed to him. They released the deck cables, pulled the chocks from under his front wheels and signalled thumbs-up. Kenji sighted down the long flat deck that rose and fell, tilting from side to side. Strapped beneath his Zero was a special bomb he had designed, a 1,000-pound armour-piercing naval gun shell. The ship's machinists had fitted it with fins to hold its course true when he dropped it. The weight was excessive, but he had planned it that way. Now he had to show the men he could take off in the foul weather even with the extra load.

A rocket, trailing green smoke, whooshed off the observation platform into the cloud-filled sky. Kenji gunned his engine until it seemed about to tear loose from the motor mounts. He signalled his crew and they knocked out the pin on the restraining cable holding the rear wheel. Kenji released the brakes. He roared down the pitching runway and over the end of the flight deck. The plane dropped instead of rising and Kenji gasped. Wind-blown spray from the whitecaps smacked his windshield and he thought he was in the ocean. He felt the lift as the plane began to rise but, looking back, he saw he was still below the level of the flight deck. He retracted his wheels and the plane gained speed and altitude. The lump in his throat melted.

He remained under the clouds, watching as one after another of his men took off and rose into the air. Satisfied they were forming up correctly, he flew over the aircraft carrier *Akagi* and saw Genda forming up his torpedo squadron. Kenji hand signalled Genda to meet above the clouds. His cousin responded with a wing waggle.

Kenji led his forty-four fighters up to 10,000 feet in a V-formation ahead of Genda's forty torpedo-planes. The fifty heavy bombers and fifty divebombers formed up in formations below Kenji's fighters.

'The Americans claimed this type of rough-weather

take-off couldn't be done,' Kenji said aloud. 'Nagumo expected ten per cent losses in launching, and only one fighter plane was lost.' He looked back at the formation with pride. 'Gods of wind and water. Gods of fire and air. Let me not disgrace my family, my ancestors or the Emperor.' Kenji slipped back his cockpit canopy and fired a red smoke rocket. He pushed his throttle forward, leading the air armada south to Hawaii, thinking of the second wave of attack planes being prepared to take off from the six carriers below the clouds around him. He looked at the picture of Raiko and Mangiro taped to his left sleeve, then moved the radio switch and tuned into the relaxing American music from Honolulu.

7 a.m., Sunday, 7 December 1941, Pearl Harbor

'Joe, this is John Whittefield. Sorry to wake you. I need someone to talk to. A lot has happened and I feel like I'm going over the edge.'

'I'll come right in,' DeCarlo said.

'No. Just give me your evaluation on the phone. There's been a change in Japanese radio patterns from the Philippines to Formosa and Japan. Heavier traffic there but nothing at all from Hawaii. Ambassador Grew in Tokyo passed on a warning from British intelligence that the Japs are going to hit the Philippines. MacArthur's answer to Grew was that there's nothing to fear.'

'If MacArthur says it, believe it,' DeCarlo said. 'He's Mr Army.'

'But there are unconfirmed accounts of Japanese troops taking over Shanghai and landing south of Singapore. Australian intelligence claims one of its scout planes sighted a Japanese armada headed towards the Malaysian peninsula.'

'All the Jap stuff is concentrated 5,000 to 6,000 miles from here. I agree they may hit us in the Philippines, but

MacArthur can take care of himself. Would you turn on my desk radio? I paid radio station KGMB to play music all night. It gives a flight of our B-17s from San Francisco a signal to home in on. They'll refuel and be on their way to MacArthur. He may need them.'

John turned the radio on and held the phone receiver to the speaker.

'Got my money's worth,' DeCarlo said. 'The Flying Fortresses should be landing in about an hour.'

'There were two sub sightings at the mouth of the harbour last night,' John said. 'This morning a double sighting of a small sub near the nets. Depth charges were dropped and an oil slick reported, but no further contact. One of our scout planes returning from dawn patrol claims to have bombed a submarine a mile off Diamond Head.'

'Sounds like the flyboys are jealous of the navy's sub sightings. What is the admiral's reaction?'

'He hasn't heard about it,' John said. 'The duty officer didn't want to disturb him. A light cruiser was sent out to Diamond Head, but there were no signs of wreckage, no sighting and no radar contact.'

'Our boys are jumping at shadows,' DeCarlo said. 'The only men with combat experience have more grey hairs than me. Why don't you call that new army radar installation on the hill? They can screen the air for 130 miles.'

'I'll do just that. I feel better having talked to you. Enjoy your family picnic.' John hung up and immediately dialled, but the line was dead. He dialled another number. 'Army communications, this is John Whittefield. I've been trying to call your new radar installation. I can't get a line.'

'They pulled the plug a few minutes ago, sir. Actually they were supposed to close down at seven but they got a scare and stayed another half-hour. There were a lot of blips.'

'Shouldn't you be concerned?' John asked.

'I checked our incoming flights. Twelve B-17s are due in from the States about now. They're a few minutes early and should land in time for breakfast. Nothing to worry about.'

60

Above the fleecy clouds, Kenji maintained an altitude of 9,000 feet and a speed of 250 m.p.h., followed by the air armada of 180 planes in perfect formation. He rolled his head in a circle, scanning the sky and listening to the radio. 'Admiral Nagumo is right,' he said. 'It's beautiful music.'

Below, the clouds began to thin. Now and then Kenji glimpsed the ocean, but concentrated on the blue sky above, expecting to see American fighter planes swooping down. Hadn't Nakajima started the Singapore landing too early? Then some idiot from the scout planes off the coal barges sank an American navy ship near the Philippines. 'Even if we do catch them asleep in Honolulu, Hino is still blocked in by fog.' Kenji laughed, knowing he was psychologically preparing for combat because he was talking to himself. 'MacArthur will catch Kido Butai with those Flying Fortresses before we can ever get clear of the north Pacific. Kido Butai will have to fight its way back over 6,000 miles of ocean. Tojo and Yamamoto may have taken every practical step to achieve success, but they forgot luck. The gods of fortune appear to be against the imperial air force.' Kenji checked his watch. They had been flying for an hour. He switched frequencies and listened for the scout planes launched from the submarines.

The single-pontoon seaplanes with American civilian markings flew a leisurely course over the naval installations at Pearl Harbor and airfields around Honolulu without being challenged. Then, at exactly 7:45 a.m. the senior scout broadcast in Japanese. 'All ships at anchor and planes on fields in designated positions as targeted.

Weather is sunny, warm and clear. No alert. All quiet below. Good luck.'

Kenji wiped the sweat from his face. Through the thinning clouds below him, he saw the green mountains of Oahu framed by white breakers and golden sand. Only minutes to the target, he watched for enemy fighters, and saw none. He switched his radio frequency to the *Kaga*'s channel and spoke the code word into the microphone, 'To! To! To!' Surprise had been achieved. He slid the cockpit canopy back and fired a black smoke rocket.

Kenji watched the formation separate. The fighters maintained an altitude of 9,000 feet and flew towards the airfields of Wheeler, Kaneohe, Bellows and Pearl Harbor. Bombers and divebombers climbed to 12,000 feet and looped right to Pearl Harbor, Ewa and Hickam fields and Ford island.

Genda led his torpedo-planes down and looped further right. His squadron would divide again into two groups attacking Battleship Row from different angles. The bombers circled right beyond Genda's planes, flying into Pearl Harbor. Yamamoto had planned to attack the Pacific fleet from all points of the compass to achieve maximum firepower in minimum time, and confuse the enemy as to which direction the attacking planes were launched from.

3:50 a.m., Tokyo

For twenty minutes beyond the scheduled time of attack, everyone in the imperial reception room watched Raiko's radio. Suddenly it came to life and she began writing, trying to repeat the words, but her throat was dry.

'Give her water,' Yamamoto ordered. 'The body heat in this room has driven the temperature up to eighty-five degrees.'

Raiko drank, cleared her throat and read, 'From Ruth

Kuhn, Pearl Harbor. Our planes sighted. Groups coming in from the north, south and east. No alert. More planes coming in low to the water. Earlier navy depth-charge attack sank one small submarine at entrance to harbour. No alert. Green smoke rocket above Pearl Harbor. Torpedo-planes flying close to rooftops and swinging wide.'

'That's Kenji's smoke rocket to signal the attack,' Yamamoto said.

Kenji closed his cockpit and holstered his signal gun. He turned his radio to the combat frequency and shouted the words his men were waiting for. 'To-ra! To-ra! – Surprise attack!' He watched the divebombers nose down and go screaming by him towards the American ships anchored near Ford island. Seven Zeros swept in from the west, another ten from the east.

Kenji saw Genda leading his first wave of torpedo-planes. Compared to the swift fighters and divebombers, the torpedo squadron seemed to crawl over the housetops of Pearl City.

Genda concentrated on his airspeed, using only his judgement for height. Down so low, the altimeter was inaccurate. He swung around, followed by three pilots off his right wing, and led them at 150 miles an hour. The four pilots reduced speed as they flew under the big ship's crane. 'Stand by to launch torpedoes,' Genda shouted. 'Make it good! We've come a hell of a long way to let these silverfish swim!' He levelled his plane over the water. 'Thirty-five, twenty-five, fifteen feet,' he shouted. 'I've got the *Oklahoma*! Fire!'

'Torpedo away,' the co-pilot shouted.

Kenji watched Genda and his planes start to climb. Below them, four telltale white trails chalked a line beneath the still blue waters, towards Battleship Row. One after the other, geysers erupted at the sides of the

Oklahoma, the *West Virginia* and *Nevada*. More Zeros swarmed in over the American ships, strafing their decks. The divebombers unleashed their missiles with deadly accuracy. Kenji saw his high-level bombers release racks of bombs on to the destroyers, cruisers and maintenance ships in the harbour.

Suddenly Kenji's plane was rocked by an explosion. Air bursts shook him. A stream of bright orange tracer bullets reached up for him from the dry-docked battleship *Pennsylvania*. A survivor of the *Panay*, the first man in the US fleet to react, had jumped to an anti-aircraft gun the moment he saw the Rising Sun on the wings of the planes above him. He knocked down two Zeros.

Kenji rolled left and climbed to 12,000 feet, watching the action below as he gained altitude. Genda led the second wave of his planes into the attack even though he carried no torpedo. He fired his machine-guns, disrupting the aim of the naval gunners now in action on Battleship Row.

Again Kenji saw torpedoes strike their targets. Realizing at the same time that the big silverfish could not get through to the second line of ships anchored directly behind the first.

'Divebombers! Divebombers, form on me,' Kenji ordered.

Eleven planes answered his call, lining up in step formation to his left. 'The targets are the inner line of ships on Battleship Row! Top four planes, take the battleship *Maryland*! Second four planes from the top, take the battleship *Tennessee*! Third group, follow me to the *Arizona*!' Kenji patted the picture of Raiko and Mangiro and touched his eye patch. 'Banzai,' he shouted. 'A thousand years to the Emperor!' He turned his plane over on its back and pushed the throttle to full power. His head slammed back against the seat. Affected by the 1,000-pound armour-piercing shell strapped beneath, the entire plane vibrated.

Kenji lined his plane up on the middle smokestack of

the battleship *Arizona*. He shouted to relieve the pressure on his eardrums and match the sounds of the whistling wind and roaring engine. The wings seemed about to rip off. Even if they do tear away I'll crash the fuselage into the *Arizona*, he thought. He raced through a wall of flak and tracer bullets streaming up from the deck of the ship. He watched his altimeter spin down – 5,000, 4,000, 3,000, 2,000. At 1,000 feet Kenji grasped the bomb-release wire and pulled. There was no response. He jerked at the wire and the half-ton shell parted from the belly of the plane. The release of weight sent the Zero screaming upwards from 700 to 1,500 feet. Kenji felt as if he had been shot from a cannon. His nose bled and he needed both hands on the control stick to keep the plane upright. He scanned the empty sky for enemy fighters. He dipped his right wing to look at his target. There was only a pall of dirty smoke where the mighty *Arizona* had been. His shell had crashed through the first three decks, hitting illegally stored bags of black powder for the sixteen-inch guns. The black powder ignited, setting off the entire ship's powder magazine and breaking the *Arizona* in half. She sank in ninety seconds.

Kenji's flat voice echoed over the *Kaga*'s radio, 'First confirmed kill on Battleship Row. The USS *Arizona*.'

Ruth Kuhn sat at her attic window, using Kenji's binoculars and working the radio key on messages to Raiko. Otto Kuhn stood behind his daughter with a car headlight connected to a six-volt car battery, flashing the same messages in simple Morse code to three of Tsubota's agents in the hills behind Pearl City. They, in turn, relayed the signals to Admiral Nagumo aboard the *Kaga*.

In Tokyo, Raiko read Ruth's messages aloud. 'First bombs dropped 7:55 a.m. Complete surprise achieved. Smoke rising from Hickam field and flying-boat basin on Ford island. Marine airfield at Ewa ablaze. Wheeler

536

airfield under heavy attack by Zeros. Much smoke. Enemy naval anti-aircraft guns now in action. Shore batteries silent. Two-man sub surfaced in harbour and fired torpedo at *Curtiss*. Direct hit. Sub rammed and sunk by enemy destroyer.' Raiko remembered the *Curtiss* as the BLT on Ruth's list.

'Request damage reports,' Yamamoto ordered.

Raiko tapped out the question and received an immediate reply. 'Battleship Row ablaze. *Arizona* sunk. *Oklahoma* capsized. Burning oil spreading over water. Ships and docks burning. Fire everywhere. Powder magazines exploding aboard ships and ammunition dumps on land. So much smoke it's difficult to see. Extensive damage. The attacking bombers and torpedo-planes are re-forming and flying south. No enemy pursuit. Two planes remaining to assess damage. One pilot taking photos.'

Raiko went cold and began to tremble.

'Mrs Ishikawa, are you all right?' Yamamoto asked.

'Kenji takes photos. That's him up there, I know it.'

'Please get a grip on yourself,' the admiral said. 'We need you to monitor the effects of our first raid and the accuracy of the second wave. The smoke will soon clear and Miss Kuhn will have a better view of the harbour.'

'Why are the planes flying south?' Raiko asked. 'Kido Butai aircraft carriers are north of Oahu.'

'To throw off enemy pursuit from land-based planes, from Admiral Halsey's three aircraft carriers and from MacArthur's Flying Fortresses in the Philippines. Hino's bombers are still not able to take off because of fog.'

'*Kaga! Kaga!*' Kenji called as he flew over the blazing harbour. 'The first wave returning. Complete surprise achieved. No enemy aircraft observed in the area. The battleships *Oklahoma* and *Arizona* sunk. The *California* is sinking and crew abandoning ship. The *Nevada* hit and taking water, but has got up steam and is fighting. She's

moving towards the main channel and should be the firs
target of the second wave. If we can sink her in the main
channel, Pearl Harbor will be closed for months. The
battleships *Tennessee* and *Maryland* are hit, burning bu
still fighting. The battleship *Pennsylvania* and destroyers
Cassin and *Shaw* burning in dry-dock. Secondary explo
sions from these ships indicate ignited powder magazines
The entire seaplane base and all aircraft at Ford island
are destroyed.' Kenji flew over the nearby airbases and
radioed, 'All enemy planes at the Ewa marine air base have
been destroyed. The hangars, maintenance buildings and
planes at Wheeler air base and Hickam field destroyed
Zeros attacking Bellows and Kaneohe airfields report
similar successes. Only ten American planes got off the
ground and two were shot down. A flight of B-17s were
mistaken for our planes. One B-17 shot down by their own
anti-aircraft fire, another two by our planes.'

Admiral Nagumo and his officers cheered but did not
respond, maintaining radio silence for fear that Bull
Halsey would triangulate Kido Butai's position.

'Kenji, you forgot to mention the battleship *Utah* sunk
by torpedoes,' Genda shouted over the radio. 'We control
the air and the sea!'

Kenji could see Genda below, zooming back and forth
through thick, black smoke. Kenji looked to the left and
was surprised to see a single-engine civilian plane flying
alongside. He had strict orders from Yamamoto against
harming civilians. A strategic decision made because the
admiral was thinking ahead to negotiating peace with the
United States. Kenji hand signalled the man and boy in the
cockpit to get away, but they only gaped at him. He banked
left and fired a burst from his machine-guns in front of the
civilian plane. It dived, and headed towards Honolulu.

Kenji looked down on the destruction below. We may
have succeeded too well, he thought. They'll never negotiate with us now. 'Genda,' he called, 'return to ship. The

second wave is coming in. Notify Admiral Nagumo mission accomplished.'

'Will do.' Genda waggled his wings at Kenji and headed south.

'Commander Ishikawa, this is group leader of second attack force with fifty-five high-level bombers, eighty divebombers and forty-five Zeros. Please give instructions.'

'Get the *Nevada*,' Kenji ordered. 'She's taken at least one torpedo hit and several bombs on the deck. She's moving in the main channel towards open sea. Sink her in the channel!'

'I hear and obey.'

61

'Admiral Kimmel, this is John Whittefield. I hope I'm not calling too early.'

'I've been up for a while. Have an eight o'clock tee-off date with General Short. What is it?'

'Three unconfirmed sightings of midget subs at the mouth of the harbour,' John said. 'Depth charges were dropped. One of our PBY scout planes claims to have bombed a regular sub off Diamond Head.'

'It's probably more false alarms, but I'll postpone golf and meet you at naval headquarters. Have the latest intelligence reports on my desk!'

John walked to the Fourteenth District Naval Headquarters building under a warm sun and clear sky. It wasn't often he spent a Sunday on the base. The peaceful, relaxed atmosphere was very different from a normal workday. He watched the navy's field-music platoon form up for the flag-raising ceremony. Men straggled towards the mess hall. Others walked to the chapel. A few, dressed in civilian clothes, hurried out of the main gate. A civilian seaplane cruised overhead and John wondered what the base rules were for unauthorized flights. He stopped and made a note to bring up the subject at the next staff meeting.

At the entrance to the Fourteenth District building, marine guards checked John's ID. Inside, the floors, still damp from swabbing, smelled of pine soap. He went downstairs to the subterranean intelligence headquarters and sought out Jeff Caspi. The navy lieutenant, a radio-traffic analyst, had been saying for weeks that the six Japanese carriers were at sea and not in southern Japan.

'What's your assessment now?' John asked.

'I still claim the absence of radio signals tells as much as the flow. Nagumo's fleet of aircraft carriers could have circled behind the Philippines and be getting ready to pounce on MacArthur from the south or south west.'

'What do your colleagues say?'

Jeff tapped his head. 'That I'm crazy.' He handed John several pages. 'Have you seen this from Washington? It's days old. This wording of Secretary Hull's turndown of the Japanese offer differs from newspaper and radio accounts. It's much stronger. And so is the Japanese reply.'

John read, then looked up. 'These demands for Japan to give up everything in China and Manchuria are pushing them to the wall. Has Admiral Kimmel seen this?'

'Just got it now because I made the officer in charge of the base post office open the mail-room. Tojo won't take kindly to Roosevelt asking him to surrender everything without a fight. You're the Jap expert. What'll it mean?'

'I think they'll react militarily. The wording of Tojo's refusal to the demands could even be meant by the Japanese as a declaration of war. They have a funny way of thinking when it comes to fighting. They attacked the Chinese and later the Russians at Port Arthur without warning. I'll take this upstairs to the admiral. What else have you got?'

The room vibrated and they heard a dull thud above them. 'An earthquake?' John asked.

Several more explosions shook the room. A cup of pencils fell from Jeff's desk. He and John looked at each other, then bolted for the door.

'I can't leave my post,' the duty officer shouted after them. 'Let me know what's happening!'

John and Jeff joined the two marine guards at the main entrance. The four gaped up at a sky filled with planes.

'Is it a training exercise?' Jeff asked.

'Bullshit, lieutenant sir!' the taller marine said. 'Those are goddamned Japs bombing our ships!'

To John it resembled a flock of angry sea birds wheeling, diving and swooping over Battleship Row. Black, oily smoke wafted up from the *Oklahoma*, the *West Virginia* and *Nevada*.

'Look!' Jeff pointed. 'Those divebombers are going for the second line on Battleship Row!'

The four men watched twelve planes with the rising sun painted on their wings scream down in a power dive on the anchored vessels. The first plane over the *Arizona* released its bomb at the last second, but the bomb did not detonate. Explosions burst on the decks of other ships. John, about to say the first bomb had been a dud, saw the *Arizona* leap from the water, break in half, and sink.

'My God,' Jeff moaned. 'There're over 1,000 men on that ship! I checked the duty roster this morning!'

'The *Oklahoma* is going over!' The taller marine unslung his rifle and knelt to fire at the planes.

John watched the battleship *Oklahoma* tilt, lie on its side, then capsize. Its slick wet bottom turned up towards the bright Hawaiian sun.

'They're tearing our fleet apart,' the second marine shouted. He knelt and began firing at the enemy planes.

Navy anti-aircraft guns roared into action.

'They got that bastard,' the second marine shouted, pointing at a divebomber trailing smoke.

The four men cheered as the plane tried to climb but its engine sputtered. They moaned when the Japanese pilot laid his plane over on its back and dived at the hangars on Ford island. He crashed into the centre hangar, blowing it up and setting off a chain reaction of explosions.

Machine-gun bullets and 20mm cannon shells tore up the lawn in front of naval headquarters. Shell casings rained down on the four men.

Admiral Kimmel's car careened up the road between shell holes. John pushed Jeff Caspi back towards the entrance. 'Get downstairs! Send out an alert to all units! "Pearl Harbor is under attack by Japanese planes! This is not a drill! Defend yourselves!"'

The admiral jumped from his car. 'What the hell is going on?'

'Japs attacking!' John pointed to the harbour. 'The *Arizona* and *Oklahoma* are sunk!'

Navy staff cars raced up to the building. Admiral Kimmel gathered his officers in a semicircle around him. Some wore colourful, flowered shirts and slacks. Two wore golf knickers and one was in his bathing suit. A Zero roared in and strafed the building, but not one man in the circle moved. They were showered with shell casings, broken glass and concrete chips.

'Come in closer!' the grim-faced admiral said. 'It's war! Defend the base and our ships! Set rescue teams to work in the harbour! Start thinking of a plan to counter-attack! Find the enemy carriers! I've got to call Washington!' Kimmel turned to John. 'I want a detailed casualty report! Have communications rig a direct line to MacArthur and Bull Halsey! We're going to kick Japanese ass!'

A short while later, John entered the admiral's office overlooking Pearl Harbor. Kimmel hung up the telephone. 'I just finished talking to the secretary of the navy in DC. He wouldn't believe what I was telling him until I held the phone out the window so he could hear the explosions!'

'There's more trouble coming,' John said. 'Our air spotters report another wave of 200 planes approaching! All serviceable navy guns are in action!'

'Damage and casualty report!' Kimmel said.

John tried to speak, but instead he sobbed, and choked back tears. 'No survivors from the *Arizona*. A thousand dead. Four hundred men aboard the *Oklahoma* believed dead. The hull is upside down and there's banging from within. Volunteers will go out to try and cut through the hull, but meanwhile there's half a foot of diesel oil on the water and it's burning everything – the men swimming, the ships at anchor, the docks.' John sobbed again. 'Almost every ship in the harbour, except the submarines, has been hit. Specific damages are impossible to estimate. The men are preparing to defend against the second attack.' John pointed out of the window. 'Sir, what is the *Nevada* doing?'

Kimmel watched for a few moments, then said, 'The skipper is bringing her about and trying to make for the open sea. He's fighting his ship as she should be fought.' The admiral shook his head. 'If the Japs sink her in the channel, it'll close Pearl Harbor for a long time.' He grabbed the telephone. 'Kimmel here. Put all your army shore batteries and anti-aircraft guns to protecting the *Nevada*!' He listened in wide-eyed disbelief. 'What the hell do you mean the army guns have no ammunition! Get it!' He slammed the phone down, picked it up again and dialled. 'Harbour master, Kimmel here! Get tugboats out to the *Nevada*! She's been hit and is trying for the open sea! Help her! Make certain she doesn't sink in the channel!'

John handed a second phone to the admiral. 'General MacArthur on the line.'

'Yes, Doug, it's true,' Kimmel said. 'We're getting our asses kicked by the Japs and it isn't over! There's another wave of enemy planes on the way! I can see smoke from our airfields! If the damage there is as bad as what I see of the PBY base on Ford island, we're naked of air cover! You've got to find the Jap carriers that sent these planes and sink them! Before they retreat to the cover of their land-based planes!'

'I'll send out recon planes,' MacArthur said. 'Do you have any idea where I should look?'

'One second,' Kimmel said, and turned to John. 'You're the senior intelligence officer. Where are the Japs?'

'In the south, I guess,' John said. 'That's the direction their planes took when they left here.'

'What about the army's new secret radio-tracking and direction-finding station? They're supposed to be able to monitor all radio conversations between planes.'

'The army pulled the plug on their telephones at the station,' John said. 'I sent a car over there. It'll take three hours before we hear anything.'

Kimmel turned back to the phone. 'Douglas, we think the Japs are south of us. They couldn't have launched this many planes in the rough seas to the north. When I get in touch with Halsey and his carriers, I'll have him scout south. The Japs here are presently out of your range. Go to Plan B! Attack Formosa with your Flying Fortresses! Bomb the Jap air bases there! You have aerial photos and everything you need. I know your new air-force Commander Bereton is for the idea. We talked about it before he flew out to Manila. If Halsey doesn't catch the Japs here, he'll chase them your way. Knock out their airfields and land-based planes on Formosa and we'll have them trapped!'

'I can't do that,' MacArthur said. 'I have an obligation to President Quezon and the Philippine people to protect these islands.'

'Are you kidding? You've got the wrong president!'

'No, I haven't. I'm employed by the Philippine government. My planes are to protect these islands by watching for enemy carriers readying to attack us.'

'Doug, your allegiance is to the United States! We're taking a beating here and there's more coming our way!'

'I have not received notice of a formal declaration of war from the president of the Philippines,' MacArthur said.

'We received one here in Pearl Harbor from Tojo!' Kimmel answered. 'Unless your Flying Fortresses take out the Formosa bases and then later combine with Halsey to wipe out the Jap aircraft carriers that are attacking us, Japan will rule the Pacific Ocean from Tokyo to San Francisco! There's nothing between them and California but you and Halsey! He's only got three carriers! The Japs must have six or more! They could tear southern California apart!'

'My planes will be used to protect Manila and our bases here in the Philippines,' MacArthur said. 'Formosa is closed in by fog. The Jap fighter planes can't reach us from there and they won't dare send bombers alone. I'll protect these islands and catch the Jap carriers on their way back from Hawaii. With Bull Halsey behind them and me in front, it'll be a turkey shoot. After that I can eliminate the Jap planes and bases on Formosa at my leisure.'

The window pane in front of Kimmel shattered. He staggered back and dropped the telephone.

'Are you hit?' John asked.

Kimmel touched the bloody spot on his white shirt. He looked down at the spent Japanese machine-gun bullet that had hit him. 'Better that it had killed me.' He picked up the bullet and hefted it in the palm of his hand.

Douglas MacArthur's voice called from the fallen receiver.

'John, hang up the telephone,' Kimmel said. 'MacArthur is going to make certain the disaster that's taking place here doesn't touch him. My career is finished. Let's see if we can salvage something from this mess.'

62

Kenji watched the precision formation of the second attack force of 180 planes divide for their assigned targets. Fifty divebombers and fighters went after the *Nevada* being guided by two navy tugs. Heavy smoke poured from the battleship's bow; fire raged from her aft gun turret. There was a gaping hole where Genda's torpedo had exploded amidships. The men of the *Nevada* remained at their guns, throwing out a wall of hot steel that chewed up the divebombers and Zeros attacking her. Army shore batteries, guns from the minesweepers anchored at the harbour entrance, joined the *Nevada*'s gunners, forming an umbrella of anti-aircraft fire over the beleaguered battleship.

Kenji radioed the *Kaga*. 'The Americans are fighting back. Six of our planes, correction eight planes lost attacking the *Nevada*. A ninth hit. He crash-dived his plane into the battleship. Two hits scored on the bow. Four more amidships. We've lost another plane.' He felt a strange kinship with the Americans who were fighting their sinking ship while it burned around them. 'No Japanese could have done better,' he said into the radio. Then he switched frequencies. 'Pilots of Kido Butai, hear this! Break off the attack on the *Nevada*! She's sinking and the tugs are beaching her. Choose targets of opportunity!'

'Bandits! Bandits!' The warning came through Kenji's earphones. 'Coming in from the south! A formation of ten P40s!'

Kenji rolled his head but could see nothing. Five Zeros

roared by him, machine-guns blazing, driving head-on into the formation behind him. The American pilots broke – right, left, up, down – the classical response of disciplined pilots trained in the previous war's methods of individual dogfights. The five Japanese planes divided, three and two, and in thirty seconds two American planes had exploded in the air. The other P-40s were pounced on from above by fifteen Zeros.

Kenji saw an American pilot purposely crash into a formation of Zeros. He heard his men salute the American, and watched the last P-40 spiral down into the harbour.

'Only two Zeros lost,' Kenji reported. 'And those to the American suicide pilot.'

'Bandits! Bandits coming from the sea and low to the water!'

'Identify and number,' Kenji ordered.

'Eleven navy Wildcats!'

'Team tactics,' Kenji ordered. 'Destroy them!' He watched the unequal battle with the interest of an engineer, not a fighter pilot. His Zeros were so superior to the American Wildcats and P-40s, it was clear that Japan ruled the skies. It was also clear to him he had lost the killer instinct of a fighter pilot. In the China war he had seen the enemy first, he had attacked first. Kenji knew he would never again lead his men in battle.

Joe DeCarlo was working off a pancake breakfast by washing the family car, with its radio tuned to KGMB. His son and daughter were playing on the lawn. He stopped working and looked at his house with pride. He had waited two years to buy into this peaceful, flower-filled neighbourhood shielded by the mountains from the noise of the air bases.

Wiping the car's windscreen, DeCarlo noticed a column of thick black smoke rising over the mountaintop. The

548

radio music stopped and he expected to hear the introduction to the song which would mean the flight of B-17s had landed.

'We have an important message!' the radio announcer said. 'The Japanese are bombing Pearl Harbor! I repeat, the Japanese are bombing Pearl Harbor! All military personnel, report to your duty stations!'

'Marie,' DeCarlo shouted. 'Get the kids into the basement!' He ran across the lawn, scooped up the children and shoved them at his wife as she came out the screen door. 'Take them to the basement!'

'We don't have a basement,' Marie DeCarlo said. 'That was the last house we lived in. Why are you crying? What's wrong?'

'I'm wrong! Everything we thought about the Japs was wrong!' He pointed to the black smoke rising up into the clear blue sky. 'They're bombing Pearl Harbor!' He bolted into the house and came out buckling his duty belt and .45 automatic over his Bermuda shorts and Hawaiian shirt. He kissed his wife and the children. 'Marie, take the kids to the Lowrys! Stay there until I get back!'

DeCarlo jumped into his '39 Chevy. The car sprayed gravel as he roared away. His and other cars raced to the base, screeching around turns of the winding road between the mountains. A half mile from Pearl Harbor's main gate, traffic slowed. DeCarlo figured the marine guards would be checking for sabotage. He could see Japanese planes circling and diving on the harbour. 'Thank God they aren't bombing Honolulu,' he said.

Three Zeros roared rooftop-high over nearby villas, their machine guns blinking bright orange. DeCarlo saw a light blinking from the window of a house on the cliff overlooking the harbour. He recognized the flashes as the simple Morse code he had learned as a boy scout, watching until the driver behind him blew his horn.

DeCarlo rolled the car forward another 100 yards, reading aloud, 'Ten of our planes down. The *Nevada* is sinking. American aircraft now in the area and attacking.'

DeCarlo spun the steering wheel, floored the gas pedal and screeched the Chevy out of the line of cars. He sped up the service road to the houses overlooking the harbour. At a mailbox labelled Ruth Kuhn, he jumped out of the car and ran to the front door. The doorknob turned and he slipped inside the house.

Suddenly DeCarlo's legs began to shake. Sweat poured down his face. 'Damn! I should have brought someone with me!' He heard a woman's voice upstairs. A man asked a question. DeCarlo unholstered his .45 and quietly pulled the receiver back. He slipped a round into the firing chamber and tiptoed up the stairs.

The door to the attic was open. An elderly man stood behind a young woman, blinking a car headlight powered by a battery. She worked a radio key, speaking at the same time. 'The *Nevada* has been beached on the south side of the main channel,' Ruth said.

Joe DeCarlo whispered a 'Hail Mary' and put his back against the wall. He had decided that if anyone else entered the room, he would shoot these two spies. 'Put your hands up,' he growled.

Otto Kuhn dropped the headlight and raised his arms without turning around. Ruth Kuhn looked into the muzzle of the .45 and tapped the letters RR.

Tokyo

'Admiral Yamamoto, Ruth Kuhn is transmitting a report her father monitored from naval headquarters,' Raiko said. 'All nine US battleships sunk or damaged. Almost every ship in the harbour hit. Six cruisers and four destroyers sunk. Known casualties at Pearl Harbor 2,000 dead, 1,000 wounded. All military airfields on Oahu inoperable. Estimate 350 American war planes deadlined or destroyed.' There was a pause in transmission, then Ruth's signal came again. 'Although the battleship *Nevada* is among those listed by the navy as damaged, I can see her limping into the channel. She is burning, and low in the water. Our second wave has attacked. American planes unsuccessfully contesting air over Pearl Harbor. They have been either shot down or chased away.'

Raiko finished Ruth's message with RR, and jumped back from the radio set, almost toppling over in her chair.

'What is it, Mrs Ishikawa?' Yamamoto asked.

'Ruth Kuhn has been captured.'

'How can you know?'

Raiko held up her writing pad. 'The RR stands for Ruth and Raiko. We arranged a signal if she was taken.'

Yamamoto patted Raiko's shoulders. 'Do not be concerned. Americans treat their prisoners well. As soon as we negotiate peace with them, Ruth will be among the first prisoners exchanged. I promise you that. Now you can go home with good news. Genda and Kenji are well. Tsubota's agents who were relaying Ruth's messages to the *Kaga* were also monitoring Kenji's radio messages. Your husband is safe.'

'Thank you, sir, but I wish to remain until the Formosa strike force has completed its mission,' Raiko said. 'I promised Lord Hiroki Koin I would find out how all his nephews are.'

'You have my permission to remain, and my appreciation for a job well done. But be prepared. The news from the Philippines may be grim. MacArthur has been alerted.'

'Admiral Halsey speaking.'

'Kimmel here. We've taken a beating. It's nine hours since the Japs broke off the attack and the harbour is still burning. Have your reconnaissance planes spotted them?'

'Nothing yet. I'm beginning to think they came from the north.'

'You'll get them,' Kimmel said. 'Yamamoto made one mistake. He proved that air power rules the seas. After today, battleships are obsolete. Aircraft carriers will determine the outcome of naval warfare. Yet he left your three carriers in his rear and MacArthur's planes ahead of him. Between the two of you, his strike force is dead.'

'Kimmel, I swear to you when we get done with the little bastards, the only place Japanese will be spoken is in Hell!'

'When you catch up with them . . .' The admiral coughed, choking back his emotions. 'Pay them for me and my men. We've taken 4,000 casualties. The Pacific fleet no longer exists. Washington will want a scapegoat and it will probably be me.'

'Admiral, sir,' John said. 'I've got Tojo on shortwave. He's about to address the Japanese people. I'll translate.'

Kimmel said goodbye to Halsey and took a seat in front of the radio. 'Wouldn't the Emperor address the nation?' the admiral asked.

'Hirohito may be Emperor of Japan but if anything goes wrong with the war, Tojo will take the blame.'

Kido Butai steamed home at flank speed. The pilots and crew of the *Kaga* gathered around the loudspeakers on the hangar deck. Kenji and his crew chief sat under the wing of his Zero. He and the others had been waiting twelve hours to hear news of the Formosa strike force. If the Philippine mission was unsuccessful, Kido Butai would have to run the gauntlet of MacArthur's bombers ahead and Halsey's planes behind.

The loudspeaker crackled, then a voice boomed. 'General Hideki Tojo, Prime Minister of Japan, Minister of War and Supreme Commander of the armed forces will now speak!'

The sound of paper being shuffled came over the loudspeaker, followed by Tojo's voice. 'People of Japan! We are at war with America and her allies, Holland and Great Britain! The American policy of Ring Fence made this confrontation inevitable! They meant to strangle Japan into submission and make us a slave state to Caucasian countries! Today, at 7:55 a.m. Hawaiian time, our forces landed at Singapore, Hong Kong, Guam and Wake island. At the same time, our planes swept to a smashing victory at Pearl Harbor! Every major American battleship in the Pacific fleet, several destroyers and cruisers, were sunk! In addition, 350 American planes were demolished! The enemy suffered 4,000 casualties! Fires continue to light the night sky over Honolulu! Our losses were twenty-nine planes and five midget submarines. A total of forty-five brave Japanese men!'

Kenji was stunned by the lopsided margin of victory. As men around him cheered, he thought of Nanking, and unconsciously spoke aloud.

'These weren't civilians,' the crew chief said. 'They were professional American military-men. We didn't touch their cities.'

Tojo's voice came over the loudspeaker again. 'Nine hours after the attack on Pearl Harbor, our pilots, flying from Formosa, set a world distance record for combat planes! They attacked the Philippine islands! Although the Americans were on full alert, our pilots swept in and destroyed General Douglas MacArthur's entire air force on the main island of Luzon!'

The cry of exultation and jubilation from the crew was deafening. The way was clear for Kido Butai. Men rushed over to congratulate Kenji on Hino's success.

Aboard the carrier *Akagi*, Genda was raised on shoulders and marched around the hangar deck.

Aboard all the ships of Kido Butai, a chant went up, 'Plan B! Plan B! – the invasion of the Philippines by troops from Formosa covered by planes from Kido Butai.'

Tojo's voice silenced the shouts. 'Our air armada caught the American fighters and bombers on the ground wing tip to wing tip! It was a duplicate of our surprise at Pearl Harbor! The American bombers, fighters and even the vaunted Flying Fortresses, were destroyed on the ground at Clark, Iba and Nichols airfields near Manila. Our losses were nine fighter planes. In the name of the Emperor, I salute the heroes of Japan! Those who died are immortal! They have left the fate of Japan in the hands of those who live! The future of all Asia hangs in the balance! Today there has begun a new order in the East, and we are its leaders! All Japanese soldiers and civilians must vow to work unstintingly for the goals of the empire as set forth by his most imperial majesty, the Emperor! I leave now for the Yasukune shrine to pray for our fallen heroes. They take their place with the gods!'

Martial music blared from the loudspeaker and the men sang the Umi Ukaba. They chanted, with fierce, unbridled pride,

'Over the seas, dead bodies in the water.

Across the mountains, corpses in the fields.

Giri repaid. Chu is owed.

Never look back on the seeds we have sowed.'

Kenji felt raging pride along with his men. Then he wilted at the thought he would never again fly another combat mission. He would ask Hashimoto for command of the flight-training school at Nagasaki.

63

11 December 1941, Tokyo

Raiko put Mangiro to sleep, then went to the salon and dialled the telephone.

'Aunt Noriko, if Uncle Hiroki is there, please ask him to listen on the extension.'

'I am here, Raiko. What is it?'

'I have wonderful news for both of you. Genda, Hino and Kenji are safe.'

'Thank you for calling to tell us,' Noriko said. 'We were worried.'

'They won astounding victories,' Hiroki said. 'Our young men have surpassed Napoleon, Alexander the Great, and even Adolf Hitler. I doubt Yamamoto or the Razor himself expected such an overwhelming triumph.'

'We have been reading all the newspapers,' Noriko said. 'We bought an extra radio to hear all the news broadcasts. Hiroki and I feel our ministry of propaganda may exaggerate.'

'How could they have caught MacArthur's bombers on the ground?' Hiroki asked. 'He had nine hours' warning after Singapore and Pearl Harbor.'

'Tsubota's agents report it was a combination of luck on our part and a sloppy US army air alert system,' Raiko said. 'Because of the fog, Hino was nine hours late when he arrived at the Philippines, about 1:30 p.m. their time. MacArthur's planes had been in the air all morning. They covered a million square miles of the Pacific, searching for aircraft carriers that weren't there. The Americans were certain no fighter plane could fly from Formosa to Manila and back without refuelling. They were positive we wouldn't send bombers alone. They brought all their planes down to refuel at the same time and sent the air crews to lunch. That's when Hino's bombers arrived. He caught MacArthur's air force on the ground wing tip to wing tip, just as they did in Hawaii.'

'That leaves only one threat remaining to our merchant shipping in the Far East,' Hiroki said. 'Sir Tom Phillips and the British task force.'

'No,' Raiko replied. 'Genda and Hino combined to sink the *Prince of Wales* and the *Repulse*. Yesterday Genda led a fleet of torpedo-planes from his carrier. Together with Hino's bombers, they sank the two most modern, powerful battleships in the world.'

'I am surprised Kenji wasn't involved in an action that important,' Noriko said.

'I received a message from him,' Raiko said. 'He has requested a position training new pilots at the naval flying school in Nagasaki.'

'We'll almost be neighbours,' Noriko said. 'But I wonder about such a decision by Kenji. Do you know what it means?'

Hiroki came back on the line. 'I've just been looking at a world map. Do you ladies realize Japan now dominates the Indian Ocean, the Pacific Ocean and several of the seven seas? The sinking of the British fleet explains a telegram we just received from the Vichy French commander of Saigon. He congratulated me on Japan's conquest of one-tenth of the world.'

'Raiko, I worry about you and Kenji,' Noriko said. 'Why don't you and little Mung stay with us in Hiroshima while you wait for Kenji's posting to Nagasaki?'

Raiko felt the floor shake and grabbed the telephone before it fell from the table. The line went dead. She raced to her baby's side and braced the crib, but there